Once Dead, Long Dead

Robert Underhill

Also by Robert Underhill

Strawberry Moon
Cathead Bay
Death of the Mystery Novel
Providence Times Three

Once Dead, Long Dead

Robert Underhill

Northport, Michigan

-Once Dead, Long Dead
copyright © 2010 by Robert Underhill
ISBN 10: 0-9798526-4-1
ISBN 13: 978-0-9798526-4-0

Delicti Press
Northport, Michigan
editor@delicti.com

Library of Congress Control Number 2010927947
Underhill, Robert
  Once Dead, Long Dead / Robert Underhill-1st ed.
  p.cm
ISBN 13:978-0-9798526-4-0
    1.Crime -Fiction 2.Capital punishment -Fiction 3. Courtroom
drama 1. - Title

10 9 8 7 6 5 4 3 2 1
Printed in the United States of America

Acknowledgments

Woodrow Lipps of the US Forest Service, Special Agent Southern Region, for his information concerning legal procedures for crimes committed within the National Forest's jurisdiction.

I am fortunate to have willing friends whose unique skills and points of view have been invaluable to me in completing this book: Susan Agar, Jim Carpenter, Trudy Carpenter, John Erb, Kathleen Snedeker and Nancy Tefertiller.

My wife, Trudy's, constant interest and encouragement has been the springboard for this project. .

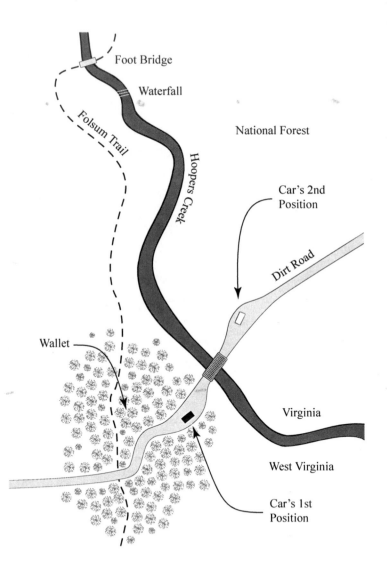

Foot Bridge

Waterfall

Folsum Trail

National Forest

Hoopers Creek

Car's 2nd Position

Dirt Road

Wallet

Virginia

West Virginia

Car's 1st Position

The massive truck sped past, forcing Kerry to take a quick step to the side to regain her balance. She braced herself as she heard the next one approach from the rear, waiting for the slam of wind and the deafening roar of engine and tires. Dust swirled around her, choking her and forcing grit into her eyes. Each time, she feared that the next truck might come onto the shoulder and hit her—a hysterical idea, she told herself, but the fact was she was moving ever closer to hysteria. She stopped and gave the backpack an upward heave to reposition the straps on her shoulders. The sun scorched the back of her neck. The forecast for the next few days was in the upper nineties and as for the humidity . . . well, she thought, better she should have gills. She ran the back of her sweaty hand across her forehead to wipe away more sweat.

Being here was surreal. Only two days ago she'd been walking along 116th Street in Manhattan. How the hell had she come to be on this stupid West Virginia highway? Well, she knew but . . . Half a dozen yards ahead of her, walking with a spring in his step was the tangible reason. Whenever he heard a truck coming from the rear, Tom wheeled around with his thumb out and gave the driver a hopeful look. So far all they'd given him back were diesel fumes. His plan had been to hitch a ride to the point, about fives miles farther on, where the trail crosses the highway, and begin their hike from there. That had been the plan, but no one had stopped and since they'd made a late start, he'd said they should start walking. That had been three miles back. Five more miles of this torture—if she made it—would just about kill her resolve to be the good mate.

Once in the quiet of the trail—if they ever got there— she was hoping to get him to face the decision about their next move. It was only the small matter of what the hell they were going to do with the rest of their lives. One thing was sure, now that he had no job, there would be no need to stay one day longer in this boring, backward, little burg. About that, there should be no disagreement.

Tom's swinging around just then to wave his thumb at a passing pick-up halted these thoughts. A sudden rush of pleasure took their place, the pleasure of possessing that handsome, virile guy.

The pickup truck swerved onto the shoulder in an obscuring cloud of swirling dirt. Tom gave a cry of victory and began to trot toward the red tailgate just emerging from the dust.

"C'mon Hon," he yelled over his shoulder as he slid his pack off and into the empty truck bed.

He helped her with her pack, then opened the passenger door and climbed in next to the driver, saying, "Hi. Thanks for stopping."

Kerry got in next to Tom and closed the door.

"No problem," returned the broadly smiling young

driver.

"We're only going a few miles to where the old Folsum Trail crosses the highway." Tom said in a buddy-to-buddy voice.

"Whooee, you'd never catch me wear'n one of them things on my back t'day, less'n it were the army make'n me do it." He laughed. "Thas why I got this ol' truck."

"I think you've got something there." Tom was being polite. Kerry recognized in his voice his sudden awareness that he was talking to someone of limited wattage. "I noticed you have Texas plates. Are you in West Virginia on business?"

"You could say that, but then I'll be head'n on home."

Kerry had settled into her seat enough to look around Tom and take in the Texan. Maybe early twenties, sandy colored hair badly cut, someone who didn't do a lot of deep thinking or spend much money on dentists.

"I'm Tom, by the way, and this is Kerry," Tom volunteered, adding too much down-hominess, Kerry thought.

"Pleased to make your 'quaintance. I'm Jerrod."

Tom said, as if really interested, "Nice name. I don't believe I've ever met anyone by that name."

"Me nether."

That seemed to allow no continuance, so they sat in silence for several minutes.

"Where you folks walk'n to?"

"We're going to hike back in the hills and camp for a couple of days. A little vacation."

"We used to camp out when I was a kid. Camp an' go fish'n up at the dam. Got a golf course there now. Wouldn't know the place now, condos an' all that."

Kerry's thoughts returned to her own problem. "A little vacation," he'd said this morning. "I need to get away." And she'd been willing at that moment to do anything to lighten his morbid mood.

Kerry wasn't the type of person who could "get away." It just didn't work for her. She had to face a problem and do something constructive to resolve it before she could relax. If a problem existed, there could be no holiday from it. Tom seemed to be one of those—this had been true of many others she'd known—who could put troubles aside and party. Good for them.

Tom pointed out the window. "We'll get off ahead there where the fence ends. That's the trail head."

The Texan pulled off onto the shoulder and stopped.

"Ya'll have yaselves a good time now."

"Thanks, Jerrod, and have a safe trip home."

They stepped out into the hot reality of the afternoon. Both coughing from the dust, they retrieved their packs. Tom gave a parting wave to the Texan, and they walked away from the highway onto the hiking trail.

It was no cooler on the trail. If anything, it was hotter, any breeze now blocked by the trees. It was much easier on Kerry's nerves, however, to be away from the tumult of the highway. They walked without saying much. Kerry felt so hot and miserable she could only reply with grunts to what Tom said. He, by contrast, was having a different experience, smiling and looking from side to side like a kid walking down an aisle in a toy store. Inwardly, was something else: he felt like a damn fool and he was sure that's how Kerry saw him also. So earlier, on impulse, he'd hit upon presenting a façade of devil-may-care high spirits to hide his true feelings, while announcing this carefree hike into the great outdoors.

He stopped abruptly and turned to face her. "How about having lunch?"

Kerry feigned surprise. "What? Then this isn't the Bataan Death March?"

"Of course it is, this is only a break for lunch. How are you doing?"

"Never better."

Tom pointed to a fallen tree. "Our dining room, Atwood."

Kerry swung first one shoulder then the other free from the backpack straps. Her fluid movement suggested athletic confidence. She took off the baseball cap she'd borrowed from Tom and shook her head, running her fingers briskly through her short, dark-brown, thoroughly sweat-soaked hair. Kerry's quick intelligence was readily apparent. The research position she'd left at Columbia University to come with Tom involved the designing of molecules with anti-malarial properties.

She sat down on the log next to Tom. He was digging in his backpack to bring out the sandwiches she'd made. He looked at her and laughed. The steady flow of sweat had established regular ruts through the grime on her face like an aerial map of the Nile delta. He leaned over and kissed her.

"That's disgusting," she said. "I'd never kiss a grimy thing like me."

"So I've revealed my perversion."

Kerry opened a bottle of water and took a long swallow, then handed it to Tom, sighing with deep satisfaction. He passed her a sandwich and took a bite of his own. "Mmm, that tastes good! You give great sandwich."

"Everything tastes good when you're hungry. I hope that holds true when we get to the freeze dried shit we bought this morning."

Tom leaned over to the pack again and took a trail map from a pocket and began studying it while continuing to eat. He laid it across Kerry's legs and pointed.

"We're about here. Not too much farther and we'll cross this road. That's a bridge just past the point where we cross the road. That creek . . . let's see, what's that name? Hoopers Creek. I believe . . . yes, that's the state line. So on the other side of the bridge is Virginia."

Kerry had been following the line marking the trail to a point where it met the creek. Her finger stabbed the map. "Look. Does that say, "Hoopers Falls?""

Tom leaned closer to the map. "You're right."

"Isn't there a good chance that where there is a waterfall there will be a . . . "

"Swimming hole!" they shouted in unison.

Back on the trail after finishing lunch, Kerry acknowledged to herself that Tom had been right; this outing was just what he needed to restore a positive mood. She was now feeling much better about what she now knew was but a delay in their need to restructure their life together.

Tom had come to this small, but booming city of Springville, West Virginia, because an architectural firm here had offered him a much better starting salary after his graduation from Cooper Union than he could have made in the northeast. In addition there was the prospect of moving up more quickly to a decision-making level with this firm, which had received more commissions last year than any other in the entire southern half of both Virginia and West Virginia. A bonus for him was the easy access Springville provided to the outdoor activities he loved: hiking, fishing and hunting.

Tom was greeted warmly at Sterns & Associates when he arrived five days ago. Raymond Stearns even helped him find an apartment. Tom then made the excited call to Kerry telling her the place and the job were all he had hoped for. She was the only missing ingredient. She in turn, having given notice when Tom had accepted the job, cleared out her desk, stored her furniture and left New

York a week earlier than originally planned. Once past the upheaval of the move, they would be married. That had been the plan!

Tom was due to begin work the day before Kerry was to arrive, but he'd received a call from Raymond Sterns the prior afternoon setting up a meeting in Stern's office for later that evening. At this meeting, Sterns told Tom that, regretfully, he was no longer able to offer him the job. An unfortunate monetary miscalculation had been made and the firm realized it could not afford to take on a new man.

This was all Kerry knew. She sensed, however, that things had become unpleasant. The fact was she didn't really know Tom very well, only having met him at a cocktail party at a West Village loft three months ago. The swift deepening of their relationship had overwhelmed her. She had never experienced anything like it, and while her cautious self would have had her hold back, as when a performer picks you out of the audience to come on stage to be his dance partner, or to be the woman he'll saw in half, another part of her said that same caution might forever cause her to lose something special. Yet, in the short time they'd been together, she'd already seen evidence in him of a trend to act impulsively when angry. She could only guess that the meeting had become ugly. She prayed that Tom's response to the news he'd been given hadn't become physical.

Yesterday, standing in the sparsely furnished living room of his apartment, her still unpacked bags at her feet, she'd heard all of this for the first time. She'd needed some input from him about the immediate future, but he didn't want to talk about it. He was affectionate but otherwise uncommunicative. He only began to talk in full sentences this morning when he announced he wanted to go camping—right now—this day. Camping was the last thing in the world she wanted to do. She stifled the impulse to pronounce the idea crazy, and instead held her tongue to see what would develop. He'd brought the minimal equipment with him from New York: small tent, one sleeping bag and a small, propane stove. They'd immediately gone to an outfitting store and bought a backpack and boots for her and some freeze-dried food, and set out.

Now as they sat eating, perched on the tree trunk, she pondered if it would be too soon to bring up the subject of their future and a job. She decided to chance it.

"You told me of another job offer you'd had."

"Yeah, but I'm sure it would be filled now. There is another possibility, though, a two-man firm on Long Island for whom I did some drafting last summer. They told me to give them a call when I finished school. Couple of nice guys. They had some interesting commissions too—and some boring ones, but don't they all.

This upbeat attitude was a relief to Kerry, so maybe the hike had been a good idea after all.

As with most places of its kind, the blended, stale smell of cigarette smoke, beer and unwashed bodies permeated the room. To this was added the cloying odor of cleaning solution emanating from the toilets and drifting to their booth. These elements they accepted as normal. Except for the wizened old guy who dozed at the bar, they were the only customers. It was a rear booth from which Clive had to raise his voice to get the waitress's attention for another round of beer. It was relatively cool here and they were hiding from the afternoon sun—and from the truth about themselves. The bulb in an overhead fixture had burned out, so a randomly flickering Budweiser sign over the booth provided most of the light, causing the faces of the two men to alternate between diabolic red and sickly pale.

Clive took the cracked plastic wallet from his pocket and, holding it out of the waitress's view below the tabletop, counted his money . . . their money.

"Enough for a coupla more rounds . . . No, maybe only one." He wasn't quick with figures. "If I get my hands on them bastards, they'll be damn sorry. Goddamn! We was be'n friendly, look'in for a good time, an' they cheated us. When I called 'em on it, one'a those fuckers sneaked up an' clobbered me. Stole most our money. Dumped us out there on the road. I tell you this, they gonna be goddamn sorry." His tone and demeanor was that of a Mafia don pronouncing a death sentence.

"No shee-it," said Lomas, his head nodding in continuous agreement like a dashboard doll. Now red, now pale, now red.

Clive's hand went up to his torn ear and the goose egg above it. He tried to arrange his oily hair so it would hide the bump.

"Be real goddamn sorry," he repeated.

"No shee-it," agreed Lomas, whose belly lay on the table of the tight booth like dough rolled from a bowl. Lomas knew the truth about last night, but a greater truth pushed this aside. That truth was his total dependence on Clive. Clive's version of last night had to be his own.

Clive had too much to drink at the roadhouse, his poker bets wild. He had lost everything. The money in his wallet was cash one of the players had stuffed in so they'd be able to buy breakfast. When the tavern closed, Lomas had to support Clive. They'd fallen and Clive's head had hit the concrete walk. Lomas had got Clive on his feet again and had struggled on with his burden, until he could go no farther and was forced to settle in a roadside ditch for the rest of the night.

Clive turned up the bottle in his hand and finished it, then called out, "Young lady . . . if you please." He straightened up and put on what he considered to be his most handsome and seductive face.

The waitress hesitated a moment, said something

to the bartender, laughed and then approached the booth with the reluctant acquiescence of one who knows she's about to deal with something distasteful.

"I don't know which is the best part," Clive oozed his rendition of suave, "this'ere beer or you. We'll have two more, Sugar."

"Oh God," the woman thought. "You better decide it's the beer," she said, picking up the empties.

"I know what it is, Sugar, it's that ass of yours. World class ass." He was pleased with his rhyme and tried it again. "World class ass. When do you get off from work, Sugar?"

She knew better than to answer him, but his sleazy smirk offended her so much she shot back, "Never, as far as you're concerned."

They have to respond this way, Clive told himself. Women were all the same. As soon as she'd left the table, he said to Lomas , "They all want it. She gotta act like that to start out."

He watched the waitress say something to the bartender.

With both hands on the edge of the table, Clive pushed his back flat against the back of the booth.

"Whad'ya bet she's askin' ta git off early."

"No shee-it."

Suddenly the bartender was standing over them. Up close he was massive.

"Get outa here you pieces of shit. Like now."

"Hey guy, we was jus joke'n around." Clive tried to make his whine sound man-to-man.

"Out of that booth. Now!"

"We jus ordered another beer."

"Now!"

Lomas was out of his seat quicker than he'd moved since he'd tried to dodge his daddy's belt. Clive tried to hold on to a little dignity in front of Lomas by moving slower, but not so slow as to provoke the bartender, who had his fists clenched.

At the door Clive turned and said, "We was leavin' this shit pit anyway. An' I wouldn't touch that slut with a ten-foot pole." Just then it occurred to him the woman might be the bartender's girlfriend or wife, and he lunged stumbling across the threshold into the glare and heat of the afternoon, looking back to be sure the guy wasn't following. When the door remained shut, he pulled himself up into a swagger. "Sombitch's afraid ta come out here."

"No shee-it," supplied Lomas.

They walked across the empty, burning asphalt of the parking lot and came to a stop at the side of the road where they stood unnoticed by drivers who passed in air-conditioned isolation.

Clive was still stinging from the humiliation in the bar, but he sensed that Lomas was looking to him for leadership, so he stared out into the distance like Napoleon contemplating Russia.

Finally, Lomas asked, "What we gonna do now,

Clive?"

Clive spat on the blistering pavement. "I'm thinkin', damn it."

"She's so pretty," murmured Gladys Tullock

"What's that?" asked her husband.

"Sharon. Doesn't she look pretty?"

"Uh huh," Ben agreed.

The newlyweds, daughter Sharon and the groom, Buddy, stood together beside the limo looking back up at the people standing on the church steps. They waved and started to get into the car but were called back by Buddy's uncle, who'd forgotten to advance the film in his disposable camera. They posed again, then with relief, climbed inside.

Such a nice looking couple, Gladys thought, and Sharon's dress looked just fine . . . at a distance. Gladys wasn't going to let pass the fact that it wasn't the quality they'd been led to expect. Bridal Blessings would have to make an adjustment in the price.

The wedding party broke up into smaller units for the drive to the Allegheny Hotel and the reception. Jimmy, the Tullocks' oldest son, gave his father's arm a squeeze as he and his wife, Laura, left to walk toward their own car.

"See you at the hotel," Jimmy yelled, "Me and Laura gotta swing by your house to pick up the presents."

Gladys and Ben were driving alone in their new Mercury. Before he opened the car door, Ben slid his hand inside his suit jacket and felt the envelope containing the twelve hundred-dollar bills. He wasn't used to having that much cash on him. Sometime during the evening he and Gladys were going to give the envelope to Sharon and Buddy. They had already given them the down payment on a house for a wedding present. The money in the envelope was a surprise for their honeymoon. Ben had heard that the airfare for their trip had cost them twelve hundred. He and Gladys hadn't been able to afford giving their other kids anything like this amount of money—at least they never thought they could. Ben and his cousin, Vernon, who died three years ago, had toiled through the years to build up their excavating and hauling business, putting most of the earnings back into equipment, and taking little for themselves—"Some day" they would. That day never came for Vernon, but his death was a signal for Ben: it was now or never for him too. He had sold the business for a good price, and now he and Gladys were positioned for a taste of the good life.

Gladys was driving, because of Ben's cataracts. He'd been advised to have the operation, but he kept putting it off. He didn't like the idea of a doctor cutting into his eyes. Gladys braked at the end of the church driveway and waited over-cautiously until no car was in sight in either direction before pulling slowly out onto the road.

2

"Quit whining, damn it," Clive snarled impatiently. "We jus gotta wait at this 'ere light 'til some ol' woman comes 'long. Then we jump inta the seat beside 'er, show'er the knife and tell 'er ta keep on a drivin'.'"

He pulled his baseball cap down so low on his forehead; he had to tip his head back to see.

"But Christ, Clive, hit's still daytime. Som'uns sure to see us do it an' call the po-lice. We only been out a month an' I sure as hell don't wanna go back inside."

"That's the beauty of it. No one's gonna 'spect to see a carjacking on a busy street in broad daylight. They'll think we're hitchin' a ride."

Lomas was incapable of pressing the point. "If you say so."

"Well, I say so."

They were standing on the shoulder of the road where the drive to the Laurel Hills shopping mall joined it. A traffic signal had been placed there to allow mall traffic to exit. Although it was Saturday afternoon, traffic was light. The oppressive heat had blunted the shopping urge of most. Drivers who did stop at the light and happened to look over at the two men saw something strange—two members of some nocturnal species out of place in the glaring sunlight.

Lomas, his bland, whiskered face registering the effort to think, pondered, then hesitatingly asked, "How we gonna be sure she's got money on 'er?"

"Hit's simple ding-dong. We pick a big new car. Cadillac or one of them Lexes."

Lomas nodded. Clive knew everything.

Half an hour passed without a likely candidate entering their trap. Clive became impatient, mumbling, "Fuckin' bastards" and "Git'n real mad here."

Suddenly he said, "Hey look! She's the one!"

A new Mercury sedan had pulled up to the light with an elderly woman at the wheel.

"But, there's an old guy with 'er." Lomas stammered.

"Don't matter. Quick now, into the back seat."

Clive did move quickly to enter the rear door on the passenger's side. His left hand went to the man's forehead, pulling his head back. His right hand held an open switchblade poised over the man's throat.

"Nobody panic. Sit real calm 'til the light changes ta green." Clive said this with a slow menace he'd heard tough guys use on TV.

Lomas had been following Clive into the back seat, but was blocked when Clive stopped and sat behind the old man. Finally figuring out the problem, he dashed around the car to the opposite door and dove inside just as the light changed and Gladys Tullock drove slowly away as she'd been told.

No other car had stopped at the light or approached it while the desperate carjacking was in progress. It had been a clumsy execution of a stupid idea, but luck was with them.

"Jus keep on doin' what I say an nobody's gonna git hurt. Now turn right at the next corner, an' drive out along the highway a piece." Clive was as confident as only those with little imagination can be.

Gladys was mute. She smelled the rancid odor of the man behind her, and this more than anything, meant to her that evil had suddenly entered their lives. She was afraid to say anything that might anger the two men.

Finally, it was Ben who spoke. "Where you taking us?"

"Don't you never mind," asserted Lomas, as if he were also making decisions.

"Hit's OK, Lomas," inserted Clive, "Hit don't hurt none ta tell 'em. We only borrowin' the car. We gonna let y'all out when we git somers where it can be done without bein' seed."

Gladys spoke up then. "We're supposed to be at our daughter's wedding reception. We should have been there by now."

"Well, y'all jus be a little late. Don't worry none, they gonna save y'all some cake." Clive laughed hard at his joke.

"No shee-it," laughed Lomas, trying to match his partner's tone.

About five miles north on the highway, Clive told Gladys to turn east on a county road. A few minutes later, he spotted a dirt road angling off to the right and had Gladys follow it. The narrow road descended gradually into a ravine, then made a sharp turn to the left and descended a steep grade. A single-lane, wooden bridge came into view. The road widened just before the bridge, so a car could pull over to let another pass. Clive told Gladys to drive onto the wide section, park and set the hand brake.

"This 'ere's as far as we go folks. This 'ere's the end of the line," he said brightly and at the same moment pulled back on the knife blade and drew it deeply across Ben Tullock's throat. Blood shot out and hit the windshield. Ben made a sound like "Hog" and flailed his arms for a moment and then went limp. Gladys screamed and choked for breath. Clive quickly pushed Lomas aside and moved over behind her, plunging the knife repeatedly into her chest. All this time she was trying to get out of her seat belt, but never did. Blood soaked the front of her new dress and puddled in her lap.

"Holy shit!" gasped Lomas. "You done went an' kilt 'em. Why'd you do that?"

"You don't think I could let 'em go after you went an' called me by my name?"

"I didn't do that... did I?" He thought he remembered Clive saying *his* name. But then maybe he was mistaken.

"Sure as hell did! Now we got ta hurry an' git their money an' git the hell outta here. You look through the old gal's purse an' I'll take the guy. Wait! We gotta be real careful 'bout our fingerprints. Let's see now, we done touched the door handles. Take that bandana a'yourn an' wipe the handles good. Same thing with the purse when you're done. Those cop scientists can identify a sneeze."

Clive was not known for the quality of his thinking, but in the next couple of minutes he achieved his personal best. He got out of the car and carefully wiped the knife he'd used on a wad of tissues from a box lying on the car's console, and then hold the knife in the tissues, he threw it down toward the fast moving water of the creek.

Lomas shaking uncontrollably, opened the front door and took Gladys's purse from the seat beside her and carefully opened it, holding it with his shirttail. He poked around inside with the knuckle of his index finger. All he found was a coin purse containing twelve dollars and a Visa card. He took the money.

Clive unfastened Ben's seat belt and rolled the body toward Gladys, so he could get the wallet out of Ben's back pocket. The wallet yielded only sixty-six dollars.

"What's wrong with these people?" he yelled. "How can they have a new car like this and no money?"

Clive took the money and then began wiping the wallet with the handkerchief Gladys had folded and placed in Ben's coat pocket after she'd tied his tie that afternoon before the wedding. Clive walked around the car to make sure Lomas was not doing something stupid. Satisfied, he walked across the road and holding the wallet in the handkerchief, he flung it like a flat stone as far as he could into the woods, aiming high through the upper branches of the trees. The handkerchief fell to the ground before going into the woods, and he retrieved it and shoved it into his pocket, mumbling, "Goddamned scientists."

It had been Clive's plan to drag the bodies into the brush and take the car. He bent into the car to take hold of Ben's body and noticed something. When he had rolled the body to the side to get at the wallet, the suit jacket had fallen open exposing the inside pocket. Clive now saw the end of an envelope protruding from it. He grabbed it.

"God damn! I shoulda knowd rich guys keep their money in the inside coat pocket. Fuckin' hundred-dollar bills." He counted. "Twelve! Twelve hundred dollars!"

"No shee-it. Leave it to ol' Clive."

Clive's jubilation suddenly passed. "We gotta problem here. We can't drive this car without gittin' covered in blood. Can't do that, cause somebody seein' that blood will be ask'n' questions."

"What we gonna do?" whined Lomas. Whenever Clive looked worried, he got scared.

Clive shoved the envelope into his back pocket and stood looking at the car, wondering if he'd overlooked anything. He reckoned not.

"What are we gonna do?" he answered Lomas. "We gonna do what we been a doin' all week—start a walkn'."

"Mom and Dad should have been here by now. I'm getting worried. Dad didn't look too good either," said Sharon, the new bride. She was standing next to her brother, Jimmy, in the hotel's banquet hall.

Jimmy walked over to a window that overlooked the parking lot. Concern showed on his face as he failed to identify his parents' car. He waited until Sharon had been called away by one of the guests and then took his wife aside.

"Laura, Sharon's right, Mom and Dad should be here by now. Maybe they waited at the parking lot and rested, but I'm going to drive back there and see." As an afterthought he said, "Don't say anything to the others. No use getting everybody upset . . . yet."

"This is my favorite kind of hiking," Kerry said.

"You mean downhill."

"Oh, that's what's different."

"Remember, in mountain hiking, what goes down must go up."

"I was afraid of that."

It was nearing seven when their path was crossed by a dirt road. The sun was beginning to release its torrid hold on the day.

Kerry stopped and listened. "That must be that stream we saw on the map. Sounds close."

"Yeah, we can't see it, because this road takes such a sharp dive into the ravine, but the bridge into Virginia must be right down there—a stone's throw from here."

They started to walk on again, Tom saying, "The booklet that came with the map says that this trail is one that the pioneers used back in the eighteenth century to cross the Appalachians through the Folsum Gap. When the Forestry Service reconstructed the trail, they put in a footbridge above the falls at the exact place where there had been one in the seventeen hundreds."

"One of the better uses of our tax dollars, I'd say."

"Kerry, I've got to take a quick trip into the woods. The rushing water has activated a primitive impulse."

Kerry walked on a few steps, swatting at mosquitoes. A minute later Tom stepped back onto the trail holding up a square object.

"Look what I found, a wallet." He walked up to Kerry while examining the wallet's contents. "No money, but there are some cards and a driver's license. Ben Tulloch. He lives in Springville."

He shuffled through an AARP membership card, a library card, a VFW membership and a Visa card.

"Looks like old Ben answered a call of nature at the same spot as I did. His wallet must have fallen out when he pulled his pants down. We'll call him when we get back."

Tom pulled her to him and kissed her. "C'mon, let's see if there's a swimming hole at the waterfall. Last one in's a rotten egg."

Jimmy Tulloch traveled the route his parents would have taken between the church and the hotel. He scanned the two gas stations he passed for their car. Finally, he drove into the empty church parking lot, where he called his parents' house on his cell phone. He let it ring eight times. He hung up and called his wife at the hotel.

"Laura, did Mom and Dad show up yet?"

"No. Where are you?"

"At the church. I'm going to drive over to their place now."

"Where can they be?" Fear was in the question.

"Don't get all worked up. They didn't have an accident along the route, so what else could be wrong?" Saying that brought the possibility of something like a heart attack to his mind, but he said nothing to his wife. "Just stay calm. I'll call you as soon as I check the house. OK?"

"OK."

Jimmy hung up and immediately called the only hospital in the city. He got a negative answer to his tensely asked question. Ten minutes brought him to his parents' empty house. He called his wife back.

"Are they there yet?"

"No, Honey, they're not."

"There's only one thing to do, call the police."

3

The natural pool cut by centuries of falling water couldn't have been more perfect on this scorching day. Their shocked cries when they first entered the cold mountain stream soon changed to giggles of delight. They splashed, they floated, they embraced. Their bodies tingled and remained cool through the time it took to make up and consume the freeze-dried chicken noodle soup.

"Hey, the top of your foot is red," Tom said pointing to an inflamed area on Kerry's right foot.

"Yeah, I see. My boot was rubbing, but I didn't think much of it."

Kerry had not brought her boots from New York. They were with other things that she had packed to be sent. So this morning Tom had insisted that she get a new pair for the hike.

"New boots," Tom observed. "I guess I should have let you wear your running shoes like you wanted to. We'd better take care of that. A blister can develop in no time."

He rummaged in his pack and found his first aid supplies. He gently rubbed some antibiotic cream over the area and then applied a broad adhesive bandage. He gave the sole of her foot a pat. "All done, Miss. Please give the receptionist your insurance card on your way out."

"Are you kidding? She wouldn't let me in here to see you without the card up front. You know, you've got a great bedside manner. Too bad it's going to be wasted in architecture."

"No, it won't. I plan to use it when I'm making sales pitches to young women."

"I don't think I like the image I'm seeing."

"You needn't worry, I'll always tell you everything."

"It's not the *telling* part I had in mind."

The teasing banter led to kisses, kisses to lovemaking.

Kerry lay awake in the tent. After they'd made love, Tom had fallen asleep. He laid breathing deeply beside her. The nearby waterfall roared steadily in the background. She was still floating upon the pleasure she'd had.

How strange it was to be here deep in a mountain forest she hadn't known existed two days ago. *Three* days ago she had walked along busy Manhattan streets. Strange again that a few months before this she hadn't known this man with whom she now intended to spend the rest of her life. Strange indeed, yet at the same time, she could think of nothing that seemed more right. No other man was imaginable. Tom was a little impulsive and unpredictable, but she knew deeply that he was a good, sincere person. She was also certain he loved her.

The heat of the day continued into the night,

but here near the falls, cooler air was thrown off as the plunging water crashed down the rocks of the cliff. Kerry was comfortable at last and content. She knew now that they would complete this diversion in a couple of days and then turn their combined attention to reconstructing their careers—and a life together.

Kerry thought she could detect a new sound above the noise of the falling water. She identified it when the sky flashed white.

She crawled out of the tent and quickly set about putting their gear into the backpacks and pulling them into the tent's small vestibule. She zipped up the entrance flap just as the first heavy drops began to strike the tent's fabric. She settled back listening to the drumming of the rain and drifted into sleep.

Sheriff Ray Royston perched on the desk in front of the room, a cup of coffee in his hand and a Marlboro in the other. He looked as if he wouldn't be fully awake until mid-morning. He took a drag on the cigarette and blew the smoke toward the ceiling. The County Building housing the Sheriff's Office was, of course, smoke-free.

Seven men and one woman dressed in the uniforms of the department sat in various attitudes of repose in front of him.

"It's a puzzler, all right. The guys on the night shift

covered every damn street in the city. No sign of the old couple. There's zero possibility that they up an' decided to go somewhere other than their daughter's reception."

"No quickie at a motel in Lewisburg?" The joker was a sandy-haired deputy in his early forties with a deeply acne-scarred face.

"That's right, Woody. So we gotta figure it as foul play." Royston leaned to one side and flicked his ashes toward a waste can. "An APB has been sent out across the state, of course." He handed the papers he'd been holding to the uniformed woman in the front row. "Pass these along, Patricia."

The long-haired blond woman, who looked more like a flute player than a cop, studied the picture she'd been handed. "This sure as hell isn't gonna be much help."

"I know. Sorry 'bout that, but the copier screwed up. We'll have better as soon as the technician gets here to repair it."

Woody chimed in. "Can't even tell if they're white folks or not."

"This department's got a non-racist copy machine," said the young man next to him. He looked to Woody for appreciation of his joke.

"Tell you what," said Royston, smiling, "You find that car, no matter who's in it, black, white or yellow, and you get yourself a nice reward. Family's offering one thousand dollars for information. We're usually excluded from rewards like this. Folks figure we'd only be doin' what we're paid to do, but not in this case: family said so."

"Why don't we start every day like this?" remarked Woody.

Royston's secretary came to the door and called him to the phone.

He slid off the desk. "Get out there now and make some good news copy for the department. Get your picture in the paper holding up that check for a thousand. On that sheet that got passed around are the details about the car, what the folks were wearing and so on. Your sector assignments are up here on the blackboard." He followed the secretary down the hall.

A tall, gangling deputy made a mock dash for the door. "I need that money for a new outboard."

Woody, Lonny beside him, stood for a moment looking at the blackboard. Woody took a pair of aviator style sunglasses out of his shirt pocket and put them on.

"C'mon boy, we gotta burn up some of the taxpayer's gasoline."

Usually there was but one deputy to a patrol car, but Lonny's indoctrination into the department had been assigned to Woody. This wasn't because Woody was the most suitable person, but because he had asked for the job, liking, as he did, to have a naive rookie riding along listening to his opinions, the sure opinions he had on any subject.

"You saw what it said on the board, spend the shift driving the roads east to the Virginia border, then north to the county line. Thought we might stop up there at Sweet Springs. Visit my cousin. Haven't seen him for a spell."

"Suits me fine," said Lonny.

"We need us a license plate an' we'll be outa here," said Clive with cocky self-assurance.

"I don't understand why you want to spend good money for a car, when we could easy steal ourselves one."

"Because, ding-dong, if we steal a car the cops'll be chasin' after us right away, an' we can't afford to git caught on this one."

"No shee-it."

"We buy the car that kid's sellin' off his front yard an' nobody's got any reason to go look'in for us. But we gotta have a plate to put on it."

"Think the County Building's open yet?"

Clive shook his head in disbelief. "We do not set foot in any fucking County Building. We steal a plate."

"Yeah, an' the po-lice'll be lookin' for the stolen plate." Lomas was surprised and pleased with his logic.

"Thas right." Clive glanced at his companion's satisfied expression. "Thas why we steal two plates."

Clive watched as confusion settled over Lomas's face like fog sliding down a mountainside.

"Two plates?"

"See, if we steal one plate, like you said, the cops'll

set out lookin' for a car with that number, but if we steal a second plate and put the first one we took on that second car and put that second plate on our car, the cops will be looking for the first plate, 'cause the owner of the second car won't have noticed his plate's missing. By the time they find the first plate on the second car—if they ever do—we'll be long gone."

Lomas couldn't begin to understand what Clive said, but it sounded real smart.

"Thas right smart," he said.

"Damn right it's smart, " Clive chuckled. "Right smart." He didn't add that he'd learned it from a fellow inmate doing time for car theft.

Still savoring his brilliance, he added, "We jus git us the plate an' go back an offer the kid two hundred less than he's a askin'. He'll go for it faster'n a whore can drop her shorts."

"There's something missing. Something like the smell of brewed coffee and the aroma and the sizzle of bacon cooking over a wood fire." Kerry stood barefoot, wearing only bikini panties and T-shirt while she sipped instant coffee and watched Tom pack up the miniature propane stove.

"What's missing is the pile of dirty dishes," Tom returned.

"Maybe someday we can cook a real breakfast in our backyard and put the dishes in the dishwasher."

"Brilliant idea. I agree as long as you dress like that."

Kerry laughed. "It depends on who our neighbors are. Actually, if you don't think the bears will mind, I'd like to wear this on the trail today. It's going to be as blistering hot as yesterday."

"The bears will be delighted . . . as well as the mosquitoes and deer flies."

"See what you mean," she said slapping a mosquito that had landed on her thigh. "I'll behave like a proper hiker, if you promise to find us another swimming hole."

"Promise them anything, my Daddy always said."

Kerry finished dressing and Tom collapsed the tent and began folding it. Half an hour would see them across the footbridge into Virginia.

4

"Whadya think happened to them folks we're lookin' for?" Lonny asked.

He and Woody were about six miles east of the city limit, having just turned north off the highway to White Sulfur Springs.

"Like Royston said, it ain't good. If they were alive an' able to, they woulda got in touch with their folks by now. Somebody musta held em up, probably hijacked their car. More'n likely they done robbed an killed em."

"Damn, that'd be a shame, right after their daughter got married an all."

"No time's a good time to get yourself killed." Woody glanced at his partner and saw that he looked pale.

"What's the matter with you, boy?"

"I was thinkin' if they're dead, I don't want to find their car."

Lonny's timidity irritated Woody. How could he be the manly role model he thought himself to be to a guy who was a wuss?

"What, and pass up that reward money?" Woody teased, hoping to kindle some spirit in Lonny. "You're right, though, it'd be ugly for sure."

Woody slowed the car as he passed a dirt road that joined the pavement.

"I been down that road before. Bottom of the hill there's a bridge. You can walk in a ways to a nice little waterfall." He backed the patrol car up until he could look down the road.

"Guess we better check it out. Other side the bridge ain't our territory. Virginia's on that side."

He shifted into drive and nosed the car down the narrow road.

"That's another thing that burns me up. Over in Virginia somebody kills somebody he gets what he deserves, gets his ass fried in the 'lectric chair, or maybe they inject 'em with that poison over there. On this side a that bridge, we pay his room'n board ten, fifteen years, then find him a job. Pisses me off. That bastard Willis Hogan, guy that killed that whole family up at Buckhannon, that's what happened to him. In jail eight years, comes up with some legal bullshit about DNA, gets a new trial, next thing he's scot-free. Makes me 'shamed to be a West Virginian."

They came to a triangular, orange sign bearing the picture of a hiker. "This here's the trail that leads on in to that waterfall."

A few yards farther, the road made a sharp left turn and angled down steeply into a wooded ravine.

"For sure no one's been over this road since it rained last night," observed Lonny, looking ahead at the smooth surface of the clay.

Suddenly, each took in a quick, audible breath as they simultaneously spotted the new Mercury parked ahead of them where the road widened a bit before a one-lane bridge.

"Son-of-a-bitch! Ain't that the license number?" Woody said in a whisper.

Lonny glanced down at the paper lying on his lap. "That's it," he said through a tight throat.

Woody pulled up behind the Tullochs' car and put on the handbrake. He got out of the patrol car and walked carefully up to the driver's window.

"Holy Shit!" He spun around. "Son-of-a-bitch!"

"What is it?" asked Lonny, climbing out of the patrol car, dread in his voice.

Woody stood with both hands on his hips looking down toward the bridge, taking deep breaths. Hesitantly, Lonny edged up to Tullochs' car, leaning forward to peek inside. He gasped, stepped back and immediately looked to his mentor for a sign of what to do next.

Woody still faced the bridge. He was sweating, but telling himself to get hold of himself. Lonny was looking to him to lead. He turned manfully back to calmly study the horrible scene inside the car.

"Cut the ol' man's throat an stabbed hell outa the ol' lady . . . God damn sick bastard!"

"Shall I call in?" asked Lonny, trying to steady his voice.

"Yeah."

Lonny, relieved to have an excuse to distance himself from the gory scene, quickly got back in the patrol car and with shaking hands began to go thorough the recently learned procedure to operate the radio.

"Wait a minute, Lonny," Woody called out. "I gotta think."

"Waddaya mean?"

"I mean jus' what I said, damn it. I gotta think a minute."

Woody stood looking toward the bridge; then he walked up the hill behind the Mercury and examined the surface of the road. Slowly he walked back to where Lonny waited and studied the anxious face of the younger man.

"What we got here, my friend, is a situation where we can be obedient, dumb assholes, or we can act the way real men do when they're in command. Any friggin' buck private can follow the rules, but the general breaks the rules in order to get done what needs gettin' done . . . then he lies about it if he has to. Always been that way."

Puzzlement was written on Lonny's face, but he said nothing, afraid of saying the wrong thing.

Woody continued, "All we gotta do is let this car of theirs roll down across that bridge an' into Virginia. That way, the fuckin' bastard that done this'll go to the 'lectric chair. We also save our state a whole pile of money."

Lonny was stunned by what he'd just heard.

"But, ain't that tamperin' with evidence?"

"The only evidence we change is the car's location.

There ain't no evidence right round here anyway—no foot prints or such. Last night's rain saw to that. I jus now took a careful look—no foot prints, all washed away." He was thinking as he talked. "We don't change any evidence in the car itself, jus' move it."

"What about the new tracks the car'll make goin' from here cross the bridge?" Lonny asked in a hesitant attempt at dissuasion.

"Done thought of that. This road's still wet from the rain. We let the Merc roll across the bridge, then we take water from the crick and wash over the tire tracks. Then we carefully drive the patrol car right over the same track. No one will be able to tell the Merc was moved. After a few minutes the water we throw on will sink in an' look no different from the rest of the road."

Woody saw that he'd got his partner thinking about the plan he'd just laid out. He pressed on. "Think of what that son-of-a-bitch did to these good people. You don't want him to get away with it do ya?"

Lonny was afraid to be a party to what Woody was suggesting, but he was even more afraid of displeasing this veteran officer for whom he'd developed a naive respect. He nodded his agreement with the plan.

"Good. Now we gotta act fast before another car comes along."

"Wait. Suppose a car has come along an' already seen the Mercury where it sets now?"

"There's no chance of that. You said yourself that no

one's been by since the rain an' that was 'round midnight. The chance that a car passed by from the time these folks went missin' 'til midnight is slim. They would'a been drivin' slow cause of the narrow bridge an' would'a seen these folks all cut up. They would've reported that for damn sure."

Lonny wasn't totally convinced, but said nothing more.

Woody acted before Lonny could raise another objection or get cold feet. He popped open the trunk lid of the patrol car and took out the pair of gloves he kept there. Wearing the gloves, he opened the driver's door of the Tullochs' car. He grasped the steering wheel in his left hand and stepped carefully onto the threshold with both feet and balanced there. He then reached across Gladys's bloody lap and turned on the ignition switch and slipped the shifter out of park and into neutral. He released the hand brake and the car began to roll down the steep incline toward the bridge, gathering speed as he steered it toward the center of the road.

The momentum carried the car over the bridge and thirty feet beyond—thirty feet into the State of Virginia. Woody steered to the side of the road. After he reset the brake, returned the shifter to park and turned off the ignition, he stepped carefully onto the surface of the road. He wiped the threshold clean of the mud from his shoes and closed the car door.

He yelled up the hill to Lonny, "Git that collapsible bucket outta the trunk of the cruiser an' come down here an' fill it with water from the crick."

Lonny hesitated only a brief moment and then began to do as he'd been told. Woody watched with satisfaction. His partner was now an accomplice in the deception.

Lonny filled the bucket and handed it up to Woody on the bridge, who began the job of obliterating the car tracks. Ten bucketfuls produced the effect he aimed for. He splashed water under the Mercury with his hand, preserving some of the tread marks, making it look like the car had protected them from the full force of the rain.

"I'm gonna get the cruiser. You guide me so my tires go 'xactly on top a where the Merc's tracks were."

Fifteen minutes later Woody stood surveying their work with the critical eye Roy Royston would give it when he arrived. He smiled. "Well done, my friend. Now I'll make that call in to headquarters."

He gave the information to the dispatcher then sat a moment studying Lonny's face. His protégé was standing uncomfortably next to the Tullochs' car, glancing furtively in at Ben and Gladys's bloody remains. Lonny's loyalty was critically important. Woody decided he needed to do some more work.

He got out of the patrol car and sidled up to his partner and put his hand on Lonny's shoulder. "The story is this. We drove right up here behind their car. We both got out an inspected it. We decided to leave everthin' jus' like we found it an' call in. Then we decided to look under the bridge in case someone was ahidin' there. That'll 'splain the footprints goin' down the bank. Then we walked up the hill givin' the roadside a once over. That 'splains our footprints up on the hill. Aside from that, we jus' been waitin' for our guys."

Woody read pale terror in Lonny's face.

"Tell ya what, let me do the 'splainin'. You jus' nod. OK?"

"Yeah, OK."

Eleven minutes later the first patrol car arrived. Soon footprints covered the scene. So engrossed was everyone with the horror of it all, not once in the ensuing activity did anyone question Woody's tale.

It took Sheriff Royston but a couple of minutes to appreciate the situation. "You were right to delay any examination of the interior of the car, Woody, because we got ourselves a jurisdictional matter here. It belongs to the Virginia State Police. We'll cooperate, of course, but we gotta wait to see how they wanna handle it. It gives the killer or killers an advantage, since it'll take the Virginians at least an hour to get here from the post in Henderson, but that's the way it is."

Woody hadn't thought of that, but he quickly dismissed the possibility that his deception had aided the murderer.

Royston proceeded to contact the Virginia police. When he returned from his car to the group of deputies who stood several yards from the Tullochs' car, not wanting to stay near it once they'd looked inside, he said, "At least we can have a look 'round on our side of the creek while we're waiting. You three men take this side of the road, and you men," he said looking back at Woody and Lonny, "take the other side. Look for anything. The killer or killers had to leave here some way. Tracks here on the road are all washed away, but maybe they stepped off the road, or broke some weeds or dropped something."

Woody believed it was just look-busy work. He was sure the killer had walked back up the hill to the main road, or else an accomplice had followed in another car, the tracks from which had been obliterated by the rain. He pretended to be making a concentrated search as Royston had ordered, but his mind was on his story, going over it so he wouldn't make a mistake. It was with surprise that he heard another deputy cry out.

"Hey, up here! There's a boot print! Here where this hiking path crosses the road."

Men scrambled up the hill to where the deputy pointed to two of Tom's boot prints that had been protected from the rain by leaves of an overhanging shrub.

"That's part of the old Folsum Trail," said one of the men. "It heads up that way to a waterfall."

"These are good prints and they're fresh," Royston observed. "Good chance it's our man. Mark them with some tape until we can get a cast made. Now let's see if we can follow them along that trail . Woody, you stay here to show these prints to the Virginia forensic team and to take any incoming calls."

Sitting alone in the Sheriff's car, Woody began to face up to the seriousness of what he and Lonny had done. His career as a lawman would come to an abrupt end if it were discovered. He managed to brush that awareness aside as he might a fly. Reassuringly in its place followed a surge of manliness. He had stepped up boldly and had acted as a *truly* responsible man must. It may turn out in the end that he'd be martyred, but he would know he had cast his lot with the great men of history.

5

"Why does one always have to climb to the top of a hill before a rest is permitted?"

Kerry's tone was pleading, her pace slowed, her steps becoming more labored.

Tom looked back at her, aware now that his hiking experience was much different than hers. It was only mid-morning, but the front of her T-shirt already showed a darker V of sweat.

"Because if you stop before you get to the top you may never get there at all. You may, instead, elect to take the easy course of turning and going back down." He said this with a mock didactic tone. "At the top of the hill the trail ahead is just as easy as the way back . . . so one advances."

"My God, I've been sleeping with Marcus Aurelius!"

Tom wiped a drop of sweat from her cheek. "No, I think it's from the Boy Scout Creed."

"It's not the Girl Scout Creed; I can tell you that."

"I didn't know you were a Girl Scout." Tom studied her as if she'd revealed a staggering fact.

"There are a lot of things you don't now about me, fella."

He raised a skeptical eyebrow. "I don't believe you. Let's hear you recite the Girl Scout Creed."

Kerry shrugged. "Hell, that's easy. The creed's simple. It says, "Girl! Don't do nothin' dumb.""

Tom laughed. "I take it back. You're genuine." He took her face in both hands and kissed her.

"Nice work Atwood, you've just managed to manipulate yourself a rest stop." He shifted his backpack. "All set? It's not far to the top."

The trail emerged from the dense woods and traversed a rocky barren slope, which reflected the heat, turning the trail into a solar oven. Finally, they reached the peak, a smooth dome of rock from which there was a wide panoramic view. They got out of their gear and sat next to each other. A fresh breeze flowed over them. Kerry soaked the bandana she'd worn around her neck with water from her water bottle and passed it over her face and neck.

"Ah, the little pleasures."

Tom checked his watch. "Eleven fifteen. Let's eat something here. Granola bar. Something light, so we can hike a couple more hours before lunch."

"Did Lewis and Clark have granola bars?"

"No, but they had bear grease patties."

"Yum. I promise not to complain again. Just don't bring out the bear grease."

From their perch the whole valley and the line of mountains to the east lay spread out before them.

"Beautiful country," Tom said.

After surveying the scene for a few moments, she said softly. "It is. It really is."

"Looks like they spent the night here. See, here's a dry spot where they put down something like a tarp." Sheriff Royston was pointing to an area of dry ground.

One of the deputies kneeling beside one of Martha's boot prints observed, "There's two of them all right. One wears about a size eleven and this one wears something like an eight, an' they're new boots. They walked all around here this morning. No sign of a fire."

"Which likely means these weren't campers," Royston said. "Looks like they planned to hike back into the National Forest and either lie low in there until they'd judge it to be safe, or else they're headed to a town, such as Allegheny, where they got a car stashed. I think the new boots means this was a planned car jacking not a spur-of-the-moment act. They planned to drive here in the hijacked car, kill them folks and get away through the forest."

Royston began climbing up the trail to the footbridge that crossed the creek. Tom and Martha's boot prints clearly showed that they had crossed over to the Virginia side.

"Well," he said to the men who had followed him. "This makes it clear that this is totally a Virginia matter." He took his walkie-talkie off his hip and called Woody.

"Woody, there are two of them. They're on the old Folsum Trail heading into Virginia. Let the Virginia Patrol know. Be a good idea for them to bring a chopper down from Roanoke. Dogs, of course. We're comin' back now."

Royston thought that about wrapped it up for his department. Only one damn thing he had to do—tell the family about their mom and dad.

"We got lucky back there, son."

"No shee-it," said Lomas.

"Clive looked into the rear-view mirror. "Road's clear. Heave that plate outta the winder as far as ya can. We don't need it no more."

He lit a cigarette and took a deep, satisfying drag. "Got us a registration signed by the seller an' his old plates. We jus' sell the car cheap to a two-bit car lot when we get ta St. Louis an' thas that. Nobody lookin' fur this car. Home safe."

Lomas was happy. He glanced over at Clive, deeply proud to be his friend.

Virginia state trooper Frank Brace glanced at his watch, twelve eleven. Springville, West Virginia could be seen below through the haze. Jim Lynch, the helicopter's pilot, had flown north from their Roanoke, Virginia base and had approached Springville by following highway U.S. 64, because they had been instructed to land in a mall parking lot near the highway.

"There's the mall, there on the right. See the Kmart sign," said Brace.

As they neared, a cordoned-off area was identifiable at the parking lot's northeast corner. Captain Lucas from the Henderson, Virginia post would meet them there to brief them and give them further instructions. Behind Brace on a shelf was the case holding the scoped Remington 700.

Frank Brace had only been with the Virginia State Police for two months, but had already been singled out as a rookie with great promise. That was not a new role for Brace. Since childhood, he had impressed adults as a take-charge kid who would come through to meet their expectations. He knew this, of course, and did his best to not disappoint. His area of greatest ability was physical rather than mental. Not that he was dull witted, but he naturally found more interest in doing rather than thinking. He had been, as his teachers and classmates expected, captain of both his high school football and basketball teams.

Frank was excited by the prospect of the chase they were about to join and had the spontaneous, self-congratulatory thought of how happy he was to be where he was rather than to be working at that Kmart down below.

Those on the ground, having spotted the helicopter, broke in on the radio to give instructions for landing.

This accomplished, a man wearing a Virginia State Police uniform, walked in under the still-turning rotor blades.

"You guys made good time. I'm Captain Lucas. The local police have found the trail of two men. They are going east on this hiking trail," he explained, handing Jim Lynch a National Forest Service map and pointing to the broken line that traced the trail. "There are indications they slept here last night." He indicated the point near where the trail crossed from West Virginia into Virginia. "Probably killed the old couple after dark and had to stop after hiking a short way, because they couldn't see the trail well enough. We have men on the trail following them now. Even with a very early start this morning they can't be too far ahead of us. Flying slowly, like you'll have to in order to identify the trail below, you still should be able to overtake them inside an hour. We don't know if they have guns—killed the old couple with a knife—slashed 'em up viciously.

"Your job is to find them and keep them under surveillance until the ground party catches up. If you see them, you could, however, send down a few rounds to make them take cover and slow them down. You can back off after that."

"From here, take a bearing of 121 degrees southeast. When they hear your engines, the ground party will guide you by radio to the trail. The trail is also fully charted on GPS. Finding the fugitives will be harder. Hopefully you'll catch them on a part of the trail that's not covered by trees. Keep the radio open and report as you proceed. Good hunting."

Lucas ran from under the turning blades, reflexively ducking his head. Lynch advanced the throttle and the ship rose above the mall. He registered the compass reading and began to fly along it. Frank took the rifle from its case and inserted a cartridge clip and racked a round into the firing chamber. As he did so, he had a brief memory of a childhood game played with his friends in the woods near his home. One person would be "it" and would have to escape through the woods, while the rest pursued him. He felt the same excitement.

After only six minutes, a voice came in over the chosen frequency.

"This is Sergeant Ross. We're directly south of you about a quarter mile. We're flashing a mirror."

Lynch banked the ship and flew slowly southward.

"I see it," said Brace, pointing. Six Virginia troopers were waving at them from a small clearing.

Ross spoke again, "I wouldn't be too ambitious if I were you. My bet is that they're armed. Just slow 'em up for us."

"Thanks. See ya'll later."

The progress was slow. Long sections of the trail were completely shrouded by the dense canopy of leaves.

"It will be a simple thing for them to take cover when they hear us," said Brace.

"'Fraid so, but like the captain said, if they're ducking for cover, we slow them up."

"If they're still on the trail at all, that is." He hoped like hell they were.

Sharon, the Tullochs' daughter, sat on the edge of their living-room sofa, her face in her hands, crying. Her husband, Buddy, had an arm around her shoulders and kept squeezing her to him in an effort to do something to ease her pain.

"We've found their tracks—there are two of them." It was early afternoon and Ray Royston had just completed the task he disliked most about his job. Yet, his avuncular manner made him the best one on the force to deliver this kind of news.

"No way they're going to get away."

He was trying now to take away some of the pain he had just delivered.

"There's this other fact. The murders were committed across the state line in Virginia. This means these scum will be executed. I give you my promise they'll get what they deserve. They deserve to die an' they will!"

"I'm going to enjoy that," Buddy exclaimed, giving Royston a smile of thanks. He added, "By the way, we appreciate what you've done—how fast your department has worked. The family offered a reward for finding Sharon's parents. Which of your men is it?"

"There were two, Deputies Youngblood and

Sheffield."

"Please have them contact me."

"I'll do that. You realize the Virginia State Police will be in charge from now on." Royston was relieved. As far as he was concerned, the case was closed.

"Why couldn't those bastards have stopped a little earlier, on the other side of that damned bridge," lamented Fitz Halloran.

"Yeah, some people don't know the meaning of considerate," joked Joe Tappan.

Tappan, the Commander of the State Police Post at Henderson, Virginia had just given the news to Halloran, the District Attorney of Henderson County. Halloran was standing at his desk in the County Building holding the putter he'd been practicing with.

"It's a bitch," Halloran continued, "But all ya can do at this point is smile an' say mah, pleasha."

Tappan smiled and shook his head. Halloran was a damned northerner, New Jersey or someplace, but he always tried to sound more southern than a native. Hell, no one around here talked that way.

"Exactly," Tappan agreed. "At least this should be a cut-and-dried case for you. The guy's wallet is missing, so it's most likely a hijacking and robbery. And that means the court will most likely end up appointing a public defender."

"Yeah, but what are you getting at?"

"It means you'll be able to assign the case to your assistant, what's her name, Rogers, and we won't have to miss any golf."

Halloran laughed. "Possibly." Some other ideas had been running through his mind, and they had to do with the next election and a possible nomination for his party's candidate for State Attorney General.

"But whatever happens, Ah'll find time t'win back all that money you stole from me when Ah had tendonitis in mah shoulder."

"Oh no. Not that phony excuse again. Tell you what. I'll give the money back if you promise to stop whining."

"That'll be the day you give any money back. You're forcin' me to remember the time the waiter gave you Jackie's change by mistake an' you pocketed it."

"I think that's slander. If you were any kind of attorney, you'd know that. Say Fitz, I gotta go, but I'll keep you posted on this case."

Fitz Halloran leaned on his desk and unconsciously traced circles on the carpet with his putter. If these killers turned out to be the scumbags he imagined they were, getting a conviction and a death sentence would be easy and make him very popular with those on one side of the state's current controversy over capital punishment—the side that backed his party one hundred per cent. He'd be very popular, indeed, because this would be an undisputed instance of justice being done, along with the clear need for the death sentence. Yes, this could become an interesting case.

6

After another hour on the trail, the hikers reached the summit of the next peak, again a wide dome of smooth gray rock. Kerry and Tom laid their backpacks under a pine tree that had somehow managed to grow in a crevice in the rock. She unhooked the water bottle from her pack and carried it out onto the open space. Tom dug his camera out of his pack and joined her. Uninterrupted forest filled the valley below.

"It looks just as it did when the first settlers made this trail. Standing here you'd never know there are such things as highways and automobiles," Kerry said.

"Or shopping malls or Monday Night Football."

"Or Microsoft."

"Or Google."

Kerry laughed. "Maybe we just dreamed them."

"I hope not. I've got fifty shares of Microsoft."

"Really, I'm marrying a financier?"

"I won them in a poker game as an undergrad."

"What a relief. I'm only marrying a gambler."

Tom raised the camera and looked through the viewfinder. "No. It really doesn't capture it." He turned abruptly and snapped a picture of Kerry, catching her off-guard.

"A twenty-first century pioneer," he announced, pressing the shutter release.

"With sweat dripping off her chin. Did you ever notice how no one seems to sweat in those early photographs?"

"They don't make ladies like they used to."

Kerry hit him on the arm. At the same time, a beating sound reached them, coming up out of the valley behind them.

Listening, Tom said, "Sounds like a helicopter. What would . . . "

The dark form of the machine rose above the trees on the last summit they had climbed and then disappeared again as it dipped down over the trail where it traversed the saddle between the two peaks.

Inside the cockpit, Frank Brace strained to pick out the course of the trail. Suddenly the helicopter was above the open rock face where Tom and Kerry stood.

"There they are!" Brace shouted.

Lynch immediately brought the ship to a hovering halt. Brace grabbed the microphone of the plane's loudspeaker and shouted with stern authority, "We are the Virginia State Police! Don't move!"

"He's got a gun, Frank!" Lynch yelled.

"What the . . . Run Kerry!" Tom shouted and made a break for the cover of the trees at the edge of the rock dome.

"Tom. Wait . . ."

"He's running for cover, take him down," Lynch screamed.

Frank Brace leveled the Remington at the fleeing figure trying to aim low at the legs. He squeezed off two rounds and saw the man fall and his pistol slide away over the rock surface.

Lynch took up the microphone and shouted for the second man to stand still. Instead, the guy ran and knelt by his fallen buddy. This second man did not seem to be armed and the pistol lay a dozen yards away.

"Tell him to stay right there and I won't shoot him," said Brace.

Lynch repeated this over the speaker then looked for a space to land the chopper. The ground party was an hour, maybe more, away. If he didn't land, it would mean hovering for that period. There was room enough, but it would be tricky; the surface slanted downhill. He also had to keep the passenger side facing the fugitives so Brace could keep them covered with the rifle. With the rotors spinning as close as he dared get to the trees, Lynch lowered the craft onto the rock with a jolt.

Brace jumped to the ground and began cautiously approaching the two fugitives, his rifle ready.

"OK you, stand up and step back nice and easy like," he said in a voice choked with the effects of adrenaline.

"Why did you do this," screamed Kerry, her face wet with tears. "Why did you shoot him?"

From the air, they had only seen the top of her

baseball cap. Now Brace and Lynch looked with horror into the face of a distraught woman, one who might well have been either's sister.

The eyes of both men fell to look at the motionless man at her feet. The total lack of movement and unnatural position of the body allowed but one conclusion. A large pool of blood had formed next to him and was beginning to run in a rivulet down the stone slope.

Brace's glance searched the man's legs for evidence of the wound he'd meant to inflict. The legs were untouched.

"You hit him in the neck," said Lynch.

"Who are you people?" wailed Kerry.

"Virginia State Police," answered Frank, incongruously polite.

Jim Lynch knelt by Tom's body and pointlessly felt for a pulse in the wrist. He was loath to touch the bloody neck for the carotid pulse. He stood up and stepped back.

"What's your name?" Frank asked, his head spinning with the knowledge that he had just killed a man.

"Why did you shoot him?" screamed Kerry.

Her attitude and her obvious confusion were not at all what Frank Brace expected. Defensively he charged, "You killed a man and a woman!"

"What the fuck are you talking about?" screamed Kerry, near hysteria.

"He was resisting arrest. He had a gun," said Brace, pointing to Tom.

"What gun?" she gasped.

Brace looked and pointed in the direction the gun had slid. The camera, which he now saw, seemed like a conjurer's trick. "It *was* a gun," he murmured. "It was. It was a gun," he blurted angrily. "Search her!" he said to Lynch. "Raise your hands over your head," he commanded, covering confusion and fear with bravado.

"No weapon," Lynch reported.

Kerry sank to a squat, her arms crossed over her knees, head on her arms, and sobbed quietly.

"I'll go and report," said Lynch, retreating to the mental safety of the helicopter.

Holding the rifle as if Kerry still posed a threat, Frank Brace backed away several steps. He really wanted to hide, to be a million miles away, to be a clerk at Kmart.

In the cockpit of the ship, Lynch made contact with Sergeant Ross. "We have the two suspects. One of them is down . . . dead actually." Stuttering between the wish to avoid saying a mistake had been made and a need not to lie, he finished his account of the action.

Frank Brace watched helplessly as Kerry suddenly leaned forward onto her hands and vomited.

7

Anyone watching D.A. Fitz Halloran's face as he listened to Joe Tappan on the phone would know he was tense. Gone was his habitual façade of negligent self-assurance. A look of anxious concern had taken its place.

"But what the hell is the girl saying? You've tried to lean on her, haven't you?"

Tappan heard blame and became defensive. "I haven't had a chance to talk to her yet, Fitz. Lucas hasn't either. They're just now arriving back here with the two of them, the girl and the guy's body. Anyway, Ross, the sergeant in charge of the ground party, said she suddenly clammed-up and says she wants an attorney."

Tappan took a deep breath before he began the bit that he knew would have Halloran shouting. "There's this. Earlier, up on the mountain and right after the guy was shot, she claimed she and the guy had only been hiking and camping."

"Holy shit!" Halloran screamed, "You're telling me you shot a god damned hiker on the Folsum Trail. Who's the moron who did it?"

"I don't have that information, yet." Tappan lied. He didn't want to give Halloran Frank Brace's name right then. He knew Fitz Halloran and he knew Halloran would publicly castigate Brace without giving him a fair hearing. Tappan also noticed that Fitz, in his excitement had forgotten to affect his down-home good ol' boy dialect.

"Well let me know, and until we know what we've got here, stall the media all you can. You know, 'a statement will be released as soon as . . . blah, blah, blah'. That kind of crap." His tone changed. "Snuggle up to that bunny, Joe, an' git her talkin' an' git back tuh me. We gotta stir this pot 'til shit turns tuh honey."

There he goes again, thought Tappan. "Right. Are you going to be at this number for a while?"

Halloran didn't like to commit himself. He enjoyed having people search to find him—important man on the go—but he wanted no delay today. "Ah'll be raht he-yah."

Halloran put down the phone and gave the desktop a drum roll with his fingers. What a fucking mess. Then he had a thought that excited him. The old couple lived in West Virginia; maybe they weren't killed in Virginia at all. Perhaps the car was only abandoned in Virginia. If so, it was not Henderson County's problem at all—not his problem at all. He felt better for a few seconds before he realized the word on the street would be that he ducked out of a difficult situation, not a good thing if he was serious about the attorney general nomination. Ah, but then he reminded himself that the murders, the couple and the guy on the mountain, came under the jurisdiction of the U S Forest Service. The Service normally handed over the jurisdiction to local courts, but he could refuse this and force the federal court to take the cases. No, that would be unusual and draw negative attention. Better leave things as they are. This way he'd be able to guide the investigation. One thing he quickly decided. If it turned out that a damn fool mistake had been made and they really were hikers, he'd distance himself. Dana Rogers, his assistant would get the assignment and they'd go for negligent homicide against the stupid trigger-happy cop. On the other hand, he reconsidered; there would be a lot of voters who would support a trooper using his gun to protect them even if his judgment sucked. Well that would have to wait until he had more information and had time to read the public's mood. In the meantime, he'd let Rogers stand in front of the cameras.

The four men standing by a golf cart were engaged in the ritual of settling bets from the round they'd just finished. The tallest—heavy set, proud of bearing, full head of carefully tended graying hair—had been the big loser. This was often the case, so he tended to treat the sport lightly, as if it required attributes not natural to a real man. After all, it was well known that he had played football at Duke and had a reputation as a skilled duck hunter. His name was Justin Dahl. For twelve years he had been a U.S. Congressman and was now nearing the end of his four year term as governor of the Commonwealth of Virginia.

The man pocketing most of the winnings was Dahl's attorney, business advisor, political confidant and probably his only real friend, Hamilton Bascomb. Political animal as he'd been early in his career, changing loyalties as easily as the fashion-conscious change their wardrobes, Ham had eventually risen to wealth and considerable power with Justin Dahl and had committed himself to staying with him now, come what may.

Two men had broken about even in the betting. Clarence Reed was a feature writer for the *New York Times*. He was ostensibly researching a piece on the current national political scene and the omnipresent struggle between conservatives and liberals over issues of abortion, gun control, capital punishment, biotech engineering, global warming, health care reform etc. He was structuring the article around the profiles of four governors. He had been following Justin Dahl around for the last four days.

The final member of the foursome was State Senator Floyd Cummins. His forty-two years in public office had carried him from being an unknown Fairfax County Supervisor from Mason to becoming the sanctified ruler and kingmaker of his party within the state. He had long ago become corrupt in the sense meant by Lord Acton when he declared, "power corrupts." He wasn't willfully corrupt any more than most of those corrupted by power. It was just that he—and those like him—had come to believe that petty rules and ethical standards didn't apply to them. It had been Floyd Cummins who had put Justin Dahl's name before the party caucus for governor. And true to Floyd's promise, Dahl's nomination had followed automatically.

The assistant golf pro, standing to the side, waited until he saw that the exchange of money was completed before he stepped up to Governor Dahl.

"There's a telephone message for you, sir." He handed Dahl a slip of paper.

Justin looked down at the name of his administrative assistant, Fletcher Eton. He knew Fletcher wouldn't interrupt him at a golf outing unless it was urgent. Eton had been his right hand man since he'd first taken public office, and they read each other like pitcher and catcher.

"I'll meet you fellas in the men's grill," Dahl said. "I gotta make a phone call."

Justin Dahl never used a cell phone; it wasn't secure enough. He breezed past Sadie, the club administrator's secretary, tossing a pleasantry in her direction, and into Curtis Langtry's pretentious office.

"Curtis, my friend, I need to use your private line for a few minutes, that possible?"

"Certainly, Governor. Sit right here. I was just leaving to grab myself a cup of coffee."

"Thank you, Curtis. 'Preciate it." That'll be the day, Justin thought, when Curtis goes to get his own coffee rather than sending Sadie. He dialed Fletcher Eton's number.

"What's up Fletcher?" he asked.

"It may turn out to be nothing, Justin, but I thought you should know. Have you heard about the couple in Springville, West Virginia, who were kidnapped and murdered?"

"Can't say I have. What of it?"

"Apparently the killing took place just over the Virginia border and our state police mounted a pursuit of two suspected killers. One of the police helicopters spotted a likely pair on the old Folsum Trail. One of the suspects appeared to be armed with a handgun. The troopers identified themselves over the chopper's bullhorn and told the guy to drop the gun. Instead, he took off running and one of the troopers fired at him intending to hit his legs. Instead, he got the guy in the neck and killed him. You following me so far?"

"Yes, and I don't like where you're heading."

"Yeah, well it turns out the guy didn't have a gun, it was a camera, and the other 'man' turned out to be a woman wearing a baseball cap. She claimed they were on a hiking and camping outing."

"Oh, fuck." Both men were silent for several seconds. Dahl muttered to himself, "And the real killers are still out there." He gathered himself. "So what are you advising?"

"Of course, we don't know enough at this time, but I wanted you to know in case a TV reporter pops a mike in your face."

"Let's see now. 'Naturally, I'm acquainted with the incident you're referring to, but at this time all the facts haven't been assembled. When they are, my office will be making a statement.' That do?"

"Admirably." Eton was experiencing *déjà vu*. How many times had he heard Justin say, "All the facts haven't been assembled."

"Thanks, Fletcher. Talk to you later."

Kerry felt acutely disoriented. Tom's death was devastating in itself, but multiplying its effect on her was the apparent continuing notion the police held that she and Tom had murdered someone. Maddening was the lack of opportunity to speak with anyone who had the authority to clear up this craziness. The people she had lamented to about the situation only half heard her—or less. They were only doing their job and processing a category, in this instance a murder suspect.

Her disorientation matched the way she'd felt the day her mother died. In the spring of her sophomore high school year she had returned home from a play rehearsal to find her mother lying dead at the bottom of the basement stairs. She'd called 911 and then sat with her mother until the paramedics arrived. She'd then moved to the kitchen table for an hour as people came and went, doing their assigned jobs. It was work as usual for them, but for her it was the end of the life she had known. How could something so devastating to her be so meaningless to those around her?

She and her mother had been unusually close, their relationship holding together Kerry's shaky adolescent ego, lending structure and a sense of continuity. Her father unfortunately created the disjoining force in her early life. With a master's degree in physics from NYU, he became a jet engine and turbine salesman for G.E., only to see a promising career dissolve in alcohol. Home life became so chaotic that Kerry's mother got a divorce when Kerry was nine to protect her and her two-year younger brother, Vince, from certain, major psychic damage. Kerry's regular contact with her father ended at that time. Although her mother had custody of the children, Vince ran away repeatedly to be with his seductive and almost criminally permissive father. Finally, when he was nine, the mother gave up and allowed Vince to move there. After this, Kerry's relationship with her brother became unpredictable. Occasionally he would call her and arrange meetings, which he would frequently miss, always having an elaborate and transparently bogus excuse.

Suddenly then, with her mother's death, Kerry found herself alone. The surety that life had meaning collapsed. In an empathic, generous and perhaps life-saving act, her school counselor took Kerry into her home for her remaining high school years. She struggled to find meaning and stability once again, narrowing her scope of interest, first to academics and then to work, two sanctuaries where if she worked hard she would be secure. She had made good friends at work, but she unconsciously limited the depth of the commitment she'd permit herself in order to avoid the possibility of another paralyzing loss. Then she'd met Tom and had dared to open herself up to the vulnerability that was part of falling in love. Now, once again she experienced the vast emptiness she'd felt sitting at the bottom of the basement steps, her dead mother's hand in hers.

She sat there in this state of mind as the police personnel went about their routine tasks, seemingly oblivious of her, as if she were in another dimension, one they could only access by way of some report that had to be filled in. She didn't hear her or Tom's name, only "suspect" and "decedent." When one of them did inquire about her comfort—the female trooper assigned to watch her—it was with quasi empathy, a gesture that was part of a job description.

After five hours, two on the mountain, one in transit and two here in this building—the sign identified it as the Henderson Post of the Virginia State Police—Kerry finally drew the scattered bits of herself together and came to a conclusion. What her sanity required would not be found here among these people. Her earlier, adolescent need to survive had caused the solidification of a character trait of moving quickly from problem to its solution with almost no stop over for regret or complaint. The overwhelming nature of the shock she'd just received, the wrenching grief and the inexpressible outrage had breached the containing nature of that trait and she had given full vent to her emotions. But now control was again established. She understood she would effect nothing talking to these people. She needed someone whom they would listen to, someone who also possessed the legal tools required. She needed a lawyer.

She asked several times to talk to an attorney. She knew no one in Virginia, so she asked for a public defender. The officer who seemed to be in charge, Captain Lucas, had acknowledged her request, but no attorney had appeared. She then demanded to talk to one. Lucas responded again as if he were going to act on this immediately. It was at this point that she discerned a sudden change in everyone's attitude toward her. The change was abrupt. While at first they had been avoiding her out of indifference or what she'd interpreted as embarrassment about having made a tragic error, now they were showing something resembling justified disdain.

A man Kerry hadn't seen before entered the room with an air of importance and authority. Captain Lucas and the female trooper followed deferentially, Lucas placing a recorder on the table and turning it on.

"This is Commander Tappan," Lucas said. "He wants to talk to you." Then speaking toward the recorder he added, "Present are Commander Tappan, Trooper Polk and myself, Captain Lucas, and Kerry Atwood."

Joe Tappan had had to suddenly readjust his planned approach to this interview. He had come away from his conversation with Fitz Halloran with the admonition to, "cuddle up to that bunny." But a recent discovery he'd made while examining the contents of Thomas Albright's backpack dictated that he would accomplish more with a hostile confrontation.

"Show her the wallet," he said flatly.

Lucas laid a plastic bag containing a man's wallet on the table.

Kerry thought she recognized the wallet Tom had found in the bushes and was about to declare this, when her recent resolve to talk to no one but an attorney stopped her.

"Your partner had this wallet in his backpack, right?"

"I'm not going to answer any questions until I first speak to an attorney assigned to me." She sat back and folded her hands on the table.

"You gave yourself away. I could tell you were about to say that you recognized the wallet, recognized it as the one you took off the man you killed."

Again there was an impulse to deny that she had killed anybody, but she swallowed it and tried to relax.

"You know where we found it too. Hid away in your buddy's backpack."

The temptation was great to say that it wasn't, "hid away."

"Ben Tulloch, he's the old man whose throat you and your boyfriend cut. I think it's only right that a person should know the name of the person she's killed. Don't you?" Tappan paused for her response, but Kerry made none.

"Lady's name was Gladys. They had just been to their daughter's wedding and were on the way to the reception when you two nabbed them."

Right after Tom was shot, the man with the rifle had said something about their having killed someone, and she'd overheard cops talking about it among themselves. She wanted to know more.

"When and how did this happen—the killing?"

"Shit, lady. Don't play games with me. You know damn well when and how it happened."

"No, I don't know. Really I don't."

Tappan laughed cynically. "You know what else? We found Ben Tulloch's blood on the wallet. How do you explain that?" Tappan was bluffing. There was blood on the wallet all right, but he didn't know yet whose it was. He decided to push the bluff farther.

"We found the same blood on other things in his backpack."

Kerry blurted out, "It must have come off the wallet." She saw her mistake even as the words left her mouth.

"So you do know about the wallet," Tappan pressed.

"Yes, Tom found it when he stepped into the bushes to urinate."

"And, where was that?"

"Just after we crossed a dirt road, before we camped

for the night."

"As you know very well, you killed the Tullochs in their car about fifty yards down that road and just across the bridge. So you know about the wallet and the fact that it had blood on it." Tappan's tone was triumphant as if he'd just sunk a twenty-foot putt against Fitz Halloran.

"You're twisting my words. I didn't know about any blood," she replied. "I'm not saying another thing until I have an attorney."

Tappan considered confronting her with the money, the twelve hundred-dollar bills. The other object in the backpack on which there was a trace of blood was one of the twelve hundred-dollar bills the police had found in the same stuff-bag where they'd found Ben Tulloch's wallet. This was about the same amount of cash that the Springfield, West Virginia Sheriff's Department had learned the Tullochs were said to have planned to give to the newlyweds for their honeymoon. The family didn't know the exact amount. Tappan had thought this confrontation would rattle Kerry. Now, seeing her attitude of determined silence, he thought he had better wait until he was sure of the exact amount of money the Tullochs were carrying. If Ben Tulloch had been carrying twelve big bills and the blood type matched, the state police were off the hook. The trooper had killed the right guy. But right now she seemed to be emotionally barricaded against being rattled. No sense in wasting his ammunition. He stood up.

"Kerry Atwood, you are being held on suspicion

that you murdered Ben and Gladys Tulloch of Springville, West Virginia."

Kerry felt overwhelmed. She managed to say, voice choking with emotion, "I formally request to speak to an attorney appointed by your court."

"I'll see to it."

The four golfers parted company in the parking lot of the Abermarle Country Club. Justin Dahl got into a black Impala sedan and left alone. Whenever he used the unobtrusive car instead of the chauffeur-driven Lincoln, it meant, according to the report Clarence Reed had had compiled by a local investigator, that Dahl was intending to pay a visit to Lorna Newby's house. Clarence Reed, the *Times* writer, glanced at the woman's address on the report, then laid it on the rented car's seat next to him. He waited until a safe interval had been established, then followed.

Dahl drove slowly toward downtown Richmond. Reed had no idea where in the city the woman's house was, but common sense told him it would be near enough to the Executive Office Building to make afternoon visits easy for the Governor—maybe even walking distance.

Reed had met Mrs. Dahl the night before at an informal dinner at the Governor's Mansion. She was still a handsome woman and she had perfectly acted the role of the gracious southern hostess. However, her script, Reed felt, was ludicrously dated. She might well have been entertaining General Beauregard. Reed couldn't recall one genuine word or gesture. He suspected that the genuine Florence Dahl would make her appearance once the Mansion's heavy front door closed behind the last departing guest. Would backbiting snobbishness then flow from the First Lady? Reed thought it likely. Lorna Newby would most likely be very different, perhaps only passably attractive, but she'd be affectionate and soothing.

Dahl's car turned into a heavily shaded street of old homes, any one of which could have featured a centennial plaque. Reed saw the Impala enter a narrow driveway at mid-block. Reed glanced down the driveway as he passed. Dahl had driven around the back of the house, only the rear fender and bumper of his car visible from the street. The house number checked. Yes, this was Governor Dahl's home away from home.

This aspect of Dahl's life didn't interest Reed greatly. It didn't figure into the piece he was working on, but it was a fact that filled out his understanding of his man. Clarence Reed was an adherent of the school of journalism holding fast to the belief that to understand any event involving people, one had to know the people themselves in great depth. Otherwise one was bound to over-simplify and thus contribute one more distortion—one more obfuscation—to the abundance that already existed. Do a careful piece of work or be quiet. One of the anachronistic wonders of the present time, Reed felt, was that his paper still permitted a journalist to do this.

Clarence Reed was not a religious man, but he did believe in something called the truth. To his thinking there were three things: truth, ignorance and deliberate bullshit. Ignorance was almost as respectable as truth, but there was no excusing bullshit.

When, as a college student, Reed had taken a serious accounting of himself—who he was and how he should spend his life—he had been fortunate enough to identify just what it was that truly stirred him. It was then that he experienced the clear epiphany that nothing would satisfy him except the pursuit of the truth. To his mind at that time, only a few paths led in that direction: Art—he had no talent, Scholarship—he didn't have the patience; Science—perhaps, but his math was weak and he was leery of confinement in a laboratory. And, finally, journalism— here he recognized the natural answer.

Over the years others had recognized this too. He'd not won, but three times he'd been on the short list for a Pulitzer. He was almost assured that his next major piece would achieve the award. What he wanted more than the prize was that what he wrote be his most significant contribution to the truth. Still, he had to admit to himself he would just plain like to win the damn prize, if for no other reason than to get it over with. Better to have it asked why on earth it was given to him rather than why it never was.

While Reed's object in examining and contrasting the four governors was to compare prevailing attitudes on controversial subjects, in the back of his mind he was always collecting material for a story he knew might never be written. It was a pet idea. He had always been interested in the phenomenon of corruption in politics, its causes and manifestations. Over the years this interest had given rise to an idea, which at first surprised and disturbed him. He began to wonder if corruption in government wasn't an evil, which the governed detested and opposed and which persisted in spite of and against their wishes, but rather that corruption existed, because of the need the governed had for it to exist. After all, couldn't the institution that supported most of the corruption in the American government be eliminated with the stroke of a pen? Campaign contribution was the main *modus operandi* of corruption in the American government.

Corruption came in two forms: direct theft for the politician's gain, and the acceptance of money—hard, soft or by any other name for the return of favors. I give you this; you give me something in return. One would have to be brainless not to see this truth. Certainly the majority of voters weren't that stupid; only the need to avoid acknowledging this truth about campaign contributions could account for their blindness.

The action needed to end to this farce was simple, he believed. The government should finance all political campaigns. Billions are spent on projects of questionable value while for a relatively small sum we, the people, could establish the basis for honest government. Plus legislators would no longer have to spend half their time raising funds for re-election. The citizenry would get their money back immediately in the increased time and ability of their representatives to study and acquire the information needed to govern more wisely. The conclusion was blatant. If it required an amendment to the constitution, so be it. No, Reed had concluded, we citizens didn't demand reform, no matter how we may protest, because we didn't really want it. But why?

Intuitively Clarence Reed knew that the exposition of this phenomenon, once he thoroughly understood it, would be his lasting bit of contribution to the truth. He had collected evidence of corruption over the years like one collects seashells: he had a garage full, but how could he use it?

8

Although Denver was not experiencing the heat wave searing the east coast, it was hotter than normal, and an atmospheric inversion caused the smog to stack up to the height of the barely visible peaks to the west.

Tony Bellino glanced at his watch. It was one o'clock. He angled the rental car he'd picked up at the airport off Interstate 70 onto Business 70 heading downtown. Bellino was on an assignment from the *Washington Post* to do a piece on the long-term consequences of civilian gun violence and wanted to interview the families of the Columbine Massacre victims. But his immediate destination was the Governor's Mansion, the present home of two of his oldest and dearest friends. It had been twelve years since he'd seen David and Jo Montgomery. A lot had happened in that period; for one thing, David had become Colorado's Governor.

Back in their college years in Ann Arbor and for a decade afterward, the three had worked fervently together on numerous liberal causes, organizing, fund-raising and marching—and partying. Separate career paths had put too many miles between them for the same intimacy to be maintained, and differing opinions about issues dear to each of them had further weakened the tight bond. Nevertheless, Tony and the Montgomerys still considered themselves the best of friends and members of the same political family. It was Tony's intention, however, to confront his friends today with an issue, which if their friendship were to continue, could no longer be avoided.

Bellino turned south on Corona Street and west again at 8th Avenue. After six blocks he slowed and turned into the mansion's entrance. The security guard checked his name on a list and then told him where to park. At the front door, a young woman identifying herself as Mrs. Montgomery's secretary met him and led him out a side door to a small garden patio. Jo Montgomery waited for him there alone. She got up from her chair and gave him a kiss and a solid hug.

"It's great to see you again, Tony."

"Same here, Jo."

Jo sat down again.

Bellino took off and hung his suit jacket on the back of a chair opposite her and appraised her as he did. He saw a woman of a like age, 49, with dark, but gray-streaked hair smiling up at him. Affection shone in her dark, forthright eyes.

Bellino experienced some inner discomfort as he took a seat at the table in this amiable setting because of his decision to bring up a subject that might be a breach of guest etiquette. But this wasn't the proper moment; Jo had just welcomed him into her home. Anyway, David had to be there too. So, he could permit himself to relax and enjoy this time with Jo.

Bellino took off his sunglasses and laid them on the polished marble table, glancing up toward the sky. "It's a fortunate thing that when on the ground here, one isn't aware of the smog over the city. I mean compared to what one sees approaching from the air."

"You mean fortunate, because otherwise we'd be forced to hold our breath."

"Exactly." Bellino chuckled, "Fortunate for our economy, not our lungs."

"You know, of course, Denver was once a place where people with lung problems came for the purity of the air. A pulmonary hospital was even established here. "

Tony felt pleased to see his old friend. He had always been very fond of her.

"What are you smiling about?" she asked.

"Reminiscing. Feeling that trite but astonished awareness that time flies—that youth is ephemeral."

Neither spoke as Tony got the case for his sunglasses out of his coat pocket. Jo watched, appraising the very effects he had just spoken of. He looked thinner, less robust than before. How long had it been? They'd talked on the phone—David, Tony and she—a couple of times a year. But when had she last seen him? It must be, yes, twelve years. David had come out to visit them right after she and David had left Ann Arbor to live in Colorado. Yes, Tony definitely looked less vital. Was the divorce responsible? To hear him on the phone one would think he had been little affected. His appearance said otherwise. Something was bothering him, or why throw out two mild insults immediately after sitting down—you've got lousy air and you're looking old.

"David didn't mention why you were coming to Denver."

"Do I have to have a reason besides wanting to see you?"

"Ah, you mean to see how time has stolen my youth?"

Tony clasped both hands to his chest as if he'd been shot. "Some things don't change. You'd never let anyone get away with anything."

They both laughed.

"OK, there's a piece I'm doing on the long-term effects of violence in a community. Unfortunately for Colorado it has become an obligatory stop when researching this topic. Unfortunate for Colorado, but fortunate for me, because I get to see my best friends and get a personal tour of the executive mansion. And . . . to see that in selective cases youth is not ephemeral."

"Well done. I'll see that you get a cookie when we go inside the house . . .er, mansion."

For a moment Tony's gaze swept across the well-tended lawns and gardens.

He looked at Jo again. "How's your daughter—still in Chicago?"

"She's fine, and yes, she's at Northwestern."

81

They both paused while a maid placed a silver tray with coffee on the table. Confirming that nothing else was wanted, she left.

"It's incredible, I mean the two of you being here. Governor Montgomery! Who would have thought? Certainly not you two. You must wake up every morning and pinch yourselves."

"This has its advantages," she said, nodding in the direction of the retreating maid. "But, truthfully, neither of us sees this as a permanent rise in status. Not a permanent address, in other words."

"Really? I understood that Dave won by a significant margin."

"Yes," she agreed as she stirred half a teaspoon of sugar into her coffee. "But it was a reactionary vote based on a single issue, the environment. It was the fortuitous revelation by an investigative reporter about the huge payoffs the former administration pocketed for zoning fraud that caused a wave of pro-environment sentiment. The public began looking for a "green" hero and there was our David standing tall. Neither of us believes this is a long-range view of voters. There's a lot of money to be made from land speculation. Growth means money for everyone. By the time the next election takes place, the itch for a high definition flat screen TV will cause many voters to choose the candidate who will give the developers a free hand. As you well know, the health of the economy does much to determine the results of an election."

"Maybe yes, maybe no," Tony countered.

"There is much that David—we—would like to see accomplished while we have the clout and, therefore, he's been working hard to build wider support than that from the environmentalists alone."

"Yes, I know," Bellino replied. He almost followed an impulse to broach the issue that had been bothering him. But he caught himself. It wasn't the right time.

Just thirty miles away in Boulder and two hours later, Piper Dahl, the Virginia Governor's daughter, still held the phone to her ear even after hearing the disconnect on the other end. Humiliation enveloped her like a hot mist. She didn't take a breath for several seconds. Greg's bored voice reverberated in her mind: "You can come over if you want to, but I'm meeting some people later." He'd meant, I can spare a few minutes to fuck you, but then you've got to leave, because I'm meeting someone I'd rather be with.

She hadn't thought anyone else was upstairs in the sorority house, and she'd left her bedroom door open when she made the call to Greg. Now, she was aware of Jody and Suzanne standing there. How long had they been listening?

"She said cheerfully into the dead phone, "Real cool, Ill be right over."

She turned and acted surprised to see the two other

girls. "Hot enough for y'all?" Those were two things she could always count on, a cliché and the southern accent she could affect. She felt at this moment there was nothing else.

The two girls left without having had an apparent motive for stopping, except to listen to her end of the telephone conversation. She closed the door and returned to sit on the bed staring unseeing out the window where campus life went on as usual. The only sound in the room was made by the small, wind-up alarm clock that she'd had since childhood. Her father had bought it for her when he'd taken her with him on a weekend speaking junket to Lexington. It was the only time in her memory of their doing something together without her mother.

She unconsciously began to seek within herself for something to sustain her. No names of others surfaced in that search. She was alone. No real friends—not since she was a child. Family? She really didn't know either her father or her brother, or maybe she knew them too well. In either case, no loving feelings flowed in either direction. Her mother? Piper's mind drew away from thoughts about her mother as one might avoid putting weight on a sprained ankle. So, if not people, what else was there she could turn to? She had no special interests, no skills as others did. Why had there been nothing that she'd developed for herself? It seemed there'd been neither time nor energy. But that was no explanation. She'd had as much time as other girls had, the future lawyers, doctors, artists—whatever. Clearly something had gone wrong, but she couldn't identify it.

The stunned numbness began to change into a pain deep in her chest. She'd revealed her helplessness just now on the phone with Greg and he'd rubbed her nose in it.

"You can come over if you want to, but I'm meeting some people later," he'd said. "Some people." What did that make her?

Piper moved from the bed to her desk, where she took her diary from a drawer. Into its pages she poured the invective she'd had to swallow while her two sorority sisters were present. She wrote giving free expression to the extremes of her feelings and what she'd like to do to Greg, ending with, "I'm going to kill him! Next chance I get." She felt a little better after this catharsis, and started to cross out the last sentences, then stopped. "Let it stand," she thought. "It's what I feel."

It came to her that she shouldn't stay in her room too long, or the other girls might wonder why she wasn't leaving to meet Greg. At the same time, in order to preserve any fragment of self-esteem she still possessed, she knew she couldn't survive any further demeaning by Greg. In spite of this certain knowledge, she could think of no other option than to docilely walk over to his rooming house.

She put away the diary and locked the drawer just as Jody called through the door asking if she could borrow her scanner.

"Sure," she answered immediately. "I'll bring it to your room in a minute." She wasn't ready yet to face her.

Piper heard Jody walk away. She took the scanner from her desktop, and as she did she caught a glimpse of herself in a wall mirror. She stopped and took a more studied look. Piper. This name, her name, she had a vague awareness, was part of the problem. She had sensed this but had never consciously come to terms with the contradiction. The woman in the mirror was not a *Piper*. Piper Dahl should be a beautiful, vivacious Southern belle—like her mother had been. Florence Bagley had possessed everything except the proper name and she made sure her daughter would have that. Unfortunately she hadn't been able to supply her baby with the required qualities to go with the glamorous name. Many times she had told Piper that she was named after a favorite movie star. On these occasions Piper recognized in the way her mother repeated this that it was said to inspire her to behave differently. Florence's frustration and Piper's sense of inadequacy invariably followed.

She didn't know the woman in the mirror. It is difficult for any woman to concede that she is homely, but it is possible to accept that one is not beautiful and get on with it. Piper hadn't been allowed to make that adjustment. Her mother identified Piper's plainness with contrariness. And then there was this other confusing element: boys like Greg—popular boys—had always asked her out. She had not been without dates. She never missed a party or dance through high school. She'd even gone steady—for a while—with some of them. But how much of that was because she was the Governor's daughter? Some female classmates had not hidden this opinion.

Jody came to the doorway of her own room when she heard Piper in the hall. She took the scanner Piper held out to her.

"What are you and Greg doing tonight?"

"We haven't decided," Piper lied. "He's got a new CD he wants me to hear. Go out to get some food later, I suppose. Why?"

"Nothing," Jody lied. She'd heard earlier that Greg had a date with another woman to go to a party this evening and she'd wondered how Piper would answer. "Have fun," she said to Piper's back as she descended the stairs.

9

"He did like I said he'd do. This new manager at the Barnhill Bank says he needs a court order before he'll let us look at the Tullochs' bank account." Sheriff Royston affected outrage and incomprehension into the phone. "When Logan Barnhill was alive, I could sit down with him and he'd tell me whatever I needed to know."

Fitz Halloran wasn't interested in what might have been.

"You're going to do that right? I mean get the court order."

"Well, it's a little complicated seeing it isn't our case." Hadn't he already gone out of his way for this Virginia DA? The man was pushy.

"Don't forget that a crime was also committed in your jurisdiction . . . like kidnapping." Halloran said this as if he were explaining an elementary fact to an idiot.

Royston was ruffled by the man's tone, but conceded that he did have a point.

"Yeah, well all right. I'll see what I can do."

"Hold on a minute I just had a thought." A pitch of excitement entered Halloran's voice. "You wouldn't need a court order to talk to the tellers who were working the day

Tulloch came to take out the cash. I imagine they knew Tulloch. Probably an old customer. I'll bet he even told the teller the money was for a wedding present. In that case, the teller is likely to remember the number of and denominations of the bills."

It did sound likely to Royston too, and in spite of being reluctant to do any favors for this guy, he reminded himself they both belonged to the law enforcement brotherhood.

"OK, I'll go talk to the tellers. Call you back."

Fitz Halloran leaned back in his desk chair. There was no swagger about him now. He was stressed and sweating and didn't know how to proceed. He still didn't know if this was a matter of a police blunder he'd pass on to Dana Rogers, or if it was a sensational murder involving two outsiders—two New Yorkers. If the latter turned out to be the case, he wanted very much to be the one in the spotlight. This could very well make the attorney general nomination possible. Not only would he be identified as the defender of righteousness and the home but he would also, by prosecuting this New Yorker, whitewash the fact that he wasn't a born Virginian. He was afraid many voters still thought of him as a Damn Yankee.

There wasn't much time to ponder this dilemma, because by tomorrow he would either have to charge Kerry Atwood with murder or turn her loose. By noon, her lawyer would be at court demanding her release. If he charged her and it turned out she was telling the truth that she and her boyfriend were only hiking and found Ben Tulloch's wallet, he'd end up looking like a jackass. And he could forget about the nomination. On the other hand, it would also look bad if he assigned the case to Rogers, only to take it back should strong evidence turn up, like finding out the amount and denominations of the cash Tulloch withdrew and the cash found in Thomas Albright's backpack matched. Taking the case back at that point, he knew, would make Rogers stand on the roof of the County Building and scream racial discrimination. He badly needed to know the exact facts about the money Ben Tulloch was carrying. He was forced to wait for that god damned, red-necked West Virginia sheriff. In any case, he should know as much as he could about Kerry Atwood and the guy. He picked up his phone and dialed Dana Rogers.

The Assistant District Attorney of Henderson County was thirty-three and African-American. She had achieved second-in-the-class rank at the University of Virginia Law School by way of scholarship and unflagging ambition. She had grown up in Richmond, where her mother still lived. Her father had abandoned the family when she was born. Her two-year-older brother had been killed in a drive-by shooting when he was sixteen. No one was ever charged. From some inner resource she had managed to put together a determined and tough will to have a better life than her beginnings predicted. Dana Rogers had the intention and energy to climb high in state office. She was vigorous in seeing that she was at the right place and made contact with the right people. She was becoming known as a very intelligent and capable person who had early in her life been dealt bad circumstances but harbored no resentment.

The only drag on her bandwagon was her looks. She was short, rotund and wore very thick glasses. She was, in fact, legally blind, but this didn't prevent her from managing her work as if there existed no handicap. She had taken the job as assistant to Fitz Halloran, because she wanted the experience. She had no intention of staying on beyond this, her second year.

Dana came into Halloran's office and sat in the chair next to his desk before he finished saying, "Have a seat, Dana."

"Perhaps you've heard about the young woman the State Police have . . . "

"Kerry Atwood, the alleged killer or the alleged hiker."

The quick reply reminded Fitz it was Rogers he was dealing with. "Ah, yes."

"Are you going to charge her?"

Halloran drummed his fingers on the desktop. He couldn't fool Rogers and he'd only make a fool of himself if he tried, but he couldn't come right out and say what he was thinking.

"Pretty sure I will. The guy had twelve hundred-dollar bills in his backpack. The old couple's family, according to what we're told by the Springville police, says the old man was carrying something like that amount of cash to give to his daughter and new son-in-law for their honeymoon—for the airfare. It's likely it would have been close to twelve hundred. There's no way in hell this can be a coincidence."

"So, why are you waiting?" Dana Rogers was smiling inside, but her face was a mask.

Damn those goggles she wears, thought Halloran. Can't make out what she's thinking.

"Any time now. You see, the sheriff in Springville is getting some information for me."

"Which one of us is going to run with this?"

Goddamn, she's calling my hand. Ballsy bitch, Fitz thought.

"I'm real busy and should ask you to take it, but I'm not sure you have the experience yet for a case like this. I'm giving it a lot of thought." Fitz hurried on before she could put his feet to the flames again. "In the meantime, whoever takes the case, we're going to have to know as much as we can about both of them, the Atwood woman and the guy . . . what's his name?"

"Albright."

"Yeah, I want you to put aside whatever you're working on and give this your best effort."

Dana gazed at her boss steadily with eyes magnified by her glasses to appear as large as a microscopist's must to a microbe.

"Since the State Police must have a great interest

in this case—like if Atwood and her buddy aren't guilty, they're in deep doodoo for killing a hiker—I'd guess they'll be willing to lend us some support—manpower. Do I have your permission to suggest that to them?"

Good God! Fitz imagined Joe Tappan's reaction if Rogers began putting the screws to him. He'd heard Tappan call her "the blind beach ball," for Christ's sake.

"I'm sure Commander Tappan would be more than happy to help us, but let me call him."

"If I'm to do 'my best effort', I need you to make that call immediately."

"You've got it."

Dana Rogers got up and left the room without another word, leaving Fitz wondering who had managed whom. He called Tappan and presented the situation.

"Working with your assistant ain't my idea of a good time," said Tappan, "but then I wouldn't be the one doing it. My impression is that she'll get all the help she wants. Everyone, right up to the top brass in Richmond is scared as hell of the fall-out from this. I'll check it out and call you back."

"Do me a favor . . . you call Rogers."

Brad Collins stood at the kitchen sink and looked through the window into the backyard of his family home in Henderson. It was dusk, but he could still see the garden well enough to discern the change. When his mother was well she attended to the flower beds with a perfection that old Sam Tobin, the family's gardener since Brad was a child, couldn't achieve now by himself, neither spiritually nor physically.

Brad had just rinsed the few dishes his mother and he had used at dinner and put them in the dishwasher. He'd taken in this view of the backyard countless times since he'd been tall enough to see over the windowsill. His mother and older sister were great cooks and he liked to hang around and talk with them and watch the meal taking shape. He hadn't minded his role as the "gopher" of the trio.

Brad had returned home because his mother was dying. He'd been staying in his old room for the past three and a half weeks. His sister had three small kids and lived a thousand miles away. Being here now, he felt, was one of the most important things he'd do in his life. He wanted to savor the last days of this relationship which had been and would always be as much a part of him as his own body's cells. At the same time, this period amounted to a state of limbo for him, a place between—between his old life and the world he was eager to explore.

He had been at the entrance to that exploration when his mother was diagnosed with leukemia. When she weakened rapidly, Brad had taken a leave-of-absence from the Washington law firm where he'd just begun to work and moved back to Henderson to help May Rutledge, the woman who had done house cleaning for them since Brad was ten. His mother was very weak, but otherwise remained unimpaired, retaining her intelligence, wit and sense of humor. During that moment looking out the kitchen window, he was very aware of the pull in both directions: outside the window lay his new life, while on the inside it was the past and its powerful attachments that waited for him. He wiped his hands on a dishtowel and went into the living room.

The room was a living room in the literal sense. He and his sister and their playmates had never been barred from it. The sturdy furniture had served as make-believe props as their ages and gender demanded. Some pieces had been reupholstered and repositioned and the plants had changed, but the room remained true to his memories.

His mother sat in her favorite, slip-covered chair, books piled on the table next to it and within easy reach on the floor.

"What'll it be, the novel Clara brought you this morning, or the biography of Voltaire?" Brad asked in an intentionally light and breezy tone.

"Oh I think Voltaire, don't you? The silly social striving, how desperate they all were to be in the important coach, the one nearest to the king's and to have the correct number of duchesses at their parties. It puts one's own cares in perspective."

Brad laughed. "It does at that."

The light-hearted smile on his mother's wan but

handsome face turned to a soft seriousness. "It's all about perspective, isn't it? We humans aren't good at it. In fact, I think it's our worst suit. We start off as infants giving ourselves and our interests too much importance and we never quit."

Her smile returned. "Something your father used to say: when you begin a task you must orient yourself. This is who I am, this is where I'm going and this is what I want to do. He said we should get up in the morning and remind ourselves that we are only one of the millions of species on a tiny planet revolving around one of trillions of stars in the universe. After that exercise one is ready to begin the day with a reasonably realistic perspective."

Brad had heard this advice many times before. He nodded as he found the place where he'd left off in the biography. He looked up and in the instant before he spoke his eyes traced the bone structure of her face beneath the depleting muscle, a long face, prominent chin and cheek bones, mouth forward from the plane of her forehead—his own face.

"I remember your having told me that before. And, I've actively tried to do it . . . several times. It works. Nothing could rile me . . . for a while. Then, before I knew it, I was back to being concerned if I were riding in the right coach."

The phone rang. Brad picked it up.

"Hello. Yes, it is . . . Yes, I am . . . you say, Kerry Atwood? OK, what is she charged with?" Surprised, Brad said, "I see. Now what is the procedure? This is my first case . . . Fine, thanks very much. Goodbye."

"Great," he said hanging up. "Now I'll be able to send my roommate my half of next month's rent."

"What was that all about?"

'The other day Jeff Goodrich suggested that I put my name down as a public defender while I'm here. Jeff's a good friend of the Clerk of the Court and thought he might be successful in getting her to insert my name into the roster near the top of the list. He told me, "The rule is that your name has to go at the end of the list, but it doesn't say which end." I thought he was kidding, but apparently not. Anyway, it pays fifty dollars an hour."

"Then this will be your first case as a lawyer?"

"Tah tah!"

"Kerry Atwood? Is that her name?"

"Yes. And she's being held on suspicion of murder. No formal charge has been made. The clerk didn't know anything else."

"Heavens. Do you feel that you're prepared to take on something so serious?"

"Murder? No, absolutely not. It wouldn't come to that. I'll just be in on the opening phase, making sure her rights are being observed during questioning and the arraignment—if there is one. She or her family would be bringing in a criminal lawyer after that." Brad laughed. "I'd make sure of it. But, there may be enough hours in this to pay my rent."

"At least we can mark tomorrow on the calendar as the day of your first case."

"If you can restrain your excitement over Voltaire until later this evening, we can mark today's date, because I'd like to go over to the jail and see her right now."

Nicely browned, the swordfish steaks were withdrawn from the broiler and placed on the stovetop. The recipe was from the *New York Times Cookbook*. Sherrie Halloran had poached the fish in a beer broth then browned it in a batter made of the reduced broth combined with butter and flour. On the granite counter beside the Viking stove waited two warmed plates already served with broccoli and parsley potatoes. Sherrie made an effort to make every one of Fitz's meals worthy of notice. It was a professional ethic passed on to her from her mother.

Fitz, when called, came into the dining room and sat down without a word. He glanced at his watch and then took up the Baccarat goblet of Chablis by his plate and washed a mouthful around his tongue. The vigor of the technique was not unlike the one he used in the bathroom each morning with Lavoris. He did all this without looking once at this wife. Sherrie was not difficult to look at. She kept herself trim through hours of working out at the gym and on the tennis courts. At forty-three, her blond beauty still turned heads at the club.

Fitz put his glass down and became aware of her smiling at him. He smiled back. He was pleased by Sherrie's appearance and liked it when friends commented on how good she looked. In his imagination, he included himself in the compliment.

She knew his approval was perfunctory, but she'd grown to accept that. Maybe she even preferred it that way, no longer able now herself to call up more than a semblance of love. She watched Fitz spear a piece of swordfish and put it automatically in his mouth. She knew he wouldn't pay attention to what he was eating.

"How do you like the veal, honey?"

He brought his attention to what was in his mouth and answered heartily, "Good. Very good."

He noticed her snide grin and looked at the fish on his plate. He laughed. "Yeah, it's nice and flaky like veal oughta be."

"I wasted my money on swordfish. I could have served hamburger."

"Hamburger's good too. OK, I'm sorry. Mind's somewhere else."

"I haven't seen you so preoccupied since you were sweating out the decision to run for district attorney."

Fitz considered this. She was probably right. That had been a big career decision and he had spent sleepless nights pacing and weighing the pros and cons. On the up side of standing for the office was his dream of being a player in the power scene. There would be more to his life than just thinking of new ways to spend the fat income provided by his law practice. More to look forward to than waiting for the next model the Mercedes designers came up with. And then there was the fact that women were more turned on by power than wealth.

On the downside was the chance of losing the election—losing and forever living with a "loser" sign around his neck.

In the end he'd decided to leave the partnership with Lloyd Farmer, his law school roommate, and run for DA.

Fitz had worked hard and fast making contacts since that first election three years ago. He was now one year into his second term and his instincts told him that if he was really going to scramble up the political ladder, getting the nomination for Virginia State Attorney General for the next election was maybe a once-in-a-lifetime window. The strategist within him also identified the Atwood case as either a giant opportunity or a fatal political blunder.

Earlier that day, Sheriff Royston had called Halloran to say that he had determined which teller had waited on Ben Tulloch, but she hadn't been at work, because she was having an MRI as part of a medical work-up for a complaint of headaches. Royston had said he'd call her when she got home from the hospital and call Halloran back to tell him what he'd learned about the cash Tulloch had withdrawn.

"Yeah, I guess you're right, Hon. I'm about as preoccupied as I was back then. It's a problem at work."

"Would it help if you talked about it?" One more attempt on her part for intimacy.

Considering her question, Fitz realized he had passed a point when he would share everything with his wife as he once had. He had come to feel that the path he now wanted to travel led to a world for which she wasn't equipped. There were actions required of him now that she wouldn't be able to understand or approve of. He had entered a realm where a different code of behavior prevailed. A non-player, even one who had been a soul mate for nearly twenty years, was no longer permitted entry.

"No, it's only a boring administrative thing, nothing you could help with."

After dinner, Fitz carried his empty plate to the kitchen where he took a clean glass out of the cupboard and poured himself a generous scotch. He announced he had some work to do and was expecting a call, so Sherrie shouldn't answer the phone. He carried his drink to his study and closed the door.

He drank the single malt and paced back and forth in front of a large print of the twelfth hole at Augusta National that hung over the fireplace. The expected call came at eight o'clock.

"Good news, Mr. Halloran. Judy, that's the teller's name, Judy Fenton. I called her at home. She remembers Ben Tulloch taking the money out day before yesterday. She's known him for years."

"And, the denominations," interrupted Fitz, impatiently.

"That's what I mean sayin' it's good news. She gave him twelve hundred-dollar bills. She put them in a cash envelope they use for gifts."

Fantastic, thought Halloran. Then he thought of something else. "And what condition was the money in?" He hoped like hell he wouldn't hear the bills were new—not circulated. The ones in the backpack showed average wear.

"Ah, yes she did say. You see Tulloch asked for brand new bills. She told him she'd have to go back to the vault to get them. Said she was the only teller working then—the other woman was on a break—so there was a line of customers behind Tulloch. She said he took a look at the line and then told her that it didn't matter if the bills were brand new and to just give him the newest she had in her cash drawer. She said she'd be happy to go back to the safe, but he said the ones she had in the drawer were OK."

"Yeah, so what did she give him?"

Royston decided to overlook Halloran's rudeness.

"She gave him what he asked for."

"And what was that?" Fitz said exasperated.

"What's that?"

"Did you ask the teller to describe the bills . . . how new were the bills she managed to find in her drawer?"

"She said he was satisfied with the ones she gave him. A couple of them were very new. Why is that important?"

"Oh, nothing." Fitz said. He'd seen the money from the backpack. And not one of those bills could be described as "very new." But there was no way in hell it could be a coincidence that Tulloch and Albright could both have been carrying twelve hundred-dollar bills that day. Fitz Halloran had made up his mind. He was going to charge Kerry Atwood with first-degree murder and he was taking the case himself.

10

It was ten to five in Boulder. Piper walked up to the white, frame house on Henry Street. Typical of a residential house converted to student housing, little money was being spent by the landlord for upkeep. It had been a frequent destination for Piper over the last two months, especially early in that period. Then, she and Greg had had sex almost daily up there in his room. Back then, she'd felt certain that he really cared for her. Piper looked up at the open bedroom window. She hesitated a moment before continuing up the walk to the house. The last time she'd been here it had been ugly and degrading. Greg had bullied her into doing things that left her feeling dirty and used.

There was only one entrance. The front door opened into a small vestibule, which was open on the one side to what had been the living room and was now a so-called study area for the two men renting the downstairs bedrooms. In actuality it was a beer hall—one without a cleaning staff. She affected self-confidence as she opened the door as if she were well liked and wanted here. She glanced into the room. One of the guys was slouched on the broken-down couch asleep. She was grateful for that.

Each time now when she came in and climbed the stairs she felt she had a sign on her back saying, "I'm going up to Greg's room to get fucked."

A dark, greasy trail on the wallpaper, made by hundreds of unsteady ascents and descents, led up the dismal stairway. Piper's ambivalence about being here made her feel twice her normal weight. She labored up the stairs.

Four, small bedrooms were crammed into the second floor. Greg's was the front room and the door was open. He lay on the bed, wearing only a pair of shorts and reading a Sports Illustrated. Piper closed the door behind her.

"Hi," she said.

"Hi," Greg repeated after a delay. He continued looking at the magazine and turned a page. Piper sat on the edge of the bed and then, after a minute, put her hand on her chest.

Greg lowered the magazine to look at her. Boredom was on his handsome, tanned face.

"I haven't much time: take your clothes off." He went back to the magazine.

Piper attempted to cover her embarrassment by acting as if a quick romp was what she'd come for. She pulled her T-shirt over her head, unzipped her shorts and pulled it and her panties off.

Greg continued to read. Piper ran her fingers over his muscular chest and then under the top of his shorts.

He began to have an erection and dropped the magazine aside.

"Suck it," he said.

She pulled the zipper down and took out his hardening penis, twisting her upper body toward it. She was still wearing her bra and Greg stretched both hands toward the clasp, but couldn't reach it while still lying down. On the table was his open clasp knife he'd used earlier to cut the wrapping off a CD. He picked it up and reaching around Piper's back, slipped the sharp blade under the bra strap and pushed the blade out, cleanly cutting through the strap.

Piper gasped and looked around. "What did you do?"

Greg was laughing. He dropped the knife on the bed and took a handful of her breast.

"Suck it, bitch. That's what you do best."

She was not able afterwards to decide what had done it. Was it the way he'd said, "bitch", or—as she'd heard it—"That's all you're good for" that did it? She couldn't decide, because she could never remember clearly the thoughts she'd had at that moment. She didn't remember seizing the knife. She didn't remember raising it and plunging it into his tanned body. She only remembered his look of profound disbelief as he gazed at it sticking straight up in his chest.

11

The second floor sitting room of the Colorado Governor's Mansion, small, oak-paneled and comfortably furnished, made a perfect setting for a reunion. There, David had joined his wife, Jo, and Tony at three o'clock. It was now seven and except for a tour of the mansion that had taken half an hour, they'd been reminiscing. Bellino so enjoyed this review of their early years together he put his intended confrontation on permanent hold.

Their mood had been initiated when David, during the tour, had opened a refrigerated closet in the basement and displayed the hundred or so bottles of champagne and other white wines that rested there at a perfect forty-five degrees. Tony had browsed and happily found several bottles of 1970 Krug Grande Cuvee.

One couldn't look at David Montgomery without thinking "active." Even at rest, his short, compact body seemed poised to begin the assault on some rocky pinnacle. His almost bald, tanned and shining head suggested more a deliberate adjustment to reduce wind resistance than a sign of aging. His mirthful gray eyes constantly examined and cataloged as if readying him for the next action. The Krug was doing its best to alter his ever-ready state. He steadied himself with one hand on the back of Jo's chair to replenish her glass from the third bottle.

"I have no idea what this stuff costs," he said with the wonder of one who had always done his wine shopping from the bargain bin.

"I do," Tony said, looking through the pale, straw-colored, bubbling liquid in his glass. "And, I doubt that you have the proper point of view to want to be told."

"And why is that?"

"First, a question. Do you believe the people really—I mean down deep and dirty—really want their leader to deprive himself or herself of the excesses they aren't themselves able to indulge in? Do you believe that down deep they respect the leader who is unable to live up to and beyond the limit of privilege?"

"I'm sober enough to know there are two questions in that question, but . . . " He surrendered to the effect of the wine and gravity and thumped down in his chair. "I'll have to give this some thought."

"On the one hand, I'm disappointed that you're not able to shout the bold answer, 'Hell yes, the people want me to drink my fill of Krug Grande Cuvee 1970'." Tony couldn't prevent a slight slur from entering his own speech as he continued, "On the other hand, I'm happy to see that you've reached a relative state of dementia—Dementia Krugiarus, as our medical friends might say."

"Somebody's feeling no pain," Jo observed. She was simultaneously amused by both Tony's quip and by how it revived memories from their past together.

"My mood is softening, but we need something . . . else. Music! Yes, of course. Something nostalgic."

Jo pondered what she and David had that would qualify. She got up and went to a cabinet that contained their library of CDs and searched until she found the Rosenkavalier Suite.

Tony had begun a loud, rhetorical declamation. "What is nostalgia, anyway? Next to orgasm and, let me see . . . and the flush of victory, it's the most pleasurable of human feelings. Wouldn't you say?"

He looked from one to the other.

"What about love?" Jo asked, returning to her chair as the music began.

David stared from Jo to Tony with a fixed smile. He was doing his best to keep up with the subject, but was failing.

"Yes, of course, love," Tony agreed He was surprised he hadn't immediately included it. "I must have been thinking of short-term feelings. Love is more long-term. Anyway, nostalgia is one of the big four . . . but just what is it?"

David struggled to concentrate on the question. Tony seemed to be serious and he wanted to oblige with equal gravity. "Good times," he supplied. "The memory of good times shared." He was pleased with himself.

Tony considered this, but wasn't satisfied. "Can't I feel nostalgia about a time when I was alone?"

David tried to address the challenge but gave up and began to drift below the surface.

"I think I know what produces nostalgia," said Jo softly.

Both men looked at her, expecting her to continue.

"My idea is rather grim—maybe not party material."

"Nothing," stated Tony with mock solemnity, raising his glass, "that Krug Grande Cuvee can't handle."

"OK then, I believe nostalgia is the memory of a time well-lived, and especially as it was experienced with others, coupled with the simultaneous awareness of the certainty of separation and death."

Silenced, Tony looked over at David, who shrugged and said, "Party pooper if I ever heard one."

Just then, the music arrived at the poignant waltz and captured their attention for a few minutes.

"Maybe," said Tony quietly, "Maybe, Jo's got it right."

Tony's cell phone chirped and he excused himself and answered, making a "who can this be?" face.

"All right, put him on." Tony looked at the Montgomerys and said, covering the mouthpiece, "Managing Editor." Into the phone he said, "Hi Chuck, what's up?"

He listened for a long time and then made a motion to Jo for something to write on. He wrote down several names and phone numbers on the note pad he'd been given.

"Right, Chuck. I'll get back to you later this evening."

Tony's mood had changed abruptly. The previous mild signs of inebriation were also gone. His voice was sober, cool. "I've been wanting to ask the two of you about something that's been on my mind ever since you were elected, Dave."

Husband and wife looked puzzled.

"In the old days," Tony continued, "You two strongly opposed capital punishment. If I'm right, however, you seem to have done an about face during your campaign. Am I right about that?"

A communicating glance passed between the Montgomerys. David had also sobered suddenly. "Our position is the same as it has always been. We're against the death sentence. We also knew it would be an issue I'd be asked about during the campaign. So, Jo and I discussed it and decided that, when asked, I'd reply that, as Governor, I would support the laws of the state."

He paused here to assess Bellino's reaction. He read distaste on his friend's face. He went on, "There was only one man on death row at that time and he'd been granted an appeal that would most likely mean legal proceedings extending beyond my term of office. In other words, we didn't think we'd ever have occasion to uphold that law. You may think that's wimpy, but we wanted to get elected, because we had things we wanted to accomplish."

"I think your hope to avoid the issue has just been dashed," Tony said acidly. "In a way that may present you with a large problem. Do you know Governor Justin Dahl?"

"Of Virginia? Yeah, I met him at a governors conference. Why?"

"Well, I was just told that his daughter, Piper, killed her boyfriend this afternoon at the university in Boulder. She's being charged with first-degree murder. The boy friend, it so happens, is the son of your state's ski heroes, Slats and Cindy Patterson."

Justin Dahl had a rule not to drink when he was with Lorna Newby; it might make it easier to stay longer than was wise. He was sure Florence was aware there was another woman, but he knew as certainly as he knew night must fall that she would not tolerate it being made manifest. An additional reason for abstaining from alcohol at Lorna's was the long daily cocktail hour he must manage once he got home. Justin had to be sober enough to control Florence's martini consumption or embarrassing situations would occur later on if there happened to be guests for dinner. Tonight, at home, he was totally relaxed as he sipped a glass of bourbon. There were to be no guests this evening.

His sanguine mood reflected his belief that his ship of life was on course. And, this was literally Justin's mental image, a ship that one commanded and steered around dangerous political shoals and toward the sunny waters of a respected retirement. The long-range forecast was for clement weather. Certainly, politically, he was secure. The majority held by his party statewide was built upon deep and long-standing voter attitudes.

His own position in his party was inviolable—as long as he had Senator Cummins backing and Cummins saw Justin as his own son. Justin was acceptable to all party factions to the degree that in spite of the inevitable reservations of some, he would remain in office as long as he liked. It was understood that after this present term as governor, the way lay open to the U. S. Senate if he wanted that—and he did.

Many in this enviable position come to think that such apparent popularity derives from their own superior abilities. Justin, to his credit, was not deluded. He was wise to the fact that the perceived truth, which frequently had nothing to do with the actual truth, was what counted. The message had been impressed upon him one day when he had mentioned to his physician brother a magazine article that listed the state's best doctors in the various medical specialties. When he heard the list, his brother commented that what the people named had in common was not superior skill, but huge egos and the will to advertise themselves. In fact, their medical colleagues held many of those on the list in low regard.

Justin was just setting out on his political career

and recognized in his brother's assessment what his path must be. His esteem with the general public would grow if he promoted it properly, regardless of his actual performance in office. Once a popular myth about a person becomes established, it could be maintained with minimal effort. Justin concluded that in those areas where we are not actively engaged, we humans like to have things summarized and simplified. Therefore, once an idea about a person is firmly established, it requires the force of a major, contradicting piece of evidence to derail it. He made sure that he maintained a sober, serious but empathic expression whenever he passed from his private sphere into the public one where a camera might lurk. He was among the first to arrive at every disaster, sleeves rolled up, appearing eager to act. He never missed church service and his voice could be heard above the rest when hymns were sung. Above all, he carefully avoided having his name linked to any controversy until it became obvious where his support base stood on the issue. Then he would appear before the cameras as a champion of "traditional values" or "progress", whichever was called for. He had played the part so well that he was frequently introduced now as "a legend in his own time."

But, Justin also realized that he'd been lucky. One can't be entirely sure how the public will perceive your actions. One can't be sure what direction fashion will take. Still, he was confident that unless he screwed up badly, and he had no history of doing that, his ship would enjoy the long sunny cruise.

Although he'd developed a tried and unfailing mechanism for maintaining his reputation, he knew he could never be comfortably sure about his associates' ability or desire to do the same. There had been examples of stupidity— appointees, employees—and he'd had to be careful to come down on the correct side of each issue. A balancing act between being a "loyal friend", and exhibiting outrage with a scoundrel. And, of course, there was one's family. Trouble there was a no win proposition. But, Justin had no worries in this quarter. Florence was a potential problem, but only if he was negligent in managing her drinking. His son, Lawson, was on his way to becoming CEO of a Fortune five hundred company and offered no problem. Piper . . . well, poor Piper didn't have the will or imagination to get herself into trouble. He'd just have to be sure that the man she chose was bright enough to hold down the government job he'd find for him.

Justin stood now at the window of the Governor's Mansion observing the last moment of twilight as the streetlights came on along Grace Street. Just then, a car turned into the driveway and drove to the parking area. Fletcher Eton, his administrative assistant, sprang out and hurried toward the front door.

"Florence, did we invite Fletcher over for dinner?"

"No, dear. No one's dining with us this evening. Why?"

"We're about to find out."

12

The Henderson County Sheriff's Department, the County Jail and the Animal Protective Service each occupied a section of a new building on a low hill overlooking a broad ravine known locally as The Bottom. Brad parked his car in the lot and walked several yards to the edge of the ravine and looked down on the wide river bottom formed ages ago by what was now only a small stream. Brad thought of the many times he and his friends had played war games on the vacant field where this building now stood. Back then the field had been creased with gullies that ran downward through the tall weeds making ideal trenches from which they pretended to shoot at the enemy. It had been the enemy's disadvantage to occupy the old, abandoned railway station.

Their parents warned them repeatedly to stay away from this part of the city. The shantytown that stood on the opposite side of the creek and the railway tracks was reputed to be home to depraved and dangerous people. That, of course, had made hanging around its borders all the more exciting. An added feature was the notorious tavern at the railroad crossing. Tales of what went on in its second-floor rooms had fueled their budding sexual fantasies.

All that had changed in the last half dozen years. The train station was now a Burger King and the shacks had given their places over to a shopping mall. Brad turned and started walking toward the jail entrance. He was smiling at the thought that the Burger King was still an easy target for a mortar attack.

He entered a cheerfully decorated waiting area, very unlike other fictional jails he'd read about or seen in films. The upper half of the rear wall of the room was thick, no doubt bulletproof glass, through which could be seen a brightly lit office. A middle-aged man in uniform looked up as Brad approached the glass partition. He got up from the desk where he'd been working and went to a metal portal through which he asked Brad how he could help him.

"Good evening, sir. I'm Bradley Collins. I'm an attorney assigned to Kerry Atwood. I'd like to speak to her if it's not too late in the day."

The man consulted a register on a counter below the glass and read Brad's name on a list.

"Sure, Mr. Collins, there's no problem about the time. Just step over to the door. You'll see a drawer in the wall. First, you gotta deposit any metal objects like keys, coins, pocketknife in the drawer. You'll be passing through a metal detector just like at the airport. Harmless things like your keys can be picked up on the inside. Something like a knife I'll be locking up before you come through the door and you'll get it back when you leave and are on the outside." He smiled. "Got that?"

"I understand." Brad put his watch, some coins and his car keys in the drawer and then passed through the metal detector. The man pressed the release that opened the door and Brad walked into the office space. The man was looking at him as if Brad should know him. He did look vaguely familiar to Brad, but he couldn't place him. The deputy's body spread downward and outward from narrow shoulders, shaping itself, Brad speculated, to the many hours he must have spent sitting at his desk. His complacency said he was comfortable with the way he'd be spending his time until retirement.

"I'm Deputy Sam Griggs," the guy announced as he looked over half glasses again with an expectation that Brad would identify him.

Griggs. Of course, N.C.'s father. N.C was one of his friends who had played those games he'd just been remembering.

"Mr. Griggs, it's been a while since I've seen you. How is N.C.? What's he up to?"

"Family man now. He lives in Chicago."

"He was going to a school for aviation mechanics the last time I heard."

"That's right. Got him a job with United Airlines."

"Say hello for me the next time you talk to him."

"I surely will."

They had arrived back at the point of tonight's business. Brad wondered if he'd have been permitted to see his client at this hour so easily if Griggs hadn't recognized him as his son's friend.

"I'll call the guard in the women's section to bring the Atwood woman over," Griggs said, turning to pick up a phone from the counter. "You can talk to her in one of them visitors' rooms across the hall."

"That would be fine, Mr. Griggs. Just lead me through the routine, if you don't mind. This'll be my first client here."

"Nothing to it. Just sign in," he said, pointing to a logbook on the counter. "And sign out when you leave. There's a call button in each of the rooms. Press it to let me know that you're through and ready for your client to be taken back. You have to stay with her until the guard comes."

Griggs punched in a couple of numbers on the phone and told the person who answered that an attorney was there to see Kerry Atwood. "Yeah, I know it's late. I'll tell you about it later."

Brad had his answer about special treatment. He said, "I was told by the court clerk that she's being held on suspicion of murder. That's all I know. Can you tell me anything else?"

Griggs went to another book on the desk where he'd been sitting. "We're not supposed to say anything except what's in the book."

To Brad this meant that Griggs knew more than he thought he should tell. How far could special consideration be stretched?

"Suspicion of murder of Benjamin and Gladys Tulloch of Springville, West Virginia." Griggs turned his back to the desk and leaned on it. "I guess there's no harm in telling you she and her partner—State Police shot and killed him—are supposed to have hijacked the couple's car and knifed them. The old people were on their way to their daughter's wedding reception." His emphasis made it clear that he thought this last fact made the crime especially heinous.

Brad was shocked. He'd had a half-formed idea of a woman who had killed an abusive husband. He was struggling with this new information when his attention was drawn to the sound of a door opening at the end of the corridor. A woman deputy was guiding a young, dark-haired woman toward him. She was shackled at the wrists and ankles, causing her to shuffle and look down at the floor in front of her feet. Brad couldn't see her face. She was slim and probably above average height if her head were raised. The guard took the woman into a room off the corridor and seated her at a narrow table. The deputy signaled to Griggs and left.

"She's all yours," Griggs said to Brad.

"The shackles, is that usual?"

"Yeah, sheriff's regulations. She's murder one suspect and hasn't been arraigned. He don't want to be faulted for an escape or anyone gettin' hurt."

Brad nodded, "OK, I'll call you when I'm through."

Kerry hadn't been told why she was being taken from her cell and, expecting another indeterminate wait, was lost in her own thoughts, running a finger under one of the cuffs. Brad's closing the door surprised her. She saw a tall man, dark hair, sharp features with dark friendly eyes. She judged him to be about her own age.

Brad sat down on the opposite side of the table and was about to extend his hand, realizing in time that it would cause an awkward moment.

"Hi, I'm Brad Collins. I'm here to be your attorney . . . That is, if you agree." He almost said, "If you'll have me." He felt embarrassed, even though the words hadn't slipped out.

Kerry raised the handcuffs, managed a smile and said, "I do, indeed, agree. What I need to do is get in contact with my brother. The problem is I don't know where he is and I expect it will take many calls to track him down. I can't accomplish this with the few calls they'll allow me."

"Your brother?" Brad repeated, taken aback momentarily by her dismissal of introductory formalities.

Kerry saw that this abrupt summary of the past hours alone thinking about a plan of action had been delivered in an avalanche. She smiled, took a deep breath and began again. "My brother is the only one I know who could help me with some money and my understanding of the legal system . . . well, I believe it would help if I had more money than I do, which is very little. My problem is that I don't know where he is at the moment, and I need someone who has more phone time available than I have, to discover that."

Brad sensed he was asking a useless question even as he said it. " Where does your brother live?"

"I don't think it can be said that he lives anywhere. He moves around."

The brother sounded like a drifter. Brad wondered how much help he could be.

"Your parents?"

"They are both dead. My mother died eleven years ago and my father last fall."

"No other relatives?" This was less a question than a hope. "Friends?"

"No one with money." She went on, embarrassed. "Look, I feel . . . irresponsible being in the financial position I'm in. I had a good job, but I've never been able to save. It's expensive living in Manhattan and then there was my father . . . I probably should have been able to budget . . . but it's not who I am."

Although this didn't affect Brad's role, as he viewed it, the lack of resources did complicate the course he had anticipated and planned on, when he learned he would be representing a woman charged with first-degree murder. This might turn out to be a huge problem, but he had more immediate ground to cover.

"Why don't you tell me what happened—from the very beginning."

Kerry paused to organize her thoughts.

Automatically she structured her story as she might approach the writing of a scientific paper. She started with a background sketch of her life in New York before she met Tom Albright, then her story took on immediacy and detail.

"I met him three months ago." She was only partly with Brad, now, and partly reliving in her mind the events she related. "I suppose you'd have to say it was love at first sight for both of us. He was just graduating from architecture school when we met. A few weeks later he was offered a good job with a firm in Springville, West Virginia."

She noticed Brad's questioning look. "It has a good reputation and is on the rise. Tom was starting at a much higher salary than he'd be offered in New York. Anyway, we decided to live together as soon as he got settled in an apartment in Springville and get married later this year. I left my job—a laboratory at Columbia— and came down two days ago. Tom greeted me with the news that the firm had reneged on the job offer. He was naturally very upset. Hell, I was very upset too. I didn't know if I should call my old boss and try to get my job back or what. Tom's solution was for us to go off for a couple of days camping and hiking." She paused to see if Brad reacted as she had at the time. "I thought this was no way to deal with the situation, but at the same time, I knew he must be feeling . . . well, I didn't know what to say or do. I was afraid to say what I thought, that the idea was crazy. Afterward, as we were hiking the second day, I came to think he was right. What we were doing emphasized *us,* us together and not the immediate problem. So anyway, we started the hike— day before yesterday.

"Are you able to follow this rambling?" she asked.

"Yeah, no problem."

"Ok, we camped one night and walked close to four hours the next morning and climbed to the peak of a mountain when a helicopter appeared out of nowhere and hovered over us. Tom had his camera in his hand. They— the two guys in the helicopter—yelled over a loudspeaker for him to drop his gun. This made no sense, of course, but Tom must have gotten afraid, because he began to run and yelled for me to run too. I was too confused and afraid to move. Tom kept running toward the trees . . . I saw him fall. I hadn't heard the shot. They were now telling me to stay where I was, but I went over to Tom. He was bleeding. I saw the wound in the back of his . . . neck."

She began to sob.

Brad waited until he could see she had regained control before asking, "He was dead?"

Kerry nodded and lifted her shackled hands and wiped her face on the sleeve of her prison dress.

"The police are talking about a man and a woman who were killed," Brad said.

"I don't know anything about that. It's all a big mistake."

Whoa, thought Brad. What the hell does this

mean?

"You are under arrest. Have you no idea why?"

"Yeah, I know what I've been told, that an old couple was killed. A state police big shot accused Tom and me of killing them with a knife. I'd better back up a bit. Yesterday, before we put up the tent, Tom went off the trail to urinate. He found a man's wallet there in the bushes. This happened just after we had crossed a dirt road. According to this cop, the couple was killed in their car near a bridge where the road crossed our trail. I swear Tom and I saw neither a car nor a bridge when we crossed the road. Tom looked inside the wallet and found a driver's license. The wallet belonged to Ben Tulloch. We figured he had done the same thing as Tom . . . well, dropped his pants in addition . . . and his wallet. So, Tom put it in his backpack, planning to call Ben Tulloch as soon as we got back to Springville. It seems that Tulloch and his wife are the people who were murdered. The police found the guy's wallet in Tom's backpack and now think we robbed them. This cop, Tappan, started in about there being blood on the wallet and I told him I'd say no more until I had a lawyer."

"Good. I'm sure they will question you again, now that I'm your lawyer. Remember to only answer the question you're asked. Don't expand on your answer, and look to me in case you have any doubt. I'll jump in, of course, if the questions are out of line. OK?"

"Yes. I understand."

Brad had been, without deliberate intention,

appraising his new—his first— client. She looked very tired, near collapse in fact. Nevertheless, in the moments when she'd managed a smile, he caught a fleeting glimpse of the impression she'd normally make: warm, bright, someone who could take care of herself in most circumstances, and . . . she was attractive.

Brad returned to a major concern of his. "Once we locate your brother . . . ah, he will be able to give you money?"

She replied, cynically, "He has the money all right."

"What kind of business is he in?"

"It's sort of . . . well . . . it's stealing."

13

"Stealing?"

"I'm sorry," Kerry said. "That was a smart-ass reply . . . although it's accurate. Vince runs scams of various kinds. He sets up phony businesses, takes in as much money as he dares and then disappears." She looked for and saw the reaction she expected—distaste. "He's always been like that. He conned other kids out of their lunch money in grade school. My parents divorced and Vince ended up living with my father, which didn't help. My father seemed to let Vince do what he wanted to and looked the other way. Vince was my mother's great worry—and embarrassment, but over the years we began to accept his behavior as if it were an organic disease, like epilepsy. You understand now why I don't know where he lives; I make no effort to keep in touch. We have nothing in common."

"Why do you think he would . . . "

"Want to help me? He wouldn't *want* to, but I *was* able to get him to send money now and then to help me with my father's expenses: his apartment rent when he was in the hospital, bills Medicaid wouldn't cover and so on."

"He's younger or older than you?"

"Two years younger."

"When was the last time you saw him?"

"He showed up at my apartment a year ago. He was in New York 'on business.' He was high on something. Consequently, he rambled on about the limitless opportunities presented by the internet. Read that as the limitless ways to bilk people. I believe he was setting up some kind of auction."

"His name is Vincent Atwood?"

"His real name, yes, but he uses many others."

Brad pondered what he'd just heard. Dismal.

Kerry guessed what Brad was thinking. "There is this possibility. I wouldn't mention it if the situation weren't so dreadful. I wouldn't mention it, because the woman has already had enough trouble from the Atwood family. Vince is addicted to her and keeps contacting her even though she has threatened him with a court order. It's just possible he's been around to see her recently. Her name is Helen Cooper. She lives in Manhattan, West Seventy-first. Her number's in the book, H. Cooper."

Brad made a note. "I'll call her. In the meantime, I'll see what I can do about getting someone good to represent you until we can sort things out."

"I don't understand. I thought you said you were to be my attorney."

Brad picked up the fear of abandonment in her voice. "I'm your attorney for as long as you need me, but yours is a serious criminal charge and you'll need additional help. But first, there are questions I need to ask you.

"You said that you and Tom Albright were planning to get married. Have you been married before?"

"No."

"Have you ever been charged with a felony, or even a misdemeanor?"

"No." Then she smiled. "That sequence makes it sound like they go together—marriage and felonies."

Brad laughed. "No parallel intended. But if one wanted to find one, the consequences of both can remain with a person for a long time."

There was a pause in which Brad was aware of a pleasant contact that had been made.

"Do you know if Tom Albright was ever married before?"

"Before what?"

"Ah, I misspoke. Was he ever married?"

Kerry knew his slip was because he thought of her and Tom as being married.

"No. No felonies either as far as I know."

"And his relatives—who is there?" Brad wondered if a source for funds might be found there.

"A sister lives on Long Island. I've never met her. We were going to visit one weekend, but her son got sick and we postponed it. She has three kids and her husband works for the post office. Tom also has . . . " she lowered her head and when she raised it again, Brad saw that tears were in her eyes. She moved the backs of her manacled-hands first to one eye then the other to wipe them. She coughed. "Tom *had* a kid brother in the navy. Tom's father retired from the post office and lives near the sister. He and Tom were on bad terms—rarely spoke.

"If you're thinking what I think you're thinking—don't." Kerry looked frankly into his eyes. "I wouldn't consider asking them for help. They are strangers and I don't want to deal with whatever feelings they have about me."

Brad sat quietly assessing his understanding of the situation. He would consult his friend, Jeff Goodrich, about a criminal lawyer he might approach to accept a *pro bono* case. And, when he did, he could be more persuasive about the case's merit if he was surer of the facts.

"Let's go over yesterday. When did the two of you decide to make this hike?"

"It seems like ages ago, but it was only yesterday morning. Tom picked me up at the airport the evening before, but waited until we were in his apartment before telling me what had happened with his job. It was the next morning, yesterday, that he came up with the idea for a hike. After I agreed, he got busy getting things we'd need, including a new pair of boots and a backpack for me. It was one or two o'clock before we actually started walking."

"Did anyone see you—say when you were leaving the apartment?"

Kerry pondered this. "Sorry, I can't think of anyone. The guy who sold me my boots, if that's worth anything. We walked out onto the highway and then along the shoulder for what seemed like miles. Plenty of people must have seen us then." She shrugged, "But who knows who they were? She brightened. "We got a ride—Tom had been sticking his thumb out. A guy from Texas in a pick-up truck gave us a ride to the trailhead."

"Great. Do you have any idea who he was?"

"Yeah, good ol' Jerrod."

"What?"

"He said his name was Jerrod and he was from Texas and on his way home."

"Texas? Where in Texas?"

"He didn't say. To tell you the truth, I wasn't paying much attention. I was hot and tired and was having trouble believing I was in a damn pick-up truck."

"How about the make?"

"Ah well, one truck is like another to me, but I know the answer to this one. He did say, 'Got this ol' Chevy headin' home' or something like that. And, it was red, a red Chevy ."

"Year?"

"Not this year or the last five. I'm pretty sure it didn't have a crank—somewhere in between."

Brad smiled shaking his head. "Great, that narrows it down to seventy years." He thought for a minute, Kerry watching the process with interest. "I hope there aren't a lot of Jerrods in Texas."

"There aren't, at least where he lives. He said he hadn't heard of anyone else named Jerrod. But for him that no doubt takes in a radius of ten miles."

"Hmm," Brad murmured. "That is something a private investigator could track down. But let's think about how this can help us if we could establish that you were, in fact, hiking at—you say you started at two o'clock and you walked a couple of miles—say three o'clock."

The answer to this question came to both of them, but Kerry said it first. "It would all depend on the movements of the couple who were killed."

"Right." Brad glanced at his watch. It was time for his mother's medication. "I have to go. I'm sure they'll want to interrogate you tomorrow. I'll be here. In the meantime, I have some things to pursue." He stood up. "I'm sorry about those handcuffs. I'll try to do something about that. I'd be surprised if using them in this situation doesn't exceed the state's code."

"Don't bother. She only put them on to bring me here to see you. Otherwise, I've been treated well. I don't want to jeopardize that."

Brad nodded. "See you tomorrow. He opened the door and called to Deputy Griggs.

Music was coming from his mother's room. Either she was waiting for him to return, or she'd fallen asleep with a CD playing. Brad peeked around the doorjamb.

"Tell me about your first client," she greeted him.

"You'll never believe this," and he related every word of the interview.

"You didn't say so, but my impression is that you think she's innocent."

"I feel very uneasy about this. You're right; I feel strongly that she is, but I'm afraid my opinion has come too fast. Yet I've never been more sure of anything."

"Indeed . . . my, my." She wasn't sure why, but Mary Collins was afraid for her son.

The eleven o'clock Denver news showed a scene that has become familiar: a person entering the rear door of a police cruiser, a cop's hand pressing down on his or her head to prevent a collision with the door frame. In this case, the woman was wearing something that looked like hospital pajamas. She was unemotional, even detached. This seeming indifference puzzled, even angered those watching passively at home in their recliner chairs.

"I feel better having him on board," Fletcher Eton said, making a note in a black, leather-bound notebook, ever alert to the reactions of his boss.

"Son of a bitch. Never thought I'd ever have dealings with that cowboy, Roscoe MacGruder. Like to laugh at that getup he wears on television, but you're right, can't argue with his record."

"As I told you earlier, I immediately called Governor Stoner—former Governor Stoner of Colorado—and asked him who could do the best job for us in the Boulder court. MacGruder was his instant answer."

"I appreciate your getting on top of this, Fletcher. I'm too undone by it to think clearly."

Eton nodded an acceptance of the thanks.

"What's your thinking on how we deal with the media?" Dahl asked.

"I believe I should be in front of the cameras. I'll say that naturally you're very distraught and won't be making an immediate statement. We wait until MacGruder has a chance to sound out the situation and decide how he's going to structure the defense. After that, your statements will support that position."

"D'ya think I should fly out there? Show a father's appropriate concern?"

Although Eton himself was unsentimental, he was surprised each time he heard this kind of cool calculation from Dahl.

"You're right, but when you'd arrive at the airport, there would be many reporters with many questions. The answers you'd think were right at that moment might not be the ones we'd prefer to have on the record later on. I think you should, with understandable distress, be forced to remain here to take care of urgent state business, while

Florence flies out to Denver."

"Florence for God's sake? You know they barely speak to one another."

"I know, but that won't be on camera. All our voters will see is the distressed First Lady hurrying to her daughter's side uttering, 'My poor baby,' as only Florence can do."

Dahl nodded. "When should she leave?"

"As soon as possible. I'll call Lyman Wright. He has always lent us Rytecorp's jet when we've asked."

Justin Dahl reached out and gave Eton's knee a slap. "Don't know what I'd do without you, Fletcher. Bless your soul."

Dahl's tribute was according to the script, the automatic flattering response, and Eton knew it. Eton knew that Dahl appreciated his efficiency, but he had no illusions about the, "Don't know what I'd do without you." Dahl would simply replace him.

14

"Now whadaya think about what we done? Them New Yorkers are gonna get what they deserve cause we had the balls to move that car," whispered Deputy Woody Youngblood across the table to his young partner, Deputy Lonny Sheffield. They were sitting in a booth at Nola's Elite Café on Springville's central square drinking their free coffee.

"Caught 'em red-handed with the old guy's wallet," Lonny contributed. He thought a moment then added, his voice also a whisper, "Wasn't strictly legal, but it turned out OK."

"Thas' it. Legal's got nothing to do with what's naturally right. What nature says is right. Right by nature." Woody had been worrying about Lonny keeping their secret. He relaxed now hearing the rookie parrot his wisdom.

"You know, years from now, when this is history, we'll be able to tell people about what we done." He laughed out loud. "We'll be legendary. Folks in the Sheriff's Department will brag on it from then on. An' jus' like it is now with us, some other veteran will be sittin' right here tellin' a rookie about Youngblood and Sheffield and the stunt they pulled off. Jus think of that!"

The café was busy with the usual morning crowd. Lonny noticed others looking around at them. "We best keep it quiet a while longer."

In another diner east of St. Louis, two orders of bacon and eggs were carried out of the kitchen by a waitress who felt she wasn't paid enough to put up with the shit she'd taken from the skinny guy. To Clive's mind he'd made another conquest.

He and Lomas had driven slowly on back roads since they'd left West Virginia, so they wouldn't draw the attention of the highway cops. It was ten-thirty, two mornings after the murders. Clive got up and retrieved a newspaper from an adjacent table. He glanced at the front page and stiffened. He read the article through, and then with a big smile he turned the paper around and pushed it in front of Lomas.

Stabbing the article's heading with his finger and speaking loudly enough for others in the diner to hear, he said, "See here, the po-lice caught them two what killed a couple over'n Virginia. Caught 'em and killed one who was tryin' to run away. How do you like that for fast work?"

Lomas mouthed his way through a reading of the article. "There weren't no . . ." he began to say, but Clive cut him off.

"Right, who woulda thought. Important thing is they got 'em."

He saw that Lomas was about to say something else. "What time did Uncle Henry say we should come by?"

Lomas's jaw dropped. Bewilderment replaced anything he was about to say.

Kerry was right, Helen Cooper did have a listed number, and information offered to dial it for Brad for an "additional fifty cents." He wondered as he dialed the number if he'd ever feel rich enough or lazy enough to take them up on it. He was using the phone in the kitchen. It was seven-fifteen in the morning. Brad wanted to catch Helen Cooper before she left for work. He hoped she didn't work a night shift and this was her time to sleep. The voice of a fully awake woman answered, but it was tinged with a note of wariness.

She was already dressed in a dark business suit, appropriate for an advertising sales person for *New York Magazine*. She was an attractive blond beginning to show the effects of chronic disillusionment. Luster had left her eyes and her default attitude was skepticism.

Brad quickly explained who he was and his mission, but she became focused on Kerry's situation and questioned him in detail. He patiently worked to dislodge her from her sympathy for Kerry to consider his reason for calling, to learn the whereabouts of Vince Atwood.

"I'm surprised that Kerry would have suggested you call me. She knows I want nothing to do with him."

"Yes, she assured me that was so, and I believe she has like feelings and that's why she doesn't know how to contact him. However, as I just explained, her defense is going to be expensive and her brother is the only resource she has. Kerry told me that in spite of your wishes, he tends to call you from time to time. She thought there was a chance th . . . "

Helen interrupted. "He hasn't called here in six months and that time I lied and said I had complained to the police about his phone calls. I read his number off from my caller ID and said I was hanging up and calling the detective assigned to my case." She paused. "This is embarrassing, because I went further and got a male friend to call the number and say he was a detective. I even went to the trouble of finding out the name of a real cop from my precinct."

"I see," Brad said, since she seemed to have ended her story.

"What I'm saying is I think it worked. I don't expect him to call again. Vince Atwood is going to stay far away from any possibility of police involvement."

This looked like a dead-end to Brad. "Well, in the unlikely event that he does call, please tell him his sister desperately needs his help and give him my number."

"I'd like to help if I can." Brad heard a serious

offer in her tone. "I don't have much, but I do have some savings."

Brad didn't know what to say to that.

"You see," she continued, "I don't know Kerry well, but I liked what I did see of her and she was very supportive when I was torn-up over Vince."

"That's a generous offer, Miss Cooper. I'll keep it in mind and I'll tell Kerry what you said."

"And tell her for me that I'm sure she'll . . . Hell, I'm not sure of anything. Just say I'm pulling for her."

"I'll tell her."

Dana Rogers had moved more swiftly than Fitz Halloran could have imagined. The moment she got the go ahead to use state police personnel she dispatched two men to New York to learn what they could about Kerry and Tom. She let them know that she was required to send a report of their performance to the head of their detective division.

Two deputies from the Henderson County Sheriff's Patrol had left early that morning to Springville, one to question Tom's neighbors and the other to talk to Raymond Sterns at Sterns & Associates, the employer Tom listed when he rented his apartment. Both deputies had returned.

"Sterns saw me right away," The first deputy

reported. "Seemed v-e-r-y willing. I'd say he had a story ready."

The deputy was a veteran with a veteran's world-weariness. He looked at Dana over his reading glasses to be sure she got his meaning.

"He said he hadn't actually offered Albright a job. Said the application was only under consideration. When Albright showed up on his own, Sterns said he didn't know what to do. If it had been an honest mistake he hated to send the poor guy away, especially since it seemed that he had given up his New York apartment. But, on the other hand, Albright's action might have been a very disturbing clue to his character. Was this an attempt to con his way into the job? Sterns said he didn't know, but since Albright had no place to stay, Sterns did make a call to a realtor friend to help him find an apartment. In the meantime he would decide how to proceed. His final decision was, and I quote, "To handle it directly and firmly." He called Albright and set up a meeting at the firm's offices that night and told him there was no job for him. He claims Albright became belligerent, threatening to make Sterns "very sorry." When he wouldn't leave, Sterns said he threatened to call the police. He waited until he saw Albright pass under the streetlight at the corner before he felt safe to leave the building. When he got home he saw by the light in his garage that Albright had "keyed" his new Mercedes from front to back."

Dana thought about what she'd just heard. "Did you

talk to anyone else at the firm?"

"No." He thought he'd done what he'd been told to do.

"Planning to?"

"Er, ah . . . "

"You said you thought Sterns had a package ready for you."

"Yeah. Right. I see what you're getting at. If he wanted me to believe his tale, there must be another version."

Rogers did not make the sarcastic reply that was sitting there like a fat pitch over the center of the plate.

"Got any ideas about where we could hear that other version?"

He'd been caught doing a half-assed job. He capitulated. "From the troops at the office."

"Sounds good. There was this question that came to mind when you were talking. If you're unsure about hiring someone and you're even having thoughts that he may be a con man, do you go out of your way to help him get an apartment? Do you let him sign a lease and then tell him, sorry no job? We may also find out something useful by contacting the school Albright graduated from."

"Sterns did mention that. A place called Cooper. Cooper University?"

"Cooper Union, a good school. I'll have someone talk to them. You get what you can from the 'troops' at Sterns and Associates and then call me."

From the other deputy she learned that Tom's neighbors knew nothing of him.

After the second man left, Dana swiveled her chair around and looked toward the window. A line of young pines had been planted down the side of the building. Looking out the window most people would see the treetops. Through her thick glasses, Dana saw a square of light, the lower portion blurred. Her mind was in New York City. She picked up the phone. One of the men she had sent there answered his cell phone.

"Thomas Albright may have a history of violence," Dana told him. "Check police records and go to his school, Cooper Union, and talk to the Dean of Students. See if they have anything related to violence in their records. From there, keep going back through his school records as far as you can."

She pressed the disconnect and dialed again. "Faith, please get a Captain Lucas of the state police for me."

The report she'd read of the investigation at the murder site failed to account for a piece of evidence. Halloran had called her last night to tell her he was charging the young woman with first-degree murder and that *he'd* be trying the case. He said that the Springville bank teller had given Ben Tulloch twelve hundred-dollar bills in a special envelope they use when they know the money is to be a gift. Since the same envelope would have been a convenient way for Tulloch to carry the money to the reception, it was safe to assume he had left the money in the envelope. That envelope, to Dana's mind, could be a more specific piece of evidence than the bills themselves. Yet, there was no mention of it in the report: not on the bodies, not in the vicinity of the car, not in Albright's backpack or anywhere on the Folsum Trail. If that were correct, she'd have Lucas search again for it. Lucas came on the line. Suddenly, she had a premonition and decided not to mention the envelope. She read off the evidence list and asked only if it was complete. She had sensed last night that Halloran wanted badly to convict this young woman. She didn't have a good reading of how eager the state police were to do the same. It came to her how easy it would be to manufacture this piece of evidence if its importance were recognized.

"Just to keep you in the picture, Fitz, I want you to know what's going on with us and Dana Rogers."

"Yor outfit gonna hep'er?"

Halloran felt a little guilty about launching "the beach ball" toward Joe Tappan.

Good God, Tappan thought. "Gonna hep'er?" where was Halloran getting this hill folk lingo? Tappan steadied himself and went on. "I called her yesterday afternoon to say the brass approved the use of our personnel for her investigation. Immediately, she sent two of our detectives to New York City to look into the backgrounds of Albright and the woman."

"Don't worry none, Joe, I know she's a slow starter. She'll get her act together pretty soon."

Tappan gave a grudging chuckle.

"By the way, Joe, I'm charging Atwood with murder one. I found out it was twelve hundred-dollar bills that Ben Tulloch was carrying—same as in the backpack."

"Shit, that's as good as a conviction," breathed Tappan gratefully. This took the spotlight off the state police. "What do you lawyers call it? *Res ipsa* something?"

"Right you are: this is a simple case of what's called *res ipsa loquitor*, the facts speak for themselves."

"Should be a slam dunk without all this extra work Rogers is laying on us."

"Like you say, but we need overkill, so keep giving Rogers what she asks for."

"Giving's got nothing to do with it where she's concerned."

15

"I've learned he's really the only attorney here in Henderson who's both capable of handling the case and likely to do it pro bono. "

"And, he outright refused? Even when you explained the young woman's desperate need?"

Brad had come home from a meeting with Lloyd Farmer and related his conversation with Farmer, not with a hope that his mother would have a suggestion as much as a need to get it off his chest. Farmer had listened politely, inquiring carefully into the details of the case before explaining that he was already committed to two other pro bono cases and didn't have time for another, especially one which would be so demanding. He had offered no names of other criminal attorneys whom Brad might approach. He had not sympathized with Brad's problem or even said he was sorry he couldn't help. He stated his position and sat silently until Brad, with confusion and growing anger, got himself out of the man's office.

What Brad didn't know was that L. Lloyd Farmer was very tempted to take the case in order to oppose his old law partner, Fitz Halloran. When Halloran had left their partnership to become district attorney, he did not leave in a friendly, gentlemanly manner, but instead left Farmer with unfair expenses and unfinished business. Farmer knew Halloran and was sure Fitz was trying the case because of the political profit he saw in it. Farmer would have liked to thwart Fitz for the hell of it. The reason he didn't agree to take on the case wasn't because he didn't have the time. He thought the case was hopeless.

Brad had been pacing at the foot of his mother's bed, while he relived the humiliating exit from Farmer's office. His attention turned now to his mother's question.

"Yeah, of course, I told him about Kerry's desperate situation. I've got to forget about him. He's no longer an option. I've *got* to find someone else."

Mary Collins's brother, Crawford, had been a criminal lawyer and the person Brad had emulated after first making an aborted beginning toward becoming a physician like his father. If only Crawford were still alive, she thought. The useless nature of that thought brought home to her how helpless, old and unimportant she was feeling. Once, she could have made a few calls and . . . That time had passed.

"You've thought of going to Richmond," she said.

"When Jeff Goodrich recommended Farmer, he also said he knew some names in Richmond. I'll call them today. The problem is there's no compelling reason for anyone to be interested in taking on a case like this for no compensation. Kerry isn't a part of their community and who wants to be identified with an outsider such as she charged with such a vicious crime?"

"When are you seeing her again?"

"I'll go this afternoon, if for no other reason than she needs someone to talk to after learning she's been charged with murder. Damn it. I wanted to have some positive news for her."

Mary looked over at the books on her bed stand and selected one. "Here, take her this from me."

The cameras and the shouting reporters were there and Florence Dahl responded as Fletcher Eton had predicted. America's heart went out to her as she looked up as if surprised to see a camera in her face and murmured, "My poor baby."

She had dressed plainly. Not the selection she'd have made, but Fletcher had insisted the mothers watching TV would identify with this simply dressed, anguish-laden woman.

Now she sat opposite Piper in a room at the Boulder County jail. A police officer stood behind Piper. Piper saw a familiar expression on her mother's face—exasperation. The look said, "I turn my back for a moment and you run off and murder someone."

Aloud Florence said with disbelieving disgust, "They say you were standing naked there in the upstairs hallway."

Piper wasn't sure how to reply. Any reply would

be meaningless. She had no credibility with either of her parents. She cancelled an impulse to shock Florence. "Yeah, I was giving Greg a blow-job." It would be wasted effort. There was no way to break through to any real communication. But, she wasn't free to just ignore her mother's question either.

"So they say."

"That's all you have to say for yourself?"

Piper had the urge to get up and leave, but instead she smoothed her hair, sighed and answered with resignation.

"The truth is, I don't remember much of that afternoon."

"Well, you'll have to do better than that if you expect us to help you. Daddy has hired the most expensive lawyer on earth. Good God, what we could do with the money it will cost us."

Piper was about to say that it shouldn't be done for her sake, but she reminded herself that her mother's concern wasn't for her anyway. Her concern was only for the "important people" in her social circle.

"I'm sorry for the trouble I've caused you and Daddy."

This apology, this supplication, mollified Florence.

"Well, it's done now. We'll do what we can. Your father always says there is nothing that can't be done or undone if you know the right people.

Piper's thoughts finished her father's familiar saying.

"That's why I go to church." It would take a resurrection to undo what she had done and she hadn't heard of any amount of prayers or connections that had accomplished that recently. Would she like to undo the moment she drove the knife into Greg's chest? Yes, of course, for her and for him. He was a pig and deserved to be hurt as much as he'd hurt her, but dying was too enduring a punishment. Guys like Greg were normal hazards of living, she now appreciated, like potholes in the road. One has to keep one's eyes open—a lesson she hadn't learned soon enough.

There were voices at the doorway of the room. Piper looked up to see a tall, tanned man fill the entrance. He strode into the room as if he were the major stockholder of the whole world. Her gaze involuntarily went upward, drawn to his full crop of radiant silver hair as one's gaze moves up a mountain to the snow-topped peak. Her eyes then moved downward again taking in the dark, perfectly tailored suit set off by a light lilac shirt and a hand-blocked paisley tie, to stop at a pair of hand made ostrich boots. He laid the wide-brimmed, gray, western hat on the table that separated the two women.

"Roscoe MacGruder. Good afternoon, ladies. I'm Piper's attorney." The voice was a sonorous bass-baritone.

He looked down at Florence and continued in the voice that he knew thrilled most women, "I'm very pleased to be able to meet you at last, Mrs. Dahl. What a shame that your daughter's crisis prevents me from being able to talk with you as I'd like to do."

Saying this, he took Florence's hand in both of his and while paying this gallant homage, he simultaneously guided her up and out of her chair and towards the door like a ballroom champion.

To the police officer he said, "Mrs. Dahl is leaving and I want to speak with my client alone."

The officer followed Florence out of the room. Piper was then alone with Roscoe MacGruder, who sat down in the chair her mother had occupied. He took a small recorder from his pocket and laid it on the table. A subtle, masculine perfume reached Piper. MacGruder smiled at her, a monument of confidence and poise.

"How have they been treating you here, Piper?"

In the past it would have been her usual behavior, when faced with a figure of authority, especially such a dominating one, to answer quickly and docilely like a good obedient child. A change had taken place in her. The obedient child had been snuffed-out, leaving her free to react with a different cadence. Instead of answering immediately, she now considered the man who sat across from her. In him, she recognized the arrogance of a Greg Patterson. There was the same assumption that he could do as he liked with her. The difference was that Greg had only dominated *her*, while this man apparently had enjoyed a much wider success.

"They've treated me well. That is, the matron of my cell unit has treated me well."

"Did the police explain your rights when they arrested you?"

Piper shook her head. "I don't remember much about that."

Adopting an avuncular tone, MacGruder said, "Tell me what you do remember of that afternoon, Piper."

No one else had asked her this. Certainly her mother hadn't. Even though he was doing it to perform his job here—and win another case for his fame and bank account—she was grateful for the question. Oddly, she felt an objective distance from that afternoon with Greg, as if she were a historian.

"I was very unhappy. It was clear that Greg didn't love me as I hoped he did. Greg had paid attention to me and I let myself believe he was sincere. He changed suddenly. I knew that he had begun to see another woman, another student. I couldn't bear to feel like my old humiliated self again. He had grown used to the easy sex, so he was willing to see me one more time. That's the way it was that afternoon. I called him and said I wanted to see him. He agreed, but made it plain that he was going out later with someone else. This humiliated me, of course, but I went anyway."

Piper was surprised by how easily she was able to describe the details of her degradation, even Greg's final words, as she'd perceived them. "Suck it, bitch, that's all you're good for." The rest was still a numb blur in her mind.

Roscoe MacGruder thought only of the weight of provocation in Greg's statement. He faced a paradox. Early in his career, such an insult to a young woman would have captured a jury's sympathy causing it to consider the insult as justification for a violent, impulsive reaction. On the other hand, her admission that she had voluntarily been performing fellatio would have done much to cancel that sympathy. Now, the oral act would not as likely undermine the sympathy, but, at the same time, neither would the insult be likely to arouse it. Or would it? However, there was another detail, which puzzled him greatly. The scene just described by his client might bring a charge of second-degree murder, but there was no evidence of the premeditation required for the first-degree charge.

"Did you say anything to your friends about Greg's treatment of you? Did you say anything to anyone about killing him?'

The question surprised Piper. Her immediate impulse was to firmly deny that she had told anyone about the deterioration of the relationship. She wanted everyone to think Greg loved her. An intruding memory surprised and stopped her.

"I never talked about it, but . . . this is embarrassing . . . I did write . . . but I didn't mean it. Even while I was writing, I knew I was only venting anger."

"Yes?"

Piper began to shake her head as if to erase the act. "I wrote some nonsense in my diary about . . . wanting to kill him."

MacGruder made an effort to keep his voice very steady. "Wanted to, or that you were going to?"

Piper strained to remember the exact words she'd written. "I wrote that I was going to kill him . . . the first chance I had. But, I didn't mean it. It's like my mother used to say when I was a child, 'If you don't come here this minute, I'm going to kill you.' Like that."

"When did you write that?" He hoped that her answer wouldn't be the one he got.

"A few minutes before I went to his apartment that afternoon."

MacGruder swallowed. He now knew why the prosecutor was going for first-degree-murder. The case was much different than he'd been led to believe by the Virginia governor's man. Could he refuse the case now? Technically he could. He had agreed to meet with Piper Dahl, but had not accepted a retainer for his service. He had, however, made a statement to the press that he was defending the girl. Withdrawing from the case at this point would be certain to lead people to the conclusion that Piper's case was hopeless. Everyone—that meant all of America—who was following the hourly TV coverage, would believe he thought the girl was guilty. Great damage would be done her defense and he'd receive a black mark too. He concluded that not taking her case was no longer an option. What then? Could he hope to convince a jury that Piper had not really meant what she had written? That would be difficult, given the short time between writing those words in her diary and acting them out. Could sympathy with her situation be stretched to cover both events? Immediately MacGruder realized, that while iffy, this was her only defense. She *did* wield the knife. He'd be laughed at if he suggested otherwise. The girl was sane in the legal sense. His only hope was to plead a period of temporary insanity initiated by Patterson's degrading treatment of her on the phone and crystallized by his remarks there in his apartment. In the throes of an extreme emotional state, she'd written the wild, meaningless statement in the diary and then stabbed Greg Patterson when his remarks further unhinged her.

MacGruder's experience caused him to be wary of another factor: Greg was the son of Colorado's Olympic heroes, Slats and Cindy Patterson. The case came with a strong built-in bias.

MacGruder turned his attention to studying Piper's amenability to instruction. At the moment her personality appeared blunted and flat, too much so to inspire sympathy. In time, and especially if she realized her life depended on it, could she cause a juror to identify with her? Maybe, but right now she was depressed, didn't seem to give two hoots if she lived or died. MacGruder had a bad feeling about the case, but he knew he'd never have another with a higher profile.

Through the window at the end of the small cell block Kerry saw puffy cumulus clouds drift slowly by against the hazy blue afternoon sky. The light-hearted appearance of the clouds seemed to mock her imprisonment as the sounds of the outdoor play of other kids had seemed to do the summer she lay bed-bound with infectious mono. The brightness of the out-of-doors meant to her people actively going about their private lives, pursuing their plans for the day and the future while being unaware and uncaring about her confinement.

She had saved a packet of saltines from her lunch and now absentmindedly opened the cellophane and began to nibble at a cracker. With anguish, she thought of how she had first planned to spend another week in New York putting things in order before coming south to be with Tom. If only she had. But Tom had pressed her impetuously and charmingly to rush down to be with him. In another week, having found out the truth about the job, he would have returned to New York. She'd still have her job and Tom probably would have contacted the firm on Long Island. If only.

This line of thinking played itself out. This was no joke or a simple mistake such as one reads about where the wrong person is arrested, because his or her name is the same as the criminal's. How incredible it was that the jail staff, no doubt normal intelligent people, could look at her and see a different person than the one she knew herself to be. They looked at her and saw a murderess, a person who could stab to death an old couple on their way to their daughter's wedding reception. Fantastic! They had put her in a cell and turned to their lives in the sunshine. They had been told she was a murderess and that is how they saw her, their judgment permanently swayed.

She was alone with another truth, one not appreciated until you're unlucky enough to be in her position. Once accused, one is not innocent until proven guilty. It was quite the opposite. You are guilty until grudgingly proven innocent.

If someone of established reputation, the mayor for instance, had introduced her to these very same people here at the jail, saying she was a friend of his daughter's, how differently they would view her. Instead, she'd been introduced as an unmarried woman from New York City traveling with another outsider, a male who possessed the wallet of a murdered man.

Such was the risk of being an outsider. One enjoyed the independence and freedom of not being bound to a group and its line of thought, its likes, its principles and positions, but for the outsider, the group's sympathy and protection is absent. More than that, one became the convenient object for the group's fear of the stranger, the alien.

To some degree, Kerry had put herself in that position much of her adult life. It had not been a conscious decision. She had had a very close and loving relationship with her mother, but lacking another loved person in her immediate world to whom this intimacy could be transferred when her mother died, she had turned inward. She unconsciously protected herself from another painful loss by investing her feelings in an abstract idea. Not in the idea of God, as many turn to in like situations, but to science and—to her—the abstract beauty and infallibility of the scientific method. She always had friendships that provided companionship for activities such as sports, movies, parties and, later, travel. These, however, never became so deep that she couldn't comfortably tolerate their termination for whatever reason. Thus, she never became an invested member of any group.

What had happened to her emotionally when she met Tom had been unique for her. She had dared to make an intimate bond—and now suffered the very pain she'd feared and avoided.

Brad sat in an interrogation room waiting for Kerry to be brought from her cell. He had no good news to give her. He couldn't even think of some encouraging bullshit. He heard shuffling in the hall.

Kerry appeared in the doorway. Her ankles were still shackled, but her hands were free now. Apparently the sheriff had decided there was no longer a danger that she might beat up one of the guards, but he must still think she can outrun them. She shuffled into the room and sat down and the guard who had brought her left.

"As you see, I'm still here." She smiled.

Her expression and quip invited camaraderie and Brad wanted to respond in kind, but he was too mired in his feelings of failure to reply naturally. There stretched a moment of awkward silence.

"Well, I've been working to find an expert in criminal law, and . . . "

"I've made a decision about that," she interrupted. With calm earnestness, she added, "I want you to represent me."

Brad's short laugh was dismissive. "Impossible— really. It's like telling a first-year surgery resident, 'I want you to do my coronary bypass.'"

His tone reflected his disbelief, but he recognized a need to modify his reaction. "Thanks for the compliment, but what you suggest is really impossible. I don't know the first thing about undertaking your defense."

She smiled patiently.

"Really," Brad insisted. "It's not remotely an option."

Kerry took the warm invitation to a working relationship off the table. She replaced it with soberness.

Actually, the decision she'd just announced had been based on a cool analysis of her position. She was sure the story of her arrest had been carried on the wire services and had been fed to the major TV affiliates, newspapers and cable news. If her brother were alive anywhere in the civilized world, it was likely he would know about it. He had not attempted to contact her. Reviewing in her mind the details of the last time she had been with him and the disdain she'd shown, she was forced to admit that she couldn't expect he'd feel sympathy and brotherly love.

"Look, I have no money and mine is not exactly a case that promises to reap acclaim for any defender. So, no money coming in, no brownie points piling up, who in his or her right mind would want to take my case? You'd be less than honest with me if you tell me you haven't found this to be the truth."

Brad didn't deny it.

Kerry paused for both of them to acknowledge this dismal truth.

"So, Mr. Bradley Collins, either you're going to represent me, or I'll have to do it myself."

They sat looking at each other. Kerry brushed a wisp of dark hair back from her forehead.

"Besides, I want you." She smiled. "I think the jury will like you. Maybe they'll feel sorry for your being shackled to the likes of me and want to do you a favor."

There was that offer of a relationship again. Brad didn't know what to say. He wasn't going to do what she suggested—that was sure.

Kerry spoke quietly. "Look, I can't blame you for thinking of your own professional reputation, or if you really don't want to defend me, or if you don't like me,

I'll understand, and I'll release you from your obligation legal and otherwise. But if it's just because you don't feel qualified . . . I won't. When you accepted my case as a public defender, you became my lawyer and I won't voluntarily release you from that commitment if it's just that you don't think you're qualified. You'll have to refuse to defend me."

In the normal evolution of a social situation Brad would be pushed in the direction of acquiescing. A very attractive woman had just told him she wanted him to defend her. After hearing that, he would tend to bend everything she said in a certain direction. When she'd said she'd understand if he didn't like her, a lifetime of romantic fiction both printed and projected pointed the way to the response. "It would be my pleasure to be your attorney. You can depend on me." But Brad's professional identity overrode the social script. He was no more inclined to agree to Kerry's wishes than that resident would have been to attempt the surgery.

"It's not that simple," he said. "It's not like asking me to help you move furniture into your new apartment. A defense in a case like yours requires skills and knowledge that I don't have. If I were to agree to what you're asking, I would knowingly be doing you a disservice—hurting you, in fact. I know you must feel insecure not knowing who will defend you, but if you can be patient a while longer, I'm sure I'll be able to arrange your defense to the satisfaction of both of us."

"I don't like to be talked to as if I'm a child. Come to

think of it, I didn't like it as a child."

This stung. He had been patronizing and having this pointed out stirred a reflexive defensive reply, "Then don't act like a child. Recognize that yours is going to be a damn difficult case to win. You need the best person available. I'm not that person!"

Kerry gave a shrug. "Then, what shall we talk about?" She gestured. "What's that?"

Brad's gaze followed her gesture and discovered he was holding a book.

"Oh yes, this is for you. My mother sent it." He handed it to her, looking at the title for the first time, *Walking Across Egypt*. "She said it was the sort of thing she'd want to read in your situation. A few laughs I'd guess."

Kerry looked at the title and laughed. "That's about as far away as you can get from what I'm doing here. Great. At first I thought it might be an uplifting religious tract.

"Tell me about your mother."

"My mother?" Brad was surprised, but he found himself saying, "She's a wonderful person, but she's dying . . . of leukemia. She's barely able to get dressed anymore." Her expression of sincere interest had tapped into this, his most emotionally laden concern.

"There's just the two of you?" Kerry asked.

"Yes. My father died many years ago and my only sib, my sister, lives in Denver. My mother has lived here alone until this illness. I moved home to help out."

"Moved from where?"

"D.C."

"Were you practicing law there?"

This was strange, answering questions about himself.

"Yes, I had just started working for a large firm."

"You took a leave of absence?"

"Yes."

"And, you're working as a public defender in order to make some money while you're home."

Brad nodded. "I have to pay my half of the apartment rent back in D.C."

Kerry raised her eyebrows. "Who is responsible for the other half?"

Brad hesitated. How had she got him talking about himself? He gave in. "A buddy from law school. He works for a government agency."

She studied him quietly. "I see," she said.

She stood up and called to the deputy, "Time to go back home."

She turned to Brad who sat bewildered by what had just passed between them.

She said, "Please thank your mother for the book." Then she said softly, "Somewhere along the line I will be in a courtroom. I'll either be standing there alone, or you'll be at my side. So long for now, Mr. Bradley Collins."

16

Dana Rogers called the friend she usually lunched with on Fridays and cancelled. She pleaded pressing work. This was true, but not department business. She had become aware of a situation that disturbed her. The cause for concern was subtle and likely would have gone unnoticed by others. First, she had discerned a change in Fitz Halloran where the Atwood case was concerned. It had been his habit to pour forth all his thinking about any case. Dana had long recognized his need to run things by her and observe her reaction. If she appeared to agree with his thinking, he would then become bold about his views. If she disagreed, he would just as readily disown an idea, even attributing it to someone else.

She noticed a difference now. He seemed to be withholding information about that case. To check on this she had sought out the Henderson County Sheriff, Jerome Prentis, and engaged him in discussing the case. Here too she had sensed evasiveness. Jerry was withholding something and was uncomfortable about doing it, uncomfortable because Jerry and she had become friends and normally confided in one another.

Halloran not confiding in her didn't threaten

Dana's self-esteem. But she wanted to know at all times what he was up to, much as a teacher keeps a wary eye on that kid who's the menace of her classroom. Dana was concerned that some action of Halloran's might besmirch her own image as she made her carefully calculated way from Henderson County Assistant DA toward the larger political stage of the state. She could not afford to passively stand by and let this happen. She had developed her own intelligence network and she now turned to it.

Shawnda Robinson, a secretary in Joe Tappan's office, Leroy Hart, a sheriff's deputy, and Faith Belclair, her own secretary, all friends, made up the core of Dana's "spy" network. From these three, the network fanned out through enough friends and relatives to keep Dana abreast of all that was happening in the county—*all* that was happening. She now made the phone calls that would fire-up her network in order to find out what Fitz Halloran was up to. She wanted to know whom he'd been talking to and what they in turn had begun doing.

Dana's assignment from Halloran had been to find out all she could about Tom Albright and Kerry Atwood. She had made progress. The profile coming together for Albright was consistent with a tendency toward impulsive behavior. His only police record was as an accessory in a car theft while an undergraduate at Rutgers. What had happened, however, was more benign than the title of the offense caused one to think. Albright and a friend went along with a third friend's idea of a great practical joke—to take a sorority girl's car for a joy ride. Pigtail pulling. The girl had gotten pissed and before the boys had finished their prank and returned the car, she'd called the police. The girl had remained pissed and wouldn't drop the charge, so a judge found Tom and his friends guilty of "unlawfully driving away a motor vehicle", but he'd given them suspended sentences. Dana imagined the judge thought he was teaching them a lesson. Not an inclination toward criminal behavior, Dana concluded, but impulsivity and poor judgment. Par-for-the-course in a male with a lingering adolescence? Perhaps. There had been other college misadventures. Albright had tried to pull off the old trick of turning in an English paper with several introductory pages on the assigned subject followed by pages from a previous assignment. The professor had not only given him a failing grade for the paper, but had made a report to the dean's office, which remained in his record. Also, the campus police had written him up for being drunk and "obstreperous" at a party. Obstreperous? The cop must have been an English grad student working the night shift, Dana figured. He probably wrote Albright up because he was angry that Albright could party, while he had to work to support a wife and child while getting his degree.

Of a more serious nature was a threat Albright made to "beat the shit" out of his boss at the electronics store he'd worked at during his sophomore year. The guy called the police, and when they took no action the guy called the dean's office and a secretary had seen fit to make a note of it in Albright's record.

One of the detectives she'd sent to New York had located and interviewed a former roommate, who said that Albright was an avid gambler, who made three trips to Las Vegas in the year they roomed together and often drove up to the Indian casino in Connecticut.

Dana knew that the personality emerging so far was not that of a cold-blooded killer, but a case could be made that he was prone to act on impulse.

Perhaps the information most useful to the prosecution was obtained by the second man sent to New York. He talked to Kerry Atwood's former roommate, Brenda Farr. It was evident to the detective that this woman was irritated with Kerry because of her sudden departure. Otherwise he thought it likely that he would have learned nothing. Although she'd left with her share of the rent paid, Brenda had the job of immediately hustling up someone to take Kerry's place. What he learned was that Brenda had been the one who introduced Tom and Kerry. She had done it with some misgiving, because she knew of Tom's explosive temper. She had witnessed two occasions when he'd become enraged over a remark and threatened to fight the other guy--once in a bar and again at a party. She had been told of other such outbursts. She said she told Kerry all of what she knew, when she saw that Kerry and Tom were becoming serious.

The second useful piece of information the detective

got from Brenda Farr was about Kerry's phone call to her on the night Kerry arrived in Springville. It was after Tom had gone to sleep that Kerry called and reported the bad news about Tom's job and that she believed Tom had gotten physical with the guy who had reneged on the offer. It was late, and although Brenda had to get up early for work, she could tell Kerry needed to talk.

Kerry had no police record. She had been given a consistent "outstanding" rating on her job performance reviews at the Columbia University laboratory where she worked. Her fellow research assistants liked her, but said she was a "private" person. The ones the detective talked with said they knew nothing of her life away from work and were surprised when she announced she was getting married.

A high school counselor remembered her well, because the brilliant, motherless student had been taken into the home of a fellow counselor during Kerry's last two years of school. That woman had since died, but the detective's informant said her colleague had liked Kerry very much; she was pleasant to be with and ever ready to pull her weight with the housework.

There existed a contradiction between Kerry's intellectual interests and cultural tastes and her choice of after-school friends. Sal Bondi was the alpha male of Kerry's class, a sexually precocious, motorcycle riding chronic truant who was almost illiterate. The counselor remembered gazing in amazement on the several occasions when she had seen Kerry perched on the back of Sal's cycle, trailed by his drop-out, biker buddies. She feared that Kerry would end up wasting her abilities and the scholarship offer from Columbia to become Mrs. Sal Bondi. Instead, the school staff had been pleasantly surprised when Kerry enrolled at Columbia and Bondi seemed to have been forgotten.

The woman was very concerned about Kerry's trouble, couldn't believe Kerry was possibly guilty and wanted to know how to contact her.

What did this history mean to Dana Rogers? She wasn't sure of the psychological dynamics that had produced this personality, but Kerry Atwood seemed to have a taste for the borderline sociopathic male. She was happy to passively ride on the back of the guy's bike. Was she also ready to go along with an impulsive plan to rob an old couple? And, when the plans soured and led to murder, would she stick by him? It was an interesting picture to develop and let a jury ponder.

Dana's interest at the moment, however, was the need to find out what Halloran was up to.

Six times Henderson County Sheriff Prentis had attempted to throw a wallet similar to Ben Tulloch's and ten times it had struck tree limbs and fallen far short of the place where the woman said Albright had found it—a good thirty yards short. He was standing at the spot where the Tulloch's car had been found. Prentis's arm wasn't what it was when he played a year of minor league ball for Knoxville. His right knee hadn't been what it was either since the skiing accident that following winter, which ended his baseball career, but Prentis still believed he could throw better than most, so when his last attempt failed, he was confident that it was impossible for anyone else to have done better. Maybe if he were forty feet or so up the hill on the other side of the bridge it would be possible, but Prentis believed that if a killer hadn't held onto the wallet as Albright did, he would throw it away the moment he took the money out. He'd throw it standing right where Prentis stood—the spot the murder had been committed. It was perfectly clear what had happened: Albright had taken whatever money was in Tulloch's wallet out and transferred it to his own wallet, and then shoved the old man's wallet containing credit cards he no doubt planned on using later into the small stuff-bag in his backpack. He then stuck the twelve big bills he took from the bank envelope into the same stuff-bag. No jury of practical folks like those around Henderson would swallow any other lawyer-invented version of the facts.

Prentis had reluctantly agreed to this experiment on which Halloran insisted. He had thought it a waste of time; dumb to think anyone might believe it was a coincidence that both Ben Tulloch and Albright were carrying twelve hundred-dollar bills. But, he admitted, if he were Halloran he'd feel more prepared by having the results of this experiment in his back pocket.

The deputy who was working with him brought the wallet back to Prentis after the last throw. Prentis took it and said, "Troy, I think we've done that enough to make a point. I'm going back to headquarters to write this up and when you come back I want you to sign it as a witness, but right now I want you to join the rest of the guys looking for that bank envelope. Like the district attorney says, it's got to be here somewhere. Tulloch, the old guy who was killed, got the money from the bank in one of those gift envelopes and is sure to have had the money in it when he was killed. The envelope wasn't in Albright's stuff, so it's got to be out here somewhere."

Dana Rogers heard all about this later that evening from her friend, Sheriff Deputy, Leroy Hart.

"What will you do now, son?"

"I wish I knew, Mom. The odds are a hundred to one that I'll find someone to take on this case, and I don't know one hundred names to call to find that one."

Mrs. Collins closed the book she was holding and gave her full attention to Brad. She waited a few moments before remarking, "Do you remember the nursery rhyme about the Little Red Hen?"

"What? The Little Red Hen?"

Mrs. Collins laughed. "She couldn't find anyone to help her either."

Brad shook his head. "A man should never return home."

Both broke out laughing.

She went on quietly, "I know you feel you can't try this case alone . . . perhaps there is someone who will help you. You could do it together."

The idea was new to Brad. He thought of his friend, Jeff Goodrich, and then rejected the idea. Jeff didn't have more experience than he.

"And just who would that be? You know, if this were fiction, you'd be suggesting an old friend of Uncle Crawford's, one who'd been a brilliant trial lawyer before a disappointment in love turned him to drink followed by disbarment for mysterious reasons. He would hear of my predicament and put whisky aside. He'd spend long hours in the law library to discover a fine point of law that would win the case."

"Maybe I had something less colorful in mind, smarty pants."

He saw that she was serious. "Sorry."

"I seem to remember that you had a high opinion of your criminal law professor. Meadows, wasn't that his name?"

Brad was surprised she'd remember that. "Yes, Ernest Meadows. I must have talked about him a lot."

"You did, and one of the things I recall your saying

was that he was very approachable."

"Right. He didn't make you feel stupid for asking what you later understood had been a stupid question." He saw his mother was smiling and nodding.

He quickly said, "Oh no. That's out of the question—outlandish. Besides, he's retired."

They sat in silence, Mary Collins watching her son with interest, while she knew he was daring to consider an "outlandish" possibility.

John Dunn felt like a coach reading the scouting report on a team he was about to face. The report on Roscoe MacGruder was extensive. Dunn stayed up late doing his homework and now knew it by heart. The case he was about to try should be a prosecutor's dream, a straightforward premeditated murder; the girl had put her intentions in writing. But there was MacGruder. Dunn wanted to tell himself that his opponent was just another attorney, but that was like saying Lance Armstrong was just another cyclist. Dunn's reading had described cinch cases for the prosecution where time and again MacGruder had walked away laughing. Dunn was competitive. He wanted to beat MacGruder more than he wanted to convict Piper Dahl. More accurately, he couldn't live with the idea of MacGruder beating him.

Dunn realized that the key to victory here would

be the public's perception of the case, because from that public the jury would be chosen, and the verdict would depend on the mood of that jury. Legally, homicide had been committed and Dunn had evidence of Piper's putting in writing her intention to kill Patterson. Clear and simple. Yet, MacGruder was sure to spin a sentimental yarn—lonely, insecure girl led on by an unscrupulous opportunist who taunts her with degrading insults until she snaps and grabs up the weapon that's at hand. This scenario would be strengthened by the fact that Piper had not brought a knife to Patterson' apartment. MacGruder would face the jury and ask, "Wouldn't a person meditating murder have provided herself with a weapon?"

The critical element in the outcome of the trial would be public bias against Piper Dahl. Public outrage would be safer. John Dunn had become jaded. Only the joust with MacGruder stirred his blood. He didn't question whether the actions he was about to take had anything to do with justice.

Sitting across the restaurant table from Dunn was Chris Tovald, a feature writer for the *Denver Evening Star*. Dunn and Tovald had traded favors over the years. It was Dunn's turn to balance the books. The conversation followed conventional small talk for half an hour: family, the Broncos, Tovald's last feature about the effect of the economy on Denver's art scene. Dunn then changed the direction of their talk toward his reason for asking Tovald to meet him. Tovald recognized the second the drift changed and knew it must be about the Patterson murder.

"I heard," Dunn began, "a rumor that it might be indelicate for me to pursue just now, but one that I thought presents a fascinating study of the psychological complexity of love relationships. You've done stories like this before—damn good ones. I remember the one about the young guy who was obsessed about Madonna. You won a prize for that one as I recall." He looked to Tovald for confirmation.

"That's right."

"The rumor is about a murder . . . "

"The Dahl case."

Dunn looked sharply at Tovald. He knew he hadn't fooled him for a moment. He relaxed and smiled. "Yeah, of course. What I'm talking about is an angle I've become aware of that has to do with Greg Patterson. You know who his parents are, of course?"

Tovald nodded.

"Well, what I heard is that the kid had been trying for some time to shed the Dahl girl, but she stuck to him like you know what. His friends say he was getting desperate, because he was serious about someone else and was afraid this Piper was going to mess it up for him."

Chris Tovald thought about this. There had been times when John had given him leads as pure gifts. More times there had been some advantage in it for Dunn. Even then, the leads had been worthwhile. Gradually, as Dunn had been talking he became aware of what it was that

Dunn wanted. He wanted this "rumor" looked into and if there was substance to it, he wanted it to be developed and fleshed out by the press, not the prosecutor's office.

"Tell me more."

"Well, what I hear is that as a last resort, Patterson had begun to humiliate her at every opportunity just to get her to leave him alone. Still she pursued him."

Tovald lifted his coffee cup to his lips and drained it and put it down. "Like you said, interesting."

17

Brad drove along the quiet street in Alexandria where Professor Meadow lived. To say the least, his feelings were mixed about being there. It took the experience of Kerry's preliminary hearing yesterday to cause him to call his former teacher. Procrastination was no longer possible. The case, as outlined by the prosecution appeared to be strong enough to convince a jury. Immediate work must be done to build a defense and Brad could think of no alternative to his mother's suggestion.

Brad remembered Meadow's house from the time he had been there with other members of the editorial staff of the Georgetown Law Journal for dinner. He parked his aging Honda Civic on the street in front of the white, two-story frame building. A porch ran the full length of the front and down one side, meeting in a gazebo-like structure at the corner. Two large hornbeam trees shaded the entire front lawn. It was now mid-morning.

Meadow had responded warmly the previous night when Brad identified himself on the phone. After the usual opening greetings, Brad told him he had a problem he hoped the professor would hear and advise him about. Meadow said he'd be home all day today and he'd expect

Brad anytime he could get there.

Was what he was about to propose to Professor Meadow wild and inappropriate or not? He had wrestled with this question so much he'd lost perspective. Would the man laugh in his face? These doubts welled up again as he climbed the steps up to the porch and rang the doorbell. Maybe he should . . . but it was too late now. The door opened.

It was Mrs. Meadow who opened it. Brad remembered her but she showed no sign of recognizing him. Over all those years of her husband's teaching, there must have been countless young men standing at the threshold as he was now. She led the way through the house to the backyard where Ernest Meadow was on his knees weeding a flower bed. It was strange to see him like this in a T-shirt. Brad had never known him except as very distinguished and immaculately turned out—dark blue suit, tightly knotted tie.

Meadow had to be over seventy, but he had the face of a much younger man. Aside from fine wrinkles at the corners of his eyes and his gray hair, he seemed more likely the age to be achieving tenure than retirement. His slow, stiff rising from his weed-pulling position did betray his age. He shed his gloves, wiped his hands on the seat of his jeans and shook Brad's hand as if he were a long-absent and good friend. It crossed Brad's mind that a year of retirement, a year away from his life-long work and position, might be making Meadow unusually happy to receive a visit from a former student, especially one seeking his help. This thought put Brad more at ease.

Meadow pointed to a wrought iron table and chairs. "How about some lemonade? You must be thirsty after the drive up from Henderson."

After they were settled with glasses of lemonade, which the professor poured from a pitcher on the table, he asked Brad why he was back in his hometown rather than D.C. where Meadow remembered Brad had joined a law firm. He sympathized when he learned about Mrs. Collins's condition. His expression altered then from that of pleasant host to the once very familiar one of the professor vis-à-vis a student.

"What is the problem that motivates you to make a three-and-a-half hour drive to talk to me?"

Brad shifted willingly into the role. He began with the story of his having signed on as a public defender, relating then in greater detail everything he could think of about Kerry's story and the description of the murder.

"The preliminary hearing was held yesterday and some of the evidence the district attorney presented was new to me and convinced me I couldn't just sit and wring my hands over my failure to find a competent defense council for my client."

Meadow listened with intense interest and this encouraged Brad, but he gave no sign of how he was reacting to the tale itself, which ended with Kerry Atwood's bold declaration that Brad would be her lawyer, or she'd go it alone. Still Meadow waited. There was nothing left for Brad to do except to say the thing he was afraid Meadow would view as a social and professional gaff, to ask his old professor for help—free help. He felt it would be easier to ask him for the loan of ten thousand dollars.

"I was wondering if . . . if I went ahead with the defense . . . you'd agree to give me advice on how to try a case of this kind?"

Meadow took his time responding. He studied Brad's face as if he were viewing a kind of person he'd heard of, but had not actually met before. He took off his glasses and massaged his eyes. He wiped the glasses with the tail of his shirt and then replaced them and adjusted them on his face. Brad was sure he was stalling to find the words to politely dismiss him.

Instead, he heard Meadow say, "Yes, I think I can see why this case is scaring you so much."

Brad wondered if he was being chastised or understood.

Meadow continued, "You feel very strongly that this woman is innocent. Your emotions tell you that everyone else should be able to see this simple truth as you see it. That set of feelings would have you simply put her in the witness box, display her to the jury and expect the case to be dismissed. On the other hand, your logic tells you the state has a strong case and without a solid defense to destroy their case, you'll be left standing sure of her innocence while the executioner leads her away."

The professor took a sip of his lemonade then concluded, "You're afraid your strong positive feelings for her are going to lead to your fucking up her chance to live."

Brad felt as if his face had just been slapped. Meadow had identified his confusion, but what were these strong feelings he was talking about? Now that it had been put into words, he did recognize his attitude that Kerry's innocence should be obvious to all—but strong feelings?

"First of all," Meadow went on, "If you look at this calmly you'll concede there is nothing about this that you haven't been trained to deal with. I'll leave you to deal on your own with the reason you panicked. Because of it you aren't seeing the facts with the detached objectivity I know you're capable of. That objectivity always leads us to ask three questions." He paused as he might have done in the classroom. "Question one; what are the facts? Question two; what is the law? And finally, what strategy does the answers to the first two questions dictate?" Meadow's face softened and he asked impishly, "Does this remind you of class?"

"Yeah, as a matter of fact and I like the sound."

Brad reminded himself that Meadow had not laughed in his face. He had given him a lecture like a football coach. "You've got what it takes to win, just remember the fundamentals!" There was still the question about whether he would be willing to participate.

"Doctor Meadow, would you be willing to discuss

those three questions with me today?"

"Of course. Today or any other day."

Good, thought Brad, now to get on with it and stop behaving like a stupid kid.

"The facts. The West Virginia couple was killed at a time and in a place compatible with my client's movements. Ben Tulloch's wallet—he's the old guy—was found in the backpack of Kerry Atwood's . . . uh, companion, Tom Albright. There were credit cards, but no money. A smear of Tulloch's blood was on the wallet and Albright's thumbprint was in the smear. Also, found in the backpack were twelve hundred-dollar bills, the same number and the same denomination, I learned to my horror yesterday, the victim was alleged to have been carrying when he was killed. It was to be a gift for his daughter and son-in-law's honeymoon. To top that off, Albright's bloody thumbprint was on one of the bills."

"You say 'alleged to have been carrying.'" Meadow interrupted.

"Yeah, the DA found out Tulloch had withdrawn that amount and intended to give it to the newlyweds at the reception—where he and his wife were headed when their car was hijacked. There is no proof he was carrying the money when that happened, but it seems likely."

"Then the prosecution had no hard evidence to back up a claim that the money withdrawn and the money in the backpack were the same?"

"That's right. They presented none."

"You saw the money?"

"Yes, I examined the bills."

'What condition were they in?"

"Mild to moderate wear, I'd say."

Meadow mumbled to himself, "The standard gift thing is to ask the teller for brand new bills." He motioned to Brad to continue.

"The police found a boot print matching Albright's boot on the trail just above the place the murder happened. They are claiming that this print was made around the time of the murders. It survived a very hard mid-night rain, because of overhanging foliage, while the other prints Albright must have made in the earth along the trail were all washed away. There is no argument about this. Kerry says they crossed the road the Tulloch's car was parked on in the late afternoon, around six o'clock. The wedding reception was scheduled for six by the way, so the hijacking had to be around five-thirty."

Meadow commented, "Nevertheless, it impresses a jury to be able to show the cast of a boot print and say. 'See, here's proof they were there!'"

"I asked about fingerprints on the car and the DA, Fitz Halloran, admitted that only the Tullochs' prints had been found. Oh yeah, the cops found what they believe to bed the murder weapon, a single-bladed clasp knife. It had been thrown into the creek. No prints on it either."

"Your client, Kerry Atwood—were her prints on the wallet?"

"No, as I said, Kerry claims Albright found the wallet in the underbrush and put it into his pack with the intention of contacting Ben Tulloch when they got back to Springville."

"And she has no idea how it was that her . . . friend had twelve hundred-dollar bills in his backpack?"

"No, she says she has no idea at all. She was surprised he had that amount of cash with him."

"Did he have any other money—in his own wallet, for instance?"

"I don't know. I didn't ask that."

"We need to know. Did Mrs. Tulloch have a purse?"

"Again, it wasn't mentioned and I didn't think to ask. I guess I was busy being overwhelmed by the coincidence about the money."

Meadow smiled. "Yes, I would have been bowled over. I know the feeling."

"The only other thing that the prosecution thinks is very relevant is the fact that Albright began to run. They claim he was trying to escape. Kerry thinks the sudden swooping in of the helicopter panicked him."

"Anything else?" Meadow asked

"Only one thing. Maybe it isn't important, but Kerry said Tom had a large Swiss Army knife. She saw it when they were preparing their meal the night before. Does it make sense that he'd be carrying two knives on a short camping trip? I think it's a point for the defense."

"Yes, I agree, but a subtle one."

Meadow sat for a time digesting what he'd heard, turning his lemonade glass around and around.

"OK, those are the facts, " he said in his professorial persona. "What is the law?"

"They are charging her with first-degree murder. That means the act was premeditated. The state must prove that she participated and that it wasn't done on impulse, but was planned before hand."

"And what do you think of the state's chance of proving that?"

"The premeditated aspect is self-evident. Whoever killed the Tullochs forced their way into the car and forced them to drive to the place where they were killed. Since Ben Tulloch's wallet was taken, the motive is almost certainly theft. Evidence wasn't presented, however, that my client participated in the actual killing."

"What about the fact that she stayed with him, camped with him, continued hiking—escaping—with him?"

"This does remind me of class," Brad said. "That she stayed with him is presumptive evidence of participation-if in fact he was guilty-but not proof."

"Try selling that to a jury," the professor said, smiling sardonically. "You'd have a better chance of convincing a cop you were speeding because you were late to the police commissioner's birthday party.

"So," he continued, "this brings us to strategy. What

shall we do?"

Brad felt heartened that Meadow had said "we." "Their case is going to stress Albright having the blood-stained wallet, plus having the same amount of money in his pack as the victim was allegedly carrying, one bill of which bore Albright's thumb print in the victim's blood. This latter, by the way, can be explained by Albright finding the wallet, getting blood on his thumb, which was accidentally transferred to his own money at the time he stowed the wallet in his pack."

"Nice thinking. It's a logical explanation, but will the jury prefer it? While the accused is supposed to be presumed innocent until proven guilty, we both know that the accused is really considered to be guilty by most. Why else has he or she been accused? So, with that prejudice already in place, would the jury prefer your explanation over the prosecution's claim that he had the blood-stained money because he is the killer?"

"You're saying my version will not be convincing, or not enough at least."

Meadow nodded ruefully. "You said this Halloran did not present proof that the sets of money were the same. What does that tell you?"

"Ah, that they couldn't come up with the proof."

"Exactly, and that must be the core of our strategy, to assert that it is perfectly reasonable for a person to be carrying that amount of money. Coincidence is a great part of our every day lives. Our challenge is to see if we can prove the two sets of bills are different in some way."

"His bank account in New York; I need to find out if he withdrew that money before coming down to Springville."

"That's a start. You also have to talk to the bank in Springville, learn more about the money Tulloch withdrew."

They parted with an understanding that Meadow was going to be an active member of the defense. Privately, however, Ernest Meadow had bad feelings about Kerry Atwood's chances. The case against her was completely circumstantial, but common sense, that same sense that told humans for millennia that the earth was flat, shouted out that the two lovers from New York were murderers. In the end it would be a matter of whether or not the jury members demanded solid proof that there were, in fact, two sets of bills, or would they be satisfied with what their common sense dictated?

He was not aware of the moment when he fully accepted his role as Kerry's lawyer for the trial. Certainly when he made the drive to Professor Meadow's house he was beginning to seriously entertain taking on the responsibility. On his way back to Henderson, "perhaps" became "I will." His mind raced with thoughts of the work to be done.

It was after Brad's next meeting with Kerry at the jail that he acknowledged to himself that he found her attractive, both in looks and personality. This must be what his mother and Meadow had already discerned. He was both inspired and frightened by the way she, soberly knowing the seriousness of her situation, calmly placed her trust in him.

Disappointment entered the interview when it became clear that she was not going to be able to help him by supplying the information he needed most. She simply didn't know the source of Tom's money. She admitted that it might seem very strange to someone else, but she had never thought about the money Tom did or didn't have. He didn't throw money around carelessly, but seemed to have enough to pay for meals at fairly pricey restaurants and other entertainment during their brief courtship in New York. She had no idea if he had a bank account in that city, although she assumed he must have had. Finally, she had no concern about their ability to provide for themselves. They both possessed valuable skills.

As far as his task was concerned, all he came away from that meeting with was a series of negative answers. It would have been foolish to leave her with a pep talk, but he did imply that he had other lines of inquiry in mind. He got into his car and sat and thought about the next move. First, he wanted to know more details about the money the prosecution was holding. Next, he had to get a Springville court order in order to question the banks about Tom's possible accounts and about Tulloch's cash withdrawal. If only it turned out that Tullooch had been given brand new bills!

Although he hadn't said so, Mary Collins knew her son had given up the search for a criminal attorney to take the young woman's case. She had very mixed feelings about this. What she hid from him was her worry that if he took the case and lost it would undoubtedly color the rest of his life, especially if he were developing the affection for the young woman that Mary believed she 'd identified. In that case, the consequences of failure were terrible. Terrible if Kerry got a long jail sentence but devastating if she . . . Mary couldn't complete the thought. Instead, she turned to the positive side. Accepting this responsibility that circumstances had put in his path and doing his best would become a lasting and invaluable part of his character. No one wants to be suddenly faced with the need to come to the aid of an injured stranger, but one must.

Mary had a lot of pain today. She tried to take as few pain pills as possible even though the doctor had encouraged her to take what was necessary. She had also been squirreling away a few out of each prescription. She rose slowly and went to the dressing table. There were only three tablets left. One of these times, when the prescription was newly refilled and the bottle was full—that and along with the ones she'd hidden . . . but that moment had to wait until she'd seen Brad through this ordeal.

18

Springville, West Virginia had three banks. The Springville National Bank was the nearest to the apartment Tom had rented, so Brad tried there first, showing the manager the order he had obtained from a Springville County judge. In less than five minutes he was told that Thomas Albright had never had an account there. This sequence was repeated at the Farmers and Commerce Bank.

Brad now followed Mr. Maynard, the manager of the Barnhill Bank into his office. He was friendly but reserved, no doubt the same, Brad figured, as any bank officer being asked to reveal confidential information about a customer's account. The first question asked concerned Tom Albright's possible account: there was none. The focus then turned to the Tulloch money. Before leaving Henderson, Brad had made a close examination of the bills found in the backpack and had copied down the serial numbers. He'd also learned from a deputy that the money had been withdrawn from the Barnhill Bank. He handed a list of these numbers to Maynard and asked if he could match them with bills that had been in the possession of the bank.

"Twelve hundred-dollar bills. That's the same amount the teller gave to Ben Tulloch. I checked the withdrawal slip and the entry Judy Fenton, the teller, made in Mr. Tulloch's account. I also checked the daily record of her cash drawer. The money she gave him came from that drawer. I have no idea about the physical condition of the notes except that they weren't new bills from the Federal Reserve Bank. She would have had to record that when she took them from the vault. We don't keep a record of the serial numbers of money that the tellers receive and dispense daily, only those of new Federal Reserve notes. I'll check your list against those numbers. Sheriff Royston asked me about the physical condition of the notes and I had to refer him to Mrs. Fenton. I know he was unable to speak to her that day, because that was the day she went in the hospital for tests."

A cloud descended over the manager's face. "Awful thing. It all happened so fast. She'd only been complaining of a headache for a few days. The x-rays or MRI showed she had a brain tumor and they operated a day later, but she's been in a coma since the surgery."

Brad was stunned. For a moment his thoughts were of the stricken woman, but quickly they turned to the problem of the money. "So you don't know if the sheriff ever talked to her."

"That's true."

An idea came to mind. "Mr. Maynard, did you tell Sheriff Royston these details you've just told me about checking the teller's records and Mr. Tulloch's account?"

"Uh, no I didn't. I only looked into it after he called."

"So," Brad thought, "The sheriff must have talked to her at some point or how would he know the amount of the withdrawal."

"Thanks very much, Mr. Maynard. This has been very helpful, but it's Sheriff Royston I need to talk to now." He got up to leave. "And, I'm sorry about Mrs. Fenton."

Many times what we consider to have been a deliberate, conscious decision has been determined long ago by needs and desires we're unaware of. Such was the alliance that had grown in the mind of Roy Royston toward Fitz Halloran. In spite of not liking the man, Royston was ready to enter into a conspiracy with him in order to convict the New York woman. It would be difficult to trace the many childhood notions of chivalry that had been instilled into his young mind, but a part-identity of himself as knight errant had been forged, emerging occasionally when the current reality seemed to call it forward. Young women, whom he perceived to be in distress, as one might imagine, triggered this persona. This particular part-identity had been instilled in most boys in the Western world, at least those of his generation and earlier. He experienced his police uniform as a suit of armor.

Might he have ridden off to the aid of the beautiful stranger from the north, who had found herself alone and in danger in his land? Very likely—if he had met her in person. That wasn't the case. He had, on the other hand, sat across from Ben and Gladys Tulloch's daughter, Sharon. He had promised solemnly to see to it that the murderers, who at that time were being pursued along the Folsum Trail, would pay with their lives for what they had done.

Unaware of all this background, he now dialed Fitz Halloran's home number.

"I got a call today from a fella, Brad Collins, who said he was the attorney for that Atwood woman. He was in town and wanted to come around to my office and talk to me. My secretary asked what it was about and he said he wanted to talk to me about what I had found out in my conversation with Judy Fenton, the bank teller. I told my secretary to tell him I was unavailable and I'd call him back."

"Then you haven't talked to him yet?"

"I wanted to talk to you first."

"Right. He, of course, wants to know the condition of the money she gave to Ben Tulloch." Halloran took a moment to compose the message he wanted Royston to get. "So, what did the woman tell you about the money? She said Tulloch asked her for twelve hundreds and that's what she gave him, She didn't remember what the bills looked like."

Royston hesitated. "That's not exactly what she

said. I told . . ."

No," Halloran interrupted, "In essence that's what you told me at the time. There was some other stuff about having to wait for the other teller to come back from a break and so on, but it's irrelevant. It just confuses things. She simply gave him bills from her cash drawer. You didn't want to question her much, because she was not feeling well."

"I guess that's about the size of it, now that you put it that way."

And Royston was primed to begin thinking that this really had been the substance of his telephone conversation with Judy Fenton. Fading away was the memory of her saying that she had looked for the newest bills she had in her drawer to give to Ben Tulloch and that two of the bills were "very new."

An analyst of doodles would face no challenge explaining the ones on Ernest Meadow's legal pad. Brad Collins was on the line going over his trip to Springville. The doodles began with a design of alternating circles and squares, then a circle with a happy face, then, they segued down the page to become a row of deeply impressed saw-teeth.

Brad gave a verbatim repetition of his conversation with the manager of the Barnhill Bank. Maynard had called him later to tell him that none of the serial numbers matched new Federal Reserve notes the bank had received in the past five years. In other words, none of the backpack money could be traced by serial number to the Barnhill Bank. It was then that Meadow doodled the happy face.

Brad then told him that the bank teller, who had given out the money to Ben Tulloch, was now in a coma following surgery to relieve pressure caused by a brain tumor. He went on to relate how he'd tried to have a meeting with the Springville County Sheriff while he was there, but the man's secretary had claimed the sheriff was too busy, but he'd been able to talk to him on the phone later in the afternoon. Sheriff Royston told him he'd been able to talk to the teller before she went in for surgery and she'd told him about giving Ben Tulloch the twelve bills from her cash drawer. She hadn't said anything about the condition of the bills she gave him, and Royston said he hadn't pressed for more information because he could tell she wasn't feeling well.

Brad then added, "I think Royston was lying to me. In his voice there was that quality of telling a story and closing it off, not wanting further discussion. Then his gratuitous addition that he hadn't pressed her for more detail clinched it. I hadn't asked if he'd tried to get more detail."

"You know, Brad, I smell a rat. Why should he lie? His role in this case is that of interested bystander. Why isn't he open with you about what he knows? One answer, and it's one I don't like, is that he's conspiring with your DA He wants the bills handed out by the bank to match those from the backpack."

It was at this point that Meadow's doodles became ugly.

"I also concluded that the sheriff had talked to Halloran, but the word 'conspire' hadn't crossed my mind. Perhaps I was too afraid to think that might be so."

"And the bank manager, what was your reading of his story about the bills?"

"He said he didn't know more than the amount. Had to look at the record of the withdrawal to learn that. I believe he's telling the truth."

"OK, so for the sake of argument, what would it mean if they were colluding? First, it means that Sheriff Royston is not neutral; he wants to convict Kerry as much as Halloran does. But what does it say about the money?"

"Logic says Halloran doesn't think, or at least doubts, it's the same money."

"I agree. And this means your examination of Royston on the witness stand is going to be a key part of our defense."

19

"I never thought I'd see the day I'd be rooting for Roscoe MacGruder, but now when I see him on TV doing his homespun bit, I say 'Go Roscoe Go!'" Jo Montgomery was eating a grapefruit half in the sunny breakfast room of the Governor's Mansion.

"I'll join that cheer," David said. "Do you share my impression that he thinks his act isn't playing too well in Boulder?"

Jo nodded. "It's those damned pieces Chris Tovald is writing about Piper's alleged obsession with the Patterson boy. That movie *Fatal Attraction* shifted people's sympathy for all time to the victim of an infatuated stalker. There was a time when the sufferers of unrequited love—Victorian heroines for example—were the ones pitied."

"So, are you suggesting that the girl's chances are undermined by the vagaries of fashion?"

"Uh huh, her chances and our chance to make it through your term without having to deal with a death sentence."

John Dunn was afraid to believe that his brief conversation with Chris Tovald had worked out so perfectly. Tovald was now, on his own, searching out students to question about Piper and Greg's relationship—from Greg's point of view. He had worked his way from one to another, until he had found one person, unknown to Dunn, who was eager to supply a detailed and vivid account of Greg's inability to shake off the "clinging" woman. It was clear to Dunn that Tovald really believed he had obtained the truth and his convincing pieces in the *Star* had his readers believing likewise, especially those who were already prepared to side, regardless of the facts, with the son of Boulder's Olympic ski heroes.

Was there anyone in Boulder County not influenced by Tovald's articles? Dunn didn't think so, and the jury would have to be picked from that pool.

Serendipity. Clarence Reed had been impressed early in his career how often, while reading of, or himself interviewing a famous or successful person, they'd told of a crucial, pivotal instance of being in the right place at the right time. Clarence's own career had sprung forward at just such an occasion. He'd been interviewing a local black minister about his plans for an ecumenical summer revival meeting when the man received a telephone call telling him of an incident of racial violence in a southern state. The minister hung up and announced he had just made up his mind to lead a protest march across that state. The minister went on to talk to Reed for an hour, expressing, for that time, very radical views about civil rights.

Reed accompanied the march from his established position as a sympathetic insider. His exclusive daily reports captivated readers of the *Times* and newspapers across the country that carried his column. This work had earned him his first nomination for a Pulitzer. Was the current moment an unexpected repetition of this kind of once-in-a-life serendipity?

As he had on that earlier occasion, he'd again established himself in an inside position, this time with Justin Dahl. Dahl had met Reed before his daughter's tragedy in Boulder, so Dahl understood the journalist had had an interest in him and his career before he'd become so newsworthy. Now other newsmen attempting to approach Dahl tended to be seen by him as opportunistic vultures. Reed didn't know how this advantage would serve his original reason for being here in Richmond. He'd have to allow opportunity to lead him. He suspected, however, that Dahl's long experience in politics counseled him against being very open to *any* reporter, so Reed looked to his next option, to cultivate an intimacy with either Ham Bascomb or Fletcher Eton. While Bascomb was the governor's best friend and likely to be the person most privy to Dahl's thoughts, he too was probably just as cautious about the press. Fletcher Eton, on the other hand, gained his intimate knowledge of his boss in the same way the king's valet once did, by being so constantly present that Dahl came to experience him as if a part of himself, taking no care what was being revealed in his presence. The king's valet may be loyal to some extent, but he may also enjoy having a new friend, especially a well-known *New York Times* features writer. While sticking close to Eton, he would come to share Eton's invisibility—what better position from which to study Dahl's campaign to save his daughter.

"Roscoe MacGruder's petition to have the trial venue changed has been turned down by Judge Claiborn." Jo Montgomery raised her voice to be heard above the volleys of rain hitting the window. She was reading the *Denver News*. Sitting across from her, David read an article in the *New York Times* about drug testing in the schools.

He looked up. "What's that?"

"I was thinking how interesting it is the way unrelated events can shape the outcome of a trial."

Bemused, David waited for her to continue.

"I'm talking about Piper Dahl's trial. Judge Claiborn has denied a petition to change the venue. Don't you just know he is remembering the outrage caused last March when the Boulder paper discovered that a Boulder judge took a payoff to change the trial venue from Boulder to

Denver in that class action suit against the Balmore Brewery. The local community was itching to sock it to the brewery for polluting their water.

"Now, if a well known lawyer like MacGruder comes along and is successful in getting a venue change for his client, Claiborn has got to be afraid everyone will cry, 'Foul.' The result is MacGruder doesn't get the trial moved to a venue where he can choose jurors from a less prejudiced community. Piper pays the price."

David was pensive. His sagging facial muscles told the story of his feelings about the case.

He said, "You're saying our odds just got longer."

"Don't give up hope yet, ol' Roscoe may still be able to live up to his reputation as a magician."

"It's ugly. Can you imagine what that girl's family must be feeling right now? I've met Justin Dahl once. I put him down as a wily politician, doing his charismatic man-of-the-people bit. But even phonies can experience genuine pain. My heart goes out to him. "

"What I've seen of the mother on TV didn't convince me of her sincerity. Her reaction seems more like self–pity. She hasn't done much to elicit sympathy for her daughter." Jo folded the paper and laid it on the table.

"Of course, an acquittal is impossible," David stated flatly. "Avoiding the death sentence is all they can hope for. She claims the guy said very degrading things to her. MacGruder can only hope he can build sympathy for her with the jury."

"Hmm. I wonder," Jo replied. "There is only her word for that and the stronger story is the one in those *Evening Star* articles painting her as a pathological leech."

David held up two crossed fingers.

Kerry's attention was fixed on the tray Flora Griggs had just brought to her cell. Decent looking meatloaf, mashed potatoes with gravy and lima beans. The matron sat down on the cot next to her, noting Kerry's obvious satisfaction as she ate. With sadness she appraised the young woman who, for a number of days had been the sole occupant of the women's section of the jail.

"Kay Doyle tries real hard to turn out good food for the inmates," Flora said.

Kerry paused a moment and considered this. The food had been consistently tasty and fresh. Was Kay Doyle one of society's unsung heroines, trying a little harder for her fellows in spite of the fact that she didn't really have to. Who, after all, would care about or listen to the complaints of Kay's customers?

"Thank her for me."

Flora had been with Kerry for many hours now and she concluded that there was no way that this young woman could have murdered anyone, let alone participated in the cold-blooded slaughter of two harmless old people.

"That tall guy going to be your lawyer?"

"Bradley Collins? I think he's finally agreed to be. Why?"

"He looks kinda young."

"He is. Too young, do you think?"

Flora shrugged. "I hope he knows what he's doing."

Kerry was surprised. She studied Flora's face. She had thought of the woman as just another one of those who'd be certain of her guilt. Had she misjudged Flora?

"I'd guess you're supposed to appear to be neutral about the guilt of your prisoners, but it sounds to me like you don't think I'm guilty."

"I know you didn't do it. I been around people in trouble too long to make a mistake about that."

Kerry was taken aback. These were the kindest words she'd heard from anyone, except Tom, since ol' Jerrod had said, "Y'all have yorselves a good time now." Even though she he knew he thought it, Bradley Collins hadn't said straight out, "I know you didn't do it."

"Thanks, Flora. I really appreciate that. But, you're not supposed to say something like this to prisoners, are you?"

Flora thought for a moment. She was one of those persons whose thoughts were written on their faces. "No, not really. Supposed to keep my mouth shut and work."

That was Flora's capsulated summary of what she'd taken away from the many "in service" training sessions she'd had to attend. Kerry was thinking of how helpful it would be if Flora could give this analysis of her character in court. Instead, it was going to fall to others to make that judgment, ones who had had no experience at all with her as a person.

"What would you do in my position, Flora?"

The matron's first impulse was to be flippant in order to deal with the discomfort the question had aroused and she started her response with, "Hell, I'd ... " She broke off the remark and said seriously, "I haven't thought about it in just that way. I got to be honest with you; the mood around these parts is heavily against you. I've told my friends they're dead wrong, but they don't want to hear it. It spoils their wish to be part of what other folks think."

"I don't stand a chance, then?"

"I don't want to say that. Of course, your best chance is if the real killer is caught."

"As I understand it, no one is looking for the real killer. He or they'd have to come in and surrender on their own. Not likely."

"The next best thing is to have a lawyer the jury will take a liking to."

Kerry nodded. "That's my thinking, too."

20

People, lined up an hour before the doors of the Boulder County Courthouse opened, quickly filed in and filled the courtroom seats. For Boulder this truly was the trial of the century: the accused, a governor's daughter, and the victim, the son of two local Olympic heroes. Adding to this drama were the two contestants: Roscoe MacGruder, nationally the best-known criminal attorney since Melvin Belli, and John Dunn, the district attorney serving his sixth term in office.

Because of the celebrity of the victim and the accused, the trial had been moved forward on the docket by the court clerk in order to ride the wave of national interest. Neither Dunn nor MacGruder had a problem with this.

MacGruder's only goal was to save his client's life. His best prospect to accomplish that had been to get Dunn to agree to a reduction in the charge from first-degree murder to voluntary manslaughter. He had failed to get that agreement. In this, he first recognized John Dunn's competitive need to disallow him even a small success, since unpremeditated homicide was, after all, the reasonable charge in this case. Of late, Roscoe had increasingly encountered opposing attorneys viewing trials as personal challenges. It was as if he were the famous old gunfighter being called out to a showdown with a cocky, young gunslinger. No apologies accepted: meet in front of the saloon, or ride out of town with your tail between your legs. Roscoe wondered if another attorney would have been able to negotiate a reduction of the charge. He thought it likely. He had always proudly thought his clients were doing the best thing for themselves by hiring him to represent them. Perhaps this was no longer true.

Sitting at the prosecution's table, John Dunn knew he had taken a big risk placing his lasting reputation in Boulder on one turn of the wheel. Throughout his previous years as district attorney he was ever ready to accept a compromise that avoided unnecessary time in the courtroom. He was well liked by local attorneys because of this—a guy one could deal with. At that time, he would have agreed to the easy charge of voluntary manslaughter. When he'd first read Piper's diary it had struck him as an impulsive, angry outburst and not a serious intention. What he'd heard about Greg's insulting remarks to the girl supported the notion of provocation, so, he would have had no problem. Still, if earlier he'd been presented with such an opportunity, prosecuting and winning a conviction of first-degree murder against the killer of the son of the state's most beloved ski heroes, it would have been tempting. Tempting, because of the doorways it might have opened, a judgeship perhaps. That time had passed. At present, he no longer had the ambition or energy for higher-level goals. He had only retirement in mind, but a new concern now plagued him. As it stood it would be a retirement knowing he had never really accomplished anything significant and knowing that's how he'd be remembered, a political hack who'd fed long at the party's trough. The thought depressed him. Then this case came along. If he took on the great Roscoe MacGruder and won, his career would end with a permanent aura of significance--cachet at any social gathering.

As the trial began, John Dunn felt no guilt about proceeding with the first-degree murder charge. His initial judgment about Piper's diary entry had already been suppressed, first because it hadn't served his purpose, but as time went on he actually began to believe in Piper's premeditated plan to kill. Such is the mind's ability to bend to our wishes, that he even began to believe what Chris Tovald wrote about Piper's obsession with Patterson, the very idea he himself had planted.

Roscoe MacGruder knew those articles of Tovald's had affected the public's mood. That was the reason he'd asked for the change of venue. That request, as he'd feared, had generated a front-page article in the local paper stating that he, the famous Roscoe MacGruder, did not believe Piper could get a fair trail in Boulder. This could be expected to create animosity toward him and his client, which became a problem with jury selection. Another problem arose if he asked each individual prospective juror if he or she had read or knew of Tovald's articles. This would tend would tend to give them importance. He was sure each knew of the articles anyway, regardless of their answer. Would those who claimed ignorance be lying to get on the jury? In the end, he'd decided to rely on his years of experience to identify those who were out to punish someone. He was far from satisfied with the jury he'd finally accepted and it is an adage among attorneys that the trial is basically over with the selection of the jury.

The clerk announced the entry of Judge Ralph Claiborn. All stood as a nearly bald, middle-aged man whose profile remarkably resembled that of an eagle settled into his seat on the bench. With eyes appropriate to the profile, he looked out over the room as the clerk proclaimed the case of the People of the State of Colorado against Piper Livia Dahl.

Judge Claiborn now turned to the jury and told them they were about to hear opening statements by the two sides. They, the jury, were not to hear these speeches as evidence, but rather as statements of the points of view of the prosecution and the defense.

Claiborn fixed the unblinking eagle eyes on John Dunn. "Mr. District Attorney, your opening statement."

"With pleasure, Your Honor."

Dunn approached the jury with a confident, matter-of-fact attitude meant to convey that the facts in the case were clear, simple and permitted but one interpretation. His smile scanned all twelve members as if he were saying good morning to each.

"This case is simple." he began. "On the afternoon of July fourteenth the defendant wrote in her diary she was going to kill Greg Patterson 'the first chance I get.' Immediately following this she went to his rooming house and, recognizing an opportunity to carry out her intent, she did just that, stabbed Greg Patterson to death. To the first police officer arriving at the scene she freely admitted that she was guilty of killing Mr. Patterson and further stated he had not threatened her or harmed her in any way. Now the defense is going to try to convince you that Greg Patterson provoked the accused in a way that justified brutally murdering him. If any person were to look into their own hearts, they could not believe any spoken words can justify taking another person's life. Piper Dahl did brutally take Greg Patterson's life. She planned to do it and wrote it down. This constitutes premeditated murder, murder in the first degree. I know that you are people with the intelligence to identify the smoke screens the defense is going to employ in the hope that you will become confused and lose sight of these simple facts. I know that you will hold on to these facts and return the just verdict of guilty of murder in the first-degree."

Dunn returned to the prosecution's table with the sure and confident air of one who had performed the easy task of distinguishing black from white. Sitting down, he looked toward the jury, favoring them with a radiant smile as if he and they had just struck a binding, mutually satisfying deal. Actually, Dunn worried about the jury's makeup. There were nine women and three men and the victim was a man. It could be a favorable ratio: women were generally more severe with other women than men were, but in this particular case . . . he just didn't know.

Cameron "Slats" Patterson and his wife Cindy sat in the gallery's front row. Slats nodded his head vigorously as Dunn completed his opening statement. The perennially tanned and smiling faces of both of Greg's parents were possibly better recognized in Boulder than that of the President. They each had brought home to the city an Olympic gold medal from the 1988 games in Calgary. From that moment it became *de rigueur* to have them on any important civic committee or fund raiser. They were Boulder's poster citizens.

The judge, who had put on glasses in order to make a note on a legal pad, looked over the half-frames and said in a conversational tone, "Mr. MacGruder. The opening statement for the defense."

Roscoe MacGruder was fitted out in his signature courtroom attire: deerskin jacket with fringed sleeves, rawhide string tie and black, lizard boots that made him stand two inches taller than his actual six-foot-two. His pure white hair, thick as a buffalo's mane, that came to the collar of his dark gray shirt appeared naturally curly and tangled, but had required an hour with a hairdresser that morning. He rose, extending himself fully, impressively, and then stood for a moment looking down at the seated John Dunn. Roscoe smiled sadly and shook his head while walking over to the jury box.

"My, my if only life were so simple," he said with a wise smile as he walked up to the jury. "On second thought maybe that wouldn't be so good. We humans are very complex and isn't it that complexity that makes our lives interesting? But it also means it's not so easy to understand what we do—or why we do it." He spoke slowly, tone intimate. "We experience almost every event of our days in a many-layered way. Every one knows this is true. If we take the time to examine the so-called simple things we do, we discover they are not backed by such simple feelings. Take, for example, the baking of a cake for the church-benefit. Many motives, many hopes and worries may be combined in the making of that cake. You may want it to be the best, as you want everything you do to be the best, because that's what you demand of yourself, or maybe you especially want it to be better than a certain other person's cake. You may be afraid you'll fail and your failure to bake a cake worthy of the congregation's praise will let your family down. Or, you may be tired and have many other important tasks to take care of and you resent having to take the time to bake that cake, but at the same time you can't afford to be seen as uncooperative by your neighbors, and you may worry that the icing won't turn out well and betray your true feelings. Looking at the cake sitting there on the table at the church sale, we can't know what human feelings lay behind its baking . . . but they were there all the same."

MacGruder paused, meeting the eyes of the individual women jurors. "Baking a cake is almost always more complicated than Mr. Dunn would have us believe." He became very sober now, and paused between each of his next words to create a dramatic effect. "You, however, are being asked to take time to analyze the elements of a much more complicated issue than the baking of a cake. The matter under consideration here involves one of the most many-layered and complex subjects we ever experience—a human love relationship—one that went wrong." This court is asking you to do that which our sacred moral code asks of all of us, to put yourselves in the other person's place, to feel and view events as he or she experienced them. That is not easy work. It can be dreadful work, but you must ask it of yourselves, because yours is the most dreadful responsibility any of us can have, to decide whether another person lives or dies.

"I will help you in that work by acquainting you with as much of the facts about these lives as I can, so you'll have material on which to base your understanding." With an appearance of burdened humility, MacGruder returned to his seat.

If Judge Claiborn were honest with himself, he'd have to admit that he resented MacGruder. Resented his celebrity. Resented the fact that as far as the media was concerned, he, Claiborn, was playing second fiddle in this high-profile case. In spite of these feelings he couldn't help being drawn into becoming part of an affected audience to Roscoe's performance and as a result, remained silent until MacGruder completed the walk back to his table, instead of stepping on the tail of his performance by calling for Dunn to begin presenting the prosecution's case before MacGruder made it back to his table.

The first prosecution witness was Greg's roommate, Todd Wolfram. It had been he who had discovered Piper alone in the upstairs hallway of the house. He testified that she was totally nude, had blood smeared on her right hand and upper right thigh and that she appeared to be stunned. Looking in through the open doorway, he saw Greg lying on the bed, motionless and bloody. It was only as he approached the victim that he saw the knife sticking in his chest. Becoming aware that Greg wasn't breathing, he considered mouth-to-mouth resuscitation, but decided it would be fruitless. He then called 911.

Dunn walked to the prosecution's table and his assistant handed him a large clasp knife, which he brought back and asked to have admitted into evidence as People's Exhibit "A". He opened the knife's blade and showed it to the witness and asked him, "Have you seen this knife before?"

"Yes, that's Greg's knife. It has his initials burned into the ivory handle." He pointed. "Right there, GP. He did that when I was with him. I was soldering a speaker wire. When I was finished, he picked up the hot soldering iron and burned those initials."

"Where did he keep the knife?"

"I couldn't say where he kept it, but I have seen it lying on the nightstand next to his bed."

"By the way, Mr. Wolfram, you said the knife was sticking in his chest. How far in? Perhaps up to here?" Dunn pointed to the middle of the blade.

"No sir. It was in all the way, right up to the handle."

"Really? This blade is four and a half inches long. A pretty determined stab, wouldn't you say?"

MacGruder shouted, "Objection, your honor. That calls for an opinion the witness is not qualified to answer."

"Sustained. Mr. Dunn I don't welcome the needless interruption of our task here by knowingly incorrect procedure."

"Yes, Your Honor." John Dunn knew that the jury typically experienced a judge's reprimands as depriving them of interesting information. He just had to be careful to avoid the type of reprimand that impugned his character or competence, or could be the basis for an appeal.

"Mr. Wolfram, had you seen the defendant at your rooming house on any other occasion?"

"Sure, Piper was there a lot."

"Can you give us a more exact account? How many times a week, for instance?"

"Earlier, before classes resumed, she was at the house almost every day."

"Where in the house?"

"In Greg's bedroom, mostly. "

"I see," Dunn said nodding his head slowly. "And how did she come there? With Greg Patterson?"

"Sometimes. Sometimes by herself. She'd come in and go straight up to Greg's room."

"And when she left, did she leave with Mr. Patterson?"

"Again, sometimes. But I'd say—at least most of the times that I saw her leave—she left alone."

"Came alone. Left alone," Dunn said. "From your own previous experience observing people whom you thought to be in love, did Greg Patterson appear to be in love with Piper Dahl?"

"In love? No. I didn't have that impression."

"And the defendant," Dunn asked, "Did she appear to be in love with Greg Patterson?"

Todd Wolfram shook his head. "I can't say that I have a good idea of what women are feeling."

This brought a surge of laughter from everyone; partly it was laughter of relief from the tension in the court. Even Roscoe smiled.

Dunn stood for a moment smiling at the witness. "You're an honest man, Todd. Your Honor, I have no more questions."

Roscoe realized he had been handed a bottle of nitroglycerine. Mishandled, it would explode. Dunn, without touching the issue of stalking, a subject on which the witness had no expertise to testify and would have brought an objection from him, had instead asked Greg's housemate to make a judgment about *love*, a subject within every person's ken. The effect was the same. The jury now had the picture of a woman who regularly came "on her own" to a rooming house, where she went up to a man's room to have sex—with a man who did not love her.

"I have no questions, Your Honor." Better to let it lie.

The second witness was the first police officer on the scene. Piper had admitted to him that she stabbed Patterson. She replied, "No," to a question of being harmed by the victim. She then became unresponsive to further questioning. The doctor who examined Piper when she was brought to the County Jail then took the stand and reported that Piper had docilely agreed to a complete physical exam. He found no evidence of any injuries and the vaginal exam showed no evidence of recent sexual penetration. He said she appeared obtunded, that is, stunned and generally unresponsive, except for asking, "Is he dead?"

MacGruder rose to cross-exam this witness.

"Doctor, you just testified that the defendant appeared to be 'stunned'. By that did you mean that her mental functioning was abnormal?"

"Yes, she did not respond to questions as a normally alert person would."

"Did it appear that she didn't know what was happening?"

"In medicine, there is a condition known as a fugue state. A person suffering this is not aware of his or her surroundings, even to the degree of not knowing who they are. At the time I examined her, I'd say she appeared to be in a fugue state." He nodded his head, saying, "Yes, I'd say that was so."

Sometimes you cast your line and you pull in weeds, Roscoe thought, and sometimes you land a big fat trout. "Thank you, Doctor. I have no other questions."

Next came the pathologist who did the post-mortem examination of Patterson's body. Dunn prompted the doctor to describe in great detail the knife's path into the body. The knifepoint had struck the superior surface of the fourth thoracic rib one inch to the left of the sternum, cutting the periostium from the bone. It then traveled deeper to sever the ascending aorta. Death occurred by massive hemorrhage into the thoracic cavity.

"Doctor, you described the knifepoint cutting the periosteum from the bone. Please explain just what that means to the court."

"The periosteum is the membrane covering the bone."

"That covering," observed Dunn, "from my experience in the kitchen, is pretty tough. Speaking medically, is it your opinion that it would require considerable force applied to the knife to cut through that tough tissue and then continue on to cut the aorta—that's the large artery that carries blood from the heart, right?"

"Yes, that's right. And yes the periosteum is tough. For the blade to have been forced through it and then to have penetrated deeper through the aorta would require considerable force—a strong, determined stab in my opinion."

"Thank you, doctor. I have no further questions."

"Questions for this witness, Mr. MacGruder?" Claiborn asked.

"No, your honor." It would only drag out the description of the knifing if he challenged the pathologist about the amount of force needed to inflict the injury he'd described.

John Dunn didn't have to hear MacGruder's opening statement to know that his defense was going to aim at getting sympathy for Piper. After all, what more did he have to offer? He knew that MacGruder would not claim she was innocent of homicide; only that she was not guilty of first-degree murder. And even if the jurors were not inclined to agree with him on that score, at least MacGruder would hope to sell them the idea that the poor girl was driven to do what she did and therefore should be spared the death sentence. Dunn had, of course, heard of MacGruder's ability to woo juries to accept a sentimental view of his clients. He could see, now, with his own eyes and ears how the bastard worked his spell. Dunn knew he must not be complacent about the sureness of his position. He had to work hard to paint Piper Dahl as an angry, vindictive woman whom Greg Patterson, try as he did, could not shake.

Dunn called Jody White, Piper's sorority sister,

to take the witness stand. She described the telephone conversation she and Suzanne Barber had overheard. She then added the detail that she had asked Piper what she and Greg were going to do that evening and of Piper's reply that they were going to listen to a new CD and then probably go out for something to eat.

"Why is it that you remember that detail?"

"Because her answer surprised me. I had heard that Greg had a date that evening with another woman."

MacGruder objected that this was hearsay.

Dunn explained to the judge that he had only asked the witness why it was that she remembered the defendant's remark.

"Nevertheless," the judge concluded, "the witness's answer is hearsay and the jury must disregard it."

Dunn went along another path. "Miss White, did you have direct information that Greg Patterson was dating another woman?"

"If the woman with whom he had the date told me is direct information, I do."

"Hearsay, Your Honor," MacGruder said.

"Yes, Miss White that would be hearsay also," Claiborn said smiling.

John Dunn was amused too. His question had been answered without his having angered the judge. He would like to ask this witness if she thought Piper was stalking Greg Patterson, but that would bring an objection that she was not qualified to answer. And since both MacGruder and the judge would know he had intentionally breached the rules of evidence to get the word "stalking" before the jury to remind them of the Tovald articles, it could become grounds for an appeal. Dunn did not want MacGruder to have grounds for a successful appeal for a mistrial. He turned the witness over to MacGruder.

Roscoe got up and approached the witness stand slowly. He stood studying the young woman's face as if puzzled. "Miss White," he began. "Do you consider yourself Piper Dahl's friend?"

This was not a question she had expected. Piper was her sorority sister and by one set of values she was supposed to be Piper's friend.

"Yes, sir."

"You just testified that you asked your *friend* what she and Greg Patterson planned to do that evening; isn't that right?"

"Yes, that's right."

Roscoe looked puzzled. "Why was that? Why did you ask her that?"

"Why, to find out what she was going to do." Jody looked around as much to say it was pretty obvious.

Roscoe's puzzlement was not lessened. "But you also said you'd heard Greg was going out with someone else that night. So . . . it couldn't have been that you wanted to know what she and Greg were going to do . . . it was to find out what your *friend* would say . . . isn't that so?"

Jody was flustered. "I don't know what you mean."

"Oh, I think you do," he said in a down home voice. "You were doin' what's called baitin' your *friend*. You aimed at putting her in an embarrassing spot, where you figured she'd lie to cover her embarrassment and give you something to tell the rest of the sorority."

Roscoe had scored. Jody's face flushed. He waited a couple of seconds more before confronting her with, "Remember that you're under oath Miss White. When Piper Dahl left the sorority house, did she behave like a person who was on her way to kill someone?"

Dunn quickly objected, saying that the witness had no qualification to render an opinion about whether a person's appearance indicated their intention to commit murder.

MacGruder replied, "Your honor, one minute the prosecutor wants us to believe his own witness's expertise on a complicated question regarding my client's motives, but now he tells us she is unqualified to render an opinion on a simple issue of her appearance."

"I am going to permit the witness to answer the question."

MacGruder returned his attention to Jody White.

"Miss White?"

A subdued Jody White answered, "No, she looked . . . unhappy."

"Angry?"

"No."

"Vengeful?"

"No."

"Fragile?"

Jody nodded. "Yes, I'd say she looked unhappy and fragile."

"Thank you, Miss White. No further questions."

Judge Claiborn busied himself making a note while suppressing a smile.

Dunn called Tracy Bauer as the next witness. He established that she was a student and that she knew Greg Patterson.

"Did you have a date with Greg Patterson the evening of the murder?"

"Yes, my parents, who were visiting from Kansas City, were taking us to dinner a eight o'clock."

"What was the occasion?"

"Well, it looked like Greg and I were becoming very serious about our relationship and I wanted my parents to meet him."

"You say your relationship was becoming serious; how long had you and he known each other?"

Tracy thought for a moment before answering. "I met him in one of my classes last spring. He asked me out for the first time at the end of the semester."

"You've been dating about two months then?"

She nodded. "Yes."

"How often were these dates?"

"We felt a strong attraction for each other right away, so we saw each other every opportunity we had.

Three, four times a week."

"Did you know that he was involved with Piper Dahl?"

"Not by name. He told me had been going with someone else, but that it was over. He said he was having a hard time getting her to accept it. She kept calling him."

"So you parents never got the chance to meet the man you were in love with?"

"That's right."

"I have no more questions, Your Honor."

MacGruder was on his feet before Dunn sat down.

In a sympathetic voice he asked the witness, "Did you know that your boy friend had been having a sexual relationship with my client?"

After a slight hesitation she said, "I thought they probably had, but I assumed it had ended when we became serious. Greg never said anything and I never asked."

"Miss Bauer, did you and Greg Patterson have sex?"

It was clear to everyone in the courtroom that she didn't want to answer. Barely audibly, she said, "Yes."

"When did that begin?"

"I guess when we became serious about each other. The beginning of the summer."

"So Greg Patterson was regularly having sex with both you and Miss Dahl without your knowing it?"

She looked down and nodded.

MacGruder stood silently looking sympathetically

at her for a long moment, letting the duplicity of Greg Patterson be felt by everyone.

MacGruder knew Dunn had been wanting to establish with Tracy's testimony that Piper had been pursuing Patterson in spite of his efforts to shed her in favor of his new girl friend. It had been Roscoe's intention to argue that the witness had no real evidence of Piper's having pursued Patterson. The ground he'd gained by impugning Patterson's character had been an unexpected harvest, so he decided to leave the jury with that impression.

"I have no more questions, Your Honor."

John Dunn hadn't appreciated the value of the point scored by MacGruder, so he was feeling good about his progress. He had made an unassailable case that Piper had killed Patterson and that it had not been done in self-defense. He felt stimulated. He was going *mano a mano* with the great Roscoe MacGruder and he almost had his man down. MacGruder had approached him before the trial started about making a deal on a reduced sentence. Dunn knew that anything except a conviction for first-degree murder would be seen as a victory for MacGruder; therefore he had turned him down. One important task remained, the conviction he sought rested upon Piper's last diary entry and this needed to be presented convincingly. He knew MacGruder would try with all his skill to convince the jury it amounted to nothing but bombast.

Dunn called a detective lieutenant of the Boulder police to the stand and showed him and asked him to identify the book. The man verified that this was the book found in Piper's room which he had taken possession of and that it bore his identifying initials. Dunn thanked and excused the man and then asked that it be entered into evidence as People's Exhibit "B".

"Ladies and gentleman of the jury, I'm going to read several entries that the defendant wrote in her diary over a period of three months."

He believed MacGruder would read the parts of the diary that spoke of Piper's tender feelings for Patterson. He hoped to deflate the effect MacGruder might achieve by reading them first. Piper's joy at believing she had finally found someone who truly loved her was evident in the earliest entries he read. Then the entries began to speak of his apparent loss of interest and the plummeting of her hopes. Dunn paused a long moment for effect before reading the entry she'd written only half an hour before stabbing him in a voice that delivered each word as a clap of thunder, "I'm going to kill him! First chance I get."

Dunn turned and looked accusingly at Piper sitting next to MacGruder, and Piper, in spite of herself, looked down guiltily at her clasped hands lying in her lap, not able to meet John Dunn's gaze.

"Your Honor, this closes the people's case against Piper Dahl."

"Thank you, Mr. Dunn. The court is adjourned until ten o'clock tomorrow."

The six o'clock Denver news opened with coverage of the Boulder trial. The first images Jo Montgomery watched were of the Pattersons, Slats and Cindy, coming out of the Boulder courthouse. The reporter's questions were couched respectfully. She asked Slats how he thought the trail had gone that day.

"I know we have to go through this trial even when we know perfectly well what happened, but I can't help feeling the whole business is a wasteful ceremony—a charade. The girl did it and she planned to do it—period!"

The reporter asked Cindy how she was holding up.

"It's very hard for me to sit so close to that…person." She broke down in tears. "She killed my boy."

In an unusual move, the reporter's face filled the screen, sparing the Pattersons from the further broadcast of their obvious pain.

"As the prosecution presented its case today, Cindy and Slats Patterson had to endure hearing the details of how their son died. Tomorrow, it may be even more difficult for them to hear the defense attorney try to convince the jury that time served in prison is sufficient punishment for Piper Dahl. This is Sandra Cater reporting from Boulder for Channel 3 Action News."

The program moved on to other local news, but Jo wasn't listening. She was pondering the fact that the news department of the station had chosen to concentrate on the Pattersons and not to interview Roscoe MacGruder. Roscoe was accustomed to leaving a courtroom and walking straight to a camera where he could be depended upon to give colorful footage. Could it also be that in the minds of the jury the contest was really Piper against the revered Pattersons? The reporter had spoken of it being difficult for the parents to hear Roscoe MacGruder work to spare Piper's life. Was it the intention of the newscast's producer to please the Pattersons? Does this jury believe that only the death sentence will please them? Jo wondered.

21

Before the trial began, as Roscoe considered his options, he was aware of the tide of public opinion that prevailed against his client. Tovald's articles in the *Denver Evening Star* had been very effective. A reader would be sure the journalist had undertaken an unbiased exploration of the human side of this tragedy, unfolding the tale of how a blind craving to be loved created Piper's obsession with Greg Patterson where her judgment should have told her those feelings weren't returned. Rage followed when his rejection could no longer be denied.

Roscoe had consulted a psychiatrist on the subject of obsessive love attachments—stalking. He was told that stalking behavior almost certainly would have been evident in Piper's previous relationships with men. In the long talks he'd had with Piper, he'd found her to be ever more communicative. Her story portrayed anything but the mental state of a stalker. She had dated a number of boys when she was in high school, experiencing a strong attraction to two of them. In no case, however, did the boy's interest continue beyond half a dozen dates. She painfully came to the conclusion that she probably wouldn't have had those dates if she hadn't been the governor's daughter. She hadn't wanted a relationship on that basis. But, then came Greg, who seemed to be genuinely in love with her. With caution at first, she opened herself to him. Roscoe knew this was the story he had to make the jury see now that the prosecution had presented its case and he was about to have his turn. He needed corroboration and turned to her mother, Florence, where he heard a different point of view. According to her, Piper was at fault. If she had only dressed as Florence had advised over and over again, and behaved differently, complimenting the boys, making them feel special, but no, Piper was plain stubborn!

Florence Dahl was a drag on MacGruder's efforts. Better she should go home to Virginia. Instead, she had established her place in the front row of the gallery, trying to get Piper's attention whenever she thought MacGruder had mishandled the cross examination of a witness. Piper, in turn, resolutely and transparently ignored her. This was a problem, because he wanted the jury to perceive Piper as vulnerable, fragile, but they saw, instead, a young woman who wouldn't be bullied.

Piper hadn't taken a knife with her to the rendezvous with Patterson. This was the strongest point of fact arguing against premeditation. Her not doing so gave Roscoe a foot in the door. He must enlarge that opening with enough convincing material to allow at least one sympathetic juror to decide Piper had acted on a provoked impulse, and with a hung jury and a retrial, he stood a chance of winning a change of venue.

"Mr. MacGruder, the court will now hear your defense against the allegations presented by the state."

Many a jury had experienced the warm, seductive smile with which Roscoe greeted them this morning. The seduction was not aimed at selling himself, but at causing each juror to abandon the portentous role of decision maker for the state and shift, instead, into experiencing themselves as neighbors getting together to work through a problem.

"You Honor, I call Kathleen Heathcote."

A self-possessed middle-aged woman took the stand.

"Mrs. Heathcote, you were Piper's kindergarten teacher, were you not?"

"Yes."

"I want the jurors to get to know Piper and I figure the best way is to let those who knew her tell about her."

Damn it, thought John Dunn. MacGruder just made what amounts to a speech to the jury and he gets away with it because of the smooth "just neighbors" manner. If I were to object, it would be like coming between two friends with the complaint that they weren't talking properly. Damn!

Kathleen Heathcote remembered a quiet, timid child, who deferred to more aggressive children, but one who willingly joined in games, songs and the like. One got the impression that Piper was pleasant but memorable only because she was, at that time, the then congressman's daughter.

One after another, creating the effect of time-lapse photography, Roscoe called on five other teachers and counselors, who told the story of Piper growing up, the testimony remaining pretty much the same throughout. Roscoe pressed them: "Wasn't there at least one time when she got angry and pushed another kid or shouted or tore up a paper—anything?" The answer was "no."

"I call Piper Dahl," Roscoe said with a mixture of pathos and deep admiration.

This was a very unconventional manner in which to summon the next witness to take the stand. It surprised the judge and reflexively he began to wonder if some kind of reprimand was called for, but Piper was already on her feet and halfway to the clerk to take the oath.

The young woman sitting now facing the court wore a mulberry cardigan sweater over a light blue scoop-necked T-shirt. Her dark hair was cut short and swept forward as if a sudden, strong wind had caught her from the rear. She fastened her dark eyes on MacGruder as he came to stand very close to the witness stand. A quick appraisal would report her to be plain, but a person investing more interest would find subtle beauty: expressive, full lips that turned up slightly at the corners, guileless sincerity in her dark brown eyes.

Roscoe began by asking general questions about her reason for being at the university and what she planned to study, following a common path taken in most first meetings between strangers, wanting the jury to enter into its acquaintance with Piper on comfortable, familiar ground. He then advanced to the subject of her meeting Greg Patterson and asked her to describe the course of that relationship. The jury, at this point, could have no doubt about Piper's love for and of her trust in Greg.

"Was there a change in your feelings for him?"

"No . . . No, there wasn't, but I became confused."

"How's that?"

"He seemed to lose . . . I could feel that he wasn't . . . eager to see me anymore."

"When did you notice this?"

"Towards the middle of the summer."

"What did you make of this change?"

"I didn't really *make* anything of it at first. Like perhaps he was busy, or his job . . . He worked for the city at one of the parks and he was having a problem with his boss. I even considered it might have been something I had done, but I was sure he loved me. Then as it became clear he was really irritated with me, I asked him what I'd done. He said I hadn't *done* anything, but he was short with me. He seemed angry with me but gave me no reason."

"This had become a sexual relationship, isn't that so?"

"Yes."

"Right from the start?"

"No . . . well, soon."

"Had you had sex before with other men?"

She didn't hesitate. "Once before. In high school."

"His treatment of you changed; did the frequency of your sexual intercourse change as well?"

"No, but when we were finished he no longer wanted to be with me. He had to go someplace, and once school started again he'd say he had to study. It . . . I began to understand he was just using me to satisfy himself."

Roscoe's tone was very supportive, avuncular. "I think we are all wondering why you didn't break off the relationship at this point."

"Why does someone whose business is failing not just lock the door? I hoped it would change. That was the reason. The business person wants to believe it's only the weather, or the economy and if he or she waits, things will return to normal."

Her analogy surprised MacGruder. He had misjudged her intelligence. She had spontaneously explained away, better than he could have elicited, the opinion that she was pathologically clinging to Patterson. He decided to continue with her analogy.

"The business man also may not want to consider that he might have a successful competitor."

Piper looked down and thought for a moment. She met Roscoe's eyes again. "I never thought of that. I guess I couldn't imagine that he would continue to want to have sex if he were involved with someone else. I never would have. As I've learned, he was seeing another woman."

"Now that you know this, can you understand the

change in his attitude toward you?"

"Well, yes, . . . but I still don't understand how he could want to do that. I began to feel humiliated when I thought he was just using me. I feel more humiliated and embarrassed knowing now that he was also having sex with someone else at the same time."

"Piper, can you tell us what happened that afternoon?"

Her face showed dismay, a painful story to be reviewed one more time, yet she must collect herself to do it.

"Greg said he'd call me after lunch. I waited until four o'clock, feeling worse with each passing minute. I felt he was deliberately ignoring me to hurt me in a way that was more difficult for me than if he'd rejected me to my face, so I had to call him, hoping he had an excuse I could believe. He said I could come over to his place 'if I wanted to', but that he was going out with some people later on. He sounded so cold, dismissive. I felt terrible, but at that moment Jody and Suzanne came into my room and I pretended that Greg had asked me to come over to listen to a new CD he'd bought. I went to his house dreading what it was going to be like. I stopped outside his house and thought of not going in, but I had nowhere else to go. So I went up and went into his room. He was lying on the bed reading a magazine, ignoring me. I sat down next to him and he told me to take off my clothes. He still kept reading the magazine, not looking at me. I found myself making as if this was really cool, just what I wanted to do." She paused, evidently reluctant to finish the story, her vision focused on the railing of the witness box. "I took off my clothes. No, I took off my T-shirt and shorts and panties and then I unzipped his shorts." Piper stopped speaking and moved uncomfortably, placing one hand on her cheek. "He began to get hard and told me to suck his penis. He put down the magazine and tried to unfasten my bra but couldn't reach far enough. Before I could unfasten the clasp, he took a knife from the table next to his bed and then pulled the strap away from my back and slipped the knife under the strap and cut it. I was shocked and I think I cried out. And then . . . then he said," Her voice caught. "He . . . said, 'Suck it bitch, that's all you're good for.'" She sat looking down at her hands. "I know I . . .did what I did, but I still don't remember doing it."

She was pale and exhausted. She covered her face with both hands and began to sob, her body heaving at each sharp intake of breath. The courtroom was silent. MacGruder waited.

"Piper," he said softly and waited until she could gain control and look up. "Piper, a lot has been made of the last entry you wrote in your diary. I'll reread it. "

MacGruder went to the clerk's desk and retrieved the diary.

"You wrote, 'I'm going to kill him. First chance I get.' Tell us how you came to write that."

Piper went over again how humiliated she'd felt

when she'd hung up the phone after calling Greg. She then repeated the explanation she'd given MacGruder the first time she'd met him, ending with, "Like my mother used to say when I was a child, 'If you don't come here this minute, I'm going to kill you.'"

As she said this she glanced toward her mother sitting in the first row of the gallery. Florence sat up, knowing she had become the center of the court's attention—finally.

Quietly, MacGruder said, "I have no further questions."

John Dunn had not expected MacGruder to call Piper to the stand, thus giving the prosecution the opportunity to cross-examine her. He would have preferred that the hour was late, so he could ask for an adjournment, but the hour was early. He killed a few moments shuffling papers, deciding on his first question. He walked over to Piper.

"Miss Dahl, you testified that you called Greg Patterson on the afternoon that you killed him, correct?"

"Yes."

"When was the last time *he* called *you*?"

"I don't know. I can't remember."

"Well, let's break it down for you. Did he call you since school resumed?"

"No."

"Did he call you in the two weeks before that?"

"I don't think so."

"Now please remember we can check the telephone

records; did you call him during that time?"

"Yes."

"Every day?"

"Probably."

"Twice a day?"

"Sometimes . . . yes."

"Miss Dahl, isn't it true that in the three weeks before you stabbed him to death, you called him an average of six times a day?"

"You see, I only got his answering machine, so I would call again later."

"I see all right. I see that his refusal to talk to you must have made you very angry."

Piper had been pushed beyond her ability to follow MacGruder's instruction to remain calm. "Wouldn't it make you angry?" she challenged.

"Yes, Miss Dahl, it would have: but fortunately not so angry I'd kill the other person . . . as you did."

Dunn paused to let that exchange sink into the jurors' minds.

"Miss Dahl, when you were in his room the day that you killed him, do you know of any witness to Greg Patterson saying those things to you which you claim he did?"

"Witness?"

"Sure. Did anyone else hear him say the things you claim made you lose control?"

"No. There was no one else in the room."

"So, we have only your word for it?"

Dunn waited a moment for the answer he knew wouldn't come.

"No further questions of this witness, Your Honor."

Good show, MacGruder thought. You managed to deliver the major rebuttal to my central argument that Piper was reacting to the humiliation of Patterson's final words. I was certain you would include it in your closing argument, but this was better. You let Piper herself admit that it was only her word that we had.

Roscoe had had Piper examined by a Denver psychiatrist. The report concluded what he'd expected, that Piper had experienced a momentary rage at Patterson's insult and acted on it. The doctor was now outside in the witness waiting room. Roscoe decided to call him, having judged him to be competent and levelheaded. As it turned out, it wasn't Dunn's cross-examination that hurt Piper's case; it was the doctor, who became a pompous ass in the theater of the courtroom. Roscoe had misjudged him. The man exuded self-importance. He bristled when Dunn questioned his opinion—which Dunn did repeatedly with relish once he discovered this weakness. The final impression when he stepped down was that he wasn't to be trusted and by association, neither was MacGruder.

It was on this sour note that MacGruder had to say that the defense had concluded its argument.

Judge Claiborn announced an hour recess after

which he would hear the closing statements. Roscoe MacGruder affected satisfaction and confidence, but he felt panic.

In his closing, Dunn was able to paint a believable picture of a bright young man on the threshold of a successful life, when he made the mistake of becoming involved with an unstable person who was unable to face the fact of their failed relationship and instead preferred to see him dead than to let him go. He discredited the point that Piper had not taken a knife to Greg's apartment by emphasizing her written words, "I'm going to kill him! *First chance* I get." In other words, her premeditated plan was to act the moment she had the opportunity. His knife lying in front of her on the bed had provided that opportunity. He ended his summary by reminding the jury, "If anyone is considering the notion of provocation in this case, please keep in mind that we have only the defendant's word that Greg Patterson said anything provocative. We have only her word and his dead body. Placed on each side of the scale of justice, which way does the scale tip?"

Judge Claiborn let that closing sentence resonate in the room for a noticeable interval before he asked for Roscoe's closing statement.

Having again made eye contact with each of the jurors, he began, keeping his voice intimate and folksy. "These trials get caught up in so much formality. Know what I mean? I mean rules of procedure, judges in black robes, the witness *stand*, the jury *box*. When you get right down to it all that's going on here is a group of folks have gotten together to try to sort out what happened on a hot afternoon up in a boy's bedroom. What happened and what should be done about it. Those of us who have kids have sat with our spouses in the evening pondering the same kind of situations. Fortunately, not with the same tragic outcome that occurred here. The teacher has sent home a note that Johnny or Suzie has punched a classmate and given him or her a bloody nose. The question we ponder at those times is this: what does this say about the character of our child and what will be the appropriate—most helpful and corrective attitude we can have and action we can take? To answer the first question we look back at what we already know about our child. Is their present act a repetition of an already established pattern, or is this punch that they've thrown an unusual act for them. As thoughtful parents, we seriously consider this question before rushing to respond as if our child is a chronic offender. I brought in here a series of Piper Dahl's teachers representing different periods of her life. You heard them unanimously testify under oath that they had witnessed no violent act in all the time they'd known her. So, the answer to that first question a parent should ask is, no, we are not looking at a chronic pattern.

"If punching a playmate is not typical of our child, then we examine the setting to see if there was something that provoked him or her. You have heard of a young man who first promised lasting love and then withdrew it deceptively, never really making it clear that his feelings had been transferred to another woman. He maintained this deception, because he was reluctant to give up the easy sexual satisfaction it afforded. So, we see that our child has been deceived and demeaned to a point exceeding her ability to hold on to her usual stable self and she has suddenly struck out like a cornered animal.

"Now that we know what happened that hot afternoon up in that room, there remains the question of what to do that is helpful. Clearly, the result was a tragedy and, unfortunately, nothing can be done to help the boy, but the young woman can, with time and support, put herself and her life back together and become a citizen once again, now made wise by having passed through the fire of an extreme experience.

"Ladies and gentlemen of the jury you have it in your power to help this young woman rebuild her life . . . Thank you."

Roscoe had no hope for a vote for acquittal. He hoped only for a hung jury and failing that, his closing description of the repentance and growth that was possible had been directed toward the trial that would immediately follow that would decide the sentence.

Judge Claiborn charged the jury with their responsibility. His tone of voice left some jurors with the impression that it was the defense that had had to prove lack of pre-meditation rather than the prosecution. The gavel sounded and it was all over.

22

A former quarterback of the Denver Broncos, who now lived in Boulder, was one of the three men on the jury that now met to consider the verdict. Every other jury member accepted that he was the natural person to be selected as foreman—as did he. He first asked if anyone doubted that Piper had killed Greg Patterson. He looked around the table and saw that they were at least unanimous on that point.

"Now is there any doubt that Piper Dahl went to his house with the intent to kill him?" he asked.

In the discussion that ensued Jane Brodrick, a woman who owned an independent bookstore in the city, began to hear remarks that suggested to her that some members of the jury had heard reports of statements made by the boy's parents to the press. But she wasn't sure if it was that, or just variations on the themes of the newspaper articles they'd all read. If they were getting this information by way of cell phone or laptop, then this would be a violation of the jury's sequestration and could mean a mistrial. Jane wasn't sure enough to say anything.

After an hour and a quarter of discussion, the foreman asked for the first vote, reminding the group that they had only the choice of guilty or acquittal of first–degree murder, that a verdict of guilty of homicide, but not pre-meditated murder was not an option. A man and two women, Jane Broderick being one, voted for acquittal.

There followed the better part of an hour of heated exchanges. The three in the minority held the prosecution at fault for not making the reasonable charge of aggravated homicide and therefore the defendant deserved to be acquitted. The majority cited the right of the parents to see the defendant punished. They deserved, these two people who had done so much for Boulder, not to have to suffer the pain of seeing their son's killer walk away free. Another vote was taken. This time Jane found herself alone.

They began to cover the same ground once more, when the foreman said they should take a break, get something to eat and drink. During this period, not feeling the pressure of the group, Jane Broderick was able to evaluate her situation calmly. If she held out, and hold out she must if she only considered the evidence, then a new jury would be faced with retrying the case on the same flawed charge. If she changed her vote to guilty, the girl would be found guilty of first-degree murder and the jury, of which she was a member, would immediately be required to consider sentencing—in other words, death or life imprisonment. Death was a remote possibility, Jane believed. Although no words had been exchanged, she felt confident that she had identified three women on the jury who would vote for imprisonment. So, the young woman would be given a life sentence. This, Jane now reasoned, would result in approximately the same jail time if the charge had been unpremeditated homicide. First-degree murder would, of course, involve more time, but with good behavior, the actual difference in the time she would serve might be little.

After the refreshment break and another round of opinions were expressed, the third vote was taken, this time unanimous.

Judge Claiborn was thinking of excusing the jury for the day when he was informed that they had reached a decision. Word went out to the parties involved to reassemble in the courtroom. In spite of his long experience, Roscoe MacGruder couldn't decide whether a jury reaching a verdict in a short time was a good or bad sign.

Now the written verdict was handed from the foreman to the clerk and carried to the judge. Claiborn looked back to the man he had seen so many times throwing a football on television and spoke the words MacGruder had heard so often.

"Mr. Foreman, what is the jury's verdict?"

The former quarterback barked out the words as if he were barking out signals. "Your Honor, we find the defendant guilty of murder in the first-degree."

For a moment the words seemed to hang in the air as if solid substance. There arose then a hubbub in the room, followed by the silencing gavel of the judge.

"Court will convene at ten A.M. tomorrow to consider sentence. The court is adjourned."

"What can I say except that this jury reassured me that the ordinary American is still the decent person we all believe in. Cindy and I love this state and Boulder. This verdict proves we are living among friends," a smiling Slats Patterson said into several microphones held by reporters who pushed and elbowed their way to get near him.

"What about the sentence?," shouted one of them, the din becoming too great for anything like an interview.

"I'd like to see this woman pay for what she did, but Cindy and I are OK with whatever this great jury decides."

"Whatever this great jury decides," mocked Jo Montgomery watching the news. "I don't think I've ever heard a jury called 'great' before, but I'm sure many have thought that after receiving an acquittal. "

"What odds are you giving against the death penalty?" David asked.

"I really don't know. I'm surprised by the verdict, so . . . I don't know."

The next morning, Judge Claiborn was carefully neutral in giving the explanation of the law and the charging of the jury before it retired to consider Piper Dahl's sentence. Jane Broderick was even able to read his attitude as encouraging a decision for imprisonment.

Great was her shock to find, after the first vote, that she was again alone in her judgment. She became furious with the three women whom she had thought shared her view, as if they had betrayed her. So emotional did she become that it precipitated an asthma attack that required using her albuterol inhaler. This physical and emotional stress resulted in her total collapse, causing her to plead that she could no longer participate in the jury's deliberation.

Judge Claiborn acted quickly, excusing her and then replacing her with one of the alternate jurors. On the next vote, Jane Broderick's replacement, also a woman, voted with the other jurors for the death penalty.

The woman sitting on the other side of the screen separating her and Piper Dahl listened intently to the almost whispered responses of the pale, young woman who had the day before learned that the jury had decided she must die. The visitor was middle aged, her solidly gray hair pulled back tight to her head, which she repeatedly tipped forward to see over the top of her glasses.

A warning announcement had already been made that the visiting time was over and that the visitors must leave.

"I'll come again just as soon as I can, Piper," she said in a louder voice than they had both been using. She stood up to leave.

"Thank you very much for coming, Doctor Aldridge. I know you're busy with classes. I never expected one of my professors to take the time to . . . well, I appreciate your coming."

"Don't mention it, Piper. I want to come and I'll be back."

She turned and walked out of the room while Piper, feeling remarkably better, watched her leave.

23

Fitz Halloran sat eagerly awaiting the moment to make his opening statement to the jury. It was a morning in late October. The main courtroom of the Henderson County Courthouse was jammed beyond capacity. Elsewhere in this quiet, southern town, those who chose not to attempt to wedge themselves into the rows of bench seats were mulching their flower beds, raking their lawns one last time or carrying sweaters from cedar chests to spread along porch railings to air out. Henderson High was unbeaten in its first eight football games, needing only three more victories to complete an undefeated season. Complacency comfortably settled on Henderson County.

Brad Collins, on the other hand, anticipated no pleasure this morning. He sat nervous and chilled at the table for the defense. He had witnessed a number of criminal trials as a student and had participated in moot court exercises. That now seemed no preparation for what he faced. He imagined that Halloran would begin by telling the jury how the evidence of Kerry's guilt was clear and irrefutable. His words would carry impact, because his confidence here this morning was irrepressible. His smugness annoyed Brad, but Brad was afraid the jury would experience it differently, seeing Halloran as representing *their* community, while viewing him, Kerry's attorney, as the outsider.

"All rise," commanded the sergeant-at-arms.

Judge Troy Anderson swept into the room his gown flapping behind him, a wisp of white hair floating from side to side on his forehead like a sailor's telltale. He affected, as always, an attitude of mild contempt for those daring to appear before him.

The clerk announced the case of the People of the Commonwealth of Virginia against Kerry Marie Atwood. This is it, thought Brad. Preparation was at an end.

Judge Anderson asked Halloran if the prosecution was prepared to present its opening statement and the smiling district attorney sprang out of the gate like a thoroughbred.

Halloran's opening didn't disappoint Brad's expectation. Fitz declared this was the easiest case he'd ever had to prepare for. The facts were so simple and straightforward that they permitted but one conclusion, premeditated and brutal murder.

"We have a Latin phrase in the law, *res ipsa loquitor*. It means the thing speaks for itself. That's the kind of case this is. The facts in this case *shout* for themselves. They are so obvious that my job is little more than having to recite them to you. The conclusion you are asked to reach, you'll realize, is as simple as looking at the red smear on your toddler's face and knowing who ate the jelly donut. The thing speaks for itself."

Sprinkled liberally throughout his presentation were such words as: butchered, heinous and barbaric as well as referring to Kerry and Tom as: greedy, pitiless, wanton and indifferent to the lives of others. "Strangers," was said four times and New York City was mentioned in the same tone as a local minister says Sodom and Gomorrah.

"They committed this vile act just because they needed a little money. Between them they had only one hundred and forty-eight dollars. Thomas Albright, the defendant's partner, had just been fired—I'll tell more about that later—and they wanted to return to New York City. The remedy they settled on? Butcher Ben and Gladys Tulloch and take their money."

Halloran then went into detail describing the wounds that had been inflicted in the murders.

"When our state police caught Albright and the defendant, the twelve hundred-dollar bills Ben Tulloch was known to be carrying to his daughter's wedding reception were found in Albright's backpack. And his thumbprint was on one of the bills—his thumbprint in Ben Tulloch's blood. Albright died trying to escape the police helicopter.

"The defense is going to object to any mention of Thomas Albright. It will contend that only Kerry Atwood is on trial here. In the state of Virginia to willingly participate in a premeditated murder is the same under the law as to have committed the murder. We admit right now that we don't know whether the defendant or her partner held the knife that killed Mr. and Mrs. Tulloch. But we will prove beyond doubt that one of them did it. Thomas Albright died trying to escape from our state police. We have Kerry Atwood, his partner in this abominable crime, to answer to the *good* people of Virginia. It is your privilege, members of the jury, to represent those good people."

Halloran had mustered the emotional drive Brad expected. Worrying Brad was the fact that most of the jurors nodded their heads in rhythm to the points Halloran drove home.

Judge Anderson asked for the opening statement for the defense.

On his mind as Brad approached the jury box was his fresh image of the look of deep revulsion he'd seen on most of their faces as Halloran had described in detail the wounds the old couple had suffered. Now he had to try to win the sympathy of these same people. Also on his mind, as it had been for days, was the idea that he wasn't capable of matching Halloran's salesmanship. These background thoughts sapped his confidence.

According to the law, all he needed to do was create reasonable doubt in the minds of the jurors that the prosecution had proven their case against Kerry. To do this, Brad and the professor had decided to emphasize two things: the first was Kerry's character, the second that the prosecution could not prove that the money found in Brad's backpack had belonged to Ben Tulloch. It was a highly unusual coincidence, to be sure, that the two parties were each carrying twelve hundred-dollar bills, but unless the prosecution could prove it *wasn't* a coincidence, then Kerry Atwood should not be found guilty of murder. To establish the first point, he would put Kerry on the stand and question her in order to demonstrate before the jurors' own eyes and ears the truth of her character. For the second point, he would cast doubt that the physical condition of the bills supported Halloran's claim. He had felt confident of this plan when he and Dr. Meadow formulated it. Now it seemed like a flimsy barricade against Halloran's force. When he'd finished giving his opening statement, unfortunately, the jury shared the same impression.

Anderson asked Halloran to present the prosecution's case.

The first witness he called was the commander of the Springville, West Virginia post of the Veterans of Foreign Wars. Halloran began to ask questions to develop a portrait of the upstanding character of the Tullochs.

Brad stood and interrupted. "Your Honor. In order to save time, the defense agrees with the opinion that Ben and Gladys Tulloch were fine people and their murder is a tragic and heinous crime. We wish to stipulate that fact and to add that we would be as happy as anyone if their real killers were found and brought to justice."

Troy Anderson said, "Your stipulation is noted. Mr. Halloran, to further query witnesses on this subject is redundant."

Halloran was surprised by Brad's move and reacted for a moment as a person would who begins with relish to tell a joke only to be told it has been heard before.

Brad's move had been pure spur-of-the-moment instinct and very reassuring to him here at the outset of his tussle with Fitz Halloran.

Halloran regrouped and called Virginia State Trooper Frank Brace. He led Brace through a series of questions establishing the purpose of the helicopter's mission.

"After Thomas Albright was shot while attempting to escape, the helicopter landed and you approached the defendant. Is that right?"

"That's right."

"Did she say, 'Thank God you came; this man killed two people and forced me to come with him'?"

The question surprised Brace. "Uh, No. No, she screamed at us and went to kneel beside him."

"In other words, she did not deny her relationship with him. She did not suggest in any way that they were not . . . a unit?"

"No. She acted like they were a pair all right."

"Thank you, sir. I have no other questions, Your Honor."

Brad got to his feet slowly. "I do, Your Honor."

He tried for and achieved a casual tone. "Officer, look across this courtroom. If a large aircraft with beating rotors suddenly appeared overhead and a loudspeaker blared, do you think some of the people in this room would become frightened and run?"

Halloran objected. "Your Honor, that is a hypothetical question. The witness can't be expected to know the answer."

The judge looked to Brad.

"Your Honor, the question deals with an area of expertise about which a member of the state police should have knowledge, namely how people might react in situations of threat."

"I'll permit the question."

Brace glanced around as if for help. "I would guess . . . "

"The question, officer," Brad asserted, "is do you *think* some people would become frightened and run."

"Yes, I think some might . . . would run."

"Would you shoot if you knew a person was reacting to fear?"

"Well, no, of course not."

"And how did you determine that Thomas Albright was not running because he was startled and afraid?"

Halloran had the knee-jerk reflex to object that Albright was not the one who was on trial, but he had already made the effort to establish that the two comprised a unit.

"Because," Brace hesitated, but it was his only defense for his action, "I thought he had a gun."

"Yes, I can see that was the reason, along with the

fact that you had been told that you were looking for two killers who were on the trail. Now, please tell the court what that gun turned out to be."

Said with pained resignation. "It was a camera."

"Yes, it turned out to be nothing more lethal than a digital camera that he had in his hand. Now I'd like to hear your opinion on something that requires no expertise to answer, only common sense. Does it seem likely to you that two desperate killers escaping from a murder scene would take the time to take snap-shots?"

Frank Brace mumbled, "I don't know."

"I have no other questions of this witness, Your Honor."

Fitz Halloran took the floor again like a pitcher who'd had his first two pitches rapped for home runs. He called Commander Tappan of the Virginia State Police.

"Commander Tappan, you were present when the contents of Thomas Albright's backpack were examined, isn't that so?"

"Yes, sir."

"Please tell the court what you found."

"We found some camping supplies: two packets of freeze dried food, a small propane stove, pot, flashlight, a map of the Folsum Trail, a bus schedule, and some Bandaids. We also found a small stuff-bag and in it a man's wallet and twelve hundred-dollar bills. The bills were loose, not in the wallet."

"Was there money in the wallet?"

"No, only two credit cards and a medical insurance card."

"What name was on the cards?"

"The victim's name, Benjamin Tulloch."

"Was there anything else of note about the wallet and the money?"

"Yes, there was a smear of blood on both the wallet and on one of the bills."

"Thank you Commander. I have no other questions, but I request that the wallet be entered into evidence as People's Exhibit 'A' and the twelve hundred-dollar bills be entered as People's Exhibit 'B'."

The judge asked Brad, "Have you questions of this witness, Counselor?"

"No, Your honor."

Halloran's next witness was one of the detectives whom Dana Rogers had sent to New York. Responding to a question of Halloran's, the man began to tell the story of Tom's impulsive behavior. Brad objected.

"You Honor, Thomas Albright is not on trial. This testimony is irrelevant."

Brad knew from Halloran's opening statement that he intended to use Tom's history of impulsivity against Kerry. He needed to prevent that.

Halloran countered, "Your Honor, the prosecution is prepared to prove that Thomas Albright and Kerry Atwood committed the murders. It is relevant for the jury to learn about the kind of person Kerry Atwood chose for a partner in order to better understand her character."

Judge Anderson looked over at Brad.

"Your Honor, using Mr. Halloran's reasoning, these tales about Thomas Albright that he wants us to hear can only be relevant to Miss Atwood's character only if she knew of them and still continued in a relationship with him. That has not been established by the prosecution."

Judge Anderson weighed the arguments in his mind. The trooper's testimony made it clear that Kerry had not claimed that she should be considered apart from Albright. Knowing what kind of friends a person chose was an accepted source of information about a person's character and testimony introduced for the purpose of establishing the character of the accused was admissible.

He said, "In my judgment, the prosecutor is not claiming the defendant knew of the allegations in this witness's testimony, but only that they serve to illustrate his character and therefore, through this association, hers. The members of the jury can each decide for him or herself what weight, if any, to give the implication. The objection is overruled."

Brad knew the defense had just sustained a major blow. Halloran and his detective witness proceeded to treat the jury to the stories of Tom's impulsivity and physical aggression. Here, Halloran indicated, was the type of person who could kill.

Halloran then called Raymond Sterns, the managing partner of the architectural firm. He was asked to describe his dealings with Tom.

"Your Honor," Brad again asserted, "I object on the same grounds; Thomas Albright is not on trial."

Anderson responded, "Again, for the same reason, I'll allow the question."

Raymond Sterns obliged, portraying Tom as a con artist, who came claiming that he had been offered a job, when he had only been told that his application had been received. He further claimed that Tom tried to hit him, when he Sterns told him to leave his office. By the light in his garage when he went home, Sterns discovered that Albright had "keyed" the side of his new Mercedes.

Brad decided not to cross-examine Sterns. He saw that Sterns would lie to support his story and Brad couldn't refute it.

"Your honor, I call Brenda Farr." Halloran, complacent, was on a roll.

Brad knew this was Kerry's former New York roommate. He'd learned this when he'd read a list of Halloran's proposed witnesses to Kerry. She hadn't been able to think of what Halloran hoped to get out of Brenda's testimony.

"Miss Farr, until recently, did you share an apartment in New York with the defendant?"

"Yes, I did,"

"Did you know Thomas Albright?"

"Yes."

"How long?"

She was prepared for this question. "Three and a half years."

"In what capacity did you know him?"

"I beg your pardon."

"I mean was he a friend, co-worker, like that."

"He was an acquaintance. I also introduced him to Kerry."

Fitz cut right to the chase. "Did you have any first-hand knowledge of behavior of his that could be called violent?"

"Your Honor, I object on the same grounds. Thomas Albright is not on trial."

"Mr. Halloran?" asked the judge.

"I'll rephrase the question, Your Honor. Did you, Miss Farr, have first hand knowledge that the defendant knew about stories of Thomas Albright's tendency toward violent behavior?"

"Yes, I told her of a couple of occasions when I was a witness to his having gotten into a fistfight. Once at a bar and once at a party. Only the other customers stopped it."

"How did those fights come about?"

"In each case the other guy said something that Tom thought was an insult and Tom lost it—exploded."

"Was Kerry Atwood present?"

"No, on neither occasion, but I did tell her about it . . . when I saw that their relationship was becoming serious."

"Why did you do that?"

"Well, she was my friend. I . . . thought she should know."

"Did your giving her this information seem to make any difference in her feelings about him?"

"I didn't think so."

"Thank you, Miss Farr."

Halloran walked back to his desk and Anderson looked at Brad.

"Yes, Your Honor. I have a few questions."

Brad began, "Miss Farr, how long did you and my client live together?"

"Almost two years."

"In that time, did you observe any behavior of hers that you would term violent?"

"Absolutely not."

"Describe her personality for us."

"She is a truly sweet person and a loyal friend. She wouldn't hurt the proverbial fly."

"Yet, you are here testifying for the defense."

"I was subpoenaed. The detective asked me some questions about Tom and I answered truthfully and," she smiled, "Wham bam here I am."

"Can you picture her taking part in a brutal killing of two old people?"

"Impossible, like totally."

"Thank you, Miss Farr."

Halloran took over again and the jury then heard how Tom had taken a Greyhound bus to Beckley, West

Virginia, and a local bus line to Springville. He had paid only part of the required one-month advance rent on an apartment, saying he'd pay the remainder as soon as the check he'd deposited in his newly opened Springville bank account had cleared. In fact, the jury was told, Tom had never opened an account at a Springville bank.

Further depositions taken in New York portrayed Tom as a talented student, but impulsive, unstable and having been fired from his last part-time job for getting into a fistfight with his employer.

Probably the most effective piece of evidence relating to Tom's character was the record of Tom's Manhattan bank account, which Halloran entered into evidence. It showed that at no time in the account's three-year history did Tom's balance exceed four hundred dollars. The account was closed the day before Tom left New York with the withdrawal of $184.38. Halloran summarized the significance. "There is no way Thomas Albright could have had the twelve hundred dollars the police found in his backpack except to have taken it from the mutilated body of Ben Tulloch."

Brad objected and the judge concurred that the statement was out of order. It was only the prosecutor's opinion and did not constitute evidence, and the jury, which of course had already heard it well, should disregard it.

Sheriff Royston of Springville County West Virginia took the stand next, describing the bloody murder scene and the discovery of Tom's boot print made before a heavy rain, placing the print in the same time frame as the murder. Halloran had the plaster cast of the print entered as People's Exhibit 'C'," which he then made a big thing of displaying to the jury.

Royston said he had discovered from the Tulloch family that Ben was planning to give the newlyweds a gift of cash at their daughter's wedding reception to cover the cost of their airline tickets. This led the sheriff to question Judy Fenton, the teller at the Barnhill Bank, who had served Ben Tulloch the day of the murder. When he first attempted to talk to her she was at the hospital having tests, but later he learned from her that Tulloch had withdrawn twelve hundred dollars in hundred-dollar bills, "to give to my kids for their honeymoon."

"Sheriff, one of your deputies found the murder weapon, a clasp knife. Please describe the weapon and where it was found."

"It was a clasp knife with a five inch blade. It was still open. It had been thrown in Hooper's Creek. The rushing water had washed all the blood away and there were no fingerprints. We believe it had been wiped because prints still might have been detectable in spite of the water."

Halloran said he had no further questions for Royston, and Brad rose to cross-examine.

With Sheriff Royston, Brad believed he needed to be careful. He was sure Royston had lied to him about the extent of his conversation with the bank teller and could lie again without Brad's having the evidence to expose the lie. He began by countering the inference that Tom's boot print had any bearing on the murders by asking Royston if the print could adequately be explained by Kerry's claim that she and Albright were only hiking and just happened to pass that way. Grudgingly the sheriff had to agree. Further, he got Royston to admit that the position of the Tullochs' car could not be viewed from the hiking path, giving substance to the idea that Kerry and Tom could have hiked past the spot immediately before or after the murders without knowing it.

"Sheriff, were the fingerprints of the defendant or Tomas Albright found at the murder scene?"

"No. No prints other than the Tullochs' were found."

Halloran hadn't presented at the arraignment what would have been a very strong piece of evidence, so Brad felt he was on safe ground asking Royston the next question.

"Sheriff, was any piece of cloth or paper which might have been used to wipe that knife found among the belongings of Albright or the defendant?"

Halloran objected. "Your Honor, Sheriff Royston did not examine the possessions of the defendant. His answer would be hearsay."

"Sustained."

"I'll withdraw the question and ask it at another time, Your Honor," Brad said, knowing he had now introduced the question in the minds of the jurors.

Brad now ventured on a ploy he had thought about, but had not until that minute discovered a way to implement. "Sheriff, you asked the teller in the Barnwell Bank the number and the denomination of the bills she gave to Mr. Tulloch. Did you ask her to describe the condition of the bills?"

"No. As I explained to you earlier, I could tell she was feeling poorly, and I didn't want to trouble her more than necessary. I planned to call again when she was feeling better, but at that time I only asked her if Ben Tulloch had withdrawn money and how much, nothing more."

"Yes, I recall, Sheriff. Most unfortunately for Judy Fenton—and for my client—Mrs. Fenton, as you know, died of her illness and can't be here to testify as to the condition of the money." This he addressed to the courtroom in general.

Turning again to Royston. "In other words, Sheriff, you learned of nothing more that would support the prosecution's contention that it was the same money found in the backpack?"

Royston, reluctant to have to agree, sat silently, until the judge directed him to answer.

"That's right, but . . . "

"Thank you, Sheriff. I have another question about the money."

Brad had learned a fact that tended to back his claim that the two sets of bills were different and he wanted to introduce that information now. The problem was that Sheriff Royston couldn't be expected to know the answers to the questions Brad needed to ask. He went ahead, knowing he'd have to pick his way through a minefield of Halloran's objections.

"Sheriff, did you learn about the serial numbers of the bills, or about what they call the 'letter seal' on the bills?"

"No."

"No, of course not, because the money given was not brand new. The manager of the Barnhill Bank checked and confirmed that Mrs. Fenton did not sign for new bills, as she must do when new money is taken from the vault. A record is kept of the serial numbers of those new bills. The money, therefore, must have been taken from her cash drawer and no record is kept of the serial numbers of those bills. Money is coming in and going out all day from that drawer. "

Fitz discerned immediately that Brad was proceeding improperly, but what he was bringing out was useful to the prosecution, even so, he didn't know where Brad was heading so he cut him off.

"Your Honor, the defense counselor is making a speech, not asking a question."

"Objection sustained. "

"I'm sorry, Your Honor. I improperly phrased my question. I meant to ask Sheriff Royston if he asked Mrs. Fenton if she knew the serial numbers of the bills she gave

Mr. Tulloch."

Anderson looked at Royston.

"Ah, no. I didn't."

"Did you ask the bank manager to check a sampling of bills taken from the cash drawers of both tellers to determine which Federal Reserve Banks issued them?"

"Why . . ."

"Why would you do that? Because, Sheriff, the money we use is issued by twelve Federal Reserve Banks. All individual banks receive new bills exclusively from the Federal Reserve in their district. Each bill bears a letter seal that identifies the federal bank that issued it."

"Your Honor, Mr. Collins is lecturing again."

"Your Honor, Sheriff Royston asked me why he would have asked the manager a question. My explanation, which Mr. Halloran is calling a lecture, was intended to help him understand what I was asking."

Judge Anderson raised an eyebrow. "Please ask your questions in a form which needs no further explanation."

"Yes, Your Honor."

"Sheriff. Did you examine the money found in the knapsack to determine, by the identifying letter, which districts of the country they were issued from?"

"No. I never saw the money from the backpack. The Virginia police were involved with that."

"Your Honor, Mr. Collins knows that," shouted Halloran. "He's engaged in trying to improperly introduce information that is not part of a cross examination."

"Counselor?" asked the judge.

"Your Honor, I don't know which law enforcement branch has and has not seen and examined that money."

"Well, you know now that the witness hasn't."

"Thank you, Your Honor. I'll come back to this issue later."

Like Mark Anthony, he had told the jurors about Caesar's will. He had tweaked their curiosity, so that when he took up the subject again during his argument for the defense, they'd be paying special attention.

"I have no further questions of the witness at this time, Your Honor."

Brad glanced at Kerry as he sat down. He felt like he had just stuck the landing on a ten-point exercise. She didn't know what he had been up to, but smiled her vote anyway.

Kerry's character was the next target for Halloran. The witnesses portrayed a young woman who went her own way, socializing little with co-workers. A similar description was elicited from a former high school classmate, who described Kerry's associating with "marginal types of students," and that she frequently was seen riding on the back of a dropout's motorcycle.

In cross-examination Brad got the witnesses to admit to knowing of no illegal acts committed by Kerry nor had there been any disciplinary problems in school, where she had been a very good student, especially in math and science.

When Brad finished with the last witness, Judge Anderson adjourned the court until the following morning.

Brad's interest now was in Kerry and how she had held up. He'd noted that she'd followed the proceeding with intense interest, remaining silent except for murmuring, "Incredible" at the end of Raymond Stern's lie about Tom's job. She smiled and gave Brad a thumbs up as she turned away to be taken back to the jail by a deputy.

Brad was very glad this first day was over. He felt he'd been in a sword duel, living by his wits, trying to parry thrusts that could end up proving fatal. He'd done his best to blunt the effect of Halloran's witnesses. Had he done enough? He had managed to deliver the first lesson in his "education" of the jury about the money. Had it been effective? He wished like hell that Professor Meadow had been able to be there. He would have liked his opinion on these points. Looking ahead he thought of how helpful it would be to have character witnesses of his own to present. That evening he learned he would have one.

Paying no attention to his surroundings, Brad sauntered and ruminated as his feet found their way home from the courthouse. A similar thing was happening that he'd experienced many times in law school. In addition to his conscious, deliberate effort to understand a complicated point of law, a parallel and unconscious process seemed to operate until a sudden new understanding coalesced in his mind. For two months now he'd been living with the fine details of this case. He'd discussed them with his mother before going to bed and he and Professor Meadow had put their heads together repeatedly mulling over the facts. Suddenly now the essence of the whole procedure of the trial stood out like a billboard. He saw that Kerry's fate depended on a sequence of compromises being formed in the minds of twelve people as they heard and saw the proceedings. Perhaps pure logic of argument counted in geometry, but so-called justice in a murder trial was the result of twelve sets of compromises between the presented evidence and each juror's own idea of reality. And as with any other person, that notion was an alloy of objective perception and subjective distortion or fiction. The prejudiced beliefs they had already assimilated in their lives made it almost impossible for the light of impartiality to penetrate. This left each of them seriously handicapped when it came to giving any question a truly impartial examination. If these jurors were called upon to make a judgment about a person they saw to be like themselves—someone holding the same views, same prejudices, same education and of the same economic class—that person would tend to be judged freer of guilt than the person they experienced as a stranger. Everyone knew this.

Yet, Brad now thought, our society holds firm to a conviction that flies in the face of this well-established fact about social prejudice. It is a conviction we hold to be almost sacred. It's this: twelve people of any intelligence and regardless of their hard-wired irrational beliefs will somehow rise above this condition over which they possess no control, and unerringly arrive at a just decision in a question so important that another person's life is at stake. It's almost like the medieval belief that a child could unerringly identify a witch.

Brad thought of the new medication his mother was taking and how we as a society demand months, even years, of study by scores of highly trained professionals and at great expense before a drug is judged safe enough to avoid a side-effect as life threatening as impaired hearing. In all of this examination of the drug, everyone's sole effort is to gather true evidence, to arrive at the unbiased truth. Yet, twelve people of indifferent intelligence and education listening to a few hours of energetically biased argument are believed to be competent to decide whether a human being will live or die.

Brad was shocked by his thought progression and its implications: he was a participant in a travesty, an archaic ritual propagated from one generation to the next. Because it had become such an accepted part of the culture, no one stood up to say, "Stop! Step back! Take a fresh look at this insanity!" The signs that the earth was not the center of the universe had been recognized and yet put aside for a thousand years before Copernicus and his supporters said, "Stop, take a fresh, unbiased look at the data."

Brad suddenly felt adrift. When he'd decided upon a law career, it was with an idealistic, crusading zeal about the logic of the law. He had his heroes both real and fictional. His uncle, Crawford, was the first real hero, and Atticus Finch of *To Kill a Mocking Bird*, the first fictional one. Coming to a halt now on the sidewalk in front of his house, he felt betrayed, as if his mentors had lied to him about the law and the real world, just as generations of soldiers in the past and present had found to their horror that their cultures had lied to them about the glory of war and its necessity and the sanctity of its purpose. The real court isn't about the truth, he thought now, but about manipulating the prejudices of the jury, and a good part of that goes into making the jury believe your client is an acceptable member of their club.

His bitter disillusionment frightened Brad. A paradigm shift had just occurred in his world, undermining his self-identity, but more importantly to him, he couldn't afford this disillusionment at the time Kerry's life depended on him. He remembered the planned meeting that night with Professor Meadows, one of his real heroes. He forced his thoughts to turn toward that meeting.

He entered his house and went into the living room where his mother sat, an open book on her lap.

"How did it go today?" they asked in unison and then laughed.

"You first," Brad said.

"My day was uneventful. I pretended to read, while I was really thinking of you in that courtroom."

"I'll give you a blow-by-blow while we have dinner. You remember that Professor Meadow is coming to

271

Henderson this evening. I'll meet him at the Laurel Inn where he's staying. I may be out late."

"Yes, I remember, of course, and do you remember you promised I could meet him while he's here?"

"No chance of my forgetting that, because he made me promise that he'd get to meet you. Let me get you settled at the table so we can eat. What did May Rutledge make for us this evening?"

"May told me lasagna."

24

Like most small southern cities, Henderson had abandoned its main street to decay while building suburban shopping malls featuring the current retail players. Only recently had Main Street been rediscovered as if it were a pearl in an oyster. The luster on the pearl was the surprisingly luxurious Laurel Inn. Folks from miles around now drove into the city to walk into the lobby in order to gape and remark, either derisively or in awe.

Brad asked the desk clerk to ring Meadow's room and tell him he was on the way up. He found the door ajar, knocked and heard the professor yell for him to come in.

Ernest Meadow greeted him with, "A piece of bad news, I'm afraid. My friend in Texas, Charlie Jackson, has come up empty handed. Remember, I said I'd call my old colleague who now lives in Austin and see if he could locate that Jerrod fellow who gave Tom and Kerry a ride. Charlie turned to a contact on the Texas Highway Patrol, who agreed to do a search through the records for a Chevy truck, of the vintage Kerry loosely described, registered to a Jerrod. No luck."

Although it didn't prove Tom and Kerry couldn't have committed the murders, placing them on the highway where Jerrod picked them up and dropped them off, put them well away from the path the Tullochs would have taken from the church to the reception at the Allegheny Hotel. Jerrod's testimony could have portrayed lovers setting out for a hike instead of a pair of desperate killers.

Brad couldn't hide his disappointment and Meadow saw it.

"Jackson said he'd place an ad in The Dallas News asking for information about Jerrod. "

"Even if he's successful, will it be in time?"

Meadow ignored the question. "Now I'd like to hear a detailed recap of the day in court."

Every word spoken that day was etched in Brad's memory. At the end of his resume he waited for the professor's judgment.

"OK. Sounds like you did effective damage control on his witnesses' testimony. I like the groundwork you laid for the serial number argument. Now about these character witnesses you mentioned on the phone."

"There wasn't much I could say to blunt the impact of Halloran's revelation that Brad's New York bank account never amounted to more than four hundred and that his final withdrawal was one hundred forty-eight dollars. I'm sure it left the jurors wondering where the twelve hundred dollars came from if it wasn't taken from Ben Tulloch. Hell, I wonder too."

"Yes, it's our biggest problem. But what about the two character witnesses you mentioned on the phone?"

"I got the call while I was eating dinner, two women Kerry worked with in New York. The woman . . . " Brad opened his notebook. "Sandy Nugent. She said she and a friend were in town, just arrived and tired. I'm meeting them at a coffee shop in the morning."

"Good. Hopefully they'll turn out to be upright, upstanding and upper class. And, although this is too much to hope for, they'll have soft Virginia accents."

There it was the very thing Brad had been thinking earlier: the object is to sell your client to the jury as one of their own. Or better yet, as Meadow had just suggested, as a perfect model of what they aspired to be.

"How did Kerry look today?"

"She looked good: upright, upstanding and upscale. I got her suitcases sent over from Springville, so she had some decent clothes."

"Excellent." Meadow made it sound upbeat, but he was afraid that her appearance might just be their whole case.

The moon was near to full in a clear sky. Brad got out of his car and stood, taking in the night. A familiar smell of burned leaves was in the air. Autumn had always been his favorite season. He leaned against the car and tried to focus on the night, tried to relax, breathing deeply the chill night air. It didn't work: his mind was like a compass needle, attempt to turn it as he might, it kept pointing in the same direction, the trial and what the next day had in store.

The phone began ringing as he entered his house, and he ran to get it, in case his mother was asleep.

"Hi, this is Brad."

A quiet woman's voice said, "Ask Sheriff Prentis if he and his men found the currency envelope from the Barnhill Bank. Ask him why it is so important that he had a number of his men looking for it for hours. What did the other employees of Sterns and Associates think of Tom Albright? Do they think the reason Sterns reneged on the job he'd offered Albright is different than the tale Sterns told? Did Sterns do it to make room for his nephew, who had just lost another job?"

The line went dead.

Brad quickly wrote the caller's exact words on a note pad. The speaker was a woman, a young woman, around thirty, refined. Did he pick up a hint of an African American accent? If only his mother had caller ID. The Barnhill Bank envelope? Brad took a glass from the cupboard and poured three fingers from the bottle of Macallan's scotch he'd brought from Washington and sat down to think about the call.

Of course! The teller would have put the money in one of those small envelopes used for a cash gift. She said Sheriff Prentis was looking for it. Yes! Why hadn't he thought of any of this? If Tom and Kerry were guilty and the money had been in an envelope, that envelope had to be somewhere in the Tulloch's car, or along the Folsum Trail.

Finding that envelope would sew up the case for Halloran. Brad wondered if the bank's name was printed on their envelopes; if so that would cinch the case. No wonder they were looking for it!

But who was the caller, and why was she doing this? Brad went to the phone and dialed the direct number to Ernest Meadow's room. When he answered, Brad excitedly told him what had happened.

"Who could she be?," pondered Meadow.

"I've been thinking. For one thing, she has inside information about both the Sterns office and the sheriff's office. A reporter would have used the information for a story. Do you think she could be on Halloran's staff?"

"If that's so, she's no fan of Fitz Halloran." Meadow became wary. "What if she's trying to set us up—lead us into quicksand?"

"Hadn't thought of that."

Both became silent. Wondering what sort of trap that might be.

"I bet anything the money was given to Tulloch in a bank envelope," Brad said.

"I agree."

"I can call the bank and talk to one of the tellers about the bank's practice."

"Yes, do that, Brad. If we believe our caller, the Henderson County Sheriff has been looking for an envelope and hasn't been able to find it."

"This is really big," Brad burst out. "If the bank

confirms that there should have been an envelope and none is found along the Folsum Trail, it points to its having been taken by the real killers. It and Tulloch's money!"

"Right, if Sheriff Prentis and his men have been searching—and you can question him about that—then the caller's intention is to help us, not to set a trap for us."

"I don't need to subpoena Prentis. Halloran has him on his list of witnesses. Since they weren't successful finding the envelope, there must be something else Halloran wants to use him to establish. In any case, I'll have him on the stand for cross-examination. In the morning I'll subpoena a couple of the architects working for Sterns."

Kerry saw that Brad was more sanguine than he'd been the day before. He stood by the defense table smiling as a deputy led her through a door in the rear of the courtroom. Her own assessment of the previous day was positive. She gave Brad a good grade for his cross-examination. To her, the only negative element had been Brad's demeanor. His voice had lacked the self-assurance needed to sell his arguments to the jury. He was more confident today. She wondered what had happened.

Halloran continued presenting the prosecution's case by having Henderson County Sheriff Prentis describe his failed attempts to throw a wallet from the location of the Tulloch's car to the place Kerry claimed Tom had found it.

"Sheriff, did you attempt to find the place where the defendant claims Albright found the wallet?"

"Yes. When the state police initially questioned her, she said her companion had left the Folsum Trail to urinate shortly after it crossed the road where the car was located. She said he went into the woods about ten yards on the right hand side of the trail. We had our dogs search this section of woods from the road to a distance of one hundred yards along the trail and from the trail twenty yards into the woods, using one of Albright's boots for the scent."

"And did the dogs identify a place where he might have done as the defendant claims?"

"No, the dogs did not locate his scent."

"I have no more questions of this witness, Your Honor."

Brad came forward to the witness stand. He was going to take a chance on a hunch.

"Sheriff Prentis, did your dogs locate Tom Albright's scent anywhere near the place the Tulloch's car was found, or along the Folsum Trail all the way up to the place where my client and Albright camped for the night?"

"Yes."

Oh, shit, thought Brad. He had to ask the next and obvious question. "And, where was that?"

"They found his scent where his boot print had been found."

Hallelujah! Brad let out the breath he'd been holding.

"And why do you think that was the only place your dogs had luck?"

"There was a very heavy rain that night. It must have washed all scent away except where the boot print was protected by some foliage."

"Yes, and therefore my client's story was not disproved by the failure to find Albright's scent where she said he'd found the wallet. Isn't that so, in your opinion?"

"You might say so."

"I might say so, how about you? You're the expert with the dogs. Did your work with them disprove her story?"

"No."

The old rule attorneys are advised to follow about questioning a witness is to avoid any question the answer to which you don't already know. He'd just disregarded that rule and came out alive, and this emboldened him to believe his mysterious caller had been telling the truth.

"Sheriff, at the time that you and your men were throwing wallets, did you also engage in a hunt for the kind of envelope that a bank uses for gifts of cash?"

The sheriff's quick glance toward Halloran's desk told Brad his information was sound.

"Yes, we did," Prentis answered.

"Did you find such an envelope?"

Halloran moved uncomfortably in his seat. How

had Collins found out about the search?

"No, we didn't," Prentis said.

"How many deputies were there looking for this envelope?"

"Four."

"How much time did they spend on this search?"

It went through Prentis's mind to give a shortened estimate of the time, but he reminded himself that the attorney obviously had been given information that would easily expose a lie.

"Altogether, six hours."

"Six hours?" Brad gasped. "Then you searched the trail from the crime scene to the place Tom Albright was shot."

"Yes."

"Four men worked a whole shift on this project . . . and came up empty handed. Yes, someone thought finding that envelope was very important to the state's case."

"Is that a question, councilor?" Judge Anderson nudged.

""I'm sorry Your Honor. Sheriff Prentis, why was finding the envelope so important?"

Prentis remained silent.

Anderson said, a smile in his voice, "I believe that really was a question, Sheriff."

Prentis's face hardened. He didn't like being put in this position . . . by either side. "I can't rightly say why it was so important. I was told to do it by the district attorney."

Brad laughed. He turned sharply to face the jury. "Sheriff, you're not going to tell these good people of the jury, people who voted for you, to believe that a man in your position is going to take orders from the district attorney that required thirty-two man hours plus eight hours of your own time—all paid for out of the public's pocket—without asking why this search was so important?"

Prentis knew he'd look like a fool if he stuck to his answer. He glanced at the judge, but got no support there.

"We had information from the bank teller that she gave the gentleman, Ben Tulloch, his money in a bank gift envelope. It was reasonable that the money would still have been in the envelope when it was taken from him."

"Sheriff, did the Barnhill Bank, the bank whose teller gave Mr. Tulloch the money, have its name printed on the gift envelopes?"

"Yes, it did."

Brad took from his pocket a copy of the gift envelope that the manager of the bank had faxed him that morning. He explained what the copy was and asked the judge if he might show it to the jury. Anderson examined the copy and handed it back to Brad, saying that he could. Brad walked along the front of the jury box holding the paper up for all to see and then returned to Prentis.

"Sheriff, why was it important to look for that envelope along the Folsum Trail?"

Prentis didn't like to talk this much. He was used to being the one asking the questions. His natural impulse was to tell the young smart aleck to go to hell . . . but he had no choice.

"If we found such an envelope along the trail, it would be strong proof that those two had taken it from Ben Tulloch."

"Yes, if they had taken it from Mr. Tulloch, you should have found it along the trail, but you didn't find it." Brad paused and repeated for emphasis, "You *didn't* find the envelope. In your opinion as a law officer, wouldn't your failure to find the envelope point to someone else having taken it and the money from Ben Tulloch, someone who didn't walk on the trail?"

Prentis shifted in the chair and couldn't control a glance toward Halloran, a glance Halloran didn't meet.

"I wouldn't necessarily say that."

"No? Well, I think you have to agree that the failure to find the envelope along the trail points away from Kerry Atwood and Tom Albright. Right?"

"I wouldn't necessarily say that either."

"Thank you, Sheriff. I have no . . . yes, I have one more question, Sheriff Prentis, you stated that you had learned that the Barnhill Bank put the money in a gift envelope. Who told you that?"

"Mr. Halloran."

"Did he say how he obtained that information?"

"As I recall, he said the Springville County Sheriff had told him."

"So, Mr. Halloran here got the information from

Sheriff Royston, and he in turn must have gotten it from the person at the bank who knew the money had been given to Mr. Tulloch in an envelope—that would be the teller, don't you think?"

"Well, I don't know, but . . . I guess that's right."

"I have no further questions to ask this witness, Your Honor."

"We'll take a break at this point. Court will reconvene in an hour and a half at one-thirty," said Judge Anderson, hammering down his gavel, springing to his feet and sweeping out of the room as if he'd been told his lunch was getting cold, leaving the unprepared clerk to say, "All rise," while everyone scrambled to stand up.

Brad and Professor Meadow sought the relative quiet of the dining room of the Laurel Inn.

"That was a very good morning's work," Meadow said when they sat down at a table in the Inn's coffee shop.

"Thanks, I thought it went well, too—thanks to our mysterious informant. Let's hope the architects from the Sterns office don't feel they must back their boss. What I really mean is that I hope I'll manage to shake them loose, because common sense tells me they'll be thinking first of their job security."

Brad ordered a salad, but he ate none of it. Meadow ate at a turkey sandwich. He understood the tension Brad was feeling. Halloran had called most of his witnesses, which meant Brad would be called upon to begin his defense this afternoon. He had seen that Brad was comfortable as a counter puncher, but what about when he had to lead?

"What do you think of Halloran?" Brad asked.

"He's no giant, no Darrow. He hasn't gained any ground on you."

What the professor didn't say was that he was afraid that Halloran had a gift for seduction. He was worried about Halloran's closing statement to the jury, the jury, which Meadow believed was on Halloran's side to begin with.

Meadow signed the bill and they went outside where the gaze of each was drawn up to a darkening sky. Brad's pace back to the courthouse pulled Meadow along as if he were on a short leash; Brad's adrenalin had taken over.

The first large drops of rain hit the pavement as they hurried up the courthouse steps.

25

Kerry was returned to the courtroom, Judge Anderson entered and the afternoon session began. Halloran called his last two witnesses. The first was a clinical pathologist who testified that there was a DNA match for Ben Tulloch's blood and that found on the wallet and on one of the bills found in the backpack. Halloran implied a scientifically certain connection between Tulloch and Tom Albright. Brad, on cross examination, had to work again to present the just as likely possibility that the blood came to be on one of the bills when Tom placed the wallet in the same part of his backpack where he kept his own money. The pathologist who had performed the autopsy on the victims took the stand last. The reason was obvious. Halloran wanted the jury to be left with the picture of horrible violence.

Now it was Brad's turn.

"Your Honor, I wish to recall Sheriff Royston to the stand."

Judge Anderson nodded to the clerk, who said, "Sheriff Roy Royston of Springville, West Virginia is recalled to take the witness stand."

The judge reminded Royston that he was still under

oath.

"Your Honor, I would like to have the court reporter read Sheriff Royston's earlier testimony. I am interested in his reply to my question when I asked him if he had inquired of the Barnhill Bank teller about the physical condition of the money Mr. Tulloch withdrew."

They waited as the reporter scrolled back through the testimony.

"I believe this is the testimony you're referring to: 'Sheriff, you asked the teller in the bank the number and the denomination of the bills you gave to Mr. Tulloch. Did you ask her to describe the condition of the bills?'"

"Yes, that's the place. Now please read the sheriff's reply."

The reporter continued, "'No. As I explained to you earlier, I could tell she was feeling poorly, and I didn't want to trouble her more than necessary. I planned to call her again when she was feeling better. But at that time I only asked her if Ben Tulloch had withdrawn money and how much, nothing more.'"

Brad looked soberly into Royston's eyes. "The teller, Judy Fenton, did tell you that she handed the money to Ben Tulloch in a bank gift envelope, isn't that correct?"

"Yes, I guess she must have. I forgot that."

"Perhaps you were pressured by all that was happening. Your department doesn't experience double murders everyday. It would be easy to forget the details of your conversation with a bank teller."

"That's about the size of it." Royston felt relieved; the guy seemed sympathetic.

"It's reasonable to understand that you forgot that you also asked her about the physical condition of the money she gave to Mr. Tulloch, isn't that right?"

Royston recognized the trap, but not before his alarmed reaction to the question was clear to all.

"No, no. I never asked her that."

"Wouldn't you have wanted to know about the physical condition of those bills? Especially because District Attorney Halloran badly wanted to match the money from the backpack and the money withdrawn from the bank. I repeat, Sheriff, wouldn't you have wanted to know that?"

"Well, ah . . . sure, but I could tell she wasn't feeling well."

"It would have been only one more question and a very important one."

Brad looked toward the jury and then back at Royston. "Sheriff, did you get a call from District Attorney Halloran requesting that you ask the teller about the condition of the money?"

Royston's jaw was set. His answer came from behind a stonewall. "I don't recall that happening."

"Your Honor, I have no more questions of this witness."

The next witness Brad called was one of Kerry's co-workers from New York.

When he'd first met Sandy Nugent and Barbara

Gorecki for coffee that morning he knew he had a problem. It was apparent to him that they were lesbian partners. Brad knew his fellow Hendersonians, and knew that many in the county would view this pair negatively. His problem: would their testimony on Kerry's behalf help or hurt her case? Brad decided he had no choice; as part of her defense, he had to present *some* positive opinion about Kerry from a person who knew her, since Halloran had done much to establish her as a loner, and loner was frequently part of the media's description of a heartless killer.

Brad had been especially concerned about Sandy Nugent. Her masculine physique and mannerisms were blatant. He'd spoken openly about his concern. Sandy was prepared for this and handled it smoothly, suggesting it would be better if only Barbara testified.

"I wish it weren't the case, but I'm afraid it is."

"Hey, don't apologize. I wasn't born yesterday and I want to do what is best for Kerry. Is it OK if I come to the courtroom?"

"Sure. I'll have a seat saved for you in the front," he'd said

Barbara Gorecki now took her place in the witness's chair. She proved an excellent advocate for Kerry, relating the high regard her fellow workers had for her. Kerry was dependable, honest and empathic. There was no way Kerry would intentionally hurt another person nor would she be a party to the mistreatment of another person. She was able to cite examples that made her testimony convincing.

What Brad hadn't anticipated was the direction of Halloran's cross-examination. Fitz approached Barbara in a friendly, chatty way, asking her if she had driven down from New York. Then, consulting his notes as if off-hand, he commented that the defense had listed two witnesses from New York.

"Barbara Gorecki, that's you of course, and Sandy Nugent. I see here that both of you have the same address, 211 West 180th. Street, Apartment thirty-four. Do you happen to live with Sandy Nugent?"

Mindful that Kerry's lawyer was concerned about revealing they were lesbians, she answered with a flustered, "What do you mean?"

"What do I mean? Why it's a simple question. Do you live with Miss Nugent? Did you think I was asking if you were lovers?"

Brad was on his feet objecting to the question, but Barbara Gorecki's eyes had gone to Sandy sitting in the front row. As did Kerry's. As did Fitz Halloran's, now, turning to stare at the stolid, defiant face of the New Yorker. Following his gaze were the eyes of the twelve jurors.

The remainder of Halloran's questions established that Barbara Gorecki knew little of Kerry's life outside of work, nor of the kind of men she chose for friends.

In Ernest Meadow's cool, objective assessment, the net effect of Barbara Gorecki's testimony was negative.

The rest of the afternoon belonged to Kerry's

side. Brad called one of the deputies who had taken part in the search for the envelope and reinforced the cross-examination of Sheriff Prentis by causing the deputy to say that they had been told that finding the envelope was "very important." Brad then asked him if he had heard that there was some question if the money recovered from the backpack was the same as that taken from the victim. Halloran had jumped in with an objection, which was overruled. The deputy was visibly uncomfortable when Judge Anderson directed him to answer the question. He stammered that he hadn't heard anything, causing a buzz to go through the courtroom.

Brad called Thelma Fellows.

"Mrs. Fellows, you are a teller at the Barnhill Bank in Springville, West Virginia?"

"Yes sir."

"Were you working the day Mr. Benjamin Tulloch came to the bank to withdraw twelve hundred dollars in cash?"

"Yes sir, I was."

"Would you please describe for the court what you remember happening at that time?"

"When I came back from a break, I noticed that several people had come in all at once and there was a line at Judy's—that is Judy Fenton's—station. Judy was taking cash out of her drawer to give to Mr. Tulloch and she asked me for a cash gift envelope, because she said she had run out. I gave her one and saw her put the money in the envelope. I was busy after that with the customers who had come over to my window."

"You say that Judy Fenton was serving Mr. Tulloch. Did you know him well enough to be sure he was the person she wanted the envelope for?"

"Oh yes, he was an old customer."

"You are sure Judy Fenton was taking money from her drawer to give to Mr. Tulloch?"

"Yes, I'm sure."

"Thank you Mrs. Fellows. I have no other questions, Your Honor."

Judge Anderson looked toward Halloran.

"No questions, Your Honor."

Brad hoped that the architects he'd subpoenaed had noticed that witnesses left by a different door than the one through which they entered the courtroom, thus making it impossible to know what another witness had testified. Even though a group can decide ahead of time to give an agreed upon and to whatever extent untruthful story, there is always the chance that the person taking the stand ahead of you will slip up, or the lie may have been exposed by evidence. Repeating the set story, in that case, put members of the group in the same peril as roped-together mountain climbers. In this case falling together as perjurers.

He need not have worried. The first architect, Terry Maltin, gave a straight account of how she and the other architects had been told that Tom Albright, a man with good credentials had been hired. They had then learned that Sterns had withdrawn the offer once Albright arrived in town.

"Why did Mr. Sterns do this?" Brad asked.

"It was in order to . . . "

"Objection. This calls for speculation on the part of the witness," Halloran shouted.

"I withdraw the question, Your Honor. Miss Maltin, did Mr. Sterns hire his nephew, Russell Tredwell, instead of Mr. Albright?"

"Yes, he did."

"Did Mr. Tredwell work for another firm before coming to Sterns and Associates?"

"Yes, he did, in Atlanta."

"Why did he leave that job?"

"Your Honor, this question is irrelevant and calls for an opinion the witness is not in a position to know," pleaded Halloran.

"Mr. Collins?" said Judge Anderson.

"Your Honor, the question has relevance to possible perjury committed by a witness. It is also relevant, because that witness gave testimony that impugned the character of Mr. Albright and therefore of my client. And, I intend to show why my witness is qualified to answer."

Brad was flying blind. He did not know if Terry Maltin had any idea why the nephew left his job, he was simply groping forward on his faith in the mysterious caller, who had implied that Sterns had lied, and if there was a reason known to Maltin, Brad wanted the jury to hear it before Tredwell testified.

"Miss Maltin, do you know why Mr. Stern's nephew left his former job in Atlanta?"

"He told me he'd been fired."

"Really," Brad said, surprised at the direct answer. Once again he groped forward. "Did he say anything related to coming to work for his uncle's firm?"

"Yes, he said he'd called Sterns that day, the day he was fired, and Sterns told him one of our architects had moved to California the previous month creating a job opening."

"Was this true, about someone moving to California?"

"Yes."

"And was this the position Tom Albright was to fill?"

"Yes."

This testimony was too good to be true and Brad had a feeling the jury would think so also. He decided to take a chance. "These are personal details that Russell Tredwell revealed to you. How was it that he did this?"

"Russell asked me out on a date the first day he was at work. He talked a lot about himself." Her tone of voice indicated that he'd talked too much about himself.

"Did others in the firm come to know this story?"

"Yes, Russell told Bill Steslicke, one of the other architects."

"Your Honor, this is hearsay!" Halloran objected.

Before Anderson could say anything, Terry Maltin added, "You can ask Bill yourself; you've subpoenaed him."

"Thank you, Miss Maltin."

When the man she referred to took the stand, he corroborated his colleague's testimony that Tredwell had come to him on the morning after his date with Terry Maltin saying, "Terry's probably already told you I was fired by Atlanta Design. It's no big deal. "

"Mr. Steslicke, according to the information initially given to you, did Mr. Sterns indicate that Thomas Albright had tried to con his way into a job at your firm?"

"No, Mr. Sterns told us that he thought we'd be happy with the man he'd been able to get to fill the vacancy we had."

Brad looked meaningfully at Judge Anderson, who nodded and then began to make notes.

"I have no other questions, Mr. Steslicke."

To his own mind, Brad considered that the point he planned to make with his next witness would completely undermine Halloran's contention that the two sets of money were the same.

"Your Honor, I call Robert Maynard."

A conventionally respectable looking middle-aged man wearing a crisp white shirt and tie and equally conventional dark suit sat down in the witness chair.

"Mr. Maynard, you are the manager of the Barnhill

Bank in Springville, West Virginia. Correct?"

"That is correct."

"When I was at your bank with a subpoena to inspect any bank records related to the late Thomas Albright, I also asked you give me a record of the serial numbers on the hundred-dollar bills currently in the cash drawers of your two tellers at the time of my visit to your bank. Isn't that true?"

"Yes, you asked it as a favor and I was happy to do it."

"You gave me a hand written list of the numbers and signed the paper."

"Yes."

Brad handed Maynard a sheet of paper. "Is this the list?"

"Yes, it is. That is my signature."

Brad looked up at Judge Anderson. "When I am finished, I would like this record to be entered into evidence as Exhibit "D", but right now I will summarize what the list reveals."

Anderson nodded.

"There were twenty-six hundreds in the two tellers' drawers. On each bill is a serial number that includes a letter. The numbers are unique for each bill, but the letter on each bill indicates the Federal Reserve Bank, which issued the bill. Springville is in the district that gets its money from the bank in Richmond, its letter is 'E'. Twenty of the bills bore the letter for Richmond. Three originated at the Atlanta reserve bank, and one each came from Philadelphia, San Francisco and Dallas."

Brad looked at the witness. "Is that about what you might have expected? The major portion of the hundred dollar bills in the cash drawers of your bank and other local Springville banks originating from Richmond, while a smaller percentage of bills make their way into Springville banks through business transactions with other parts of the country or from travelers?"

"Yes, I wasn't surprised by the distribution."

"Your Honor, I want to certify that the list of numbers that are on this sheet of paper, which I want Mr. Maynard to examine, are identical to the serial numbers of the twelve hundred-dollar bills making up People's Exhibit 'A'. "

Brad showed the paper to the judge and then took it to Halloran's desk.

"Your Honor, I ask if Mr. Halloran will stipulate that the numbers on the list I just gave him are the same as the serial numbers of twelve hundred-dollar bills found in Albright's backpack?"

Fitz compared the list with one he already had. "Your Honor, I so stipulate."

"Now, Mr. Maynard," Brad said, "you will see that nine of the bills on this list bear the letter 'B'. The New York Federal Reserve Bank issued these bills. Two have the letter 'C'. They are from the Philadelphia bank, and one bears the letter 'D'. It's from Cleveland. If twelve bills with these serial numbers were withdrawn from a local bank, what would be your conclusion about the district in which that local bank is located?"

Halloran yearned to be able to object and stop this answer, but he had no grounds.

Maynard replied, "I'd consider it likely that the bank was in the New York district."

"Yes, Mr. Maynard, so would I."

Brad hadn't cried, *"touche'*, but that's the way he felt. He had just given enough proof to convince any rational jury that the money Tom carried was not the Tulloch money. He put aside in his mind his knowledge that a jury in Los Angeles had ignored irrefutable DNA evidence in a famous trial that should have dismissed any thoughts of innocence in the minds of those jurors.

"I have no more questions for this witness, Your Honor."

But Brad had been too quick to count up his points for the day. Halloran was on his feet and approaching the bank manager.

"Mr. Maynard, wouldn't you agree that the composition of those twenty-six bills was a matter of chance? I mean, it would be unlikely that the distribution of districts would be the same on every day."

"I understand you. Yes, it would vary."

"Now just suppose a cattleman from New York had come to Springville to buy a prize bull and paid for it in cash, and that Springville rancher had taken the money to your bank that morning and deposited it. Then suppose I had come in and asked for twelve one hundreds to give to my daughter for her honeymoon. After looking at the serial numbers on the bills . . . "

"I object, Your Honor. This is a hypothetical question. We are not talking here about prize bulls. This question is irrelevant."

Judge Anderson nodded. "Sustained. The jury will disregard the question."

Thank God, Brad thought. He was afraid Halloran was on his way to knocking the stuffing out of his argument.

Halloran was not pleased. "No more questions, Your Honor."

Brad had one more witness. He wanted to leave the jury with this final impression. First he said, "Your Honor, I ask that Thomas Albright's camera that the police took possession of the day he was killed, and I have asked to have brought to the courtroom be entered into evidence as Exhibit 'F'."

When the formal procedure was completed, Brad held the silver-bodied camera up for the jury to see.

"This is the 'gun' that led Trooper Brace to shoot and kill Tom Albright. Tom had inserted a new memory card into the camera when he came to Springville—to start of a new life."

He turned toward Judge Anderson. "Your Honor, I call Fay Dunfee to take the witness stand."

A young woman carrying a manila envelope sat and took the oath.

"Miss Dunfee, please tell the court where you work."

"I'm a technician at the Virginia State Police Forensic Laboratory in Roanoke."

"At my request, you made photocopies of the images that were recorded on the memory card of this camera. Isn't that so?"

"Yes, I did."

"I presume that envelope contains those pictures."

"Yes, it does."

"Please give that envelope to Judge Anderson. Your Honor, I ask that the jury be allowed to see those pictures."

Anderson opened the envelope and began to look at the prints.

"Miss Dunfee, how many pictures were on that— uh—roll?"

"There were only six."

"Have I seen them before, or did you tell me what was on them?"

"No. No one besides me has seen them, and you never asked me what the pictures were of."

Brad laughed. "So, I must be pretty confident of what the jury will see when I ask that they be allowed to see them."

The judged handed the 8" by 10" prints back to

Brad and said it was all right to show them to the jury if the prosecutor agreed. Brad took them to Halloran's desk. Fitz had never thought of any pictures being in the camera and felt embarrassed as he handed them back to Brad and nodded his agreement.

Brad leafed through them as he walked to the jury box. He saw three views of downtown Springville, two of the Appalachian mountains taken from one of the peaks along the Folsum Trail and a close-up of Kerry's face.

As the jurors passed the photos around, Brad returned to his witness and asked, while facing the jury so they would clearly hear him, "Miss Dunfee, if you had just taken part in the killing of two people and anticipated the certain pursuit of the police, can you imagine yourself taking these pictures?"

With a look of disbelief, Fay Dunfee shook her head

Brad was pleased . . . by the smile Kerry gave him as they led her back to the jail. He'd put her on the stand tomorrow as his final move to let the jury see for themselves how absurd the charge was.

Ernest Meadow wasn't ready to agree to the wisdom of Kerry taking the stand until he had a chance to interview her. So, the program for the evening was to have dinner with Brad's mother at the Collins home followed by a visit to the Henderson County jail.

26

In the first few moments of talking with Kerry that evening, it became clear to Ernest Meadow that there was an almost palpable substance flowing between Brad and his attractive client. Meadow knew his would be the only reliable opinion on whether it would be wise to put Kerry on the stand to face Halloran's attack during the cross-examination.

For the next hour and a half, he led Kerry through the complete tale of her association with Tom Albright, down to the concluding moment of his death. When he rose to shake her hand to wish her good night, his impression of the young woman was close to Brad's.

Kerry looked rested and self-possessed taking the stand the next morning. Brad then asked the questions, which had elicited the same story she had related to Professor Meadow the night before. A neutral observer would have heard an intelligent, unguarded account of a normal, growing attraction between two people. The only part of her tale that might raise any doubt was her lack of knowledge that Tom was carrying twelve hundred dollars, or where he'd gotten the money. The idea that one might not know this about one's intended spouse challenged the credulity of every member of this small town jury. Apart from that, her testimony was a convincing story of an innocent victim of tragic fate. Brad and Meadow were satisfied.

This was also the appraisal of Virginia representatives of national civil rights groups and anti-capital punishment organizations present in the courtroom.

Fitz Halloran was well aware that Kerry seemed to have the sympathy of the jurors. He decided he needed to tread lightly to avoid appearing to be bullying her. He didn't give a damn about the international press, but he didn't want to say anything to cause a juror to switch sides. He was sure he had them on his side at the start of the trial. He now employed his natural acting skill. He managed to achieve a neutral tone and expression, no hint of the caustic sarcasm he was capable of. Rather, he looked tired like a patient but tired parent might, when repeating a lesson to a young child. A dialect coach would applaud the very subtle down-home inflections in his voice.

"Miss Atwood, I listened with interest to your tale of your innocent hiking trip. A couple of parts don't gel in my mind. First, you and Albright were poorly equipped for camping out. When you were apprehended, you had a tent and one sleeping bag, a tiny Primus stove, a one-pint pot, a half-gallon plastic bottle of water and enough freeze-dried beans and instant oatmeal for three hungry days on the trail—barely enough to get you to Allegheny, Virginia, if you refilled the water bottle from streams along the way. In Albright's pack was a trail map on which he'd circled Allegheny. There was also a schedule for the local Appalachian Bus Line, with the departure times for buses traveling between Allegheny and Springville underlined. In other words, your equipment and supplies point more to two desperate people bent on a hastily conceived escape that was meant to *look* like a hiking trip. It wasn't a set up for a good time—not the type of hike anyone in this room would like to take. Why, Miss Atwood, such spare provisions—just enough, if you went hungry, to get you to Allegheny?"

How to explain the hiking trip? She couldn't fully explain it in her own mind. She had just accepted it.

"It was a spur of the moment idea of Tom's. It wasn't well planned. He had just had an emotional setback over the job and wanted to get away—outside. I didn't know of a plan to take the bus from Allegheny, if there was one."

"You know, this just doesn't sound right. I'm sure it's hard for folks to believe that you had no idea of . . . See, we'd like to know what your plans were for the immediate future."

Halloran leaned forward with an exaggerated attitude of interested expectancy. After several beats, he prompted, "Yes?"

Kerry was perplexed. "I'm not sure how long . . . another day or two, that is hiking. As you said, we didn't have food with us for more. "

Now Halloran looked puzzled. "You mean you had

no plans? You didn't talk about this? I'm sure the jury is having as difficult time understanding this as I am. A man has just been told he has no job and he and his mate don't discuss it?"

Ernest Meadow gripped the arm of his chair. He recognized the way Halloran had picked up on and was pursuing a point upon which the jury most likely agreed. This maneuver caused them to believe they and Halloran held the same sensible view of things. And, by asking a second question before she could consider her answer to the first question, he had confused her, causing her delay to sound like evasion.

"Miss Atwood, you flew down from New York didn't you?"

"Yes."

""Did either you or Thomas Albright have an automobile?"

"No, we didn't."

"How much money did you personally have with you when you arrived?"

"A little over two hundred dollars."

"Did you have a bank account in New York?"

"No, I closed it before I left."

"And after you closed the account and bought your airline ticket, you had only a little over two hundred dollars?"

Kerry became cautious. She figured Halloran's complacency meant he was on to something.

"That's right," she answered.

"We checked your credit cards. You have a Visa card with a four hundred and thirty-two dollar balance, two hundred ten of which was carried over from last month." He looked over at the jury and delivered the next question in its direction. "You were broke, weren't you, Miss. Atwood?"

Before she could answer, he continued, "As I've already brought out here in court, Albright's finances were in the same sad shape. Apart from the twelve hundred-dollar bills we've been talking about so much here, he had only forty-seven dollars in his wallet. What I'm getting at is this; you two badly needed Ben Tulloch's twelve hundred dollars, didn't you?"

Brad rose to his feet to object that Halloran wasn't giving his client time to answer his questions, but Fitz was already walking back to his chair.

That evening Brad and the professor huddled over the composition of the closing statement. Interfering with their concentration was their disquieting feeling that Halloran had caused the jury to be left with a distrust of Kerry. He had very deftly amplified the very weakest part of their case; where did the money come from if not from Ben Tulloch?

They decided together that Brad must stress the main point that one was innocent until proven guilty and the prosecution had failed to prove Kerry's guilt.

Specifically, had failed to prove the money in the backpack came from Ben Tulloch and Brad had demonstrated with the bank manager's testimony that Tom's money had probably come from a bank in the New York Federal Reserve district. About this latter, Brad had misgivings. At the time he had been making this logical argument, he saw puzzlement on the faces of many of the jurors. They didn't get it. He'd discerned their reaction but pushed it aside. Still, Brad and the professor parted talking a good game.

Later, alone in bed, Brad began thinking of tomorrow's contest with Halloran. They'd be two Olympic skaters doing their free program and then awaiting the judges' decision. Twelve people would listen to his and Halloran's words—words carefully chosen to mold the jurors' thoughts and individual prejudices into a fiction all their own, called a verdict.

A familiar social compromise would be arrived at, the kind that occurs when any group reaches a joint decision. And, as in any group, a leader or leaders would emerge who'd want to prevail. Brad knew that the smart advocate, be he prosecutor or defense attorney, would have identified those leaders and would direct the main manipulative effort toward them. Some lawyers were legendary for this skill. They'd have picked them out as early as the jury selection and throughout the trial they'd have further divined the particular prejudices the leaders in the jury held and would court these jurors as well as Cyrano could find the words to win the lovely Roxane. The easiest job was to convince someone of something he or she was ready to believe.

Brad knew Halloran had him outmanned at this game. He tried to tell himself it was because he wouldn't let himself stoop so low, but his self-honesty vetoed that comfortable idea. Being a skillful manager of people was the name of the jury trial game and he just didn't possess the skill.

The fundamentals of the case came to this: Kerry's life could well depend on the jury believing her character was such that she was incapable of the monstrous act she was accused of. Against this was the perceived near impossibility that Tulloch and Albright were both carrying the same large amount of cash and in the same denominations. Tomorrow, Halloran would use all his tricks to cause the jurors, and especially its leaders, to believe that thinking coincidence could explain the facts was about as stupid as believing a pickpocket's claim that it was only a coincidence that the Rolex found in his pocket was just like the one missing from your wrist.

Sunlight from the courtroom's tall east windows streamed across the floor, creating a light mood in those who began filing in to take their places for the trial's final drama. Fitz Halloran affected an attitude of total confidence, conversing easily with court personnel. Brad nervously sorted papers on his desk. The clerk's "Hear yea! hear yea!" brought sudden silence, and Judge Troy

Anderson swept into the room in his usual manner. He asked Halloran if the prosecution was prepared to give its closing statement.

Halloran rose, answering in the affirmative with exaggerated politeness. He approached the jury of eight men and four women. One man was an African American in his mid twenties, the rest middle-aged and white.

"Ladies and gentlemen of the jury, much has changed since you and I were children. You can remember when it was safe for a teenager to hitchhike, safe to leave the doors unlocked at night, safe to let a child walk alone to the corner store for an ice cream. How many of your grandchildren are able to live today with that kind of freedom?"

Fitz held out both cupped hands in a gesture that begged a response and searched the eyes of each juror. He smiled ruefully and performed a weary, disconsolate shrug.

"Sadly, those times are past. What has happened to bring about this change? You people haven't changed. You still hold in your hearts the values of your parents . . . your grandparents. Our community would be safe in your hands." Here, his voice took on a note of indignation.

"What has happened is that our community has been poisoned from without. Values contrary to our own have been insinuated into our lives by the subtle influence of the media. Our children see movies and television with content that all of you reject, content that undermines the good values we'd like them to hold. We are not asked what we want our children to see and hear. Just pressing a button tunes our children into moral decay."

Halloran had the jury's attention, had the attention of everyone in the room. He made them wait while he walked to his table and poured and drank some water. He returned to the jury box, grasping the railing with both hands.

"Whose fault is it that this has happened?" He looked each and every juror in the eye. "It is our fault." This solemn verdict fell on them like the judgment of God. "Our fault, because we let ourselves be lulled into a state of passivity. We let this abomination seep into our lives, our community, like the unheeded waters of a rising river until we awake one morning to find all has been destroyed in the flood."

He shook his head in self-accusation. "Understand me; I am as responsible as any one here in Henderson County. I let myself fall asleep while this was happening to us."

His head hung in an attitude of culpability. He raised his gaze to once again meet every juror's eyes. "Is it too late? Must we acknowledge that we have lost for all time the heritage our forefathers worked so hard to leave to us?"

Imperceptibly he had drawn himself up into a defiant stance. Challenge flashed in his eyes. "I'm here today for one reason; to bring the message to you that it's not too late. We can throw off the insidious infection of this moral decay. But we have to make a start. We must have a symbol of our goal." He paused for emphasis. "This case is just such a symbol. The callous disregard for the lives of innocent people is what this case is about. To viciously sacrifice those lives for crass personal gain is the epitome of the foreign thinking that has poisoned our lives. What type of thinking has this evil taken the place of? Our parents and grandparents would have no problem answering. They lived by the principle of working together to help each other, ready to come to the neighbor's aid in bad times, ready to share what little they had."

Fitz'z voice had risen to a crescendo. He became suddenly solemn. He waved a dismissive gesture toward Kerry. "This woman's behavior is an example of the worst poison that has entered our lives. She wanted the money that Ben and Gladys Tulloch had saved to give to their daughter and her new husband to start a new life together. And, just because *she* wanted this money she was coldly ready to wipe away their lives and destroy the happiness of the whole family."

Halloran walked the length of the jury box and back. He looked up and recited quickly and almost dismissively, "The evidence is clear. Her accomplice had Ben Tulloch's wallet in his backpack. In the same pack he had the money Ben had withdrawn from the bank. The good honest blood of the Tullochs' that this woman helped to spill was on both the wallet and the money." He gripped the railing once more until his fingers. His tone was of desperate appeal. "Ladies and gentlemen of the jury, help us all. Help us find our path again." His voice choked. It appeared that he wanted to say more, but couldn't. With tears in his eyes, he turned and walked back to his table, where he composed himself enough to say, "Your Honor, The Commonwealth of Virginia rests its case."

The room was as silent as if it were empty. Fitz's listeners had experienced a personal epiphany. By internalizing this experience they had taken on the obligation with which he had charged them. Clean up their community by cleansing it of foreign, evil taint—by ridding it of the likes of Kerry Atwood.

Brad heard the judge call his name. He had been lost in the realization of how effective Halloran's speech had been. What could he say to neutralize it? It was as if he, Brad, had now to follow Henry the Fifth's speech at Agincourt and talk the army out of its white-hot fervor.

He did the best he could to appear confident of Kerry's innocence. He reviewed the many ways in which the prosecution's case was built upon pure circumstance. He emphasized that the certain logic of the serial numbers indicated the two sets of bills could not be identical, reminding the jury that the accused was innocent until *proven* guilty.

"Why then, " he implored with incredulity, "would the prosecution try to convict Kerry Atwood in spite of the lack of evidence? Simply to win, that's why. To have a feather to put in its cap. Maybe to build a personal reputation in order to run for political office. Only you, ladies and gentlemen of the jury, can make this trial about justice."

Brad sat down. Again there was silence, but it was of a different sort than that which followed Halloran's speech. It was an embarrassed silence, such as follows an impassioned and awkward plea for clemency.

Kerry sat and heard Judge Anderson charge the jury with its duty. She sensed that something seemed to have changed—that a signal had been given that the remainder of the program was now to follow a familiar script already agreed upon. The jury would deliberate for a seemly period and then return. The judge would ask if a verdict had been reached and the foreman would affirm this. The written decision would be handed to the judge and he'd ask the foreman what the verdict was. The foreman's response: "Guilty as chargeed."

This was Kerry's premonition. It was also what happened . . . exactly.

Amidst the commotion, which broke out in the room, Kerry heard the gavel rapping again and again, heard the judge talking about a second trial that by Virginia law would immediately consider the matter of sentence. Finally, she understood acutely this was all taking place in real time and the deputy was at her elbow wanting her to stand to be led back to her cell. She wanted to get Brad's attention to reassure him that he had done everything he could, that she thought his closing statement had contained all that was necessary to prove the correct verdict to the jury, but he was putting papers in his briefcase and did not look her way.

In truth, he could not at that moment face her. He was busy lambasting himself for not being equal to the manipulative power of Halloran's closing statement. The raw fact that the trial had not been about a competition between Halloran and him settled in painfully and left him feeling emptied. It had been totally about saving Kerry's life, and on this point, he had failed miserably. What vanity it had been to think he was able to defend her.

She hesitated, making the deputy wait, while she continued to look at Brad. He felt her gaze and forced himself to meet it. As one might say, "Have a good day," he told her not worry, because he would file an appeal of the verdict. He felt as he said the words that he was compounding his fraudulent garnering of her trust, since he didn't know if a meaningful appeal could be framed. Certainly an appeal for clemency would be made at the sentencing trial. Halloran, judging from his closing statement, would be pushing for the death sentence.

Ernest Meadow wasn't traveling this thought line. He knew Kerry had had no other option. Brad had done a competent job. He had undone the prosecution's circumstantial case convincingly to any juror willing and able to listen and think. True, Brad hadn't all the tools of demagoguery. Young lawyers had to learn, as did young surgeons. Kerry didn't have the luxury of choice, didn't have the money. She had fared better than most in her circumstances. At least her court appointed attorney was bright and had the conscience to seek counsel.

As far as an appeal was concerned, Judge Troy Andrews had made no mistakes. He had allowed testimony about Tom Albright's character to be introduced even though he wasn't on trial. It had, however, been introduced as an example of the kind of person with whom Kerry was intimate, therefore reflecting upon her character—deceptive, but legally permissible. The verdict had come down to a judgment call for the jury members and there was evidence, while circumstantial, which provided a rational basis for their decision. The Court of Appeals would have to abrogate the considered opinion of twelve citizens—not likely. Injustice done disturbed Ernest Meadow, but no longer enraged him. He had become inured, but not indifferent. One just came to accept that this was the way the system worked and one got on with one's job, as one might not become emotional over a flat tire and kick it, but instead get out the jack to change it. In this vein, he was thinking now of the influence of the press and how that might best be engaged. He had heard from a couple of anti-capital punishment groups who'd been following the case. He would get in touch with them immediately after leaving the courthouse.

If the jury returned a death sentence—and he thought they would, given the vicious double murder—criticism would pour forth from the international press, which was fond of faulting the US on that score. He would work with Brad to prepare a press release with an aim of raising criticism to the level of outrage. It was still possible that the Virginia Supreme Court, which must review a death sentence, could be influenced, and change the sentence to life imprisonment. Looking ahead, and it kept Meadow balanced to look ahead, an appeal to the parole board in five years time pointing out the absence of unimpeachable, concrete evidence just might achieve Kerry's release. In the meantime, the real killers might make a mistake.

27

It broke her heart watching Kerry brush her hair before being taken to the courtroom to hear the decision of the sentencing trial. Flora Griggs felt like going into the cell and taking Kerry in her arms. For a moment she allowed herself to imagine Kerry standing bravely before the judge, but it was too much. She busied herself with a needless walk to her station at the end of the hall.

Kerry left with two guards and Flora started pacing. She could not concentrate enough for anything but pacing, sitting, getting up and pacing again.

One glance at the bloodless face of the young woman who was brought back said everything. Once the guards had gone, Flora entered the cell and wrapped her arms around Kerry and hugged her tightly. Kerry's control collapsed and she sobbed without control, burying her head in Flora's generous bosom.

"There, there. It will be all right." The words came out automatically, like, "Tell Mommy where it hurts." Flora knew it wouldn't be all right, but she dared not think more.

Jo Montgomery, returning to the Governor's mansion from a dental appointment, stopped by her secretary's office.

"If those are my letters, June, I can save you a trip up the stairs."

"Sure, but it throws off my calorie schedule. Ten round-trips a day are figured in," she said, holding out the letters.

Jo shuffled the pack of letters as she climbed the stairs. "Urgent Bulletin" on the outside of an envelope from the International Sentinel for Human Rights Violations caught her eye. She opened it first when she sat at her desk.

"The jury in Henderson, Virginia has found Kerry Atwood guilty of two counts of first-degree murder and determined the penalty would be execution by a choice of lethal injection or electrocution. Our Board of Review is strongly opposed to both the verdict and the sentence. It's objection is based on the independent judgement of Southern Law Watch. An automatic review by the Virginia Supreme Court will now follow. We urge everyone to write letters of protest to the judges of the Supreme Court and to the governor, Justin Dahl. An example message as well as relevant addresses are enclosed."

Jo, lost in thought, placed her letters on the desk.

Abruptly, she opened the desk drawer and withdrew her address book. She looked up Tony Bellino's direct number at the *Washington Post* and dialed. She heard his familiar voice.

"Tony, this is Jo. I need to ask a favor."

Bellino heard the urgency in her voice. "Ask away."

"I got a notice from a civil rights watch group, The International Sentinel, about a murder trial in Virginia . . . "

"I've heard about it. New York woman. What about it?"

"They believe the woman is innocent. While I trust this organization's intentions, I don't always trust that the conclusions are unbiased. I'd like another opinion, that of a hard-nosed reporter. I'm hoping you can put me in touch with someone."

"Why, may I ask?"

"No, you may not."

Bellino laughed. "Fair enough. I'll see if I can find a reporter with a hard nose."

The return call came at 7:30 p.m. Denver time.

"I talked to our stringer who's been covering the trial, as world-weary and cynical a person as you could wish for," said Bellino.

"Good, and his or her opinion?"

"There is convincing circumstantial evidence against her."

"Such as?"

Bellino went on to explain the details of the case as summarized by his colleague. "But he is of a mind—based mainly on his nose, hard as it is—that the woman's innocent. He strongly feels she's just not the type to be a party to a bloody murder. But he said he thinks that for the jury it came down to what kind of crowd you run with. The money I just told you about: is it common for you and your friends to carry around twelve hundred dollars or isn't it? If it had been fifty dollars that the victim was missing and fifty that was found on the accused, nobody on that jury would think it significant. But twelve hundred-dollar bills? No way. They'd sooner believe a politician's promise. As Einstein said, 'The evaluation of evidence is relative.'"

"Yes, well, of course I knew he said that. Can't thank you enough, old friend."

"Still going to hold out on your reasons?"

"Wasn't I always a girl who could hold out?"

"Let me think a moment."

"Good night, friend."

Brad's dejection from having lost the case was not the recommended state of mind needed to engender the energy to turn to the task of fighting the verdict and sentence. He and the professor had framed an appeal based on the prosecutor having aroused irrational emotions in the jury through his inflammatory closing statement. They figured it held out their best hope, since there had been no egregious errors made by the judge to warrant an appeal on other grounds. Ernest Meadow had been pessimistic about their chances from the start, and his evaluation proved to be justified: the appeal was not granted. Now the only hope of relief rested with Virginia's high court, whose review would only deal with the justification of the death sentence. Statistically, this court stood out as being one of the most deaf in the nation to appeals of the death sentence. Next came an appeal to Governor Dahl. This man had a history of turning down every request for clemency since he'd been in office. After this there remained only an appeal to the U.S. Supreme Court and it was unlikely that it would interfere with the decision of a Virginia court unless it were on constitutional grounds, and the Supreme Court had already rendered the opinion that capital punishment was not cruel or unusual punishment.

What was needed was new evidence. The problem, besides there being none, was the—to most intelligent minds—absurd Virginia "twenty-one day rule." This stated that the Court of Appeals could not consider any new evidence after twenty-one days from the date of the murder verdict. That time had now passed, so if they found evidence proving Kerry's innocence beyond doubt, it would not be heard. There existed, in fact, a case where the defense had miscalculated the time and came with evidence two days too late—too late to save the condemned. There was still the chance, however, that such evidence *might* influence the Virginia high court or the governor as far as the sentence was concerned.

Meadow had returned to his home and began to work his Washington contacts to arouse the interest of the international press corps. Hovering over his efforts was the question he asked himself: Would media pressure influence the Virginia high court or governor, or would it cause the justices to close rank against outside interference?

"This sushi is excellent! This place was a good choice, Clarence." This statement was proclaimed at near full volume, each syllable proclaimed precisely—the normal German conversational tone. The speaker was Gerhardt Zeissler of *Die Frankfurter Allgemeine Zeitung*. Of the paper's Washington bureau, he had been alerted to the trial in Henderson weeks before by a colleague who had seen Kerry testify and was convinced of her innocence. Since the unjust application of the death sentence had become good press in Europe, he contacted his home office, which assigned him to follow the story. He quickly learned he was not alone, since the trial and the verdict had suddenly become newsworthy across the European Union. Zeissler's first move was to contact his friend, Clarence Reed. He was delighted to learn that Reed was acquainted with one of the attorneys for the defense, Ernest Meadow, and that Reed was in Richmond working on a story that included the Virginia governor. Nothing could be better. He then set up a lunch meeting in Richmond with Reed and Meadow.

After each had eaten enough to satisfy their hunger, they focused on the issue.

"Your goal of getting a unanimous response from the European press should be easily accomplished, Ernest," said Reed, "Will the Virginia Supreme Court and the governor care, that's the question."

"No one likes criticism, regardless of the source," said Meadow.

"True, but how much displeasure will the foreign press cause those worthies so comfortably entrenched in their secure positions?" asked Reed.

"Clarence is right," boomed Zeissler. "European objection to capital punishment is easily rationalized by Americans. 'Those jealous Europeans are ever ready to find fault with us.' The substance of the criticism can then be ignored."

Ernest Meadow imbued with the scholar's curiosity, wondered aloud, "Are Europeans jealous of this country?"

"To some extent, yes," answered the German. "For many years America was ascendant in so many spheres. It is natural to want to find something one can feel superior about. Any thinking individual sees the death penalty as archaic, brutal and inhumane. In short, it's practiced only by the inferior. So, the equation is 'You may be successful materialistically, but morally you behave as a

Neanderthal.' Did you know, by the way, when the UN adopted a protocol in 1989 banning the death penalty for minors, it was signed by 192 nations. Two nations did not sign: the United States and Somalia. Your position today on the death penalty clearly places you with Islamic and Asian countries and not with the West."

Gerhardt emptied his sake bottle and waved to the waitress for more. "But," he resumed, "there is something which might go even deeper to explain the complaint of other countries against the US. We must remind ourselves that even though all the EU countries have banned capital punishment, for many it was only accomplished in recent memory—Britain only abolished it for high treason in 1998 and most of the former Soviet bloc countries in the nineties. An exception is The Netherlands. The Dutch did it in 1870, but they always were ahead of the rest of us in human rights. What I'm getting at is that a psychoanalyst would point out that there is no one more intolerant of an irrational practice than the person who has just given it up."

"That's interesting. Where did you read it?" asked Meadow.

"You mean where did I read what I just said? I didn't read it at all," he replied with a smile. "I know it from examining myself." Becoming serious, he said, "A question has come to me as we've talked. I hope you are not offended, Professor, but I'm curious if you held your present strong attitude toward capital punishment before it became a real threat to your client."

"You don't fool around do you?" Meadow laughed. "The answer is, yes. I have long been against the death sentence for one specific reason. One hears many arguments against it—among them, one that impresses me is the contention that a society that incorporates killing as part of its structure instills violence in its members. I think that's true, but my objection is quite simple. I believe that the very central purpose of forming governments is to insure the safety of its citizens. For a government through its official actions to falsely kill one of those citizens is the single most damning thing it can do. By doing so, it nullifies its reason for being. In fact it commits murder itself. Since, as it has been demonstrated time and again, the mechanisms we have for determining guilt are badly flawed—the DNA based reversals are proof of what must be only a small portion of wrong verdicts that have sent innocent people to their deaths—there is but one option, to abolish the death sentence. When and if an error is identified, it means nothing if there isn't a living person to be exonerated. Some may argue that the errors are few and in the great majority of cases guilt is certain. I would answer that even in cases where guilt appears to be certain, we have found out later that we were in error. My question is: can a just and good society afford even one such case? We are willing to have many die to rescue one comrade on the battlefield. How is it that we are willing to let even one innocent person be executed?"

Meadow realized that he had become more impassioned than might be appropriate for a lunch with a stranger in a busy restaurant. "I'm sorry," he said smiling, "but as you've just seen, this is a topic I have trouble talking lightly about."

Gerhardt spoke out, "Nonsense, I was very interested in what you said. It moved me, so I can promise you I will work the phones tonight and I predict in the next days you'll find expression of your views appearing across Europe." Zeissler raised a hand in warning. "You realize, of course, this will undoubtedly be used as a further condemnation of your 'society', as you put it."

"If it would only wake us up."

Gerhardt turned to his friend Clarence Reed. "Clarence, you have been very quiet."

"Oh, I'll take a stand along with both of you. The death sentence is an ugly, primitive holdover from the past. But I was thinking of a proposition a colleague of mine at the *Times* came up with. It was only intended to be provocative. It's this: to be fair, the judge and jury in cases where an executed person is later found to have been innocent should themselves then be executed."

"That's provocative all right!" exploded Gerhardt.

Meadow nodded, "Yes, yes. At present the jury is now in the position of those speculators who use other people's money for their ventures. If the jury was put in the position of the average investor who puts his money on the table . . . " He began to laugh. "They'd be as careful with another person's life as they are with their money."

Gerhardt Zeissler was laughing too. "You'd never get anyone to serve on a jury."

The waitress put down the bill and Meadow reached for it, but Zeissler grabbed it first.

"I will gain the most financially from this meeting. *Die Allgemeine* will gladly pay."

May Rutledge was talking with Mrs. Collins in her bedroom. Brad, having just returned from visiting Kerry, sank onto a kitchen chair. He wanted a moment of rest from the obligation to respond to another's needs. His mother's voice sounded stronger today. There had been a change of medication and they all hoped, in spite of knowing better, that the improvement would last. Brad's own pain over Kerry, however, seemed permanent, the frustrated agony unbearable. He understood for the first time how a person could be driven to suicide to escape such deep misery.

The phone rang. He didn't want to speak to anyone, but he got up and went over to the extension on the kitchen counter and answered. Meadow's voice, buoyed with enthusiasm, rolled right past Brad's subdued greeting.

"I've just talked to my friend Charlie Jackson in Austin. He called to say that the Highway Patrol Captain—Captain Rote—who'd checked on the truck registration for him, continued on his own and found the guy who gave

Kerry and Tom a ride. His name is Jerrod Bush. He lives in Coleman, Texas. The captain hasn't made contact. It's our move."

"How did he find him?"

"Charlie didn't know the details."

"I'm going down there," flew out of Brad's mouth. Without thinking it, he felt a window of relief open up. He didn't know how much his talking to Jerrod would help Kerry, but he'd be doing something.

"Unfortunately," Meadow cautioned, "the twenty-one day rule prohibits any consideration of new evidence, but his testimony could be a juicy morsel for the press, and that might influence the governor and the Supreme Court."

"Right. I'll call about an airline ticket. Maybe you could put the addresses I'll need into an e-mail."

"I'm sure Charlie would be happy to pick you up at the airport."

"Great. I'll be in touch."

Brad wanted to rush emotionally forward, giving his new hope free rein, but his knowledge of the legal reality tempered this. Not helping were the delays in the flights caused by equipment problems and an unexplained raising of the security risk level. Finally, he was shaking the hand of Charlie Jackson ten hours after he'd left home.

Jackson drove Brad to his home, insisting he spend the night and start the three-hour drive to Coleman in the morning using the Jacksons' second car. On the way to his home, Jackson related the details leading to Jerrod's identification. It was the river that Kerry remembered the young Texan describing, the river where he went camping and fishing with his father, a place that he'd said had since been incorporated into a golf course. Captain Rote had located three possible candidates for this physical description. Next he perused the state's driver's license database, where he found two hundred and forty-one Jerrods. Forty-nine of these men fit the age Kerry had estimated. Betting that the site of a fishing trip with a young child would be no more than a two-hour drive from home, he inscribed circles with a one hundred mile radius from each of the three possible golf courses. He had now reduced the list to fourteen Jerrods. Studying the map before him, he noticed that thirteen lived within a few miles of one of the other Jerrods. Rote suddenly remembered a detail from the story Kerry had told Brad and which Brad had recorded. Tom Albright had remarked that he had never heard the name Jerrod before, and the young man had replied that he hadn't either. The Jerrod Bush, who lived in Coleman, was more than ninety miles from any of the others. A call to the local police chief in Coleman had furnished the rest of the information. The red Chevrolet truck was in the Bush family all right, but it belonged to Jerrod's brother-in-law, explaining the failure of the title search.

It was eleven the next morning when Brad passed a sign that told him that Colemen had "the friendliest people in Texas." He hoped it was true. The local policeman Rote had talked with said Jerrod lived with his wife and two kids north of town on Crawford Wash Road. Brad had the map of Coleman he'd printed that morning off MapQuest lying on the seat beside him, but he'd decided to drop in and speak with the chief of police before venturing out to the house.

He pulled into a gas station on Walnut Street near the center of town. He considered asking the attendant if he knew Jerrod, but the guy's reticent manner suggested the answer he'd get back could well be, "Who wants to know?"

Coleman was small. The odds were good the police chief—O'Bannon was the name Captain Rote had mentioned—knew more about Jerrod Bush than the fact that he drove his brother-in-law's car.

Brad's movie-based image of a Texas lawman was a cross between John Wayne and Tommy Lee Jones. The man he met when he stepped into the chief's office was a tall version of Woody Allen. It took Brad a moment to adjust.

"So you think our Jerrod could be a witness for your client?" O'Bannon said as he waved Brad to a chair.

"Are you familiar at all with the case, Chief O'Bannon?"

"Not much really. I got a call from Captain Rote of the Highway Patrol, so I know you're lookin' for an alibi for your client. Young woman convicted of murder."

"I'd like to fill in that picture, but first let me ask you if you saw a notice in the *Dallas Morning News* that stated we were looking for a man named Jerrod who owned a red Chevy pick-up?"

"Guess I missed that."

So, maybe Jerrod missed it too. Brad hoped that explained his silence. He began, then, to relate his condensed version of the facts about the case. O'Bannon constantly interrupted this recitation with questions.

"I don't know if Bush is your man, but it seems likely. I know a little bit about him. His wife, Debbie, is a second cousin of mine. Nice quiet lady. She's known around here for her baskets—real works of art. Jerrod works for her family's feed company. Debbie's brother owns the red pick-up. But, I didn't hear of any reason that Jerrod would have been up in Virginia."

"West Virginia. Any business angle for the feed company?"

"Not that I know of. I think I see what you're wondering; if he did read the notice in the Dallas paper, why didn't he come forward?"

"That's it."

"I might be able to get some answers. Problem is, if I start askin' questions, word will get out . . . I have an idea." He picked up the phone. And pressed one of the express dial buttons.

"Hi Hon, I need some information about Jerrod Bush. Uh huh. Well, what I'd like to find out is if he took a trip up north in . . ." he looked over at Brad.

"July thirteenth."

"In the middle of July. Did he drive up West Virginia way in the pick-up truck that belongs to Leonard? I don't want to ask him directly, if you know what I mean." He listened a moment. "Right. Thanks."

"My wife," O'Bannon said when he hung up. "She's going to work the gossip grapevine. She said it could take an hour. Maybe you could get some lunch and come back in here at one."

"Really, Chief, this is way more than I expected . . . "

"No problem. See you after lunch."

Brad walked north on Commercial Avenue past the Chamber of Commerce office and turned west on Pecan Street, making an eight-block circuit back to Walnut Street before entering and taking a seat at Frieda's Fries. Frieda took his order for a grilled cheese sandwich while politely quizzing him about his business in Coleman. Brad parried her thrusts in an amused, but unyielding way. Finally, she asked him directly if he was the agent for the new shopping mall rumored to be destined for the city. He assured her he wasn't. It wasn't the answer she'd hoped for. Not convinced, she left him and went to refill another customer's coffee cup.

At one o'clock Brad again took the chair opposite Chief O'Bannon.

"Jerrod made a run up to Cleveland back in July to

deliver a number of his wife's baskets to a gallery that sells them there. West Virginia wasn't on the schedule. I'd say that's quite a coincidence, but what would take him that far off the normal route?"

The same idea occurred to both men at the same time, Brad voiced it. "Do you suppose he had a little something going on the side?"

O'Bannon leaned back in his swivel chair. "It would account for his not coming forward when you advertised— if he read it."

"This is exactly why I wanted to talk to you first before I attempted to see him."

"I may be able to help you a bit more. If we were to drive up to the feed store in my patrol car, it figures to shake up the confidence he'd need to stonewall it."

"But I don't want to cause any trouble for him if he's not my man."

"Nobody has to know what you ask him. He was a witness to kids starting a fire in an abandoned barn several weeks ago. If anybody asks, he can say you're an insurance company adjuster."

The Jessup Feed Company was located on Ranch Road just beyond the city limits. Jerrod Bush was in the warehouse shifting pallets of feed sacks with a forklift. O'Bannon introduced Brad and then walked a short distance away.

Jerrod fit Kerry's description, but then so would a lot of other men.

"Mr. Bush, as Chief O'Bannon said, I'm a lawyer from Henderson, Virginia. Last summer you were in Springville, West Virginia, driving your brother-in-law's pickup truck. You gave a young couple a short ride to the trailhead where they were going to begin a hike into the mountains. The woman has been convicted of a murder she didn't commit and faces execution. Many people are sure she is innocent. It would help her more than I can say, if you were to make a statement describing the ride you gave them. It would place them away from the spot where the murdered people were abducted. I'm not exaggerating when I say it could save her life."

The effect O'Bannon had hoped for was evident on Jerrod's face. He was alarmed and frightened, and Brad had no doubt that Jerrod Bush was the man he had searched for.

"I don't know what you're talking about."

"I don't believe that. The Chief doesn't either."

"I ain't never been to West Virginia. I only went to Cleveland."

Brad said quietly, "How did you know I was talking about the time you went to Cleveland?"

Jerrod shook his head vehemently, "No sir! I ain't never been to West Virginia."

"Did you go there to meet someone you don't want your wife to find out about?"

Jerrod's head shot up. His face was livid.

Brad hurried on, "You can make a written deposition

this afternoon and I'll take it back with me. No one here needs to know what our business is or who I am."

For a brief moment the trapped man seemed to consider this offer, but then stubbornly repeated his disclaimer.

Brad became angry. "I could go to your wife and tell her the story and ask for her cooperation."

Jerrod looked fiercely into Brad's eyes. "Don't you go near my wife mister. Now git!"

O'Bannon had overheard much of the exchange and walked over, "Jerrod, this is very serious. A young woman could die for something she didn't do, and just like Mr. Collins said, no one here will ever know."

Back when he'd read the short article in the Dallas paper, Jerrod had been afraid someone he knew would put his name and the description of the truck together. That never happened, or at least he was sure his wife never learned of it. He'd realized at that time that it couldn't be proven he'd been in Springville. He just had to stick with his denial. Debbie would believe him, because she'd want to. He climbed back onto the seat of the forklift.

O'Bannon saw that Brad was boiling mad, so he intervened before Brad said something which would make it impossible for Jerrod to change his mind.

"Thanks for giving us the time. We'll be heading back to town, but please give more thought to this."

In the patrol car he continued, "I'll stop by tomorrow and talk with him again. From his reaction, it's clear he was in Springville. It's hard to admit he was cheating on Debbie and for sure that best explains his attitude. Too bad no new evidence is admissible; a subpoena would be in order. I promise I'll do what I can."

On the road out of town, Brad passed Coleman's boastful sign again. At least two of the three people he'd met in Coleman answered the description.

The dread that had been temporarily lifted by taking action returned as he boarded the plane in Austin for the return trip home. He felt as if a large, heavy animal had climbed onto his shoulders.

28

"You've heard, I assume, that Roscoe MacGruder presented his appeal before the state Supreme Court this morning," Jo Montgomery said as soon as she closed the door to David's office behind her.

"Yes, I did." David Montgomery read acute agitation in his wife's voice. "One of my aides called me." David recognized that Jo had something on her mind and he waited.

Jo raised an imaginary glass in a toast. "Here's hoping he succeeds." She took off her jacket and laid it across a chair. "First there was the verdict, then the jury decided on the death sentence and now the high court is the last chance, my dearest one, before you face the big question."

"True, and I don't hold out much hope that the high court will help me. Bert, who called me, described the court session. MacGruder's appeal is based on his claim that the newspaper articles prejudiced the jury. His petition for a change of venue was denied by the judge, therefore, he claims, t was unjust for the trial to be held in Boulder."

"I'll buy that."

"One of the justices pointed out that MacGruder

hadn't questioned a single prospective juror about his or her knowledge of the articles, and if that had been his concern at the time of the trial, he could have had those who admitted reading the articles dismissed for cause. Another justice mentioned the fact that the articles had been in a Denver paper and not the local one."

Jo huffed. "That's silly, as if the paper isn't read across the state. He's saying an article can only affect a person's judgment if it's printed within the city limits. If that's an example of the kind of logic this court is capable of, we're in deep trouble."

David didn't comment on her reasoning. "Anyway, it's Bert's reading that the odds are against any reversal." He went to a coffee carafe and poured each of them a cup before he continued. "I know you, and I know you have some plan germinating. I can tell from your body language. The last time I saw it, you had that crazy idea that I should run for Governor of Colorado. Are you going to let me know what's on your devious mind?"

She was taken aback for a moment by how transparent she was to him. "Plan? What plan?," she laughed.

"I didn't pursue it as vigorously as I should have. If we'd brought in a guy who said he'd given you a ride to the trailhead, the jurors would have had the image of two lovers off on a hike, instead of the two predators Halloran sold them."

Kerry's thoughts were pulled in two directions, what might have been had Jarrod testified, and her recognition of Brad's painful self-reproach. One direction caused her to want time rolled back, picturing the effect on the jurors of Jerrod's testimony; the other direction caused her to brush her face with her hand as if to wipe those thoughts away.

"I think you're probably right, it would have made a difference, but then if my parents had bought Apple stock in 1980 I'd be rich today. We tell an unfair lie about ourselves every time we say, 'I should have.' I think we all do the best we can at every moment. If we avoid or neglect something which we later come to recognize would have been advantageous, it's because for many reasons we couldn't have done it differently at the time. This isn't Pollyanna thinking. It's a fact. You, I . . . We didn't go after Jerrod, because, number one, you were fully occupied with other issues that seemed and no doubt were more important, and number two you and Professor Meadow did cause an article to appear in the Dallas and Austin papers. The truck registrations were searched and you never really abandoned searching for him. Other concerns were more immediate. But then, what rational person in the Western world would think a state could have a law banning additional evidence in a murder trial after twenty-one days?"

Brad listened and nodded. Hearing her say these things helped.

"You're right, neither Meadow nor I knew of that law. The professor blames himself, of course, but his expertise was in the general rules of evidence not the laws of a particular state."

"The point you were making," Kerry said brightly, "before you began the self-flagellation, was that the news that Jerrod really does exist and is not a feeble lie I concocted might influence the Supreme Court and the governor toward clemency."

Brad knew it was too late for the Supreme Court. The justices were meeting at that very hour, but he refrained from mentioning the fact. He and Meadow expected no relief from that quarter and there was no reason to add unneeded tension to that which Kerry already felt.

"*If* we can persuade him to admit it," he said. "As I told you, the chief of police promised to work on him. He thought that one-on-one and the family connection might eventually bring a change of attitude. In the meantime, I've had another idea. I'm placing an ad in the Springville paper urging the person whom a Texan named Jerrod Bush visited last July to call me."

"Neat angle. I never thought of that. The question is, what kind of person did ol' Jerrod drive out of his way to see?"

By coincidence, the high courts of both Virginia and Colorado arrived at their decisions regarding the murder cases before them within a couple of hours of each other. In both cases no reason was found to overrule the verdicts of the lower courts. As far as the judicial branches of the governments of both states were concerned, each had done its job and had closed the books on the fates of Kerry Atwood and Piper Dahl. The condemned could now only look to the clemency of the executive branch. Only a governor's clemency now stood between each of them and the executioner.

The moment she heard that Piper Dahl's sentence had been upheld by the Supreme Court, Jo Montgomery went to her computer and googled "richmond virginia newspaper." She clicked on the address for *The Times Dispatch* and then entered "supreme court verdict Kerry Atwood," but the latest article only dealt with Kerry's conviction. She did the same search for the Henderson, Virginia paper and clicked on the *Henderson Register*. The front page headlines told her what she wanted to know; "Supreme Court OKs Atwood Sentence." The story had more relevance for Henderson and they must have had a reporter on the spot. It was time to approach David with her wild idea.

He held his second martini as he paced in front of the picture of the Augusta National's twelfth hole. Fitz Halloran was worried. The wheels of justice had turned to produce the exact result he'd wanted. He'd won his case and he'd just heard that the Supreme Court had approved the sentence arrived at by the jury in the sentencing trial. Fitz's main aim, however, had not been to see to it that the woman was executed, it had been to win the case, and use that victory as the vehicle to advance his chance for the attorney general nomination. Now, she was going to die. This presented unexpected complications. The foreign press had started a hue and cry, which had been picked up by the national liberal press. This in turn had given renewed vigor to the anti-capital punishment factions in Virginia. His role in the case had demonized him with that crowd—and it was no longer such a small crowd. What if his party decided to back away from this hot issue? His name, then, would be a liability on the party ticket.

Halloran had tried to get a fix on where State Senator Floyd Cummins, the *de facto* party boss, stood on this issue. The word he got back: Cummins was standing firm for capital punishment. This was good, and Fitz was the candidate with the correct profile. On the other hand, if the party suddenly, because of the dust stirred up by the press, decided to soft pedal . . ..

The hell of it was he couldn't do a damn thing except pace and have another martini.

When he had visited the Montgomerys in Denver, Tony Bellino had not pressed them about their position on capital punishment. They had been having too good a time to spoil it with rancor. David admitted that when asked during his campaign for governor he had answered that he would uphold the laws of the state. For weeks now, ever since the verdict, the question of David's stand on the issue kept intruding into Tony's thoughts. Well, he'd find out soon enough now. News of the Colorado Supreme Court's ruling had just come into the newspaper office. He had an impulse to call David and ask him if he was going to commute the sentence, the action he'd surely take if he were still at heart the old David of the early days of their friendship—the only David—when it came down to it— with whom Bellino cared to be friends. Now that he faced a stark fact, would David bend toward what he knew to be the opinion of the majority of voters, or would he take the step which might very well defeat him at the next election. Bellino knew what the old David would have done, but Tony had long since ceased to be surprised at what the power of public office can do to change a person.

"I should call him and remind him of his old self,"

thought Bellino. "But if David has had to bury his humane feelings under some rationalization, would he welcome my interference, or even hear it?"

David Montgomery hadn't expected a call from Justin Dahl. His secretary had paged David and informed him of it while he was doing a tour of a new state drug treatment clinic. He continued the tour, but his mind kept drifting to Dahl and what he might want. It would be terrible to be in Justin Dahl's position, about the worst thing David could imagine. What could be worse than to be a parent waiting for and witnessing the execution of your child? People talk about the death sentence upholding the rights of the victim's family to see justice done and to relieve their feeling of loss. No one mentions the feelings of those other victims, the innocent members of the family of the one executed.

He had only met Justin Dahl once before, at that governor's conference. He'd played a round of golf with him and three other governors. But he'd ridden in the cart with one of the others and hadn't really talked to Dahl much. Still, in Dahl's position one might turn anywhere for commiseration. Well, he'd certainly be more than willing to commiserate. Strangely, it never occurred to him there might be more that Justin Dahl wanted.

Back in his office in the late afternoon a thought of

returning Governor Dahl's call crossed his mind, but he pushed it away. He caught his move to procrastinate and admitted to himself that he wanted to avoid the difficult call, avoid the pain the other guy was feeling. What does one say? Sorry to hear . . . No, of course not.

"Ruth, I want to return Governor Dahl's call. Would you see if you can reach him please?"

He put down the phone and sat waiting, doodling a picture of a golf club. He snorted. "Easy to see what I'd rather be doing," he mumbled to himself.

The phone buzzed and he picked it up. "Thanks, Ruth." And then, "Hello Governor, David Montgomery. I'm sorry I wasn't here when you called earlier. I heard the terrible news, of course."

"Thanks for callin' back, Governor. I never got the chance to tell you what a pleasure it was to meet you at that Williamsburg conference and play a little golf with you. My golf, as I recollect, was less than a pleasure that day."

"Thank you, the pleasure was all mine."

"Governor, I want to tell you right off that I realize it takes grit to call a man back knowing the difficult thing you're going to have to talk to him about." Dahl paused for a second and then went on with a catch in his voice. "I thought I had prepared myself for the sentence they gave my daughter—I thought I had, but it hit me right in the gut when I got the news. I can't really bring my mind to contemplate it. I won't let myself think that thought."

"Nothing can be harder for a parent to deal with.

Nothing! Absolutely nothing! "

David's heart went out to Dahl. He tried to imagine being in his situation, but just as Dahl had said, his own mind refused to form the image. He groped for something to say. He had the impulse to assure Dahl that his daughter would not die, but caution made him draw back. He needed to talk to Jo, needed to go about such a commitment with more thought. Dahl's call had caught him unprepared.

"Does MacGruder have a plan for further action?" David asked.

"What further action can he take? He's taken a big hit also. He's not used to losing when he's had as reasonable a case of unpremeditated homicide as is my daughter's case. Anybody with an ounce of . . . but that's water over the dam. What I called about was to reassure myself that you understand this, that there was no premeditation. I know you can't think this timid little girl is a calculating killer."

It was clear what Dahl wanted. He wanted more than an assurance of clemency for his daughter. Justin Dahl wanted to come away from this conversation with a quotable phrase to the effect that the Colorado Governor disagrees with the sentence of the court. This was dangerous territory to enter. He didn't want to go in that direction for sure.

"This must be very terrible for Mrs. Dahl. Please tell her I understand."

Dahl didn't intend to be diverted. "There was considerable prejudice in Boulder. The whole city was identified with the boy's Olympic hero parents. I'm sure every member of the jury wanted to please the boy's parents. I'm sure you see that."

Here was another land mine: Colorado Governor says jury was prejudiced. Evasion was no longer possible.

"I can't comment on that, Justin, I hope you understand."

"It makes a world of difference to my daughter, you know, David, if her unfortunate action is viewed as an act of momentary passion, or if it's seen as premeditated."

Montgomery was aware Dahl had now put it on a first name basis and was back on the theme about which he wanted to be able to get a quotable reply.

Dahl backed off. "Hell, of course I know you have to be careful what you say right now. The purpose of my call was to talk to you, to tell you one father to another, one governor to another that my little girl is no killer. She is a girl who was terribly humiliated and struck out. I hope you see that."

David squirmed as if he were facing a relentless chess champion who had made a move toward cornering him to a square from which no other defensive move was open. He had directly told Dahl that he couldn't comment, but Dahl continued to press for that quote that would commit him to clemency. At the same time he knew the pain the man was in and naturally wanted to console him.

"I understand that you love your daughter and want to do everything you can to help her. Every parent in the country sympathizes with you in that."

Justin Dahl recognized that he had been given something and it was all he was going to wring out of David Montgomery today. The politician within him was dissatisfied; the father was grateful for the kind words.

Dahl closed with a few homespun phrases of gratitude leaving David Montgomery alone in his office with the portraits of Washington and Lincoln, which hung on the wall. George was staring off to the left in an attitude of indifference to the previous conversation. Lincoln, however, was looking at him with a quizzical expression. Yes, David thought looking at George, you're above a problem such as I'm facing. You are secure in your knowledge of being the first president. No one can take that away from you. You had only one big decision to make, whether or not to cross that damned river and it was an easy decision. All your men were about to leave to go back to their farms.

His eyes shifted to the other portrait. "You," he murmured, "You know what difficult decisions are all about. That look you're giving me. Are you wondering if I've got what it takes?" David met Abe's gaze a long moment. "You and me too, Mr. President."

He laid his briefcase on the desk and slid some papers and a booklet into it. After telling his secretary he was going home, he left the office by the door that led into a short hallway and to the private elevator from his office to the basement garage. Descending, he thought about

Justin Dahl. The Virginia Governor was mounting a step-wise campaign to manipulate him into commuting his daughter's death sentence. Dahl had first established the fact that they were fellow governors, who had even shared eighteen holes of golf. He then introduced the idea of his daughter's having been falsely charged and therefore wrongly sentenced and tried to get David to make a statement to that effect. Dahl had been careful not to press him too far. David knew he'd be getting another call from Justin Dahl.

29

She waited until they had finished dinner and had taken their cups of coffee into the small second floor sitting room, the same room where she and David and Tony Bellino had spent the evening together back in the summer.

"Remember a few days ago, the day Roscoe MacGruder made his presentation to the Supreme Court, you asked me what was on my mind?"

"Of course. I asked if you were hatching some plan and you denied it."

"Well, you were right, as if you didn't know. I was waiting to see if the situation would develop where my plan made sense. It has. Today both the court here and the one in Virginia affirmed the decisions of the lower courts. Both Piper Dahl and a young woman in Virginia named Kerry Atwood are going to die."

"Kerry Atwood?"

"Yes, I learned about her case through the Human Rights Sentinel and checked it out with Tony's help. The death penalty is wrong, period. We both firmly believe that, but it is especially so in both of these cases. The Virginia verdict is based on circumstantial evidence and many informed observers think the woman is flat out innocent."

"OK." David listened, wondering where Jo was going.

"You intend to commute Piper's sentence, right?"

"Yes, of course. We discussed this before I ran for office and agreed that if it ever came up while I was governor, I would commute every death sentence to life imprisonment. "

They both expected that such a course would probably mean the end of David's political career and he would be accused of dissembling, because the perceived view was that he had pledged during his campaign to support capital punishment. They had both been surprised that his promise to uphold the laws of the state where the death penalty was concerned had so readily been interpreted this way. After all the law also allows the governor to offer clemency in capital cases.

Jo hesitated to present the body of her plan. "Well, I see a way . . . that you can also save someone else from execution."

David stared at her with furrowed forehead.

She plunged ahead. "You can offer Justin Dahl his daughter's life for the life of the Virginia woman."

"Good God!"

"Wouldn't you save someone else if you could?"

"This is bizarre, Jo. I can't believe you just suggested it."

"It's only bizarre at first. Believe me, it grows on

you."

"What?"

Jo sat holding her coffee cup in both hands looking silently at him over the brim.

"Bargain with a man for his daughter's life? It sounds like Faust."

Her eyes merely continued to smile over the brim of the cup.

David gave a mirthless laugh. "Dahl called me. He was angling for my commitment to clemency."

"Did you agree?"

"No. He didn't actually come out and ask. At first he wanted a statement critical of the courts, but he moved on. He didn't come right out and ask me to commute his daughter's sentence, but he might as well have. He'll call again."

"But you didn't commit yourself."

"No. I hadn't had time to consider how and when or what I would say. I certainly didn't want an announcement to come from Justin Dahl."

"Good."

"Good?"

"It sounds monstrous, but—if you agree to my plan—he mustn't be *given* anything. He must be made to agree to a deal."

David laughed aloud at the outrageous idea. "Can you imagine what the press would do with this?"

"Who's going to tell them? Not you certainly. And

not Dahl either."

David shook his head, He didn't want to hear more of her "plan", but he knew he would.

"This will have to be planned very well," she began. "I'll hate myself if I have to look back after Kerry Atwood is executed and know that it happened because we didn't go about this in the right way."

Jo's use of "we" was no problem for David. Although he was the one who had been elected, they had been political partners since college and any important political decision was discussed and made together.

For a minute, neither spoke, Jo waiting for her proposal to sink in, David gradually allowing himself to consider it as serious. Jo judged the moment ripe to continue.

"The deal will have to be presented in terms that are vague enough so that Dahl—we have to assume he will be recording the conversation—will have no proof, should he see it in his interest to go public," she said.

Each could read anxious anticipation in the expression of the other. They were like an affluent couple on the cusp of a decision to leave a high six-figure job to buy a small farm and try their hand at raising llamas.

"I've never done this kind of bargaining before," David said. "The closest was when I'd offered to do my sister's math homework if she'd lend me her car. That had to be clandestine also, or our old man would have turned us both in, my sister to the school and me to the police for driving without a license."

Jo saw that he was on board. "We'll have to wait until he calls again as you predict."

"Hmm. Intuition tells me I should put him off, at least on the first call." David shook his head as if to wake up. "Jeeze, I hate to do this to the man—the spot he's in!"

"Of course you do, but the suffering due to the delay in giving him relief is nothing at all compared to the suffering that poor Atwood girl will suffer if you don't do this. His record is grim on appeals for clemency. Appeals 4, Clemency 0."

"I distinctly remember your once saying, 'The end justifies the means is the reasoning of scoundrels.'"

"That's right, we're about to become scoundrels, and I don't know about you, but I feel invigorated."

"I can see now that Freud was right. The super egos of women are more malleable than men's. He said it was because they didn't have the threat of castration hanging over them."

"Baloney, or rather Viennese wurst. But, maybe he was onto something. I know I've always felt that morals are relative; if your kids are starving you steal. Absolute morals are for those without human problems—the immortals."

She stood up, walked over to his chair and kissed him on top of his head. "So, try on a woman's superego for a time. You could come to like it."

The expected call from Justin Dahl came after three days. David had walked down the hall to discuss a small matter with his executive assistant. He returned to have his secretary greet him with her rendition of the Virginia Governor. "Appreciate a call when Guvna' Montgomery has a minute."

David went into his office and waited to be connected as one awaits the serve of a good tennis player, not knowing what speed, spin or direction is coming your way.

"Thank you for calling back, David. I hope your weather out there is better than the cold drizzle we're havin' here today."

Dahl moved from observations about the weather to an inquiry about David's "lovely lady" before he segued into the subject of Piper's sentence. David recognized the moves of the instinctive, political animal and this helped him assume the ready position for the coming bout. He returned the opening remarks in kind and waited. Justin began a review of the case and the unfair verdict. David in turn sympathized while not disputing the conclusion of the court. Dahl then directly said he hoped David would act to "remedy" the injustice.

"Remedy?"

"Yes, the authors of our state constitutions, in their God directed wisdom, provided the head of the government with the power to correct the muddle-headed or even

355

malicious actions of the lower branches, much like the role of a father to keep a family on the straight road—the power to remedy."

'The remedy in your daughter's case is clemency, a commutation of the death sentence. Is that what you had in mind, Governor?"

"Yes, I'm asking it as a father, one father to another."

"As I've assured you, I couldn't be more sympathetic, but you yourself are well aware of how impossibly difficult it is to set aside the serious deliberations of two courts. The question is, when can we afford to let our personal feelings take precedence over the considered opinion of so many good people?"

"I'm with you there, David," said Dahl. "That's the burden of leadership. That's why the executive branch was created. It was so that individual exceptions could be made when called for."

The man was relentless. What a salesman he would have made, David thought. He also must have scored at will in his youth. What young girl could have rejected his campaign?

"This is the first death sentence to be handed down since I became governor. You've been in office much longer than I: How have you handled these cases?"

There was a pause. "Like I said, one has to look at each case individually. Consider its merits. Now if you put yourself in my daughter's . . . "

"Governor," David interrupted, "I'm asking you to help me now by letting me follow the course of your own thinking when an appeal for clemency has been made to you. What factors have caused you to go against the ruling of the courts?"

"I'm afraid I won't be able to help you much; you see in each of the cases I've had to consider, the evidence of guilt was so compelling I knew the court had been right."

"I see," David said, "But there is a case I read about of a young New York woman who has just been sentenced to death in your state. The article said that the evidence was only circumstantial."

"No appeal for clemency has been made to me."

"It will certainly happen, however. How will you go about deciding what you'll do?"

"It's impossible for me to tell you until I see the transcript of the trial."

Justin Dahl said this with assurance, happy to be on solid reasonable ground.

"Then you read the transcripts in each of the previous cases."

The flavor of mendacity again entered his voice. "Well, certainly!" Following a few moments of silence he added, "This woman you're talking about is guilty without a doubt."

"Since no appeal has been made to you, it figures you haven't read the trial transcript yet."

"That's right, but I certainly will."

"You can say she's guilty beyond doubt before you've read the transcript of the trial?"

Dahl knew he had wandered into a trap and wondered how the conversation had spun away from his intended direction.

"My daughter's situation is worlds apart from what you're talking about. No cold-blooded motive of profit. Only a betrayed and angry little girl giving momentary vent to her humiliation."

"Going back to the case of the New York woman for a moment; it would be your inclination to deny clemency?"

"It was a heartless, vicious murder."

David decided enough had been said for one day. Let Justin Dahl stew and wonder.

"Thank you, Justin, for sharing your thoughts with me. This has been very helpful. I'll get the transcript of your daughter's case. As you read the details of the trial of that woman there in Virginia, you'll know that I'll be doing as you advise. Who knows, maybe after our informed consideration, we'll arrive at the same decision. Goodbye and please give my regards to Mrs. Dahl."

He hung up and called Jo.

"I need to know about these things, Fletcher. The fella began talking about this case and I didn't know diddly."

Fletcher Eton waited patiently for his boss to cease his tirade, then pointed out that several days ago he had included an outline of the case and the impending, inevitable appeal for clemency in his daily briefing.

"I'm not surprised you missed it with all that's on your mind," he added.

"That so? Well. I'm sorry then. What's this thing all about anyway."

Eton gave the governor a capsule review, finishing with the clamor the foreign and liberal national press had been able to stir up.

"Have those foreigners started voting in Virginia when I wasn't looking?"

Eton laughed.

Dahl opened the refrigerator beneath the wet bar in his office and took out and poured a glass of mineral water. Eton noted that Justin looked very tired. More than that, he looked depleted. He was attempting to maintain an attitude of supreme confidence, but Eton knew that Piper's conviction had all but crushed the man.

"What about the death sentence, where do we stand on that . . . I mean with the voters?" Dahl asked this as if he were talking about the effect of a sales tax increase.

"Two factors to be weighed: public attitude and the party's position. A recent poll indicates that a slight majority of voters favor abolition. The pollsters' opinion suggests, however, if adjusted for the people who are really likely to get out and vote, the majority would be for continuing capital punishment."

Justin took a cigar from a humidor on his desk and removed the band. "And the party?" He added *soto voce,* "As if I didn't know."

"Firmly for, and Senator Cummins very firmly for."

Dahl began puffing clouds of smoke.

Eton inquired quietly, "Did this talk you alluded to prompt these questions?"

Fletcher Eton knew that must have been the case, and was curious about what had been said. Ham Bascomb, Dahl's attorney would have asked, "What the hell is this all about, Justin?"

Dahl grunted in reply.

This really prodded Eton's curiosity. Usually Justin withheld little from him.

"Fletcher, get hold of Floyd Cummins for me . . . see if I can lunch with him."

"Certainly." Eton knew now it was serious.

The ad Brad placed in the *Springville Clarion* brought immediate results. A woman who said she was Ellen Barnes called the day the ad appeared, and Brad made an appointment to meet her that evening in Springville.

He parked in front of a small, frame bungalow on the southern fringe of the city. A pickup truck with an elevated frame and huge tires sat in the dirt driveway.

Work was apparently in progress on the steps to the porch and stacked cement blocks served the purpose in the interim. A light shone through the front windows. A man in his twenties answered Brad's knock. He was barefoot, wearing jeans and a black T-shirt with writing that Brad couldn't take in with a quick glance.

"Yeah?" the guy challenged.

"My name is Brad Collins, I have an appointment with Ellen Barnes."

The man stood thinking about this for a long moment, then stepped back, calling out, "El, some dude here to see you." Without another word he turned and went back to the couch where he'd been watching television.

Brad stood self-consciously until a young woman came into the room from what was probably the kitchen. She paused, looked at the man in front of the TV , then picked up a jacket that hung over a chair back and putting it on said, "Let's sit in your car."

Brad followed her outside, shutting the door behind him. The woman's chestnut hair fell to her mid-back. She walked with a self-assured stride to his car, where she opened the door and slid into the passenger seat. As he went around the car, Brad thought that here was a woman who was very comfortable dealing with strange men. Also aware of and comfortable with her sex appeal. Cocktail waitress?

"Hi, I'm Ellen. I think I'm your girl."

It flitted through his mind that under other

circumstances and at another time he might have heard that statement with interest, but he had but one thing on his mind.

"Thanks for answering so promptly. I'm Brad Collins, the attorney for Kerry Atwood. She's . . ."

"Yeah. I've read all about the murders. It's been big news here, as you might imagine. I know one of the sons of the murdered couple; went out with him a few times. "

"Then you know that Kerry Atwood has been found guilty and now faces execution."

"Sure. I've got to tell you that the attitude of people here is she's getting what she deserves." She took time to scan Brad up and down, an automatic process of evaluation. "It has never sounded right to me. I said so at work and had a couple of the salesmen yelling at me. I'm the service manager at the local Ford agency." She was prepared for the look of surprise coming from Brad.

"My older brothers were always tearing down and rebuilding engines when I was growing up. They're both on the Darryl Slater Racing Team now."

"I was relieved when you called. I was afraid the information I wanted might be seen as too personal for . . ."

"A woman to admit? Yeah I think you'd be right in most cases. This Jerrod didn't mean anything to me and nothing happened that I'd be inclined to deny. I met him at a stock car race in Dallas. Well, at a bar after the race, actually. We'd won and were celebrating. I'd had a few and here was this good-looking Texan hitting on me. Ended up spending the night with him. I didn't think I'd ever see him again, but I must've told him where I lived, because he showed up here last summer." She shrugged. "A Texan while we were celebrating in Texas was one thing, but I had zero interest in messing with him here and I told him so."

Kerry had described Jerrod as being cocky and upbeat. "What time of day was it when you told him you weren't interested?"

She thought a moment. "After work. He was parked in the driveway when I got home."

That explained it. Jerrod still had high hopes when he picked up Kerry and Tom. Brad brought out the driver's license picture O'Bannon had given him and showed it to Tracy.

With a sardonic smile she said, "That's my little buckeroo."

So far so good. Brad then made a decision to share his problem. "Here's the situation; we need Jerrod to admit he gave Kerry and her fiancé a ride that afternoon before you saw him. We want him to describe them, their mood. We prefer him as a friendly and not as a hostile witness. I talked to him down in Texas. He denied that he was here. You might not know this: he's married and has a couple of kids, which explains why he won't admit he took a detour on a trip to Cleveland to see you here in Springville. In order to give us the testimony we need, his wife is sure to find out about that detour. Got any suggestions?"

Ellen settled back into the space between the seat and the car door and drew her left leg up onto the seat.

"If she knew, she might make him testify," she said.

"I can see that, only we need a friendly witness. We want him to remember the good feelings about the young hikers he picked up. If we anger him by telling his wife, who knows what he might say to get even."

"I know!" A bright smile bloomed on her face. "Ol' Jerrod came by here to see one of my brothers about getting a job with the race team. He'd met my brothers in Dallas and they'd hit it off. He figured that a job on the racing circuit would be a lot better than busting his ass riding in rodeos."

Brad was startled by the rodeo bit, but only said, "Would your brothers go along with this tale?"

"No sweat."

"Let's see, he didn't want to tell his wife until he actually was offered the job and your brothers had told him, 'Can't be done this year. Wait until next.' So, he went home and kept his detour to Springville to himself."

"Sure, wouldn't you?," she said laughing.

"Ellen, you're the answer to the prayers of a maiden in distress. I can go back to Texas now and make ol' Jerrod an offer he can't refuse."

She held up her hand for him to slap a five.

Brad rode off with renewed hope. He hadn't thought it wise to tell Ellen that Jerrod worked in a feed store. She'd given herself one night to a rodeo hero.

This time Jerrod Bush listened. Brad laid out his choices and he was smart enough to see that one choice led to a certain crisis in his marriage while the other would only result in his wife, Debbie, scolding him for acting like a silly kid dreaming of traveling the stock car circuit.

"All we'll do at this time is have you tell me your story here in Coleman. Chief O'Bannon will be one witness and his secretary the other. I'll take this deposition back to Virginia and include it as part of our appeal to the governor."

His problem solved so nicely, allowing his burden guilt to be lifted, Jerrod became talkative.

"I hope this works out for you. I knew them folks never did nothin' like murder. Guy was real friendly, lookin' forward to a little time off. She was lookin' hot and sweaty. Lord it was a hot day. She didn't have robbery or murder on her mind, only how could she cool off. Bet that girl woulda done anything for a swimming pool."

"That's fine, Jerrod. Wait until I get this set up with Chief O'Bannon and I'll want you to tell me all this again."

"He's on line two," announced David's secretary.

David was prepared to present his *quid pro quo*. "Yes, Justin, how are you?"

"I'm fine. Thanks for asking. Reason I'm calling is that I'm coming out there to see Piper. I'd like to meet with you where we can talk without nosy people taking notice. Know what I mean? I'll have me a room at the Marriot in Denver on Thursday and go on to Boulder next morning."

"I think that would be a good idea. Where and when would you like to meet?"

"It's your city."

"How about my picking you up in front of the hotel at 8:30 in the morning. I have a green Jeep Cherokee."

"I'll be there."

David thought about the call when he'd hung up. Dahl wanted no witnesses and didn't want to talk on the phone. He must be ready to make a deal, or he would have made his bid again for clemency just now.

Approaching slowly, hoping he'd remember what Justin Dahl looked like, he searched the faces of the men around the entrance, but didn't recognize him. He noticed, then, a man step out to the curb some thirty yards further down the street, who, looking directly at David, made a subtle wave of his hand. It was the man he'd played golf with in Williamsburg, who evidently wanted to avoid a doorman remembering him getting into David's car. Good,

David thought, he intends to deal.

Dahl opened the door and got in. He didn't look well. In Williamsburg he had been bluff and hearty; today the word was haggard.

"Good morning, Governor. Nice to see you again."

"Likewise, David. I only wish it was only golf we had on our minds, like last time." He followed this, clearly not able to delay the question, "I hope you've given serious thought to relieving a father's heavy heart."

David expected this approach from Dahl. He intended to see what he could get through sympathy, before he got around to serious deal making.

"Nothing would give me more pleasure than to be able to do that, Justin."

"Hell, that's easy and I can call Florence and tell her the good news."

"You, Justin, know better than anyone that we public servants often aren't able to do what we'd like to for friends, because there are rules and procedures that tie our hands."

David drove into an empty parking lot adjoining some public tennis courts, parked, turned off the engine and turned in his seat to face the other man.

Dahl was uneasy. "What procedures are you speaking of?"

"First of all the one you suggested to me, reading the transcript of your daughter's case carefully. I assume by this time you have done the same regarding the case of

Kerry Atwood, the young woman in your state."

"Now that you mention it, yes, David, I did that. My conclusion is that there is much to be said that questions her guilt."

That was more direct than David had expected. The ball was in play and was now in his own court. His impulse was to say that he was going to grant clemency to Piper, but something made him hesitate. Perhaps the hook wasn't set yet. Dahl was as wily an old trout as there was in any stream.

"It's certain your daughter is guilty of killing the man. I haven't had time—I only got the transcript yesterday—to give it a close reading. I can tell you that in doing so, I'll have a definite bias toward clemency."

"David, I'm on my way to Boulder to see my girl. Surely you're going to make it possible for me to reassure her that you are not going to let her die."

David had enough objectivity to be able to wonder what the average number of times a normal person could hold out against pleas such as this before capitulating. That last one almost swallowed him up. He steadied himself.

"Believe me, Justin, I know how much you'd like to reassure your daughter, but before I can say anything, I have to confer with advisors. It would be cruel to give your daughter false hope."

"Advisors?" Dahl said with incredulity. "I figured you for a leader who only listened to his own council in important decisions. I know I'm right about that."

David would like to have been able to laugh out loud. He had just been offered the distinction of being a forceful leader, or the converse to be forever dubbed a milquetoast.

"No, Governor, I always try to keep my people in the loop. They don't act without conferring with me, and I believe in including them . . . unless it is something which shouldn't be shared."

Justin Dahl looked dismally through the windshield. "My trip here has been wasted. I had you figured all wrong."

The guy was relentless. Time to be more direct.

"Justin, you said you looked at the record of the case that has been appealed to you and you said you saw room for doubt about the verdict. Have you made the bold decision that you're advising me to make. Have you decided to commute her sentence to imprisonment?"

"Well now, I must take a closer look. If I'd heard here today that which I was expecting, then I'd be more inclined . . . "

"Governor, your hearing what you want to hear from me is going to depend entirely on your taking that action. What is more, you will have to make that announcement before I make mine."

Justin Dahl stared in shock. He couldn't remember the last time he heard someone say, "check and mate."

30

State Senator Floyd Cummins had his lunch most days at the private Capitol Club. Members knew that his was the corner table by the window and although it was not formally reserved for him, no one considered sitting there unless it was by his invitation. Governor Justin Dahl pulled out a chair and sat down.

"Justin, I'm so happy you called me. I've wanted to tell you how Sally and I are terribly distressed 'bout Pipah, but we didn't want to intrude. Is there anything at all we can do to help?"

"Nothing, other than my being able to talk with you. I've always come away from our talks with a sense of resolution to a problem." His voice then abandoned the tone and cadence of social exchange to those of personal intimacy. "It's been very hard, Floyd. First the dreadful news of what had happened, then the trial and now . . . very hard."

It was support that Justin Dahl was looking to Cummins for, support to be able to take the path that would make the deal with that bastard in Colorado. The time was ripe for his move to the U.S. Senate. Senator Rice had announced that he wouldn't seek re-election. His party's nomination was open. Even though he had much power within the party, he didn't want to test it against the power of Floyd Cummins. To oppose Cummins and fail meant he'd end up being as popular with fellow party members as Clinton was with Democrats post Monica. It was not the way he wanted to end his years in politics.

"I can tell you, Floyd, seeing the death sentence from the point of view I've been forced into, puts the issue in an entirely different context." He glanced at his table companion to see if sympathy was still alive. "Florence and I have only one hope now to save Piper, the Colorado governor's clemency. Floyd, I've got to tell you I got down on my knees to that man."

Cummins replied in a tone a shade more reserved than moments before. "I can understand that, Justin. It's the right and natural thing for a parent to do." Now he became preachy. "Just as it's natural for parents to go to a teacher and beg for a failing child to be passed."

Dahl felt a jolt. Asking to have one's daughter spared from death was, to Cummins, the same as asking for a change of grade. The implication was that the requested favor was undeserved in either case. He forced himself to rally.

"Just the same, Floyd, it makes one think hard about the sentence itself. I really don't think Piper deserves to die for the mistake she made . . . awful as it was."

"Yes, but . . . after all she did take a life . . . that's so isn't it?"

This wasn't the issue that Justin had come to discuss. He needed to get back on track.

"There's no question, Floyd, as you say, but what about those times when there is a question. Times when there is doubt about the validity of the verdict?"

Cummins now assumed an attitude of the elder with wisdom. "Justin, nobody's perfect. We have to rely on the good Lord to guide our juries and judges to a just verdict. We can't question his guidance . . . can we?

"If we could only be sure."

"This also is a natural reaction to personal tragedy, Justin, to question the Lord's ways."

Cummins's position was pretty clear, but Dahl needed to be sure.

"An appeal of the death sentence has been made to me in the case of Kerry Atwood, the New Yorker . . ."

"Yes, yes, I know. I've been listening to that bunch of foreigners and atheists scream. One of their evil lot is exposed for the hateful trash she is and they can't stand it. Thank God Virginia remains a place where decent God-fearing people stand together against their kind."

Dahl had his answer. It had been phrased in religious terms, but this was commonly Cummins's way, he always let the Lord do his dirty work. His main authority for the positions he took on most issues was scripture—more so the more remote the issue stood from spiritual matters. His stated reason for supporting the tobacco industry was that God wanted tobacco to grow in Virginia. "Else he would have made it native to Arizona." Actually, Justin knew that in every case Floyd's position was the simple reflection of the interests of the party's wealthy and powerful backers.

As if to remind Dahl of his loyalties, Cummins changed the subject. "I was also wanting the opportunity to discuss the next election and your candidacy for senator. Our party's man will easily defeat that cipher the other party seems bent on nominating. That is if we don't create any dissension in our own ranks. In spite of your personal problems with your daughter, God bless her, my choice is you. This tragedy, and the sympathy you'll garner with voters could work in your interest. Heaven knows you'd gladly forgo that sympathy if this had never happened, but it did and the sympathy will be forthcoming."

It became crystal clear, sitting there smiling back into Floyd Cummins's smugly smiling face, how he'd have to deal with that tail-twisting bastard in Colorado.

The anchorman told those watching the six o'clock news, "Governor Montgomery, today, commuted the death penalty of the University of Colorado student, Piper Dahl, to life imprisonment. The reason he gave was he believed there was insufficient proof presented at the trial of prior intent. Slats and Cindy Patterson, the parents of the victim, stated that 'the change of sentence made a mockery of the laws of the State of Colorado.'"

The familiar face of Slats came on next. Angrily he said, "It's the same old story, it's *who* you know that counts. It's transparent that Montgomery did this because that girl is the daughter of the Virginia governor. From what I've heard already from people I've talked to, Governor Montgomery can forget about another term."

The picture reverted to that of the TV anchor who, looking up from papers on his desk, said, "There has been a six-car accident on Interstate 25 near Northglenn."

His shoes off and his feet on an ottoman, his unknotted tie askew across his shirtfront like the stole of a disillusioned priest, Justin Dahl swirled the ice cubes in a just emptied glass of lemonade. He was spiritually spent.

Lorna Newby, seated on part of the ottoman, messaged his foot and waited. She recognized his state of mind.

"That was yesterday afternoon. I told him I had called a press conference for this morning to announce that I was commuting the Atwood woman's sentence." Justin chuckled. "And I did have Fletcher set it up too, but I told Fletcher it was to announce my candidacy for the Senate seat, but for him to say nothing about the purpose of the conference to the media. Said I wanted it to be a surprise to the media. I figured that asshole Montgomery would check to make sure I really had scheduled a press conference as I said I would. I also figured he would want to be the magnanimous one and make the announcement first."

Lorna looked puzzled and Justin saw this, "Don't you get it? Last night in time for the news, he went ahead and announced he was commuting Piper's sentence. When I heard that, I told Fletcher to cancel the press meeting he'd set up." He began laughing until tears ran down his cheeks. "I outfoxed him and he was trying to be so foxy with me. Fool!"

"What did Ham say about it?"

"Haven't told Ham. Don't intend to either."

Not once in the dozen years she'd been intimate with Justin had she heard of anything he failed to run by Ham Bascomb. There had been many occasions of political double and triple dealing he'd told her about, things that totally jaded her view of government. All these had been shared with Bascomb. Justin, she thought, must really feel shitty about this particular deception.

"What can this . . . governor do about this?"

"He'll do nothing. There are several things he *could* do. He could reveal the agreement we had, but he won't. He won't do a damn thing except keep calling me."

"Why won't he go public?"

"He's smarter than that. He's a reformer and an idealist, but he's not suicidal. He'd know I'll deny the deal, act insulted. I'd be outraged that he implied I would betray the trust of the Virginia people, etcetera. Besides he can't admit he made that kind of deal. He might even get himself impeached. He can't rescind the clemency either. No, Lorna my dear, I've saved my little girl . . . and I haven't made waves here at home, waves that most surely would have upset my senate boat."

Lorna was not of the same mind. She'd always been offended by the amorality she'd been privy to for years. But still, in that same way of parents who can never see their children as *really* bad, she'd loved Justin in spite of his faults. Much as one might say, "Boys will be boys," she said to herself, "Politicians will be politicians." She even thought of Justin's openness with her as a virtue. A person who confesses a wrongdoing is not fully guilty. There exists after all a long, accepted history of confession having the magical ability to transmute.

"What about Kerry Atwood? I'm told there was an article in the *Post* a couple of days ago that strongly said you should grant a stay of execution."

"Yes, of course, I know. If I were running for re-election instead of running for the senate, I think commuting her sentence would be a good move. I can sense a change in the wind among voters. No one in the party, not even Floyd, could block my candidacy. The senate's another matter. There's this here billionaire businessman who'd love to be the party's candidate. He is willing to spend a huge part of that billion to get elected. It's only my relationship with Floyd, who as you know sees me as a son, which insures that I'm the candidate. One more time, I've got to suck up to ol' Floyd."

Justin got up and went to a cupboard and did something rarely did while at Lorna's; he took out a bottle of bourbon and poured a reassuringly full portion. "So, at least until I'm through this next election, Floyd's way is my way."

Lorna needed one more bit of information to fill in her understanding of this current "peccadillo."

"Do you think she could be innocent, this Kerry Atwood?"

Justin smiled at her in the way an adult smiles when a child asks, "If you don't have money, why don't you just go to the bank and ask for some?"

"You can't afford to get bogged down in questions like that. It'd drive you out of your mind. There is procedure in place for a fellow to follow. It's the rule for covering your ass. They can fault you, but they can never condemn you for following the rules. Have you ever seen a wide receiver, who knows damn well that the ball touched the ground, argue with the referee who sees it as a fair catch?"

Here Justin became uncomfortable. The note of braggadocio left his voice. "Piper called me after Montgomery made his announcement. She was begging me to grant clemency for the Atwood girl. She'd read about the case in the fuckin' *New York Times*."

"And?" Lorna prompted.

"Well, I told her it couldn't be done. I couldn't interfere with the verdict of the court. She pointed out that

Montgomery had done it, set aside the court's decision. I reminded her that hers was an entirely different matter. There was no premeditation in her case. But she went on and on. I finally told her I had to go."

In her heart, Lorna knew that she too had avoided delving below the surface of the issues made known to her over the years. The direction of further inquiry lay away from the comfortable, secure and important position she enjoyed. Her acceptance of this prompted her next thought.

"I expect it's not too soon to start looking for an apartment in Washington. That will be for six years at least. Do you think I should rent this place or sell it?"

Flora Griggs brought the morning newspaper along with breakfast, and Kerry was pondering the headline, "Colorado Governor Grants Clemency." Brad, when he visited the night before, hadn't mentioned this as a possibility. He had only talked about the "package" he and Professor Meadow had sent Governor Dahl containing the deposition by Jerrod Bush. Kerry dared to let herself think of the favorable mood the news from Colorado could cause in Dahl. Wouldn't you, after another governor had just saved your daughter from execution, have forgiveness in your heart?

She was sure Brad would be coming any minute to

repeat the same sunny speculation with her. She spread jam on a piece of toast. Better get breakfast out of the way before he arrived.

"The bastard lied to me. He said he'd called a press conference for this morning. Now I learn he's canceled the conference and is avoiding my calls as if I'm soliciting money for the ACLU." David laughed ruefully, "He suckered me. Suckered me and all the while I thought I'd been so clever. Unfuckingbelievable!"

"Me, too," Jo said. "I was so focused on getting him to agree, that it never occurred to me that he would just thumb his nose at us." Defeat was in her voice—and awe. "We thought we were dangling bait in front of him and all the time he was setting us up. I feel so badly. I accomplished nothing for that kid in Virginia. I'll never forget that."

"And there's not a damned thing we can do. Any step in the direction of exposing his deception is a step into quicksand. If our "deal" were known, I might well be impeached, which would be worth it if it saved the Atwood girl, but it wouldn't. He would deny everything and step away self-righteously. The Virginians would rally around a leader who is seen as the object of a smear by outsiders."

"Yeah, well, this game isn't over yet," Jo replied. "I agree about your assessment of *your* coming out with an accusation. What if someone else, someone interviewing him for instance, were to do it, Joe Bellino, for instance? What if he surprised Dahl with, 'I have been told you cut a deal with Governor Montgomery of Colorado and then backed out.'"

David laughed with disbelief. "You're totally wild."

"I'm serious."

"So am I," a subdued First Lady said, "OK, got any better ideas?"

"I'm afraid the only leverage that will move him is political. He obviously believes it's to his political advantage to be a 'hanging judge', and to save my . . . or rather to save Kerry Atwood's life, I can't think of an angle that would bring the kind of pressure to bear that he'd feel. Especially in the little time remaining."

They looked at each other in frustrated silence.

"In the meantime, I plan to keep trying to talk to him," David said.

"That's like saying the only way to avoid bankruptcy is to keep playing the lottery."

"Hey, that hurt and I'm on your side."

"I'm sorry. You know I didn't mean . . ." She had gone over to him and embraced him, her head on his shoulder. "I'm just so very sad."

It was early afternoon in Richmond. A waiter from Binny's Bistro on Canal Street was leaving Fletcher Eton's office after having delivered sandwiches.

Eton's secretary brought in a carafe of coffee and left. That morning Eton, who had gradually been forming a closer tie to Clarence Reed, described an unusual tension he'd observed in his boss, equal to the tension he'd displayed when his daughter's life was still in jeopardy. After the Colorado governor had made his announcement Justin had experienced profound relief, but now the tension had returned. Eton speculated that this had something to do with the appeal Justin had received from Kerry Atwood's attorneys. If so, he didn't understand it, because he'd witnessed Justin's calm dealing with past appeals, rejecting them with no alteration of his usual hearty demeanor.

Fletcher knew that Governor Montgomery had been trying to reach Dahl and Dahl had been avoiding the calls. He had a growing hunch the avoided calls and the anxiety he read in Dahl's behavior went together.

Through the open door, Eton heard Barbara, Dahl's secretary, say in her telephone voice, "The governor is in a meeting. If you can hold for a minute, I'll see if the meeting is still going on. OK, I'll check."

The secretary pressed the hold button and came to the door of Eton's office.

"Fletcher, Governor Montgomery of Colorado is on the line. This is about the fifth time he's called today wanting to speak to Justin. Justin said to tell him he's busy and can't talk. Lord, the man knows I'm lying. Lying a little bit is part of my job, but this is becoming embarrassing.

Justin's away having 'lunch.' (The innuendo on "lunch" meaning Lorna's place) What do you advise, Fletcher?"

Eton put the sandwich down and thought about what she'd just said. She prompted, "Do you want to talk to him?"

"Sure, I'll take it." Curiosity led him to agree.

The secretary left, closing the door.

The light of his extension went on and he picked up the phone. "Hello Governor Montgomery, this is Fletcher Eton. I'm Governor Dahl's Executive Assistant. Governor Dahl is still in the meeting. But perhaps I can help you."

David's repeated calls were intended to keep reminding Dahl of his betrayal. He had abandoned the goal of actually being able to talk to and persuade Dahl. With Eton on the line, he came to a quick change of plan.

"Mr. Eton, Governor Dahl and I have an agreement which he has arbitrarily chosen not to honor. I recognize, of course, that the meetings and so forth that have allegedly prevented him from taking my calls are just dodges. I'd appreciate it if you'd tell him that and that I will never forget our agreement. Never."

Whoa, thought Eton. What's this all about? "Never" sounds pretty damned serious.

"What, may I ask Governor, is the agreement you have with Governor Dahl?"

"I'm not at liberty to say. It's between him and me. It is so far, at least. I'd just appreciate your letting him know we talked. OK?"

"Yes sir, I surely will."

"Goodbye, Mr. Eton."

"Goodbye, Governor."

Eton leapt to his feet and opened the office door and looked out. Barbara was not at her desk. She hadn't been listening in to the conversation. He went back to his desk and turned over what he'd just heard. An agreement. To Eton's knowledge, the only thing linking the two men was Piper. Had there been some "agreement" for Montgomery's grant of clemency? An agreement means a deal, a *quid pro quo*. Money? No, Justin would have paid. He always paid his debts. Besides Eton couldn't believe Montgomery would have been so crass. Some kind of favor then. He'd known Justin to dodge and weave—to rationalize—to go back on his word. Then what was the *word* in this case?

The Atwood appeal! Like an anagram appearing in its proper form before his eyes, it came together. Justin had asked him about the voters' attitude about capital punishment. His asking had come at the time of the Atwood appeal and before Montgomery made his announcement.

"Jesus!" he said aloud. "He made a deal, Piper for the Atwood woman." AND, now he's backed down. This explains his sudden change of mind about the press conference to announce his candidacy for senator. Son-of-a-bitch, he promised to announce clemency for Atwood the morning after the other guy made his announcement. He had never intended to announce his candidacy that morning. Eton had thought it strange to suddenly decide to do that without his customary hashing over the subject of timing with Bascomb and himself. Son-of-a-bitch!

The clarity of the business became complete as if he were hearing it dictated to him. All along, Justin had intended to cancel the press conference he, Eton, had been asked to arrange. Having a meeting scheduled made it look to Montgomery as if he were going to keep his part of the bargain. If Montgomery had had any doubt, a check with the Richmond media would have reassured him.

"Son-of-a-bitch!" Fletcher threw the pencil he was holding and hit the opposite wall.

The back corner booth at Binny's was open as he'd hoped. Fletcher gave a waitress his order for a Guinness and headed there. His mouth was dry. He was eager to talk to Clarence. He had always kept the inside information about Dahl as close to his chest as if he was making a nothing-hand bluff with his last thousand in the pot. Without his being consciously aware of it, a shift of allegiance was happening, which little by little had made Clarence Reed a confidant. This change had been brought on by Dahl's tendency over the past weeks to exclude Eton from his intimate thoughts. Eton felt it as a slight and had reflexively looked elsewhere for closeness. Clarence Reed was there on the rebound.

Fletcher saw Reed enter the restaurant and look around. He waved to him. Reed and the waitress with the

Guinness got to the table at the same time.

"I think I need one of those," Clarence said. He sat down and continued, "So what's the news from the throne room?"

The offhand question was too much for Fletcher to resist. "You'll never guess." Sudden doubt followed saying this, since it was so unlike his usual, Teflon-coated manner of deflecting questions about his boss. At the same time, he was conditioned since childhood to follow "You'll never guess" with the telling of a secret. So, with hesitation at first, but with ever-greater freedom, he revealed his brief conversation with David Montgomery and the epiphany that followed it.

"No wonder he hasn't been his old self," Reed commented. "So you think he hoodwinked Montgomery into going ahead with his announcement by scheduling that press conference."

"I know he did in the way a mother knows her baby wants her breast."

Reed grew pensive. He said, barely loud enough for Fletcher to hear, "Hmm. Out to save both his daughter and his candidacy for the senate." He gave a rueful laugh. "Makes you wonder which he would have chosen if he'd had to make a choice, Piper or the senate? And Montgomery is pissed, needless to say."

"I think he'd kill Justin with his bare hands if he could get away with it."

"A friend of mine with the *Post* knows Montgomery

well, went to school with him."

The waitress came with Reed's drink and took their orders.

Eton stared into the middle-distance. "I'll say this for Justin, he isn't feeling proud of this caper, or else he'd be bragging about it."

Reed raised his glass. "Let's give him that."

While they ate, Reed reviewed in his own mind that he'd been right about there being a good story here in Richmond if he had patience. He didn't allow this appraisal to show. He didn't want Eton to realize and feel the magnitude of the story. He instead began telling Fletcher of a movie he'd just seen and wanted to recommend.

Leaving the restaurant, they parted and Clarence continued walking along Canal Street. The full potential of the story was exciting, the ramifications dilating in his mind. Handled correctly, the story had the makings of . . . he tried once but failed to push the words aside—a Pulitzer.

31

Wednesday. The daily calendar on his mother's kitchen counter proclaimed the "word of the day to be, "Blithe. (bli*th*) adj. Lighthearted." No less appropriate word could be found for this particular Wednesday. Monday, tomorrow was the day set for Kerry's transfer to the Waverly prison and Virginia's death row. It had been a very full month since their appeal containing Jerrod's affidavit had been sent to Governor Dahl. Dahl had remained obdurate. To the press, he was presenting himself as someone holding to a difficult but moral course. To Brad, who couldn't understand how Dahl could hold to his position after his own daughter had been spared from execution, he became more of a monster with each passing day. According to a person close to the governor's office, who asked to remain anonymous, Dahl had isolated himself from all except one of his "most respected friends, a state senator."

Brad's pain was constant and deep. He not only suffered the conviction that he was responsible for Kerry's inexpressible ordeal; his mother had begun the terminal phase of her life. She was hanging on, Brad was sure, to be there for him when Kerry died. She was on continuous, strong pain-killing medication, which did seem to control her pain—the one positive element in all this.

One very surprising development had brightened Brad's hope for the governor's clemency. A statement had been made by the assistant district attorney for Henderson County, Dana Rogers, to a group of purposefully assembled reporters. After reassessing the merits of the state's case against Kerry Atwood, she said, she did not believe the evidence presented by the prosecution obviated reasonable doubt. She made it clear that this was her own opinion and did not represent the opinion of the District Attorney's Office. In answer to a reporter's question asking for more detail about why she had come to her conclusion, she cited the prosecution's failure to prove that the money found in Tom Albright's backpack was the same money taken from the victims, and without that proof the state's case was "not sufficiently compelling."

The impact of this bold statement did not, oddly or maybe not so oddly, alter Justin Dahl's position. It did, however, as she'd probably known it would, stir up speculation about the future of her career. Rumor had it that she would be fired as soon as the dust settled after the execution. Fitz Halloran was busy making "What a crazy bitch!" faces to all the people who counted.

Brad looked into his mother's room. She slept peacefully. May Rutledge dozed in a chair, her hands still holding knitting needles. Brad stood for a moment watching his mother's shallow breathing. He tried to absorb the very movement of her chest. What would life be like when it stopped?

He had come to tell his mother he was going to the jail and to ask her if she had a message for Kerry. She always had a message.

Deputy Griggs saw Brad enter the waiting room and got up from his chair and opened the door to the secure area. The normal procedure, including a walk through the metal detector had been dispensed with some time ago. He called the cell block to have Kerry brought up front, while Brad signed in.

It occurred to Brad, at that moment, how easy it would be to wait until Kerry, long unshackled now, was brought to the interview rooms and the guard had returned to the jail, to overpower Griggs and make an escape. The idea excited him for a moment, until he confronted the inevitability of being caught. Still, what did it matter if they were killed trying to escape since she was going to die anyway. At least they'd be doing something and doing it together. Just as suddenly, he thought of his mother and knew he could never do this to her, the terror it would cause and her grief if he were killed.

Kerry looked over his way as she and the guard passed the doorway. He threw a "Thank you" toward Sam Griggs and followed her.

He expected her certain disappointment with him to show on her face. It didn't. She was sober, but still capable of humor.

"Do you think the governor is holding out for a

bigger bribe? Can't we convince him I'm not the Atwood who owns all those race horses?"

Brad managed a bitter chuckle. Silence came between them like a third party.

"Everything here OK?" Brad asked knowing it was dumb.

"Sure," Kerry answered with a straight face to help him out. "Flora Griggs is a sweetheart. Yesterday they put a woman who'd stabbed another woman in the leg in a bar fight in the cell across from mine. She began baiting me when she learned who I was. I figured she needed to find someone she could look down on. Flora heard her and yanked her out and moved her to the end of the hall. I heard Flora talk to her in a menacing tone. Didn't know what she said, but the lady shut up."

Brad was finding it impossible to find the way to a normal conversation—whatever that was in this situation. His tension mounted to an unbearable level and he began to pace.

Kerry plunged ahead. "Tomorrow, as you know, they are moving me to the Waverly facility where they do their dirty work. See if I can take Flora with me." With a worried smile she went on, "Cheer up, it makes it easier. It will be hard, but it will come to an . . ." She realized the bad choice of words. "I mean . . .well you know. Remember those dreaded exams, or the solo you had to sing in front of the whole school. You knew there was no way out, but somehow you got through it."

She was thinking of Brad's wait and his "getting through it." She wouldn't come out on the other side of this experience. The mood flattened to a deep solemnity. She made her voice take on a business-like tone.

"Look, I want you to know I'm fully aware that I pushed you into this, when your better judgment told you to stay clear. I'm the one who brought on this horrible situation you're in. I need you to know that I sincerely . . ." She made Brad meet her eyes and hear her. " . . . sincerely believe you and Doctor Meadow presented an excellent defense. You made a solid case for their lack of proof. The assistant prosecutor has admitted this was so. It was not your fault that the jurors were moved by Halloran's appeal to their fears and prejudices . . . and that they couldn't believe Tom's having the money was a mere coincidence."

"Since that verdict, we've entered another dimension haven't we, the dimension of politics." She shook her head slowly in puzzlement. "One tends to give it no thought until one finds oneself in my place, but the American legal system sucks. If you say that, you'd be quick to hear, 'Yes, it's imperfect, but it works most of the time and anyway it's the best there is.' That seems to satisfy everyone. We nod in wise agreement. I say it sucks. The belief in the jury's wisdom and open-mindedness sucks. The power given to the judges sucks. The advocate system sucks. Party politics sucks most of all."

The silence following her diatribe was as impenetrable as a concrete wall. Kerry vaulted over it.

"Hey, I got that off my chest. How's your mother today?"

Brad respected Kerry's wish to move on. "She was asleep when I left. She's hanging in there. Feeling less pain, actually."

"I love her. I feel like she's *my* Mom."

He could barely get the words past his emotions, tears filling his eyes. "She thinks of you in the same way."

"Strange isn't it, that you can have such strong feelings toward someone you haven't met."

Brad reached across the table and took her hand. His effort to maintain the proper professional distance had ceased. They were now only two desperately unhappy people and at the same time two people feeling the best possible human emotion.

"Kerry, I love you."

"I know. I love you, too."

They rose from their chairs at the same moment and immediately became locked in an embrace. They kissed hungrily. Their tears flowed and the kisses tasted of salt.

Sam Griggs made some loud banging sounds in the outer area. He must have come and observed them through the door's window, and while not intruding directly—hadn't had to contend with a lawyer and client kissing before—he decided it required some action on his part.

The two became aware of Griggs's problem and reluctantly parted, laughing.

Brad's heart was surging, enthralled by his feelings

of love. He could not, would not tolerate an end to it. He was suddenly impatient to be on his way to action that would insure its continuance. What that was, he had no idea. He only knew it must be. Another kiss and he flew out of the building. He was half way home when he faced the question soberly. He would go to the President! The final resource, the caring parent. He'd start by calling Meadow. Maybe he knew someone who had the President's ear.

Coming into the kitchen he went straight to the phone and called the professor. Meadow answered and listened. He heard the joy in Brad's voice and wondered at it. The current reality couldn't explain it, and then he guessed. He'd known of Brad's feeling for Kerry from the outset, since that hot summer day when Brad brought his problem into Meadow's backyard.

"Have you talked to Kerry today?" he asked.

"Yes, I was just there. When I left her it came to me that we should appeal to the President. Dahl would listen to him. I was wondering if you knew anyone close enough to him."

Meadow took a deep breath. He felt like a surgeon who had to tell hopeful relatives that their loved one had died on the table.

"Brad, it's a good thought. As a matter of fact I thought of it myself and I made some inquiries. I wasn't going to say anything unless I got positive feedback. The short tale is that the President passed on it, or rather one of his advisors passed on it. As I heard it, he considered the value it would have politically to please the liberal sector, but the deciding factor, my contact informed me, is that the European press has been especially critical of the President's foreign policy and the advisor doesn't want the White House to appear to be influenced by their criticism."

"You're telling me that because of a concern about appearances this person's willing to let Kerry die? That's absurd," Brad screamed into the phone.

"But, wait. You said this was only a lackey, not the President."

"Right, but this man is not acting on his own. He represents the administration's position."

"OK, then it's back to the Governor Dahl. I have this feeling that if . . . "

"Brad. Brad. Don't make me be the voice of doom, but if the White House feels strongly enough that it's good politics at present to appear to be deaf to Europe, don't you think Dahl is aware of that. They belong to the same party, after all. If there's one thing I'm sure of it's that Justin Dahl is very politically savvy."

"Ernest, I'm not going to let them kill her."

Frank Waldrum cleared the dinner dishes, while his wife, Beth, rinsed them and put them in the dishwasher. They were looking forward to watching a **DVD** from Netflix, a Hitchcock classic starring Cary Grant and Grace Kelly that they hadn't seen since they were in high school.

Frank, in the living room to set things up for the film, heard the phone ring in the kitchen and then heard Beth talking. He let her answer these days if possible, because he was having increasing difficulty hearing over the phone. Beth came to the living room door and said the call was from his department's answering service.

"I'm not on call. What are they doing calling me?" he said not so much with annoyance at being disturbed as miffed by the failure to follow protocol.

"This is Frank Waldrum."

"I'm sorry to have to call you at home at this hour, sir, but the caller—he said his name is Homer Sheffield— wants to talk to you and no one else. He said his son is a deputy sheriff, who has something to tell you. "

"A deputy sheriff named Sheffield? Don't know him. I'll be pis . . . uh, unhappy, if this is some kind of joke. OK, give me his number."

The phone was answered on the first ring by a man who claimed his son wanted to confess his part in a "wrong doing." When Frank tried to interrupt, saying that the correct procedure was to take his problem to the sheriff, the guy said he would only talk to Frank, the Springville County District Attorney, because he didn't trust anyone in the Sheriff's Department. And, he and his son would only talk to him in person and that there must also be a witness present.

The man's voice, while tense, was level and dead serious. Nevertheless, what he was saying sounded to Frank like paranoia.

"Very well, why don't the two of you come to my office first thing in the morning, nine o'clock. I'll make sure there is a witness." Frank was thinking maybe two or three witnesses with restraints.

"That's not good enough. This is an urgent matter. It can't be put off, and I also know what it's like getting involved with a bureaucracy, secretaries deposit you in a waiting room and by the time anyone pays attention to the fact that you're there, the person you came to see has gone to lunch. No thanks! It's got to be now. We'll meet you at your office in an hour. And no one from the Sheriff's Department is to be there. Just my son and I and you and the witness. The witness can be a two hundred and fifty pound karate expert armed to the teeth if you'd feel better. OK?"

"OK, I'll be there, or rather we'll be there." Oddly, the guy suggesting he bring someone along for protection made the whole business more rational.

Frank immediately called Jim Carpenter, his assistant. Carpenter's wife redirected Frank to a local fitness center.

"Jimbo, a really weird thing has come up. I've got to meet a guy and his son at my office in an hour and I'd like to pick you up to come with me. Is your son Rob at the gym with you? Good . Invite him along. I'll tell you all about it when I pick you up."

When they got to the County Building, two men, father and son, were waiting for them.

Waldrum and the two Carpenters, both in warm-up clothes and physically imposing, approached with a wary attitude.

The elder Sheffield took this in at a glance, but didn't appear to be concerned.

The five men entered the building and after signing in with the night watchman, took the elevator to the DA's office. It was only then that anyone said anything beyond a grunt.

"Mr. Waldrum, thanks for seeing us. I think when you've heard what my son, Lonnie, has to say, you'll know why I called you the way I did." He looked at his son. "Lonnie here came to me this evening to ask my advice about what to do. He's been keeping a real bad secret since last summer . . . well, I'll let him tell you. I wanted him to tell someone outside the Sheriff's Office, 'cause they might think first 'bout saving their own hides."

The young man, dressed in jeans and a sweatshirt, uneasily shifted his eyes from his father to the other men. Lonnie Sheffield began to talk, but his mouth was so dry and his throat so constricted that only a reedy croak came out. He cleared his throat and began again. He had thought of telling this tale so many times that he had a script in his head. Now, with three stern men facing him, he forgot how it went.

"I know what we done was wrong. I should never have went along with Woody, but he was my teacher and I thought I had to do what he said. I know better now—I know him better now— and wouldn't do it now."

Waldrum heard the guilt-ridden preamble of a young man finding himself way off base for the first time in his life.

"What is it, son? What was it you and Woody did?"

Lonnie took a deep breath, his well-rehearsed script coming back to him. "I had only been on the force two weeks last July when the Tullochs were reported missing. Sheriff Royston had us spread out searching the county the next morning. I'd been assigned to be Woody Youngblood's partner for my first month and we were given the eastern border from the city up to Sweet Springs. Well, we drove down Hooper's Creek Road, intending to go as far as the bridge, the Virginia state line, and then turn around. We saw the Tulloch car, a new Mercury, parked about twenty yards above the bridge—the West Virginia side of the bridge. We parked and investigated." He shrugged and in a barely audible voice said, "We found them all cut up . . . blood everywhere. I went back to our patrol car and was going to call in to headquarters when Woody said to wait. He said he'd figured out that if we moved the car to the other side of the bridge into Virginia, the killer, when he was caught, would get the death penalty—get what he deserved. He also said we'd be saving our state a lot of money, cause we'd have to pay for him to be in jail for years."

Lonnie had gotten it out. He studied the faces looking at him to judge their reactions. He saw three poker faces.

"I said it was wrong, really I did, but Woody made me feel like I was . . . like I was a stupid kid if I didn't go along."

"What happened next?" Waldrum asked.

"Woody released the brake on the Mercury and let it coast across the bridge. The I guided Woody as he drove our car right over the Mercury's tire tracks and then we washed away the tracks that we needed to with water from the creek." He shrugged. "Then we called in."

"Why didn't you come forward sooner?" Jim Carpenter asked angrily.

"I don't know. At first I was thinking like Woody, and then, when I faced the truth, that it was wrong, I just got plumb afraid. With that woman going to be executed, I had to talk."

"Did you tell Woody you were going to talk to your father?" asked Waldrum.

"No sir."

"We need a sworn statement from you." He turned to Carpenter. "Jim, let's hit Youngblood hard: arrest warrant, interrogation setup, the works."

"My pleasure."

Waldrum didn't want to exonerate Lonnie just because he had confessed. After all, he might not have done so if he hadn't had a sympathetic father to talk to. At the same time, he didn't want to say anything that would make the father regret he'd brought his son in.

"As you admit, son, you did a very wrong thing, but thank God for everyone you went to your father in time."

Appropriate is an adjective that all who knew Brad Collins would agree described him well. Maybe not perfectly behaved, but well within the standards of his group. Even though devastated by his failure to protect Kerry, those who knew him well had no doubt that in spite of his great pain, he would steer a steady, appropriate course through the coming months and emerge in a few short years a changed, but competent and successful attorney living a normal life with a normal family. He should get out of the car he had just parked at the door of the County Jail, go in and console Kerry once again this evening and then make the regular drive to Waverly to visit her until the very end. That, however, was not the way he had it planned.

There can come a point in a person's life when accumulating events catapult him or her into a new self and world-view, a new and altered reality. The always stable and self-satisfied acquaintance we have known for years can suddenly become so sure of his or her worthlessness that no course seems open but suicide. Similarly, a new and dominating reality had taken possession of Brad's thinking. All other values were forced aside. He now couldn't—wouldn't—live without Kerry!

Earlier in the evening he had noted how much Griggs had relaxed the rules. Later, sitting at the kitchen table at home, he obstinately decided it was impossible to docilely allow the system to kill the woman he loved. These two thoughts merged: Kerry must escape! Earlier he had rejected the idea of escape out of fear of the effect it would have on his mother. Now, it must happen regardless. The only chance for this to be successful was to take action before she was transferred to the maximum-security prison at Waverly. It had to be tonight! He got paper and wrote his mother a note, telling her not to worry, he had a good plan and would contact her as soon as he was able to and in the meantime she should not talk to the police about anything. He quietly entered her room where she was asleep and put the note on her pillow next to her head. He stopped outside the guest room door and listened for a moment for the sound of May Rutledge snoring. Fortunately, she had now come to stay at the house full time.

Brad went to the garage, where his mother's '94 Cadillac Coupe de Ville was parked unused since his father died twelve years ago. First he lifted the hood and checked the engine oil. It measured up to the mark all right, but he had his doubts about its lubricating properties after all this time. He knew the gas tank was empty; several years ago, knowing the car was not going to be driven, he'd siphoned out the gas and then run the engine until it stopped as a mechanic had advised him in order to avoid ending up with a tank of stale gas that might never start. He now poured an almost full two-gallon can of gasoline for the lawn mower into the Caddie's tank. After moving lawn chairs, the lawn mower and flower pots to the back wall to make room, he drove his Honda Civic into the garage beside the Caddie and attached the jumper- cable he kept in the Honda's trunk between the cars' batteries. Now came a critical moment in his plan. Four times he turned the key in his mother's car and let the starter grind through several revolutions of the old engine without the hint of a start. Brad's heart sank. On the fifth attempt the engine gave a cough, and then on the sixth try it put its coughs together into a steady roar. Brad was as elated with the sound as he had been when he'd been given permission to borrow the Caddie for his high school prom.

Brad's father, a very practical do-it yourself type, had bought a heavy-duty air compressor that over the years had served to inflate footballs, rubber rafts, sleeping bags and bike and car tires. All of the Caddie's tires were slack. Brad had re-inflated them from time to time over the years to keep them from going completely flat and had found them to hold air well for months at a stretch. He started up the compressor and brought the tires up to pressure. Buoyed by his success so far, he hurried into the next task, switching the old and potentially attention-getting plates on the Cadillac with those on May's car, which was parked in the parking area at the side of the house.

He went back into the house to get the duffle he'd

packed with clothes and items collected from the kitchen: bread, cheese, apples, cereal and a two liter bottle of Coke, and put them in the Cadillac. Next he replaced the Cadillac's battery with his own, and then jump started the Honda. Driving his Honda, he went to his bank's ATM and took out the maximum withdrawal. After this he went to a gas station where he was known, filled the tank and went inside to pay, drawing attention to himself by acting nervous and rushed. The Honda was then driven to the mall near his home where he parked and locked it. It was a thirty-five minute walk back to his house, giving him time to go over the details of his plan again. Once home, he started the Cadillac and backed out of the garage and onto the street. Here he paused and looked toward his house. This could well be the last time he'd see it or his mother. He broke away from the wave of sadness and refocused on the immediate future. He shifted the Caddie into drive.

At the mall near the jail, was a large gas station with several rows of pumps. He filled the tank at the pump farthest from the office/convenience store, and paid with his mother's credit card. He was ready for the last phase of his escape with Kerry. Everything had so far gone smoothly. The only disconcerting element: driving the large car felt like he was driving his living room.

He knew that once he arrived at the County Jail things would move very fast. The plan was simple. He was going to ask to see Kerry again. He was sure, knowing that she was being taken the next day to the execution site at

Waverly, Deputy Griggs would allow the extra visit. When Kerry came to the front and the guard had returned to the cells, he would overpower Griggs, first using the pepper spray that had been in his car's glove box for a few years, origin no longer remembered. He would tie Griggs up with the length of cord he'd brought with him and was now stuffed in his back pocket. The moment the escape was discovered, the police would go to his home, where he hoped his mother would first notice and read his note before talking to them. After this, they would put out a bulletin on his car, which would not be discovered in the mall lot until at least after closing time when the cars parked there thinned out. By that time he hoped he would be across the North Carolina border. He planned to drive along the winding, scenic Blue Ridge Parkway, which had a low speed limit and not the road one would expect an escaped felon to take. In Asheville, he would seek out a car-filled lot where, unobserved, he could swipe a Carolina plate to replace the Virginia plate. His final destination was the Mexican town of Pozos in the state of Guanajuato; there one of his best friends lived and painted. A mining camp in colonial times, it was now an abandoned relic where a few artists worked in quiet isolation. The details of crossing the border hadn't been worked out. Maybe they'd do a reverse wetback and wade across the Rio Grande. The other detail he hadn't considered was whether Kerry was willing to go along with all this, but what other choice did she have?

Brad parked the car next to the entrance door and left the engine running. The waiting room had to be empty if his plan was to work. He walked in and looked all around. Thank God. Without realizing it he'd been holding his breath. He let it out and took in a lungful of air before he shifted his attention to the glass barrier wall behind which Deputy Griggs sat. Griggs looked up and saw him and raised his hand in greeting.

Brad walked up to the glass and said, "Hi, Sam." His voice sounded strange to him, as if he were forcing the sound through a wooden larynx. He had to relax or Griggs would sense danger.

"Sam, I got so emotionally overwrought when I was here earlier that I completely forgot to tell Kerry something I'd like her to know. I'd like to see her again." That sounded better.

"Sure, Brad, I understand."

"Thanks. This will . . . uh, be the last time. You've been very helpful."

"No need to thank me. I'm just very sorry . . . that's all."

Griggs picked up the phone and talked to the cell unit asking to have Kerry brought to the interview area.

Brad saw Kerry coming along the hall and put his hand in his pocket, rolling the pepper spray cartridge over so his finger fit onto the trigger release. The guard put Kerry into the room across the hall from where Brad stood and began walking back toward the cells. Brad waited until he heard the door close behind the guard. Now was the moment!

The phone rang and Griggs turned to answer it. He had turned his back, making it easy for Brad to bring the small canister out of his pocket. As soon as Griggs turned back around so the spray would hit him in the face . . .

"Yes sir, I'll do that. Her lawyer is standing right here. Do you want to talk to him? OK, I understand."

Shit! Brad thought, what's going on?

Griggs turned around. Brad hesitated.

"That was Sheriff Prentis. He said there has been a development and Miss Atwood is not going to be transferred to Waverly tomorrow. He didn't say what, but he said something has come up in Springville, West Virginia."

Brad was so focused on the escape that he could only hear this as an immediate dilemma. Shouldn't he proceed with the plan? It was now or never. But, Griggs seemed to be elated. He hadn't noticed anything in Brad's hand and Brad moved the hand behind his back.

"Don't you realize what this means? It means there's a delay. Prentis said 'everything is on hold.'"

Brad wasn't interested in a delay. "On hold?"

Griggs was frustrated. Brad wasn't getting the significance. "You see there was this thing about his voice, the sheriff's voice. I mean like some really big thing has happened."

"I've got to know what this is about. I'd like to use your phone."

"Sure." He turned from Brad and Brad returned the pepper spray tube to his pocket.

"Do you have the district attorney's number?"

"No. I don't," Griggs lied.

"OK, tell me the sheriff's number."

"I can't do that, Brad. Not allowed to give out numbers."

"Come on, for Christ sake, Sam. This is important."

Griggs looked unhappy. "Sorry. Got in trouble before."

"May I see the phone book?"

Griggs took it out of a desk drawer and put it on the desk.

"Please tell Kerry I'll be a minute, Sam."

Brad looked for and didn't find a number for Fitz Halloran. Must be unlisted. Same for Jerome Prentis. Then Halloran's assistant came to mind, the person he and Meadow had speculated was their "Deep Throat." What was, oh yeah, Dana Rogers. Her name was in the book and he dialed it.

"Hello."

"Is this Dana Rogers?"

"Yes."

"This is Brad Collins, I'm . . ."

"I know. I just left a message on the answering machine at your home. Have you heard the news?"

"I heard the transfer to Waverly was cancelled for tomorrow. Something about Springville, West Virginia."

"That's all you know?"

"Yes." Irritation had entered Brad's voice.

"Oh happy day! I'm the one who gets to tell you! I got my information from another source and called Fitz Halloran to confirm it. I asked if he had called you and he told me he wanted more information and would wait until tomorrow. I told him you should know immediately. He said he was waiting. Hell, that doesn't mean I gotta wait, so I called you and left the message. Lord, you still don't know. Kerry is free! The trial and verdict is null and void!"

"Null and void?" Brad was reeling. He wanted to believe what he'd just heard, but how could the trial be null and void? What was this shit?

Dana sensed his total confusion and hurried to explain in detail what had happened.

"So you see," she summarized, "It was discovered that the murders took place in West Virginia. That, of course, means Virginia does not have jurisdiction. Probably just as important is the fact that it wasn't in the National Forest either, so the jurisdiction belongs solely with West Virginia. There is a question of whether or not West Virginia will seek extradition, but my money says it won't happen, because the case against your client is very weak. I know you must be cautious after what you've been through, but trust me, you can rejoice."

Brad let this good news flow over him like a warm, soaking summer rain.

"Incidentally," Dana continued, "I have personally called the warden at Waverly to tell him about this. And I sent a registered letter to the Governor. There'll be no fuckups!"

Who was this woman? She came on like a Bradley tank. It was clear whose side she was on. Hallelujah! Brad told Dana he was at the jail and needed to tell Kerry.

"I can't tell you how much I appreciate . . ."

"Get along and tell your client."

Brad burst into the interview room, swept Kerry out of her chair and began kissing her. Deputy Griggs, standing in the hallway, drank it in.

"Kerry, it's all over! No execution, no jail. Never!"

Kisses, hugs, explanations all mixed together. Finally Griggs told Brad that he probably should go. Brad promised to keep Kerry apprised of the situation tomorrow. He'd have so much to do, maybe a trip to Springville, maybe to Richmond.

When he got outside after shaking Griggs's hand until it hurt, he was surprised to see his mother's car standing there. Why was the engine running?

32

War, sports, business and politics: the object of each is winning. Clarence Reed was in a contemplative frame of mind. The unique combination of forced non-participation plus his inclusion in Justin Dahl's inner circle provided the ingredients for detached analysis. Dahl had called a morning meeting. Ham Bascomb arrived at the same time as Fletcher Eton and Reed. As the three went into Dahl's office, Bascomb cast a look of doubt in Reed's direction, but let it pass.

The topic this morning was the question of the governor's response in the light of a stunning revelation in the case of Kerry Atwood. Dahl opened the meeting with a declaration that he had planned to commute the woman's death sentence this very day and had scheduled a press conference for that purpose. His tone of voice, however, carried a wink. Bascomb smiled and nodded. He went on as if he were at a press conference, saying he had waited until now, because he had been deeply engaged in reviewing the transcript of the trial. He had come to the conclusion that the evidence was not strong enough to warrant the ultimate punishment.

This statement and its cynical delivery shocked

Clarence Reed. He thought he'd heard everything. His thoughts, then, matched the governor's cynicism. In sports, he mused, the way you won mattered if the referee was looking. In war, the way you waged your campaign became accountable only if you lost. In business, the way you won mattered if you were audited. In politics, the way to victory was irrelevant as long as you didn't embarrass your party.

"I'm going to tell you something personal," Dahl confided, "What really tipped the balance in my decision to commute this woman's sentence was a phone call I got from my daughter begging me to do it. She said she couldn't stand to think that this other person was going to die when she had been mercifully spared."

Reed was astonished to the point of amusement. He had an urge to ask more about the alleged phone call, but maintained, instead, the role of fly on the wall. The amazing thing to Reed was the way that, what only a moment before had been Dahl's announcement of the cold-blooded lie to be handed to the press, had become a myth of his daughter's intervention, which it appeared Dahl really believed. An angel came down from heaven and whispered into his ear.

"Justin," said Bascomb firmly, "We need to release the commutation thing immediately, and we need to have you on camera for the noon newscast, but the part about Piper's call we should . . . ah, keep that to ourselves."

Clarence understood Bascomb's wish to have Dahl on camera. What the three had just heard him say with

411

a cynical wink was not what the viewer would see and hear. He or she would be watching a compassionate head of state claim he had already decided to grant clemency when the news arrived from West Virginia. The fact that the case should never have been tried in a Virginia court would be overlooked. Justin Dahl would profit politically. The anti-capital punishment sector, not being able to rule out the possibility that Dahl really had planned to change the sentence, would experience a Dahl-positive moment. Those of the opposite stripe, having wanted the woman to die would be feeling a little chagrin right now and welcome the opportunity to think they had backed an omniscient governor.

Dahl and Bascomb, their heads together, began drafting the press release. Fletcher was on the phone arranging for TV coverage. It occurred to Reed that something else was about to happen in Virginia politics. State Senator Floyd Cummins, whom everyone equated with an unequivocal demand for the death sentence, was about to be marginalized. Party leadership was about to pass to Justin Dahl with the next news broadcast.

The call came through on his private extension, meaning it was either the switchboard or someone to whom he'd given the number.

"Bellino here."

"Tony, it's Clarence Reed. How are you?"

"Clarence! Good to hear your voice. What's up?"

"I'm working on a story . . . more than that a helluva story. I need some information and I believe you may be my man."

"Really, tell me more."

"My story, right?" Clarence said laughing.

"It's that good?"

"Here it is." Reed talked and Bellino listened without interruption.

"You're right about it being a helluva story. You'll have a problem backing it up, but I know you'll work that out. How can I help?"

"Governor Montgomery; I think he's a friend of yours if I remember correctly, college roommate or something."

"Good memory. David and his wife, Jo, and I were at Michigan together, and shoulder to shoulder in all of the good liberal causes of the day." He laughed, "Marching and toking side by side. Relevant to what I see your interests are at the moment, they were both absolutely against the death penalty. I was troubled when I thought they'd abandoned their stand in order to get David elected governor. David's setting aside the execution of Dahl's daughter showed me it was needless worry. If what you're telling me is true, that David also tried to cut a deal to protect Atwood, it makes me proud of my old friend." He had an alarming thought. "Clarence, these are good people, who

413

have a goal to accomplish good things in Colorado. If this story broke, it could hurt them a lot politically."

"Didn't he take that chance when he attempted to make the deal with Dahl?"

"Sure, but he probably figured he was only dealing with Dahl, and Dahl had his own reason to keep it secret. You can bet David never thought you'd learn about it."

Reed's voice took on a harder tone. "Are you telling me I shouldn't write the story?"

Bellino knew there was nothing he could do. "No. I can't . . . won't tell you that. You'll have to resolve that issue yourself." He lightened the mood. "We need to get together, Clarence; it's been too long."

Tony had been checking the *Times* online everyday, anticipating Reed's article. And here it was, **"Sorry Governor, We Don't Buy It,"** with Reed's byline.

He began to read with dread.

"Last Saturday Virginia Governor Justin Dahl treated all of us to a virtuoso performance. The night before, it was dramatically revealed that the killing for which Kerry Atwood was being tried had actually occurred in West Virginia, giving that state jurisdiction and voiding the trial and death sentence she had received in Virginia.

Even before this, the nation's civil rights

organizations had strongly protested the verdict and sentence, citing lack of evidence. Governor Dahl ignored their arguments when time came to consider an appeal made to him for clemency, preferring instead to court the pro-death penalty contingent of his party, whose support he needed in his bid to be the nominee for the U.S. Senate in the next election. Among those who pleaded to save Ms. Atwood's life was Governor Montgomery of Colorado, the man who had recently granted a commutation of the death sentence of Governor Dahl's own daughter.

The stellar performance referred to earlier was Dahl's claim on Saturday morning, the morning after the jurisdictional error was discovered, that he had intended to commute Ms. Atwood's sentence that very day, saying that he had instructed his executive assistant the night before to call a press meeting for that purpose the next morning. He claims he took that action before he was informed of the unexpected development in the case. He also says he is "overjoyed" by the news, because of his strong doubt about Ms. Atwood's guilt .

Now the facts: I made extensive inquires and found no one who knew of any intention Governor Dahl had of commuting the sentence before the mistake concerning jurisdiction was discovered.

The executive assistant was not told before the discovery to gather the press. Also, several sources told me the governor had readily voiced his opinion that the young woman was guilty up until the moment he was informed that he no longer had a prisoner to execute. One person heard this from him only two hours before the startling news reached the governor's office.

You made your choice to allow the execution of Kerry Atwood, Governor, and it was wrong. Go down with your ship. It is embarrassing to see a man try to run the winning colors up the mast and sail into the harbor with the victors."

Bellino closed the *Times* site, thinking, "You're a good man, Clarence Reed."

"Roy, I need your help. I've got to make a decision and I hope to God I make the right one."

Claude Waldrum, the district attorney of Springville County, had known Sheriff Roy Royston since grade school and in Waldrum's opinion Roy was a decent man, who seriously applied himself to his job every day, maintaining discipline and morale among his deputies. Waldrum had to decide whether he was going to charge Kerry Atwood with the murder of Mr. and Mrs. Tulloch, now that she was being released from custody in Henderson. The deposition made by the Texan, which Atwood's attorney had rushed over to him along with the trial's transcript describing the young couple he'd given a ride, supported the contention of the defense that the two were merely on a camping trip. The whole case, as Waldrum sized it up, came down to the question about the two sets of money.

"Roy, I want you to know that this conversation is confidential. Just between us. I looked over the transcript of your testimony. Roy, I'd like you to forget all that and describe to me, one old friend to another, what you know about that money that Ben Tulloch got from Judy Fenton."

Royston had always liked Claude. He'd stood in line next to him when they'd had their physicals for the draft. He remembered how he'd lied to the doctor when describing the severity of his asthma symptoms and had confessed this to Claude at the time, who'd replied, "I wish I'd thought of that. But don't kid yourself, they don't go by what you tell them"—and they didn't.

Royston began to repeat what he'd said in the trial, but then he stopped, his voice becoming tightened and he broke down and began to cry. He got control quickly.

"Sorry. I don't know where that came from."

"I believe there's something you'd like to get off your chest, old friend. There's only the two of us here, Roy."

"Claude, that Virginia DA, Halloran, put words in my mouth. Now don't get me wrong, I'm not saying it was all his fault, but he sort of bent what I told him and before

I knew it I was going along with him . . . and then it became too late to change my story; we were into the trial and I had testified. Her lawyer put it straight to me and I couldn't . . ."

He searched Waldrum's face for a sign of disgust.

Waldrum saw that there was need here for reassurance. "It can happen all too easily in court, taking sides. Many has been the time that I've seen a witness manipulated by an attorney into making a statement he or she didn't wholly believe, but one he or she became wedded to once it had been said." He looked directly and steadily into Royston's eyes. "What did that DA push you to say, Roy?"

"I've been over this so many times in my mind." Suddenly he blurted, "Damn it, Claude, it won't do for me to tell you and then have you say it wasn't so bad." He was almost shouting. "It couldn't be worse, man! I was about to let that woman be killed and it would have been because of me. I couldn't bring myself to say anything. I'm a goddamned coward. I'm an evil person and I don't want you to say dif . . ." He began to sob convulsively.

Claude Waldrum had just made up his mind about Kerry Atwood. He saw that he had two tasks at hand, to begin looking for the real killers, a difficult one considering the cold trail, and the immediate task of putting his friend together again.

"Roy, are you listening to me?" He waited until Royston got control and nodded. "None of us are perfect. Things happen we don't expect and we discover ourselves reacting in ways we never suspected. Believing otherwise is pure fiction. It's bullshit. Sometimes when we get overwhelmed like that we end up looking good, like we knew what we were doing. Other times it comes out pretty bad. The decent people are the ones who straighten things out when they've had a chance to think it over—make good on their debts. You got lucky, Roy. You're still have a chance to make it right."

Royston got up from the chair. He had complete control now.

"Here it is short and simple. Judy Fenton told me Ben Tulloch asked her for brand new bills, ones fresh from the printer. She said she would have to go back to the vault and get them and Ben told her not to bother, but to give him the newest ones she had in her cash drawer. Said he was in a hurry. Judy told me she did that and most of the bills she ended up giving him were crisp and new. The money found in the guy's backpack didn't fit her description."

"Thanks, Roy."

A week later, Roy Royston announced his resignation as Springville County Sheriff, taking an early retirement. The reason given was his wish to join his brother in running the family turkey farm up near Sweet Springs.

The last time he made the trip to Denver, he had an article to research about the long-term effects that violence causes in a community. He had taken the time then to visit David and Jo. He had come this time just to see them. He was pleased when it was the maid who answered the door. He gave her a package and some instructions.

Half an hour later the three friends were sitting around the patio table on this pleasant, spring day. Tony Bellino looked up at the sky. It seemed bluer than last time.

Jo watched him. "We're working on it," she said.

"They say that Rome wasn't built in a day," David added. "But, come to think of it, maybe their senate was dragging its feet too."

Abruptly Bellino changed direction. "Guys, I came all the way out here to tell you that I'm proud to be a friend of yours. I learned from a colleague, Clarence Reed, about the deal you tried to work with Justin Dahl."

A startled look passed between the Montgomerys.

"Don't worry, no one will know."

Tony explained how Reed had listened to Fletcher Eton's deductions about Dahl, which led in turn to Reed's *Times* article and the reason it didn't mention any deal.

"You've got 'class', my friends," Tony said.

The two moved uneasily with embarrassment.

"I read the article aloud to David. It felt good after our frustration with that bastard, Dahl."

"Yes, I bet it did. In spite of it, you may have noticed, old Justin got his party's nomination for the senate seat and will probably win it."

"I'm sure you realize that the complete story Clarence might have written may have won him every journalist's dream."

"You mean a Pulitzer. Yes, I can see that now," David said.

"Don't worry, he'll get one before he quits, but I'm certain nothing can replace the good feelings he had about himself for deciding to write it as he did."

"Not even a Pulitzer?" prodded Jo.

Tony laughed. "We'll never know."

"OK now, I've got to tell you one part of what you did that made me unhappy." It was a sober look he gave each of them.

"Oh, oh, now what? I see and hear my father."

"Your motive couldn't have been for a better cause, but how could you allow poor Piper Dahl to suffer, thinking she was going to be executed, while you negotiated with her father for Kerry Atwood's life?"

"Oh, is that all?" David said ironically.

Jo was nodding. "Of course, that would have been cruel, Tony. The first thing we did after she was found guilty and the death sentence was handed down was for me to go to the prison and lay it all out for Piper. I told her David would commute the sentence no matter what happened with an appeal and our supreme court. I asked her to not say anything to anyone and especially not her father until David actually made the public announcement of the commutation.

In the event that the supreme decided against the sentence, no one would have to know what David's intention had been. She understood this was important to him politically. At that time, the plan to try to make a deal with her father was only beginning to germinate in my mind. Piper was and has remained a real brick. She's kept our secret."

"Well, I'll be damned," Tony murmured.

"Jo had already prepared for that visit before the verdict came down, getting fake ID showing she was a U of C professor named . . . " he looked over at Jo.

"Aldridge. Dr. Aldridge, who also had to go and buy a wig."

The maid came in carrying a tray holding three Champagne glasses and the bottle of Krug Grande Cuvee' Tony had handed her at the front door.

Tony pulled the cork and poured. He held up his glass. "Good friends and good times."

.

33

Earth knows nothing more lovely than a sunny spring day in southern Virginia. Joy is the name of that mixture of scents from the warming soil, the flowering trees and the soft air lapping down from the Appalachians. This particular May Saturday afternoon was a model. The Collins's home had seen hurried comings and goings all morning as preparations proceeded for the four o'clock wedding. Now, everyone involved was inside awaiting the arrival of Judge Raiford Spruell, an old friend of Brad's uncle, who Mary Collins had insisted be the one to lead Brad and Kerry through their vows.

May Rutledge and a friend had worked late into the night and again all morning to prepare the food for the reception. All was ready. Upstairs, Flora Griggs and Brad's sister Tallie fussed over Kerry's dress; Sam Griggs stood discussing fly fishing with Ernest Meadow; Jeff Goodrich, Brad's best man, tossed a Frisbee with Brad's two nephews and niece, the boys making diving catches, while the nine-year-old girl's main concern was her party dress; Brad's brother-in-law, Jack, poured scotch in the kitchen while pumping Brad with questions about the trial and getting distracted answers, and Mary Collins was in her room talking to Laura Meadow.

May Rutledge came bustling into Mary's room to say it was time to get into her wheel chair and join the others, since Judge Spruell and his wife had just arrived.

The men gathered around the judge, a tall, spare, bright-eyed old gentleman, who in spite of wearing hearing-aids, needed everything repeated. Mrs. Spruell complained to the ladies that once again Raiford had made them late.

The moment had come. Kerry came downstairs with her attendants and joined Brad. The others found one of the chairs Jeff and Jack had arranged facing the fireplace at the end of the room. Judge Spruell couldn't find his glasses and his wife raised her voice to tell him they were in his jacket pocket. Finally he got them on, opened the book he held and cleared his throat.

The doorbell rang. Ernest Meadow, nearest to the door, got up and opened it. His gaze went immediately to a pair of huge eyes looking at him through very thick lenses, then to the woman's brown face and short, round body.

"Excuse me. I'm not an invited guest, but I would very much like to attend the wedding, if I may."

"Yes, certainly. You're just in time," said Meadow, who had recognized her from the trial. He stepped aside and pointed to an empty chair.

Brad and Kerry looked around at the newcomer, then at each other and smiled, then turned back to the judge, who cleared his throat once more.

"We are gathered . . . " began his deep, cultured voice.

The stranger listened to the familiar words of the ceremony, words that spoke of the best of the human spirit, of love and trust, of dedication. She drifted into a reminiscence of the words heard many times seated as a child in a church pew beside her mother. The cadence and the words transported her into that warm state of mind created by people taking time out to be mindful of these values. She was brought back to the present when she realized the judge was speaking the joyful words, "You may now kiss the bride." Her poor vision only enabled her to see two shapes merging into one. The others began clapping and so did she.

LaVergne, TN USA
06 July 2010
188452LV00001B/1/P